About the Author

Raised mainly in West Africa, Dahlia Moore received her PhD in social psychology. Having worked all her life in academic settings, teaching, and researching issues of equality, justice, and gender, she published many professional books and articles. In her latest position, Prof. Moore served as vice president of Tel Aviv academic college. She now devotes her time to literary writing, her dream for years. She lives on the cliffs overlooking the Mediterranean with her husband and dog. This is her first novel. Her next one will be a historical fiction manuscript set in World War II.

Inadvertent Encounters

Dahlia Moore

Inadvertent Encounters

Olympia Publishers
London

www.olympiapublishers.com
OLYMPIA PAPERBACK EDITION

Copyright © Dahlia Moore 2022

A CIP catalogue record for this title is
available from the British Library.

ISBN: 978-1-80074-412-7

First Published in 2022

Olympia Publishers
Tallis House
2 Tallis Street
London
EC4Y 0AB

Printed in Great Britain

Dedication

To Moti, my twin soul

Acknowledgments

Thank you to my editor, Valerie Valentine, for her wise and insightful comments, meticulous work on the manuscript, and her belief in the book. Thanks to all the people at Olympia Publishers who worked with me on this project. Thank you to all my family and friends for their constant encouragement and support, especially Eyal Benbrry and his thorough reading and observations, and Jonathan and Aviva Moore, for their suggested changes, their forbearance, and forgiveness. I'm immensely grateful to my best friends, Amalia Tamir and Judith Stoffman for critically reading several versions of the manuscript, offering thoughtful improvements, always dependable. My deepest thanks are to my husband, Moti Ravid, my staunch, unwavering supporter, who believed in me from the moment I decided to write, trusted my abilities, inspired me, and bolstered my spirit when it flagged, encouraging me to continue. Thank you for always being available, reading and rereading the manuscript, forever being there for me.

1

Olivia turned off her computer and looked out of the window. Dark, heavy clouds met her tired eyes. It seemed too cold for September in San Francisco. Her mood was just as dark.

Home, time to go home... can't postpone or avoid it any longer.

Looking outside, Olivia thought her domestic life in the past five years was less than she would have wished for: Less fun, less fulfilling, less intimate. Her job was rewarding, her sons were great and doing well, but at home...

Getting slowly to her feet, she felt her shoulders tense, as if the heavy burden she'd ignored throughout the day had now landed heavily on her back.

How I wish...

But what could she wish for? That he was well?

He never would be well again, she knew.

That it would end?

It was not something she felt she had a right to wish for. Elliot was a caring and involved husband and father before the colon cancer struck five years ago. The "disease" as he called it, had brought helplessness and misery into their home.

His depression bothered her more than anything else.

I can't face the silent abyss, the total lack of movement or reaction, as if he was conserving every ounce of energy, Olivia thought. *He'll be in the same slump I left him in when I went to work in the morning—staring at the TV, but not seeing or hearing anything.*

Sighing heavily, Olivia inserted her laptop into her oversized handbag. All was quiet outside her office. There seemed to be no one in the building; everyone but her seemed to have somewhere else to be or something else to do.

Stop it. No self-pity! She scolded herself. *You're an academic director of a prestigious economics graduate program, and you'll manage!* She took a deep breath and shook her head, as if trying to rid herself of the despondency that threatened to engulf her. She'll manage... that's what she does, these days.

Unable to delay her departure any longer, she exited the building and made her way to the dimly lit parking lot. The sidewalks, full of young lives and activities in the daytime, were now deserted. The green central courtyard surrounded by trees was serene.

She loved it all, even when dark and abandoned. The university was one of the primary sources of joy for her these days. That and her sons.

She unlocked her car and settled in with a sigh. "You can't have it all, can you?" She said aloud and started the car. Still, she could not ignore the considerable discrepancy between her home life and work.

Elliot's cancer influenced the entire family. Olivia understood her sons distancing themselves. It was difficult for them to see their father's deterioration and suffer the depressing atmosphere at home.

Must be why our friends avoid us, too. Although she was frustrated with their friends' inattention, she knew that they just didn't know what to say or how to act. The process of people withdrawing from them began when Elliot was first diagnosed with cancer.

For an outgoing person like Olivia, to lack of a social life was painful. *How long can I maintain my sanity just going to work and returning home?* She gave up everything else—concerts, theatre shows, movies, friends. At least she had the walks with Pinky, her sweet little dog, who was always loving and undemanding.

Traffic was heavy despite the late hour, and drizzle and fog slowed the congested roads. By the time Olivia neared home, a storm was raging. She'd forgotten to take her umbrella this morning, so she sat in the car, waiting for a break in the rain to dash to the door, peering at her home.

The house was dark, listless. None of the windows indicated life within. She expected only a small dim lamp to be on in the living room, and the blue, flickering light of the TV. Even the porch lights were not on.

Her gaze turned to the front yard, which looked neglected. The gardener came once a month, but Olivia thought it had been longer since he'd last arrived. The grass needed mowing, and the shrubs required pruning. No seasonal flowers had been planted this year, and Olivia missed the pansies and English primroses the gardener usually replenished when the weather cooled. Elliot didn't do anything any more, and she had no energy to spare.

Impatient, she drummed the steering wheel, looking up at the low-hanging black clouds, as black as her mood. The short footpath beckoned, but she hesitated—it was flooded and muddy.

On impulse, Olivia decided to run across the yard and up the few steps to the porch. When she got to the front door and entered the dark hallway, she was wet to her bones.

"Hi, I'm home," she called, hoping she managed to disguise her solemn mood and the distress she felt at the dark loneliness that seemed to permeate the house. "Sorry I'm late."

Pinky, the small, tan crossbreed, came rushing to greet her, jumping with delight. Olivia had found her at the SPCA dog shelter and brought her home as a present for Elliot's sixty-fifth birthday three years ago.

"Hello, little one, how have you been? Were you good?"

Wagging her tail vigorously, the dog seemed to smile. Well, Olivia always assumed this facial expression was a smile…

"Why didn't you turn on the lights, hon?" Olivia asked as she bent to kiss his forehead.

Elliot just shrugged, the light from the TV enough for him.

He was sitting in the same position she'd left him in, as she knew he would be.

"How was your day?" she asked.

"Usual," he grunted.

"Shall I arrange some dinner for us? Would you like some of the vegetable soup I cooked yesterday?"

"Nothing for me," he said.

"Come on, Elliot, you've got to eat something! Did you eat anything today?"

He's lost a lot of weight, she thought, *and he's not even trying to help himself…*

Ruby, their daily cleaning lady, probably prepared some tea for him, maybe even convinced him to have some yogurt. But that would have been hours ago.

Olivia warmed some soup for herself and brought some for Elliot. She sat down on the couch, close to the heavy armchair he occupied. He placed the bowl on the side table without tasting it.

They sat silently in front of the TV, watching the news. Hardly paying attention to the presenter's words, both were lost inside their private worlds.

Olivia looked at her husband's profile, searching for any response: to the news he watched, her being there, or any emotion at all. Nothing registered.

Olivia was trying to figure out if he was sad or afraid. If he was aware that time was running out… *Why can't he express what he feels?* His upbringing was the only explanation she could come up with. The only child of elderly, overworked, silent parents, Elliot must have learned not to show his emotions.

At the beginning of their relationship—and when their boys were growing up—Elliot talked more, shared his thoughts. But even then, it was as if he was always holding something back.

"Did Adam or Tom call today?" she tried drawing him out of the lethargy that enveloped him.

"No." Laconic. As usual.

Adam, their firstborn, now twenty-seven years old, lived in Palo Alto, but Olivia and Elliot only saw him and his wife on the weekends. Both were high-tech engineers who worked very long hours.

Their younger son, Thomas, was a twenty-four-year-old computer science Ph.D. student at the University of Washington and lived in Seattle.

They are like their father, she mused, *reluctant to demonstrate their feelings… and if I want to hear from them, I have to call them. But they are kind, caring, and willing to help if I ask them.*

Olivia wondered whether to ask them to call their dad, not sure if it would make Elliot happy or just burden him.

Taking a deep breath, she got up and took the soup bowls to the kitchen.

"Do you want some tea?" she called.

"No, thanks," came his feeble reply, "going to bed."

"I'll join you in a while," Olivia said, walking toward him with a smile, "I need to check my emails first."

Loading the dishwasher, she was lost in thought.

I can't take this unresponsive glumness much longer; it's so oppressive! But the thought of leaving Elliot never crossed Olivia's mind.

She looked at the clean, seldom-used kitchen… and yearned for a change.

Still, if I'm honest, I do have some outlets—my work, my friends. He has no source of self-fulfillment, or challenge, or pleasure.

Olivia turned the lights off and went to her study. She took her laptop from her bag and opened it.

Is this extremely urgent, or am I delaying going to bed so he'll fall asleep before I enter the bedroom? With a wry, bitter smile, she sat down and lost herself in the more immediate attention-demanding aspect of her life.

***

It was past midnight when she next looked at her watch. She got up slowly and tried to stretch out. Her spine refused to straighten.

Going to the gym was another thing she missed terribly. She looked lovely for a woman over fifty, she thought. Not great, but OK. She was still quite slim, her complexion clear, with big, very bright, very blue eyes. But she needed to work out if she wanted to remain "reasonably well maintained" as her friend Sarah used to say.

I've got to make time to work out, just have to! She missed her morning aerobics and exercises. She felt she was withering, drying out, stiffening… and helpless. Olivia hated feeling she lacked control, unable to find a way to make time for herself. *It wouldn't be selfish, would it?*

She vowed to herself to get in a good long walk with Pinky in the morning, then turned out the light and went upstairs.

Elliot was snoring softly.

2

"OK, OK, Pinky, just wait a minute!"

Olivia wished she could linger in bed, but knowing the little dog was getting desperate, she got up, feeling tired. Elliot was still asleep. She put on a faded T-shirt and jeans, thrust her feet into the old sneakers by her bed, and took her coat and keys.

The dog beat her to the door, jumping impatiently, and bolted outside as soon as the door opened, even before she managed to get the leash.

Olivia followed, the leash dangling in her hand, strolling, deep in thought. Her mind focused on her schedule.

***

The park was cold but lovely in the early morning hours. The rain had stopped during the night, and the weak sun rays managed to break through the clouds. Autumn blooms shared their delicate colors with the early risers.

Hemmed in by the well-appointed cottages on two sides and the fancy apartment blocks on the other sides, the park was quiet and serene. Until the kids filled it with laughter and their young voices in the afternoons…

She loved the peaceful walks at first light, the people who kept the same morning routine she did, and the easy camaraderie that pervaded her meetings with the other park users.

Several of her neighbors, wrapped up in their hooded coats, were already in the small park with their dogs or jogging around its perimeter. Some waved, others smiled their welcome.

Olivia started walking toward Sarah, her best friend and neighbor. Sarah's dog, also a crossbreed, was already running to meet Pinky. Sarah and Olivia met at university as undergraduate students, and they hit it off right away. They became close friends despite the differences between them. Sarah was daring, free-thinking, and quirky, whereas Olivia was studious, more withdrawn, and intellectual. Still, both were unpretentious and honest, and their friendship was based on deep trust, counting on each other's help in all spheres.

Although Olivia had gotten married and moved to Sacramento, they kept in touch and met as often as they could. Once Olivia and Elliot considered returning to San Francisco, Sarah was the one who found the perfect house for them, close to hers.

When Sarah's husband died, Olivia was there supporting her, helping her regain her balance. And when Elliot was diagnosed with cancer, Sarah was there to help with Pinky, with shopping, even finding Ruby.

"Hi, Olivia, haven't seen you here lately." She heard a deep, cultured, masculine voice on her left.

Olivia turned.

Close to the park's fence, Mark Wallace, her tall, aristocratic neighbor, was standing alone, away from other park users. Tish, his Labrador wagging its tail, ran toward them, welcoming Pinky.

His clothes—the best high-end brands—were perfectly ironed, she noticed, his utterly white hair impeccably cut and combed. His posture was both elegant and relaxed. As always, he seemed aloof, even standoffish.

Her first impulse was to wave in response and continue toward her friend. However, something in his tone urged her to react differently. She changed direction and walked over to meet Mark and Tish.

"Hi, Mark. How are you?" As usual, whenever she saw him, her first reaction was dread. They'd met over thirty years ago, in an unpleasant encounter. She was a very young twenty-two-year-old at the time, and he seemed considerably older, already famous through his TV appearances. She remembered the incident—and him—very well, but he didn't seem to remember her. She hoped he would never recall it.

Professor Mark Wallace was a well-known internist, considered one of the best in California, the medical director of a major medical center for many years. She knew he arrived home very late every evening.

"I'm usually an early riser," he said as she drew near, a small smile tugging at his lips, "By the time most people come to the park, I'm already playing tennis or at the hospital. But I slipped during a game last week and broke a finger. No tennis for a while…" He smiled again, lifting his bandaged hand.

A shy smile? She wondered. *Hesitant…?*

She took a closer look, trying to decipher his mood. Despite his smile, he seemed tense, overworked. His work was time-consuming, but was that the only reason he worked such crazy long hours? *Is it because he is too lonely at home?* The unbidden thought popped up in her alert mind.

"Must be frustrating for you. Do you go to the gym instead or enjoy waking up later?" Olivia bent to pat Tish and missed the shadow that crossed his face.

"I use the time to answer emails," he shrugged, "And to give Tish longer walks... and to give myself some time to think."

What was the undertone she sensed? She didn't think she had a right to question him on that. *We're just neighbors, not close friends,* she reminded herself, but she felt he would have liked her to ask, to show interest.

"What do you think about?" Olivia asked, gazing into his sad, blue-gray eyes. He seemed surprised, and she thought she sounded too forthright.

"Cutting to the chase, hmm?" A slow smile reached his eyes. "I think about work, mostly."

The wan smile vanished.

"No, that's not entirely true." Shaking his head, he lowered his eyes.

Olivia waited for him to continue, giving him space to organize his thoughts.

"I think a lot about Helen, and how she died..." He sighed deeply.

Helen, his partner of fifteen years, died eight months ago. A sudden, unexplained death. No autopsy was done, so the cause of death was not known. She'd wondered why he didn't insist on an autopsy. *Doesn't he want to know?*

"She was miserable for so many years... and I keep thinking—was there something more I could have done?" Mark paused, thinking. "For years, I tried to help her. To draw her out. Alleviate her unhappiness. With all my heart. I even tried to bring her new clients."

Olivia remembered that Helen was an employment lawyer and worked from home.

"Did she still work... before she died, I mean?"

"Not really." Mark shook his head. "Helen used to enter her office in the morning—not very early, of course... She sat there, going over notes of God knows which case, writing letters... there was always a vodka bottle under her table." The pain in his eyes was apparent. "I believe she began drinking as soon as she entered her office."

Olivia's hand rose to touch his arm in sympathy, but she dropped it before reaching him, not daring to bridge the gap between them.

"Oh, well… I'll never know…" Mark murmured and shrugged. Then fell silent.

Years ago, Olivia consulted with Helen when she had a minor problem with one of the professors in her department: he thought he should have been promoted and was angry someone else was promoted before him. The two women liked each other and developed a good rapport. At that time, Olivia didn't see any signs of alcohol abuse or a lack of professional concentration. However, she couldn't miss the heavy smoking.

Does he want to continue talking? She mused.

He didn't seem to be in a hurry, but she was. She didn't even shower yet and needed time to help Elliot get organized and on his couch. *I can't be late for the morning meeting, so I must move soon*, she thought.

Mark saw her sneak a look at her watch. "You need to go. So do I. Ciao for now."

Olivia wanted to say she still had a few minutes, but Mark had already turned to leave, his long strides crossing the soft grass to the park gate.

3

Sarah walked over to Olivia and stood by her side, looking at Mark's retreating figure.

"I think Mark is very lonely since his wife passed away," Olivia said.

"In a way, it's not a huge surprise her health gave out, considering her habits, you know," Sarah responded, a trace of cynicism in her voice, "She smoked heavily. And drank even more… Betty, my next-door neighbor, used to be a very good friend of hers, and she says Helen smoked at least two packs a day and was usually drunk by lunchtime. A dicey combination."

Olivia nodded. "I knew something was wrong. I met her several times in the evenings, taking Tish for a walk, and we always talked a little. She seemed not herself, but I didn't know she drank so much. Her death was so sudden! Unexpected… she was about our age, wasn't she?"

"She was your age. I'm two years older, remember? To die at fifty-two is terrible…" Sarah looked pensive. "You know… Betty told me the rumor is that Helen killed herself. Maybe she didn't mean it to be final. Maybe she took some pills as a sort of desperate cry for help, but her pretense act became a fact, and she ended up taking her own life."

"I heard that. But I find it hard to believe. Maybe Helen was too drunk to know how many pills she took? Or maybe she had a heart attack?" Olivia looked doubtful. "I guess we'll never know. Anyway, it doesn't matter. She's dead, and he seems confused and sad and lost."

Surprised, Sarah looked at Olivia. "Him? Sad and lost? He seems to me to be as arrogant and reserved as ever. You are the only one he talks with; did you know that?"

"That's not true, Sarah. I often see him talking to neighbors. Many people go to him for medical advice. And as far as I know, he's never charged any of them for the consultations."

"Well, maybe." Sarah looked doubtful. "But what I meant is, he's not talking to people. Discussing their medical problems is altogether different. What did you two talk about?"

Olivia averted her eyes. "Nothing much…"

20

"Ooooh-kayyyy…" Sarah drawled.

"I've got to rush," Olivia said, suddenly uncomfortable, "Early staff meeting. See you!"

Hurrying out of the park, she thought about their conversation.

Why didn't she tell Sarah what they spoke about? Probably because Sarah was such a gossip. Olivia liked her a lot but was aware of her inability to keep a secret. Also, for some reason, she was certain Mark would not want other people to be privy to their conversations.

Despite his image of unapproachable detachment, and their embarrassing encounter in the past, she enjoyed talking to him.

And I feel empathic. The thought surprised her.

Empathy for an iceberg? She hid a small, sardonic smile. Nevertheless, how could a person not feel sympathy toward someone who lost his wife like this, with no warning signals?

Olivia heard he found Helen dead in their bed when he returned from work. It must have been dreadful for him. Especially for a doctor who specialized in complex and critical situations. And she died undiagnosed and alone…

In his place, I probably would have felt shocked, terrified, devastated, lost, distraught, helpless, deserted, lonely, sorry, regretful… the adjectives flooded her mind.

It will be my turn to mourn soon, and I'm convinced I'll feel all that.

Oh, Elliot, she longed to be able to say to him, *I'll be so sad when you go, but I know it will end your misery, so there will be a relief, too.* Olivia felt like crying.

Pinky whined, looking at Olivia as if sensing her mood. For a change, the little dog was not running ahead of her but stayed close. *Talk about empathy,* she thought…

Olivia reached her house and unlocked the door. Dark and gloomy, as she'd left it. She opened the curtains and the windows, letting the outside world join her internal thoughts, taking a deep breath of the fresh air that filtered in.

She entered the kitchen and turned on the Nespresso machine, gratefully inhaling the smell of fresh coffee. Skimming through the newspaper that she brought in from the porch when she returned home, she sipped the strong, aromatic coffee, leaning on the kitchen table.

She washed her cup a few minutes later and filled Pinky's bowl with fresh water. *I think we need some more milk and fresh bread*, she thought, and left a note for Ruby to buy some on her walk with Pinky.

She went into the bedroom to help Elliot get up and into the shower. He could still manage the rest on his own. "Let me know if you need any help, OK, hon?" She said before leaving him there. She hoped she sounded cheery.

Getting dressed was becoming harder for him, she knew. But he refused her aid. Nor was he willing to accept paid help. It took him ages to do things by himself, but then—he was in no hurry. Had nowhere to go and nothing to do. Locked in his own, secluded world, he hardly communicated any more.

"Strangers in the night, exchanging glances, wondering in the night." The song came, unbidden, to her mind every time she felt the growing alienation between them.

She hummed Sinatra's song as she entered the guest bathroom, which she had turned into her own. She couldn't wait for Elliot to finish in their en suite bathroom every morning.

"You OK, Elliot?" She called half an hour later. He was still in the bathroom…

"Fine, don't worry," he responded.

"I'll call you later to see how you are, but it's going to be a hectic day, so I'm not sure when. And I don't know when I'll be back. Ruby should be here around noon, and she'll take Pinky for a walk."

Ruby used to come twice a week, but a few months ago, when Elliot's illness worsened, Olivia asked her to come every day for a few hours. She didn't want Elliot to be alone for the entire day.

She left the silent house, turning to look at it, sorrow heavy in her heart. She realized she couldn't stay with Elliot, but also that she didn't want to stay. She needed her life, work, challenges, colleagues, and students. People at work thought she was a brilliant researcher, a great academic director to work with, imaginative and creative, and a considerate person. At home, Olivia felt as if she was dying a little. Her energy dimmed, and her outgoing personality was subdued. Enduring all this in the evenings was as much as she could handle.

Distracted, Olivia listened to the news on the car radio while thinking of the busy day ahead: an urgent meeting with the academic council, a crucial meeting with the board of directors. She hoped to gain their support for the new graduate programs she planned. They would bring new students and contribute to the community.

Traffic was congested, as always, but she had enough time to arrive punctually.

4

The weather cleared, the wind sweeping the leaves back and forth in a crazy dance. Olivia realized that, again, she'd forgotten her umbrella, and she hoped it wouldn't rain in the evening.

Her secretary was already in. "Some students are waiting for you," Sophie said.

"Students? For me? Do they have an appointment? There's nothing in my calendar!" *I don't have time for impromptu meetings today…*

"Did you tell them they should first turn to the dean of students with their problems?" She asked.

"Of course, I did," responded Sophie, "but they insisted they had to talk with you."

"Why does it always have to be me?" Olivia asked, exasperated. "We have such a capable dean of students." *He is not always very sympathetic, but he is reasonable and fair!*

"OK, I'll see what they want." Olivia entered her office as Sophie went to the waiting room to get the students.

***

"Well, well, what a delegation!" Olivia smiled at the three students entering her office. "Please, do sit down," she said, indicating the spacious meeting table. "I don't have much time—there's an important meeting in a few minutes, but you told Sophie it was urgent, so—what is it?"

The students exchanged nervous glances. One of the young women— Olivia didn't know her—took the lead, though Mason, the head of the students' union, was also there. He usually took the initiative in students' meetings with her.

"My name is Natalie," she began in a small, timid voice. She seemed agitated. Her hands were twitching nervously in her lap, "I'm a good friend of a student who isn't here right now. She didn't come in today."

"Go on," Olivia encouraged her.

"She's pregnant!" Natalie blurted and looked at Mason. He nodded, indicating she should continue.

"That's getting right to the point," Olivia said, shocked. Her students were primarily young and unmarried.

"She has an abusive boyfriend," said the third student, a bright young woman called Madison.

"I see…" Olivia uttered with a sigh.

"No, you don't." Mason took the lead. "It's true—she is pregnant, and she does have an abusive boyfriend, but that's only part of the problem… She had an affair with one of our teachers, and—"

"Mason!" cried Natalie, sounding fearful. *Was she warning Mason not to betray the teacher, or was she unsure whether to trust me?*

Olivia froze. This was a grave allegation.

"And Ruth believes the baby is his…" Natalie said, her agitation growing, her hand flying to cover her mouth. She clearly hadn't meant to use Ruth's name.

"Her boyfriend doesn't know—about the baby, I mean," added Madison. "But also… he doesn't know about… the teacher."

"We're afraid of what he might do if he finds out," Mason explained.

What a terrible mess! What a complicated problem they've laid on my desk.

"OK, guys." Olivia spoke authoritatively, but she had a compassionate look in her eyes. "I've got to go to the academic council meeting right now; it can't be postponed at the last minute. However, this is too important to treat lightly or without due consideration. And I need more details, too. Shall we meet back here at four p.m.?"

They seemed worried and looked at each other.

"I won't say a word to anyone before we have a chance to speak again," Olivia promised, understanding their unspoken hesitation.

The students nodded and filed out of the room. Olivia moved back to her desk and sat down heavily.

Can it be true? Of course, it's possible… She knew that some students were immature. And some of them were irresponsible enough, or stupid enough, to make reckless choices.

Some of the teachers were young enough to be as irresponsible as their students, Olivia had to admit.

"You have to leave now, or you'll be late!" Sophie called.

Olivia took a deep breath, exhaling slowly. "On my way," she muttered, picked up her smartphone and her notes, and made her way to the department's boardroom.

***

Focusing on the issues at hand was difficult, and her colleagues noticed she was miles away. She decided not to propose the changes she so wanted to implement. *I need a clear head for this, to tackle any opposition.* Some of her colleagues had a problem with changes, no matter what they were and how necessary. She'd have to convince them how beneficial the adjustments could be.

The meeting allowed each faculty member to express themselves, socialize, and object to any suggestion not discussed before the gathering. Olivia brought the meeting to an end as soon as possible, without offending her associates.

"What's wrong?" Andrew, the dean of students and a good friend, walked by her side. His kind, observant eyes were examining her face. She wanted to say "nothing" but knew she couldn't fool him.

"Something that a few students brought to me earlier this morning. I can't discuss it yet. Gave them my word."

"But you are worried." A statement, not a question.

"Yes. Very…" Olivia admitted.

"It will be something we'll need to deal with in one of the coming council meetings?"

Olivia nodded. "I'll talk to you later, Andrew. Got to get ready for the board of directors meeting."

"A waste of time." Andrew smiled.

But unavoidable, the thought fleeted through her mind.

***

It was almost four p.m. when Olivia returned to her office. The students were already huddled in her waiting room. They stopped conversing when they heard her approach and stood up.

"Come on in." She indicated the open door. "Please, sit."

"Let's begin at the beginning. And this time—including names. I need to know—Who are we talking about?"

Mason nodded, and she realized that they have decided to trust her in the hours since she met them. "We're talking about Ruth Dickson, a sophomore. I think you know her. She's taking your seminar."

Olivia was stunned. "It can't be!" Ruth was as brilliant as she was beautiful. Hard to miss.

Natalie nodded her head, affirming the impossible revelation.

Mason swallowed hard and said quietly, "And the teacher is John Kendrick."

Olivia felt faint. John was one of the best teachers she had. He was also married, and his wife was expecting their second baby.

"Oh, God, what a mess. Does John know Ruth is pregnant? How long has this affair been going on? Do you know what they plan to do? Did any of you speak with her?"

The three students seemed relieved. Finally, they had someone who'd take responsibility; the load was, in an instant, off their young shoulders.

"John knows. Ruth told him yesterday. He said she couldn't be sure the baby was his, but in any case, they needed to get rid of 'the problem' immediately, and she was devastated. She's not convinced she wants to keep it, but his reaction tore her heart…" Natalie was crying softly.

"Why didn't Ruth come to me?" She looked at the three in front of her.

They shrugged and raised their palms, indicating their helplessness.

"Did she seek advice anywhere?"

Three head shakes.

"No?" Olivia ascertained. "How many months, do you know?"

Again, the head shakes.

"I'll need to think about all this. And talk to John. And Ruth, of course. Will you ask her to call me or see me?"

Three vigorous nods.

Olivia assumed that they related all the information they had, which was not much. She thanked them and said, "You did the right thing."

She looked into their eyes and saw their relief. "And thank you for caring so much. And for trusting me," she said as she walked them to the door.

The three students nodded again and walked out.

"Thanks," each of them said as they passed her on their way out. They seemed reassured; their steps were lighter than when they came.

Natalie turned at the door. "Thanks, Professor Anderson, I know you'll find a way to help." And she was gone.

Will I? Olivia shivered. *What a mess…*

I'll need to talk to Ruth… I can't believe John did such a stupid thing… Then it occurred to her that, without a doubt, he'd have to leave the university. But what about Ruth? What will be best for her?

Olivia decided to help Ruth get away from that boyfriend if he was as abusive as they said. If she had a relationship with John, she's probably looking for a way out anyway… did she think John would leave his wife for her? What did he promise her?

Well, it's too late now to do anything. Olivia decided to ask Sophie to get Ruth's phone number tomorrow.

With a heavy heart, Olivia sat down again, gazing at the sleepy campus outside her window, her eyes caressing the dewy grass and the tall, dark trees surrounding it. She was exhausted; it was a stressful day.

She packed her bag and left the office.

Ambling, deep in thought, she failed to see the lone figure seated on the edge of the bench on her left.

"Good evening, Professor Anderson." A strained, soft voice.

Startled, Olivia raised her head.

"Ruth, hi," she said softly, "I'm happy to see you. Shall we go to my office and talk?"

"I'd rather sit here, if it's all right with you." Ruth slid to the end of the bench, still tense and on edge. As if expecting a rejection.

"Fine, OK." Olivia joined her on the bench.

"I hope it's not too uncomfortable for you here." Ruth mumbled. "I prefer the darkness, if you don't mind… It's so difficult."

It must be… poor girl.

"It's fine. I'm glad you came to talk with me."

"So many mistakes… I can't believe I was so stupid… my life is a mess… I don't know what to do. How to deal with this chaos. It's like I've got a huge ball of leftover wool threads, like my grandmother used to have, and I don't know where to start pulling to untangle the mess… I wish she were still with us, but grandma passed away a couple of years ago… she always found appropriate solutions."

The tears Olivia noticed hanging at the corners of Ruth's eyes slid down her cheeks. Olivia pulled a small pack of tissues from her handbag and handed it to Ruth. The girl's hands were trembling.

"Tell me," Olivia said quietly. "Tell me, like you would have told your grandmother. Arranging your thoughts and putting them into words will help you clarify things for yourself and paint a clear picture for me. Then, together, we'll find a solution."

Ruth nodded. She was silent for a while, and then the floodgates opened.

She talked about Rolf, her boyfriend, and how sweet he was at first. So attentive and loving. He wasn't a student at the university, she said, but that was not a problem, not at first. After a while, he started criticizing the long hours she spent studying... then the mocking began... and the derogatory comments. Lately, he became more demanding, and if she did not comply, or not quickly enough, he turned offensive. Cruel, even. She was often frightened of him.

Her grades deteriorated. She was more withdrawn and avoided most of her friends and classmates.

"Did you talk to anyone? Your parents? Friends?" Olivia asked, gently laying her hand on Ruth's.

"My parents are divorced, and both have remarried. And they are miles away from here. Not that they'd care, even if they lived close by." She sounded bitter and sad.

All the elements which are necessary to set the stage for a classic drama. *What a cliché...* Olivia thought.

After a while, Ruth resumed talking. Natalie was her best friend and saw what was happening to her, so at least she had someone to talk to. But Natalie couldn't help. She didn't understand why Ruth didn't leave Rolf right away.

"Do you understand?" Ruth turned to Olivia; a pleading look in her tearful eyes.

"Yes, I do," Olivia replied. She realized Rolf's continued harassment diminished Ruth's self-esteem and repressed her willpower. And she was afraid of what Rolf might do if she decided to leave him.

"Natalie suggested I talk to one of our teachers. Maybe a more experienced person will be able to help." Ruth continued. "That's when I approached Professor Kendrick."

John was sympathetic, Ruth said. He was encouraging her to stand up

29

for herself. They met during his office hours, but after they got close, they started meeting in one of the small coffee shops away from campus. He was so nice to her, so understanding. And their intimacy grew. And one day, it became more than just talks.

"Did you know he was married?" Olivia asked. She guessed the answer, and her compassion was evident in her voice.

"Of course, I knew! But by that time, I was totally in love with him." Ruth grimaced. "Somehow, I convinced myself he loved me as much as I loved him… one of my biggest mistakes."

She paused again, gathering her fragmented thoughts.

"The moment I suspected I was pregnant, I went to the doctor, and she confirmed it. I told John… and realized how wrong I was about his feelings for me. He was terrified and wanted me to get rid of it immediately." She fell silent. The pain on her face was unmistakable.

A rude awakening, Olivia thought.

"I tried convincing him that I love him and need him, and…" She fell silent.

"And?" asked Olivia after a while.

"He said, I couldn't be certain the baby was his. It could be Rolf's. And then he said I shouldn't call him any more; he wants nothing to do with me and my childish irresponsibility."

Olivia was horrified and trying hard not to show it, knowing she'd have to confront John. "He blocked your calls?"

Ruth nodded dejectedly.

"I tried talking to him in his office, during office hours, but he just seemed angrier. He asked if I was trying to ruin his life. How could he think that? I love him so much. That's the last thing I wanted!"

"Do you want the baby?" *Careful now…*

"I don't know. I'm so confused. I didn't plan for something like this. It's not how I pictured my life… how will I manage on my own? A twenty-one-year-old single parent, with no family support, with hardly any income? And what about my studies? I can't stay here and see him on campus every day and have everyone know he is the father!"

"You've thought a lot about the situation, the various options open to you, and their possible consequences, didn't you?" Olivia looked at the young woman, uncertain of her maturity and internal strength.

Ruth nodded. "But there are so many elements to take into account…

it's so difficult."

An idea began to crystalize in Olivia's mind.

"May I suggest something?" Olivia asked.

Ruth looked at her, expectant.

"Will you write it all down, arrange the options, the pros and cons of each, the price to pay for each of the possible choices? When you have it all written down, come and see me again, and I'll help you decide what to do. The decision will be yours, but I'll help to ensure all the possibilities are on the table and fully considered. Then, I'll help you find the best way to carry out your decision."

Ruth turned to face Olivia. Her brow cleared a little, Olivia saw, despite the darkness deepening around them.

"Thank you, Prof." Ruth called her by the nickname that many affectionately used for Olivia. Her voice choked, trembled with emotion. It was clear that she was relieved to have someone to lean on.

Olivia stood, extending her hand. Ruth took it and pressed hard, with both of hers.

"Come soon," Olivia said. "We'll find a way."

***

What a day, Olivia mused. She walked to her car, ponderous. Weary of the additional burden waiting for her at home.

And tomorrow I have to take him to the hospital again. Chemotherapy. The eleventh time… eleventh! He undoubtedly doesn't give in.

5

The familiar, "Hi, Olivia," sounded from his usual corner in the park.

"Hi!" She was surprised to see him. "It's been a while!"

"Yah... I was busy with the renovations, you know how it is—you begin, but you don't know when it will end... I'm learning new architectural terms every day."

Mark told her that he and Helen had bought a house in Seacliff. Now he had to learn all about architects, constructors, and building plans. It was a project Helen started a couple of months before she died, and she'd made all the major decisions with the architect.

When he went to look at the house, Mark told her, he found that all the internal walls were torn down, with no flooring or bathrooms—just the shell remained. The whole building was waiting for Helen's new plans, and Mark had to deal with the reconstruction. It was not an easy task for a very busy man who knew nothing about choosing drapes, wood paneling, and bathroom fittings...

Olivia was amazed to learn that he had left all the decisions to Helen in the past. He claimed she had excellent taste, and what does he know about her needs in the kitchen or color schemes for the bathrooms?

Olivia thought he also wanted to give Helen something to sink her teeth into, keep her busy, maybe drink less.

The plans Helen had approved were detailed, but not all to his liking. Now that he didn't need to please her, he wanted to change some things. The architect, a close friend of Helen's, objected. She wanted to keep the designs the way Helen approved them, as a memorial to her unique taste and creativity. Reluctantly, Mark fired her when the arguments became too much for him and hired another.

"How is it all coming along?" Olivia was amused by Mark's thoroughness, even in such areas as interior decoration.

He noticed her amusement. "You'll be surprised!" he said. "It's getting to be sort of fun!"

"Well, if you're enjoying it." Olivia looked at him. "How's the new architect?"

"Good, fine," said Mark. "Well, maybe he's not very creative, but at least he listens to my choices and preferences, and he doesn't argue so much."

"How about you?" Mark asked, looking deeply into her eyes. "How's Elliot?"

"He's frail." Olivia shrugged helplessly. "He hardly eats, hardly moves. Most days, I have a hard time getting him out of bed."

Mark had been very supportive when she came to ask for his advice after the colon cancer was diagnosed, and he was still following the treatments. She always listened to his recommendations and suggestions.

"I don't understand how he can take it. The chemo, the weakness, the depression…" Olivia believed she would have stopped fighting long before she reached Elliot's condition.

"It will end soon… You do understand that, don't you?" Mark's eyes were still on her, but there was a soft kindness in his tone.

Yes, she knew. She nodded and shrugged helplessly. Elliot's suffering would end. But he was only sixty-eight… Too young to die. And she'll be a widow. What a terrible word… Was she ready?

After about thirty years with him, she'll be alone. On her own. Of course, the boys will be there for her, but they had their own lives to live.

"When Helen died…" Olivia stopped. "I'm sorry! I shouldn't have… I don't know if it's OK."

She was horrified. How could she? It's probably still a raw wound. So insensitive of her!

"I'm so sorry," she repeated.

He just stared ahead and then turned to her.

"It's OK, Olivia. Really. It doesn't hurt so much any more, after nine months. I was devastated at first, but you learn to accept the inevitable. And in a way—it is also a relief. She was so miserable."

Mark hesitated, then continued. "Friends, clients—they all avoided her. She was quite obnoxious when she was drunk. Aggressive, even."

The anguished expression returned to his eyes. Olivia placed her hand on his arm, saying nothing, just being there, sharing his pain.

"She had nothing to fill her days, as she lost more and more of her clients," Mark continued after a while. "With my very long hours at work, she was lonely and frustrated… and that may have exacerbated her drinking and smoking."

Olivia was stunned by his openness and frankness. The dignified, reserved man she was familiar with was replaced by an open, sincere, hurting person. She thought it was very uncharacteristic.

Helen had no family at all. Mark, was all she had, Olivia recalled. She had no children; her only brother died years ago, and his wife and kids wanted no contact with Helen.

Olivia remembered the gossip: Mark had two grown-up daughters when he began seeing Helen. She had never bonded with them. Some said his daughters disliked her because they believed she tried to weaken the deep connection they had with him, resenting her for claiming a piece of their father's heart. Was that why he never married Helen? They lived together as partners for fifteen years or more…

"It must have been terrible for you, too," Olivia said. "Seeing her in such a state. Helplessly observing her deterioration. I'm certain you tried to convince her to drink less, to stop smoking."

"Of course, I tried, but she would get even more aggressive." From the faraway look in Mark's eyes, it was apparent that he remembered some very unpleasant confrontations. "The last five years were truly challenging. The past *ten* years, if I'm honest." The faint smile was back in place, and Mark shrugged.

"Well, like me, you'll have to deal with all the issues you tried to avoid," Mark said. "For me, it was all the home stuff like shopping, paying the maid, the renovations."

Olivia nodded. "For me, it will be dealing with insurances, the banks… it was easier to let Elliot handle all that. He was good at it. And it freed me to work, pursue my career."

They fell silent. Each engrossed in thought, looking at the dogs playing among the trees.

They sighed simultaneously, which made them laugh, embarrassed.

"Time to go…" Again, in perfect synchronization, and once more, they laughed.

Companionably, this time.

6

Olivia was on her way home from work. Dusk was setting, and the light was fading fast. The sky was gray, laying a cover of soft, low clouds on the dark land below them. *As dark and gray as my mood,* Olivia pondered dejectedly.

Going home was getting more and more difficult. She dreaded the vacuous, depressing evening ahead.

She was thinking about his chemotherapy session in the morning. It went as well as could be expected, with Elliot putting on a brave face, joking with the nurses as if everything was fine.

Always the pretense in front of others, Olivia recollected.

He wouldn't let them see him lean heavily on her when they walked the short distance from the car park to the clinic. Before entering, he'd straighten up and put on a jovial mask. Did he not realize they could see through the bravado?

He'd lost a lot of weight, yet his face was puffed up because of the steroids they pumped into him before each chemo session. He looked sick. Still, he kept up the pretense and acted cheerful for the medical staff.

After the chemotherapy session, on their way home, she could see how much the act had cost him. Lethargically, he slumped in the seat next to her, not saying a word, as was his habit nowadays.

Does he want me to talk to him, tell him about my day? He certainly has nothing new to say to me. Will he ever again share his thoughts, feelings, or fears with me? It's as if he's already parted with me, she admitted sadly and wondered why he wanted to keep going for treatments.

***

Olivia was surprised to realize she'd arrived home. She was driving automatically, without paying attention to the road. Terrible habit... a dangerous one...

The house looked dark, as usual, but she could hear Pinky barking hysterically inside.

Odd… Why is she barking like this?

She rushed in. Pinky ran to her and then, still barking madly, ran back inside.

"Calm down, girl; what's the matter with you?" Olivia's alarm grew. That was so odd! And where was Elliot? He was not in his usual position in the armchair.

"Elliot?" Olivia called, panic in her voice. "Hon?"

She followed the little dog and heard her barking in the corridor leading to the bathroom. Elliot was on the carpet, lying on his side. He moved his arm. *He's alive,* she realized…

"Oh, God, Elliot, what happened? Let me help you up." Olivia bent and extended her arms.

"I can't," he whispered.

"You can't stay on the floor like that!" she said, distressed.

She tried to pull him up, but he was too heavy. She wouldn't manage without his help, she knew, and he wasn't helping.

Olivia stood up and turned the lights on. She almost fainted. There was a pool of blood close to his mouth and nose, congealed blood around his lips.

She ran back to look for the bag she had dropped when she entered the house.

Taking her phone out, she dialed frantically.

"Hi, I need an ambulance right now!" she said to the female voice on the other side of the line and gave her the address.

"What is your emergency, ma'am?" asked the operator.

Olivia explained clearly, choosing her words with precision to minimize further questions.

"Thank you, ma'am. The ambulance will be there in about ten minutes."

Olivia ran back to Elliot, who was still lying, curled, on the carpet. He hadn't moved. Bending to him, she verified he was breathing.

She brought a pillow from the bedroom, raised his head gently, and placed it under his head. With his eyes shut, he licked his dry, blood-encrusted lips.

"Ambulance is on its way, honey. I'm so, so sorry I can't lift you. I'm not strong enough… I'm so sorry," she mumbled over and over again.

36

Helpless, she sat heavily on the carpet next to him, patting his back.

They were silent, waiting—her fear mounting. *I should call Adam*, she thought. She needed him with her. And he'd want to know...

Her phone rang. Adam's name appeared on the screen.

"Unbelievable," she said. "I was just thinking of you."

"What's wrong, Mom? I can hear in your voice there's something wrong."

"It's your dad. I just got home. He's on the floor. I can't lift him! The ambulance is on the way."

"Slow, Mom, slow down! Did Dad fall? Is he hurt? Can't he get up on his own? Why an ambulance?" Not waiting for answers, he said, "OK, I'm on my way!"

The call ended. She felt tired and empty.

"Did you hear that, hon?" she went back to stroking his limp arm. No response. She didn't expect any...

Her back ached, but she didn't move. Pinky! She remembered the little dog needed to be taken out. She thought of her neighbor Sarah. Pinky knew her and wouldn't be frightened, but Sarah had no key.

She called Sarah, still sitting on the floor.

"Sarah, hi," she said hurriedly.

"Hey!" came the immediate reply, and Sarah started talking.

Olivia didn't listen.

"Sarah!" she said sharply. "Please listen! I need a favor. Please—can you come and take Pinky for a walk, and then take her to your place? Please—right now!"

"Of course. What's wrong? Olivia? What happened?"

Olivia was crying softly.

"It's Elliot, isn't it?" Sarah gasped. "Coming right over."

The doorbell. Pinky started barking. Olivia got to her feet and walked to the front door; her legs were numb.

"Please, come in," she said to the two paramedics on her doorstep. "My husband is on the carpet, in the corridor. He can't get up, and I couldn't lift him on my own. We need to take him to the hospital. He's a cancer patient at the medical center in this area."

"Don't worry, ma'am. We'll take care of your husband." The man said

"Sir, can you hear me?" The female paramedic turned to Elliot.

No response.

"Sir?"

"We'll move you to the stretcher now, OK?"

Elliot groaned and made as if to get up. "Don't, sir. Don't move. We'll help you."

It wasn't so easy. Despite his weight loss, Elliot was still a heavy man. Trying to slide the stretcher under him took some maneuvering.

"Where's the blood coming from? It looks dried. How long was he lying here?" The female paramedic looked at her.

"I don't know," Olivia said miserably. "I wasn't home."

"And he was all alone? In his condition?" The male paramedic looked at her, and Olivia could see the accusation in his eyes.

"The cleaning lady left earlier. He was alone for a few hours," Olivia explained.

The woman was about to say something, but there was a call, "Olivia!" The front door was open. Sarah walked in.

Elliot was still on the carpet, and Sarah's hands flew to cover her face. "Oh, Olivia…" was all she managed to say.

Olivia sighed.

Sarah walked toward her miserable friend and hugged her.

"I'm so sorry, Olivia," she said. "Truly sorry. But a deterioration was expected, wasn't it? You knew it was bound to happen soon, didn't you?"

Olivia was crying silently, her shoulders shaking. Her hands trembled as she tried to wipe her eyes.

The paramedics managed to place Elliot on the stretcher. His eyes opened when they started to wheel him out, vacant and unfocused. Olivia and Sarah followed.

The paramedics were almost out the door when Adam arrived.

"Dad!" he sounded anguished.

Elliot turned his head, his eyes focused for a moment, and he smiled feebly when he saw his son.

Adam grabbed his father's hand and pressed it tightly. "Don't worry, Dad, you'll be fine. We're here with you." Elliot closed his eyes and missed his son's horrified look when he saw the blood smeared on his father's cheek.

Olivia hugged her son tightly, unwilling to let go.

"What happened?" he asked quietly, his eyes searching hers.

"I don't know," Olivia admitted, "I came home about twenty minutes ago, no lights were on, but that's not unusual, and Pinky was barking hysterically… I found him on the floor…" Olivia sobbed. "I couldn't lift him… It was like trying to lift a sack of potatoes twice my weight."

"We're good to go," said one of the paramedics.

"I'll go with them," Olivia said to her son, "Take my car and follow us, OK?"

She turned to Sarah, who stood in the doorway, looking as miserable as Olivia felt.

"Don't worry about Pinky. She'll be fine with us. I'll keep her at my place for as long as you need me to." She smiled at Olivia. "Go. Take care of Elliot. And yourself. Call me when you can, and let me know how he's doing."

Olivia nodded and took the spare key and Pinky's leash from the hook on the wall by the door. She handed both to her friend and mouthed "Thank you," holding her palm over her heart.

She stepped into the ambulance and took a seat next to her husband's head, taking his hand in hers. He opened his eyes, smiled wanly, and closed them again.

The female paramedic had a form to fill in and started asking questions. Olivia answered patiently, but her mind was a million miles away.

Olivia called Dr Orlansky, Elliot's physician, to let her know they were coming to the hospital she worked in, and asked her to meet them there.

"Certainly," was the terse response, and the doctor hung up.

Olivia took a deep breath, exhaling slowly.

She had a bad feeling about this. It was not the first time Elliot fell, but this fall seemed different. She couldn't say why. Was he bleeding internally? Did the last chemo cause the bleeding? How bad a sign is it? A million questions tumbled around in her mind.

The paramedics were conversing quietly, leaving her alone with the fear and the sorrow. Not knowing what to expect, being unable to predict the course of the disease, and the lack of control she was experiencing were unsettling.

Olivia lowered her head tiredly. She should have anticipated the deterioration; she knew how the accursed disease progressed. But when the decline in his health happened, she was unprepared…

Dr Orlansky was waiting for them in the ER when the ambulance stopped at its entrance.

"I've arranged a bed for him. Take him to internal medicine," she said to the paramedics.

"We need to check him in, go through the formalities of admission," the male paramedic said.

"No time. I'll take care of the details." Dr Orlansky pointed at the elevators' bank, her tone commanding.

"OK, doc." The female paramedic said, directing her partner to move on. "Don't mess with the bitch," she hissed under her breath.

The doctor didn't hear, or she pretended not to. Olivia smiled wryly and followed the stretcher. Orlansky entered the elevator and said, "Evening, Olivia, Elliot."

Adam came running into the emergency room and continued at a quick step to the elevator to join them.

"Dad," he looked anxiously at his father, "Dad, can you hear me? How do you feel?"

"Fine… Just great, son…" Elliot tried to keep his eyes open.

"Lovely to see you, too, doc." He tried to reach his habitual joking tone with the doctor.

Orlansky always said she wanted to see him cheerful and vigorous. And he complied, but Olivia saw the high cost…

They liked each other immensely. Orlansky said she didn't get attached to her patients, but Elliot got to her somehow, and they enjoyed each other's quick minds and their banter.

Orlansky tended to be brusque and was often perceived as insensitive and inconsiderate. It was her way of dealing with the imminent death of most of her patients, Olivia knew. Colon cancer was a severe, deadly disease. Still, she was considered one of the best experts in her field, so she had many clients despite her callous bedside manner.

Elliot was in bed in no time. A nurse came in and drew blood; an IV needle was inserted, an infusion attached. He lay covered to his chest; the light blue blanket was tucked snugly around his body, his hands resting on top. Adam pulled a chair over and sat by his father's head.

Dr Orlansky left the room and went over to the head nurse at the nurses' station. They stood close to each other, speaking in low voices. Watching them from afar, Olivia noticed the doctor did most of the talking, the nurse nodding her head. She went to join them, and the doctor introduced her.

"This is Professor Olivia Anderson, the patient's wife," she said, then turned to Olivia. "I asked for a few tests, and he'll probably get some blood transfusion tonight. We'll know more by tomorrow. We'll talk."

Curt, as usual.

She turned, looked at Elliot again, nodded to herself, and left the department.

Olivia returned to Elliot's room, observing the father and son tableau.

"Dad, what happened to you? Were you dizzy before you fell? Did you faint?"

Elliot closed his eyes. "I don't know… I fell."

"Some water, Dad?" he asked.

Elliot weakly shook his head.

"Just a little, to wash your mouth, your lips look parched." Adam pleaded, bringing the cup close to Elliot's mouth, and he raised his father's head.

Elliot sipped and lowered his head to the pillow, groaning.

"OK, Dad, just rest…" Olivia could see Adam was making an effort not to cry, willing himself to put on a brave face. Not to show Elliot how desperate he felt.

Another nurse came in to dim the lights. "You'll have to leave soon," she said. "Let him rest. We'll take good care of him for you." She smiled compassionately and left.

Adam got up and moved to sit on the bed so Olivia could take the seat next to Elliot.

She stroked his messed hair as if trying to bring some order into the chaos the illness caused.

They sat for a while, Olivia and Adam talking quietly. He wanted to know what had happened, but Olivia couldn't help him. She told him, again, how she found Elliot on the floor when she got home. The pain in Adam's eyes was apparent.

"How long do you think he just lay there?" he asked.

"I can't say," Olivia responded miserably. "Could be minutes before I came home, could be a few hours."

She was tormented by guilt. Guilt because she had a life of her own; guilt that she went to work every morning, leaving him alone; guilt for enjoying so many things in life while he couldn't…

Adam understood, though she said nothing aloud. She was not surprised. Often, intuitively, he grasped her feelings or moods.

41

"We'll have to go soon, hon," she said to Elliot. "But I'll be here bright and early, OK?"

Elliot pressed her hand feebly.

"Right," Olivia said and turned to Adam.

"Shall we go?" She looked at her son, and from him—to the door.

"In a minute." Adam walked closer to his father and leaned down. He took his father's palm in his and seemed to be whispering something in his ear. Then he straightened and nodded to his mother.

"OK," he whispered wretchedly.

"What did you say to him?" Olivia asked.

"Nothing much," came the evasive answer, and Olivia realized he was holding something back. She knew him well enough to understand that Adam would tell her if and when he was ready, not before.

Tears were coursing down his cheeks, and looking at him, her eyes misted, too. She took his arm.

"Are we losing him?" he looked at her as if imploring her to deny the unavoidable reality.

"Maybe," she murmured, "I don't know."

They went to the car park, deep in thought. Overwhelming sorrow engulfed them as if creating a barrier that separated them from the human bustle around them. No words were necessary right then. Both were aware of the deep bond and understanding they shared.

"Will you come to the hospital tomorrow?" Olivia asked before they reached her house.

"Of course, I'll come." Adam said. "Around four p.m., I guess."

They hugged tightly and parted. Adam walked a few steps toward his car and then turned back.

"Mom, do you think we need to call Tom, let him know? Maybe tell him to come home?" Adam was, as usual, looking after his younger brother.

"No… not yet, love. Let's wait for a while. We'll decide tomorrow when we know more."

"Right," he said. "Good night, Mom." He waved and was gone.

7

Olivia went inside. The house was cold and eerily silent; she turned all the lights on. Although it was past midnight, she was wide awake.

I haven't even eaten, Olivia remembered suddenly. But she had no appetite.

Instead, she prepared a gin and tonic and added a few ice cubes.

She sat at the kitchen table, her elbows on the table, her head resting heavily on her palms. She stared at nothing; her gaze turned inwards.

Her long habit of organizing and prioritizing "to-do lists" kicked in. There were so many things to do, issues to solve... However, the first thing on her list was obvious: Call or text Sophie. Her secretary will take care of the work side of her schedule for tomorrow.

It was too late for a call, so she texted her secretary, knowing that Sophie would see the message in the morning. *"Cancel all my morning meetings."* She wrote. *"Elliot's back in the hospital. We'll talk when I have more info."*

Sarah was next on her priority list. Olivia started texting her friend when her smartphone vibrated.

"I saw you were WhatsApping." Sarah said breathlessly.

That's a funny verb, "WhatsApping." Olivia thought.

"Yes... I just got home," she told her friend. "Oh, Sarah, I left him there, alone... he looked so frail... so miserable."

The two women fell silent.

"I'm coming over." Sarah's tone meant, 'Don't even think of arguing.' So Olivia didn't. She was familiar with her friend's intense determination.

Olivia could hear Pinky's shrill, happy barks a few minutes later. She went to the door and opened it before Sarah reached the porch. Pinky rushed in, jumped up at Olivia, her tail wagging so vigorously that her hind legs were wobbling. She left the two women standing there and darted past them as if looking for Elliot. Not finding him, she came running back.

Olivia believed the little dog's eyes were questioning: *Where is he?*

She bent down and picked up the dog. "Don't worry, little one," she said, "He'll be back soon."

"Is this you, wishing, or what the doctors say?" Sarah asked, her tone implied, "No nonsense, please."

"Just me, talking nonsense." Olivia sighed. "Drink?" She asked her friend.

"I see you're having one, so yes. Thanks." after a brief pause, Sarah added, "Just a small one, and I'll be out of your hair; you need to get some sleep."

She followed Olivia to the kitchen.

"Honestly, how is he?" she asked, again in the "no-nonsense" tone.

"Frail... he's been growing weaker and weaker, and the last chemo..." Olivia halted. "It was his eleventh session..."

"Wow." Sarah looked at Olivia with a faint smile, "He's unyielding! Won't let go, ha?"

It would have sounded insensitive from anyone else, but not from Sarah. She was such a decent person, a steadfast, fully committed friend.

"What will you do now?" Sarah inquired. "About work, I mean. You can't neglect your job... the graduate program, your research!"

"I know," Olivia said, sighing deeply. "I'll drive to the hospital in the morning. And get to work from there. I'll try to finish work earlier, and on my way home, I'll pass through the hospital again... Who knows how long it will take?"

"If he does pull through, you'll have to hire someone to be with him during the day." Sarah said emphatically.

"Obvious to you and me, and the rest of the world, but not something Elliot will agree to!" Olivia said, desperate.

She tried to persuade him weeks ago. His reaction was always a complete refusal. When she struggled to understand his refusal, his obstinate response was— "I don't need any help. I don't want anyone hovering over me!"

"Well, things will have to change," Olivia said determinedly. "Ruby is a fantastic cleaning lady and a lovely person, but she can't stay the long hours we'll need, and he will not accept any help from her, anyway. He's too proud."

"A friend of mine has contacts with the best private nursing company, and I can ask her to find a suitable nurse for you."

Sarah was the best "go-to" person Olivia could wish for. Whenever

Olivia needed something—from a gardener to information concerning stain removal, from travel agencies to the best food processors and where to get them—anything at all, she could always trust Sarah to find the right, immediate and cheapest solution.

"We'll see. I want to see him back home first."

"Yes... Right... Agreed." Sarah stood to go. "It's late. Try to get some sleep. I'll meet you at the park in the morning, and then take Pinky with me. She can stay with me until you get back in the evening. Rex would love to have her." Rex was a big, beautiful, mixed German shepherd, and tiny Pinky loved him.

Olivia looked at her friend gratefully, relief flooding her. One problem solved. She wouldn't have to worry about Pinky. It was the best solution possible.

"You sure you don't mind?" she asked, even though she knew the answer already.

Sarah made a mocking face, as if she couldn't believe Olivia bothered to ask.

Sarah had free time. Her husband died several years ago, and she never remarried. Moreover, she was not interested in forming a new relationship. Olivia presumed, from vague hints, that the marriage was a troubled and stormy one, but she never asked for details. She assumed that Sarah was too embarrassed by her weakness, or wanted to leave the sad story behind her, and, therefore, didn't elaborate. Her son and daughter lived somewhere in Texas and hardly came to visit. Twice a year, Sarah traveled to see them and her grandchildren. That was more than adequate, she always said.

Sarah relished her freedom too much, she said often enough. She worked as an accountant in a successful firm and enjoyed a good pension, and was well off; she filled her days with diverse courses, her evenings with concerts and ballet shows. Or TV, which she loved.

The two women hugged, and as Sarah walked to the door, she said over her shoulder, "Sleep! You need it!"

Taking the glasses to the sink, Olivia thought how right Sarah was. *I do need it.*

On her way to the bedroom, she saw the bloodstain on the carpet, and her heart missed a bit. She sprayed some carpet cleaning fluid on it, deciding to deal with it tomorrow.

Her thoughts returned to Elliot. *I hope you're OK, hon, and that you sleep well, too.*

8

Sarah and Rex were already in the park when Olivia and Pinky came through the gate the next morning. Pinky ran over to greet her friend. Olivia walked more slowly, and Sarah hurried to meet her.

"How was your night? Sleep well? Any news from the hospital? Did you talk to them? How is Elliot?" All in one breath. Typical Sarah.

"I had a hard time falling asleep," Olivia said, "But I slept OK when I finally managed it. Didn't get much sleep, though…"

It'd be challenging to concentrate on anything today, she knew.

"And, yes—I called the hospital earlier. Elliot had a rather uneventful night. No drama. But they gave him another blood transfusion. His red blood cell count was still too low after the first dose he received."

The added blood transfusion was not a good sign, but Olivia didn't want to say this aloud.

"This doesn't sound good, does it?" Sarah looked closely at her friend.

Olivia shrugged helplessly. "I don't know yet. I'm going to the hospital from here, and I'll talk with his doctors."

"Did you talk to the famous Professor Wallace about Elliot's condition?" Sarah asked.

Olivia was surprised by her sarcastic tone, not liking what she heard. She stared at her friend, expecting an explanation.

"Oh, come now, you know what I mean." Sarah said, taken aback by her friend's reaction.

"No. I don't," Olivia said, still looking at Sarah, waiting for clarification. "Tell me!"

Sarah looked away, watching the dogs playing, then turned to Olivia.

"I'm sorry, I meant no offense… Maybe I resent the fact he seems so arrogant and condescending… Well, it feels that way to me and to many of our neighbors."

Olivia burst out laughing.

"Are you jealous because he talks to me in the park?" she asked Sarah. "I brought my dad to him when he seemed to decline, and I went to see him and ask for his advice about Elliot's cancer when it was first diagnosed a few years ago. Mark put me in touch with Julia Orlansky, who's considered one of the best in the field. So, he talks to me because he knows Elliot's case and is nice enough to show interest! Shall I introduce you?"

Sarah seemed to regret her critical tone, shrugged her shoulders, and the air between them cleared.

"Well, look who's here… you can introduce me right now because here he comes, and he's walking right over!" Despite her disparaging remarks, Sarah appeared eager to meet the tall man walking toward them.

Mark was dressed impeccably, as usual. His light blue shirt made his blue-gray eyes seem more luminous. His clean-shaven face and high, lined forehead created an intellectual look, enhanced by a cultured voice.

"Good morning, ladies," he said politely. He talked to both of them but was looking at Olivia.

"This is my friend, Sarah, who lives in number twelve, right by the entrance to the park." Olivia hurried to include Sarah in the greeting and fulfill her introduction promise.

"Hi," Mark said courteously and extended his hand, "Nice to meet you. Am I disturbing a very private conversation, or may I join you?"

Not waiting for a response, as if he was confident his company was welcome, he turned to Olivia. "You seem preoccupied. What's wrong? Is it related to the ambulance I saw next to your house yesterday evening?"

His eyes were filled with empathic concern.

Olivia nodded.

"It's Elliot," she said and told him what she found at home when she returned from work.

"Hmm…" his look of concern deepened. "What did Orlansky say?"

Mark knew Orlansky since she was his intern years ago, and had suggested her as a case manager.

Olivia informed him of the tests and the blood transfusion, saying that she planned to go to the hospital to learn more.

"Would you like to share the information with me later today?" he asked. Olivia knew he could get all the information by making a single phone call, but he would not do so unless she asked.

"Yes. That would be great." Olivia felt relief. Whatever she encountered at the hospital, and whichever options they suggested, she was confident Mark would help her make the best decisions.

"Call me when you have the information," he said and walked away.

"Nice of him to be so interested." Sarah said, but the moment he was a few paces away, she added, "He hardly said anything to me. Completely uninterested!" Sarah was not used to being ignored. "And then he turned his back on us!"

"Maybe he wanted to give us space? He did see us in conversation, and perhaps he didn't want to interfere?" Olivia questioned. "Anyway, I hope he will help me with this new situation."

Olivia checked her watch and gasped.

"Listen, I must run. Take good care of Pinky for me, will you? I'll be in touch later and let you know what's happening."

Sarah was still upset and hurt by what she perceived as Mark cold-shouldering her.

"You're wrong about him, Sarah," Olivia said. "I believe his heart is in the right place. He seems to be a no-nonsense kind of guy, but not one to snub people. Certainly not without cause. And it feels like the distant, unapproachable façade is just that—a guise he hides behind. Especially in front of women."

"How did you come to this brilliant insight?" Sarah demanded, looking astonished.

The scene she saw at Helen's funeral flooded her mind.

"I saw how women swamped him at Helen's funeral—drawn to him like bees to honey. It seemed they were pushing each other to get close to him. They were all over him, and he seemed lost. He's a famous physician, handsome, and well-to-do. And now he's free. That makes him a highly eligible bachelor! Did it occur to you that any female attention may seem threatening to him?"

Sarah seemed amazed by Olivia's interpretation of Mark's behavior. It took her a moment to assimilate the new perspective and then refute it.

"So why is he not avoiding you?" Sarah asked, triumphant.

"Because I'm no threat! Oh, Sarah, don't you see? First, I'm married, and my husband is terminally ill. Also—I'm neither rich nor beautiful, and I do not belong to his social circle. Maybe he finds me interesting to talk to for a few minutes when he's walking his dog, but I will not try to snag him!"

"Well…" Sarah said. "You are brilliant, and you are good-looking, but I agree with you—you're undeniably not the high society, glitterati type he's associated with. That's true."

They smiled at each other.

Sarah seemed somewhat mollified. "Let me have Pinky's leash and go. Don't worry, I'll take good care of her. You take care of your Elliot."

Olivia smiled warmly, hugged her friend, and left.

9

Although she texted her last night, Olivia called her secretary when she was on her way to the hospital, getting her voicemail.

"Sophie, good morning," she said, "I hope you got my message last night. I'm on my way to the hospital. Elliot's condition deteriorated last night. I do not know if I'll be able to come today. So please cancel my appointments. I'll be in touch later and let you know what's happening. Thanks."

Olivia walked quickly down the corridor from the hospital's entrance, worried about Elliot.

She entered the department and stopped at the nurses' station. The nurses had changed, of course. The morning shift seemed busy and already deep into the day's routine.

"Can you please tell me how Elliot Anderson is doing?" She asked the nurse who came to the station. "I'm his wife."

"Hi." The nurse acknowledged her with a smile. "I'm Nurse Laura."

Olivia smiled back, but she was impatient and worried.

"He's not doing as well as we hoped. He's weak and frail. We gave him another blood transfusion and took another count this morning. His red blood cell count is still very low, his creatinine—rather high. Doctor Orlansky will be here later and decide whether to give him additional blood. For now, he's getting some fluids, and we added iron to it, to strengthen him."

"Is he in pain?" asked Olivia, her voice strained.

"No, he's not. We'll give him something if and when it becomes necessary." The nurse patted her hand. "Go, see him. He'll be happy to see you. He asked about you earlier."

Olivia nodded and turned.

She took a deep breath, fixed a smile on her face, and entered Elliot's room.

The curtains were open, the room filled with soft light. Elliot was on his back, breathing quietly, an oxygen mask covering half his face. He was motionless and very pale, his eyes closed.

"Hi, hon," she said quietly as she sat down next to him, taking his hand in hers.

He opened his eyes for a second, looked at her, and closed them again. He pressed her fingers, acknowledging her presence. A faint smile hovered fleetingly and was gone.

Olivia wanted to believe that her presence reassured him.

She tried to focus her stream of thoughts. What needs to be done now? Can she handle her job and deal with Elliot's illness and treatments at the same time? Does she need Ruby to come every day now that Elliot is not home and Pinky is at Sarah's? Should she call Tom and tell him his father's condition deteriorated, and he should prepare to come home? Or maybe it was too soon? How long will the hospitalization last? What is the actual prognosis?

Olivia failed to isolate a specific thread of thought to pursue in order to reach a decision; she was unable to choose an action plan and follow it.

She needed more information, and she had to create a system to arrange all the problems at hand so she'd see how the issues were interdependent, then determine priorities.

A few minutes later, she heard the nurse's voice outside the room. Dr Orlansky's voice responded, and she entered Elliot's room.

"Hi, good morning!" she said, her voice raised. "Hey, Elliot, I said good morning! Don't be impolite!"

Olivia looked at Elliot. No reaction at first, and then he opened his eyes as if it was a great effort. The same faint smile, but this time it looked more like a grimace.

Orlansky checked the monitor, the drip, the data in his computerized file. She shook her head, unsatisfied. She bit her lower lip and considered all the data she had, trying to create a coherent picture.

Determinedly, she turned to Olivia. "Come outside," she said.

Olivia followed her out.

"The situation is not good. I'm sorry to say this, but Elliot's condition may deteriorate rapidly, and you need to know this. His kidneys are not working efficiently; the red cell count is still too low; oxygen saturation is insufficient. In short—the internal systems are beginning to fail." She paused, looking at Olivia, gauging her reaction. "We'll try to fight it with another blood transfusion, but I'm not sure if that will be sufficient."

Olivia stared at the tall, stout, dark-haired, and intense-looking doctor, her heart beating wildly. "If I understand you correctly…" She couldn't continue, her voice choked, and her eyes teared.

Orlansky looked at Olivia. The slender, blond woman in front of her was the opposite in looks, but a match in intelligence and resilience.

In a softer tone, she said, "I'm sorry. I'm truly sorry. It's sudden, I know, but these sudden deteriorations often happen in cancer patients, and their condition becomes acute and irreversible… but listen—don't give up hope yet. He may still surprise all of us. He's a fighter… and improvement may yet happen. Encourage him to fight."

She let Olivia absorb the meaning of what she said.

Olivia nodded. Her sadness was apparent. "I'll tell our boys…" She said softly, her tone under control again.

She went back to Elliot's room and sent a text message to both Adam and Tom, telling them their dad's condition was less than great, the doctor not very optimistic, and finished with, *Call me when you can.*

Adam was the first to call. "Is it that bad?" he said. "I can read between your lines. What, exactly, did Orlansky say?" He sounded devastated.

He'd be affected more than anyone, she knew. He understood Elliot more than anybody. They were both introverted, observant, and highly sensitive. Adam was the one who could interpret most of Elliot's gestures and nuances.

Olivia summarized her conversation with Orlansky, and then, her voice sounded tired even to her ears, she said, "We'll talk later, son, I need to get going—"

"Please, Mom," Adam interrupted her, pleading, "I'm almost at the hospital, Mom. Please don't leave before I get there."

"Oh! OK, son. OK… drive safely!" She was afraid he was too distressed and would not concentrate enough.

A few minutes later, Tom called.

"I'll be right back, love," Olivia said quietly to her listless husband as she moved away to stand by the window of Elliot's room.

"Hi, Mom, I just saw your message. How are you?" A very different approach, so unlike his brother.

"I'm OK," Olivia said. "It's your dad I'm concerned about… His condition has worsened."

"I see…" Tom said, hesitating a moment, and then asked softly, "Is it the end?"

Olivia heard sadness in his voice, but no surprise, no shock, not the depth of anguish Adam's voice revealed.

"It's too soon to say, but it seems to be," Olivia responded. "This time, his hospitalization seems different. I can't put my finger exactly on why it's unlike the previous times I brought him here, but I believe it is—"

Adam entered just then and kissed his mother before walking over to his father's bed.

"Tommy, your brother has just arrived. I'll call him out of the room and put you on speaker so that I can update the two of you."

Adam joined her, and they huddled away from Elliot's room, her phone between them.

"Hi, bro." Adam said. "You OK?"

"As OK as can be expected, considering what Mom just told me… Do you think I should come right away? I can't stay for very long, so if he's not critical, maybe I should wait?"

"I think you have time, but not long. So, you should get ready. Let your people know you may need to leave suddenly, and soon… I'll call you when we know more." Adam took the lead, as always, knowing his younger brother would heed his advice.

"OK. Let's hope Dad will improve soon," said Tom. *Forever the optimist*, Olivia thought.

"Yah… let's hope… I'll call you. Take care, brother."

"Come on, Mom," Adam said, "Let's go for coffee. The coffee shop won't be crowded at this hour, and we'll talk."

The thought about the heavy workload awaiting her crossed Olivia's mind, but considering Adam's need to talk, she decided to stay. Sophie would take care of any emergency and contact her if she needed it.

They walked together, silent and deep in thought. The hospital's coffee shop was, indeed, almost deserted. Olivia chose a table in a remote corner and sat down laboriously. Adam went to get their coffee, and she noticed him examining her. She put on a smile for him. Carrying the two Styrofoam cups and two muffins, he walked unhurriedly back.

"You probably had nothing to eat," he said.

True, Olivia thought.

They stirred their coffee in companionable silence. Olivia decided to let him take the lead so she'd learn what troubled him.

He straightened and raised his eyes to hers. "You OK?" he asked softly.

Olivia nodded. A small, sad smile hovered over her lips. "You?"

Adam shrugged. He seemed pensive.

"Dad seems worn out…" he said. "He's been fighting this cancer for almost five years… I think he's had enough. He doesn't seem to care any more. Do you think he's ready to give up the fight?"

Olivia searched her son's face to see how he was dealing with realizing that his father may die soon. "I don't know, son," she said softly.

She took a deep breath, deciding to be honest with her son. "I believe he's tired of it all, but I'm not certain he's ready to let go… yet. One thing's clear—he won't be able to come home in his current condition, and I can't see him ever improving enough to return to the previous arrangement we had. He'll need constant, professional care. And he'll detest it."

Adam was turning his cup between his palms, hardly drinking.

"So, we'll take turns sitting with him every day while he's here, and see how things develop?"

"Do you want to do this?' Olivia asked.

Adam shrugged, signaling he didn't see any other option.

He's not ready to let his father go, Olivia realized. She felt that her son had a deep need for closure, as if there was unfinished business between him and his father.

"Do you want to spend more time with him?" She inquired.

"He's not responsive" Adam's pain was apparent. "I wish I could talk to him. We haven't had a meaningful conversation for ages! He's so withdrawn, uncommunicative most of the time."

Olivia remained silent, just nodded her agreement, waiting for Adam to continue.

"I tried to make him talk to me. To understand what he was thinking… to know if he is afraid. If he's worried about us or he's proud of our achievements. Or thinking about the huge parts of our lives he'll miss…" Adam said quietly, and his anguish brought tears to her eyes.

"Your father was always a type of loner. It just got worse in recent years. I don't think he knew how to talk about his feelings, fears, or hopes… That doesn't mean he wasn't a loving parent. He didn't know how to say it, but he tried to show you and Tom that he loved you very much… And he was very proud of both of you."

"It hurts, Mom…" It sounded almost like a moan. Olivia was helpless, wanting to help her son, but unable to find the words to ease his pain.

"Maybe it's his upbringing," Olivia tried, "You know… he used to say his parents were silent and undemonstrative."

Adam shrugged helplessly. "Whatever the reason, he doesn't respond to anything I say to him… And I'm unable to reach him. It's too late now… it's too late…" A sob escaped his clamped teeth, and he hurriedly covered his face.

Olivia withdrew a tissue from her pocket and held it out to her son. Their intuitive insight and comprehension of each other's thought processes made words unnecessary.

"We've been dreading this day, but we knew it was coming. In the past weeks—I was expecting another decline," Olivia said, her voice low, her gaze concerned. "You remember the previous sudden drops?"

Adam nodded, listening to her calming voice.

"Well, I was expecting an additional one. It was bound to happen. Each night, on my way back from work, I dreaded what I'd find at home. It was like a huge rock would settle over my heart and lungs. And yesterday, it happened. The position I found him in made it even more horrendous… Not knowing whether he was still alive."

"Will you be relieved when he dies, or will you be sad?" Adam asked.

"Both, I guess," Olivia said without hesitation. It was something she often thought about and could answer clearly.

"I'll be glad to know he's not suffering any more, but I'll miss him, and I'll be sorry he won't be in your lives. You and Tom are too young to lose your father."

"So, you do think the end is near?" Adam looked at her, his eyes sorrowful.

"I'm afraid so. I tried to prepare the two of you as best I could. Of course, nothing can prepare you for this, but still… At least you have Ann to share it with. I hope Emily will be there for Tom. Do you think she is the one for him? It seems to be a good and strong bond between them, but I have doubts sometimes because they're so young."

"Don't worry, Mom." Adam's smile was a genuine one, the first since he came to the hospital. "Tom is handsome, with a good job, fantastic prospects, and an easy-going, open personality. He's a great catch, and Emily will not let him off the hook. She's too bright for that. And he loves her. I believe she loves him, too. They are a good match."

Olivia agreed. She was glad Tom had met someone like Emily, who was a sweet and patient young woman, a good match for Tom's reserved nature.

"I hope so. I like Emily. Let's go back, see if he woke up," Olivia said, getting up slowly, reluctantly. "Do you want to stay with him for a while, or do you have to go back to work?"

"Yes, I'll stay." Adam said.

"Then I'll go and verify everything is running smoothly in my department, despite my absence. I'll be back later."

Elliot was dozing when they came back, but he opened his eyes when Adam sat down next to him and called his name. Adam took his hand, and Elliot pressed it and smiled, surprising his son, whose face lit up. "Good to have you back, Dad," he said.

"I'll leave you guys to manage on your own for a while and come back later." Olivia was relieved and felt she retrieved some balance. "Be good!" She said before she left, her step lighter.

Is this a real change? Has the sentence been postponed? She did not delude herself to think it was a reprieve, but maybe they have some more time. She wanted this for her sons.

For herself, she wasn't sure if she wanted the saga to be over or not. But she desired to breathe freely again.

Other than her work, she had no life of her own. Every minute of her time outside work was subjugated to his needs: The chemotherapy schedule, taking care of all the aspects of the house, the cars, the banks…

The burden was getting more substantial as she grew more worn-out and frustrated. And, on top of all the responsibilities, Elliot's depression was weighing her down. She didn't blame Elliot; she was aware it was part of the accursed disease and the medication, but she wanted her life back.

She never said a word about how she truly felt. Not to anyone. She could not deny a selfish element behind these feelings, but she wanted to believe she was not entirely egotistic.

Olivia also knew she owed him a lot. When she was offered the position at the University of San Francisco, he was very supportive and immediately said she should take it. Elliot suggested they move to the Bay area, and when they told their friends and colleagues that they were planning the move, many of them—especially among Elliot's partners—raised a questioning eyebrow. Others thought he was very feminist to allow his wife her career, which annoyed her. She believed that sacrifices were something partners did if they cared about each other.

Ten years ago, they moved to San Francisco. Living close to the university was a great advantage for her. However, his electronics company—installing mainframe computers in corporations—was still in Sacramento, and he had long drives, between the two cities. Route 80 was a nightmare, sometimes... Elliot rarely complained, and she was sincerely grateful. He wholeheartedly forfeited his comfort for hers.

Now it was her turn to give up her needs for his. Still, although there was a significant element of sacrifice in taking care of him, Olivia was also away from home for long hours every day, longer than was necessary. She didn't leave him alone in the evenings to go out, but her work gave her the legitimate outlet she needed during the days.

Because he refused any help other than hers, he was alone when she wasn't home, except for a few hours with Ruby. But that was his choice, she pointed out to herself. Elliot refused paid help because he didn't want people to know how dependent he had become. And maybe he was a little selfish, too, wanting her to be there.

Her closest friends would probably understand her need for space and be supportive, but she felt that uttering the words aloud would be a betrayal. Other people only saw her loyalty and devotion. They may have guessed the difficulties such a total commitment entailed, but they couldn't know how hard it was.

She needed to keep a segment of herself for her needs, too, or she'd crack.

10

"Prof!" Sophie cried. "What are you doing here? I didn't expect to see you today! How's your husband doing?"

Sophie always called her "Prof", an affectionate nickname, but one that maintained her respect for Olivia. Amused, Olivia knew it was espoused by many of her colleagues and student.

"Things seemed to have improved a little, so I allowed myself to leave. And Adam is there for a while, so Elliot is not alone." Olivia paused, gathering her thoughts.

"Listen, Sophie. We need to cancel my meetings for a couple of days until I know more clearly what to expect. I know it's the middle of the semester. Still, the doctors won't tell me exactly what to anticipate, so I do not know how the situation will develop. Elliot is sort of stabilized, for now. Still, I don't know if this is temporary and will deteriorate in a few days or a true reprieve. The Academic Council should be notified. If urgent matters arise, you should ask Andrew Kent to fill in for me; I'll talk to him and let him know. But I want to be informed if anything crucial occurs, so I won't have to deal with unpleasant surprises once the situation with Elliot is resolved."

"Sure, Prof." Sophie said, a concerned look on her face. She'd known Olivia for a long time and understood things were bad, even terrible, if she relinquished authority and responsibility.

The two women stood silently, looking at each other, sharing a deep understanding.

"Well, I'm glad you came." Sophie was the first to break the interlude. "There are so many issues you need to deal with! The CFO's office sent some questions about the graduate program budget, and Professor Andrew Kent wanted to know if you're OK. I don't know what you wanted him to know, so I said you'd let us know when you came in."

It wasn't about Elliot, Olivia knew. Andrew was an old friend and realized something was bothering her after the meeting with the students concerning their friend, Ruth.

"There is also a student looking for you. She had already called twice to see if you'd arrived. She sounded distraught. Breathless. I asked her what the problem was, but she refused to say. I told her she should make an appointment with the dean of students, and she refused. You are the only one she'll talk to. She said you'd know what this is about."

Ruth.

"Yes, I guess I know… if she calls again, put her through, will you?"

"OK," Sophie said, hesitantly, "Are you sure you need more problems on your plate right now?"

"Do I have a choice in the matter?" Olivia smiled softly, understanding Sophie's desire to protect her, then added, "It's fine… I know the girl, and she truly needs help."

Not entirely convinced, Sophie shrugged, her hand on the door handle. "I'm going for some coffee. Do you want some?"

"I'd love a cup of coffee," Olivia admitted gratefully.

Sophie turned to leave, and Olivia pulled her laptop from her bag when she heard a startled "Oh!" from Sophie.

A moment later, Ruth was standing, trembling, in the doorway. "May I talk to you?" she said, close to tears, obviously distressed.

"Of course, come in, come in… what happened?"

Ruth entered, timidly, and sat nervously on the edge of the chair. She looked at her feet, her leg jerking. Olivia waited patiently, and after a few minutes, Ruth raised her head, her eyes wet and red.

Olivia froze. An angry red mark was visible on Ruth's cheek.

"He turned violent," Olivia said. A statement, not a question.

Ruth nodded miserably.

"I told him I wanted to leave… I thought I could pretend to be assertive, and convince him it's not working between us, but my words only made him angrier."

Sophie entered, carrying Olivia's coffee and a glass of water for Ruth. The young woman looked up gratefully, as if even a small act of kindness was unexpected.

Her self-confidence reached rock bottom, Olivia reckoned. *She's just a kid… A traumatized kid…*

"You did the right thing, leaving immediately," Olivia said.

The girl nodded, unsure. She tried to stand up for herself and failed. Olivia assumed the experience contributed to Ruth's sense of powerlessness.

Something had to be done swiftly. Obviously, Ruth couldn't return to the apartment she shared with Rolf. An idea was forming in Olivia's mind.

"Ruth, can you confide in either of your parents? Can you go live with either of them for a while?"

"No! Definitely not!" Ruth exclaimed, horrified. "I don't even know how to tell them! I suppose they'll think it's all my fault."

So, staying with her parents was not an option, either.

Olivia looked at the frightened young woman. *How old is she?* She mused. *Twenty-two? Twenty-three? She had important decisions to make— life-changing choices—with weighty consequences attached to each option. Her pregnancy was not showing yet, but it wouldn't be long before it did…*

Ruth shook her head weakly, her indecision apparent.

"I think you still have time to make your mind up before you're left with fewer options," Olivia said gently. "Tell me, do you have any other family here, or somewhere else? Family members that you feel close to?"

"Yes," hesitantly, "Sort of… my aunt, Mom's older sister. I always loved to visit them as a kid… the summers with them were the best! They have a vineyard in the Napa Valley and a huge house. We stopped going to visit when my parents separated; I don't know why… so I don't know how close we still are."

"Can you call her, check if she'll be willing to have you for a while? Until you decide what to do? Perhaps even help you to decide?"

"I don't know if it's such a good idea," said Ruth, "I don't know what happened between them and my parents. And she probably has enough work with my cousins, the vineyard… I think there was a problem with her youngest daughter, but I don't know what, I didn't keep in touch."

"Well, you won't know unless you try," said Olivia. "People often surprise you. Positively, I mean. If you give them a chance."

Ruth looked unconvinced. Her recent experiences were rather the opposite of positive surprises.

"Call her." suggested Olivia. "What have you got to lose?" *Nothing but another rejection,* Olivia thought gloomily. Still…

She looked at Ruth. "No one can do this for you. You have to find the strength within you, and just call her."

Feeble hope emerged in Ruth's frightened, weary eyes. "Can I do it here, with you? It will give me the courage to do it."

The vulnerable look again. Reluctantly, Olivia nodded her assent.

Ruth's cellphone was in her hand straight away, as if afraid that Olivia might change her mind. In an instant, she found the correct number and rang her aunt. Olivia realized the speaker was on, and she was forced to participate.

"Aunt Judith, hi." Ruth said, her voice tearful and shaky.

"Ruth? What's wrong, baby?" came the immediate, warm response.

Ruth choked, the tears now streaming freely down her face. Gasping for breath, she tried to speak and failed.

"Come on, girl, take a deep breath, and talk to me." A warm, pleasant voice.

Ruth extended her hand, holding the phone to Olivia, her face imploring.

Shaking her head, Olivia rejected the pleading in Ruth's face.

"Ruthy? Ruthy, talk to me, love, please… are you still there, love? Please, you're scaring me!"

Ruth's arm was still extended. She placed her phone in front of Olivia and lowered her face to her hands. Olivia put the tissues she kept on her table next to Ruth.

With a reluctant, heavy sigh, Olivia picked up the phone, saying, "Hello, Ms—"

"Just Judith, who's this?" came the reply.

"Hi, Judith. This is Professor Anderson, I'm the academic director of the international economics graduate program, and your niece is my student. She is in my office right now. You're on speaker so Ruth can hear our conversation."

"Oh, my God, what happened? Please! What happened?" The woman was anxious. She hadn't heard from Ruth or her family in a long time, and now this hysterical phone call.

"She's a bit distraught, so it's hard for her to speak right now. I suggested she call you, as she can't confide in her parents right now. I got the impression she feels comfortable with you."

"Of course, of course, what happened to Ruthy? What can I do?" Judith asked, sounding worried.

"Can Ruth come and stay with you for a while? She'll tell you whatever she chooses, at her own pace, but right now—she needs a place to stay, and be loved and nurtured."

"Yes, of course… yes, we'll be happy to have her for as long as she wants! Ruthy, take the first bus to Napa… Do you remember how to get here? We'll take care of everything when you get here. Don't worry about a thing. Just come!"

The soft, caring voice and the support it offered caused Ruth to cry even harder, but she vigorously nodded her assent.

"Ruth says yes…" Olivia said. "I'll check the bus schedule and take her to the station."

"Thank you, Professor! Thank you! I do appreciate it… Ruthy, call me when you know what time your bus leaves; I'll be at the station. By then, your old room will be ready."

"OK. Thanks, Judith. Bye now."

Olivia hung up and looked at Ruth. "She seems a very nice person."

Ruth nodded.

"And she's a person you can count on, a strong woman…" Olivia added.

Again, Ruth nodded.

"First, we need to find you that bus. You're not going home for your things. We'll deal with them later when you decide what you want to do."

Olivia called out toward the doorway, "Sophie, I need your help."

"I'm already on it!" came Sophie's reply.

"Ha? On what?" Olivia asked.

"On the bus schedule!" came the immediate response.

She'd heard them. Ruth didn't close the door when she came in, and nosy Sophie, who loved gossip, left it open. Olivia tended to forgive her prying because she was such a good-hearted woman.

A few minutes later, Sophie came in, saying, "There's a bus in forty minutes. I'll take Ruthy to the Embarcadero, so she'll be there on time."

"Do you have enough money on you?" Olivia asked.

Ruth blushed. "Probably…" she said.

Olivia took out one hundred dollars from the department's petty cash box, told Sophie to remind her to replace it later, and handed the money to Ruth.

"It's too much," she protested.

"Perhaps," Olivia said. "But you may need to buy a few things once you get there."

11

Olivia woke early. The pale gray light of early October, filtering through the blinds, indicated that it was still hours before her alarm clock would sound. Even the birds had not woken up yet, and only a few chirps of some early-rising sparrows could be heard.

She slept badly. She could not subdue the clamor of thoughts in her mind for several hours. When she finally fell asleep, it was a sporadic, light, unsatisfying sleep.

Olivia closed her eyes, listening to the silence in the house, letting yesterday's events flood her mind. This time, she was in control of the flow, able to stem the maelstrom from swamping her conscious mind.

One thing at a time, that is what she wanted. If she was to function rationally and effectively, she had to deal with issues one at a time. She thought of Ruth, and her grandmother's massive ball of leftover wool threads, trying to find a lead to pull to untangle the mess—Precisely what she felt right now.

Well, Ruth was one of the issues. And she was sorted out. Olivia hoped she'd be okay with her supportive family.

Her trip up north was uneventful. Ruth's aunt was at the station to greet her and take her home. They called Olivia to let her know Ruth arrived safely; they were together, in her aunt's kitchen, talking. Judith said she'd help Ruth understand all the aspects of each choice and reach a decision, considering the consequences of each option. Whatever Ruth decided, Judith would support her. She would also deal with her sister, Ruth's mother.

Olivia was relieved to hear Ruth would be able to stay with her aunt's family for as long as she wanted. They were well-off and ready to care for Ruth, even if her parents did not contribute to her upkeep. Judith and her husband would take Ruth to her apartment to gather all her belongings at a later date. No hurry.

For Olivia, this was only part of the equation. She still needed to deal with John, the possible father of Ruth's baby. That matter was not resolved yet. He'd probably be fired; she had no doubt the university law consultants would be involved. However, he had a wife and a kid… He was an excellent teacher, and students loved him. But what he did was inexcusable. She left a message in his voice mailbox.

She realized she'd have to tell Andrew Kent about this. He already suspected something had happened, and the old-school professor may have encountered such occurrences in his long history in academia.

She called Kent's phone, and he answered before she had time to arrange her thoughts and decide how to present the issue. So, she chose the straightforward way she tended to favor and divulged the facts. Andrew didn't interrupt her, uttering "Oh" or "Ah-ha" now and then to indicate he was listening.

"I'm sorry to bear such terrible news, but Ruth agreed that you must know. And I think you should join me when I talk to John, listen to his side of the story…" she finished.

"Of course," Andrew replied. "Of course, I'll be there with you… tell Sophie to call me with the date once she gets hold of him."

"Thanks," Olivia said, relieved.

"How's Elliot doing?" Andrew Kent knew and liked her husband.

"Not good," she replied, "I'll tell you about it when I get a chance.

She hung up.

Her mind turned to the main critical issue she had to deal with: Elliot, and the possible routes open to her concerning treatments, developments. She needed Orlansky to be more explicit about the prognosis. What was she to expect?

He's not going to be well. That's a given. Not ever. But is this the end? Will he come out of the hospital, and if so—how soon? Do we need to look for a hospice for him, or will it be possible to return him home? There will probably be no more chemotherapy. Will it be a palliative treatment only? No one can say how long this may last, but maybe a time frame could be defined so that I can prepare for the inevitable?

Olivia knew she'd have to talk to Orlansky today and get more precise answers. Then, she'd have a clearer picture and would be able to make decisions and preparations.

And the boys? What should she tell them? Should she tell Tom he needs to come home now? She'd leave the decision to him, of course, but he needed to have enough accurate data to make a decision. But she didn't have the information yet. She'll call him after speaking to Orlansky. With his clear, rational, intelligent mind and high emotional capacity—he'd be able to make a decision. A decision that would be right for him. A decision he'd be able to live with, afterward.

Adam, she knew, would be more strongly affected by whatever she decided to do. He was close to his father and more devoted to him than Tom. She'd share the information with him. Maybe she should even ask him to join her when she met Orlansky? She was convinced he'd be by her side throughout the ordeal.

I'll have to get him ready. To steel himself for what I believe will happen shortly. He has probably begun the process on his own. He's brilliant and must have figured it all out by now...

She wished she could talk to Elliot about these matters as well. *What does he prefer? What does he want?* She didn't even know if he was mentally suffering, in physical pain, wanted to be left alone, or desired to have them close by...

He had shut them all out a long time ago. Living with the vacuum he created was difficult for Olivia, but she respected his right to choose it.

I'll not bother him with all this now, she decided. *I'll try to figure what's right for him and hope to get it right. If not—I hope he tells me so.*

Her alarm clock sounded, signaling it was time to get up. Pinky was immediately by her side, tail wagging enthusiastically.

"I know, baby, I know... you need to go out... just a few minutes..." Olivia spoke to the little dog. *It's good to have someone to talk to,* she thought, amused.

She hurriedly brushed her teeth and combed her hair. Put on a clean, though worn-out jumpsuit, pushed her feet into the old trainers by her bed, and moved toward the door, the little dog jumping excitedly by her side.

Pinky rushed out the moment Olivia opened the door and relieved herself close to the bush at the end of the yard. Olivia put the leash on her and walked slowly, still deep in thought.

"Olivia, Hi!" Sarah called to her when she entered the park. "How are you? How's Elliot? What's new?" Breathless, as ever. Her outgoing, cheerful personality was shining bright and clear, even at seven a.m.

Olivia was still struggling to control her thoughts, and would rather have had tranquility at the moment, but she smiled at her friend, aware that the noise came along with a big, warm heart.

"I'm OK," Olivia responded. "Though I didn't sleep well... too much on my mind, but I'm OK. Elliot, too, as well as could be expected, under the circumstances... I hope he had a better night than yesterday... how about you? You OK?"

"Fine, I'm just fine." Sarah waved her hand as if brushing away the topic. "Did you hear the news?" Sarah changed tack abruptly, her eyes bright, her tone excited.

"What news?" Olivia tried to draw her thoughts away from the hospital and concentrate on the new topic of interest her friend brought up.

"Your 'friend' has a new girlfriend!" Sarah declared triumphantly.

Olivia looked at her blankly. "Which friend? What girlfriend?"

"Professor Mark Wallace, who'll hardly speak with any of us—except you—was seen several times at social functions with... Cynthia Morgan, the bitch!"

"I'm glad for him if he found someone!" Olivia said. "But who is Cynthia Morgan?"

"No, no, no!" Sara's voice was charged, her face animated. "You don't wish *her* on *him*!"

Olivia looked puzzled. "Why not?"

"Do you remember I told you about my friend Cora, whose husband left her for a younger woman? It was years ago. The younger woman was *her*, Cynthia, the bitch, Morgan!"

Olivia had a vague recollection of Sarah's story. She raised her hands, palms flat, open, and facing outwards, indicating she needed help with the anecdote.

"Cora and Steve were married for years. He's a rich building constructor, a very, *very* rich constructor... and out of the blue, he wants a divorce. Cora was devastated. Totally! She didn't know what hit her, or where it came from. She didn't see it coming!"

Sarah took a deep breath and continued. "Well, he said he met someone and fell in love; the romance was going on for quite a while, and now he wants to marry her. *She* wants marriage, he told Cora. And Cynthia, the bitch, knew he was solidly married when she latched on to him!"

Sarah was bubbling. "Anyway, that's not the whole story! Steve divorced Cora and married the bitch... But!" Sarah stopped for dramatic effect. "A couple of years ago, he wanted to divorce the bitch and go back to Cora. Cora agreed to take him back, the poor thing. After all, he's the father of her children, and she didn't remarry."

"So, the story has a happy ending." smiled Olivia.

"Only partly." came the immediate reply. "Cynthia, the bitch, only agreed to set him free if he gave her the fantastic villa they lived in and a huge sum of money. Nobody knows how much, but rumor has it she stripped him… Like she did with her first husband!"

Sarah was enjoying herself.

"I'll be honest with you—and I have to admit—the bitch is gorgeous." Sarah continued. "One of the most beautiful women in town. She's about fifty-six now, and still well-maintained. Obviously, she had help —a facelift, a nose job, a little Botox here and there—but she's beautiful. And now she's rich, too… So, you'd think she'll be considered a good catch, right? But NO! Most men know she's greedy! And—it is a well-known fact that after Steve divorced her and went back to Cora, she attempted to destroy a few other marriages to get herself another husband. In some cases—the marriages of her good friends!"

A real predator, if all this is true, Olivia thought.

"Moreover, everybody knows how she forced poor Steve away from his children, and even stupid men understand the risk the bitch represents and avoid her!"

She stopped for a second, and Olivia understood she wasn't through, the drama still unfolding…

Sarah looked at Olivia and shrugged. "That's why I thought it strange when I heard Mark Wallace was seen with her. He's the next in line, the last gullible in town, her newest conquest. And she spreads the rumor throughout town to strengthen her hold and scare away any competition!"

So that's the punch line, Olivia realized.

"Pure gossip, obviously!" Olivia protested.

"Not really! Everybody knows already. They were seen at parties, at the cinema… I'm telling you—they are dating!"

'Everybody' doesn't include me, I guess, thought Olivia.

"Let's say I buy this story—what of it? They are both adults. And it's over six months since he lost his wife. She's been divorced for many years…"

"Two," interjected Sara, "Two years. But that's not the point, don't you see?"

The look on Olivia's face clarified she didn't understand.

"She's a man-eater! If she sank her claws into him, he's doomed! She's been 'starved' for years and just dying to find a mate. Nothing is sacred to this bitch. Mark has two daughters, doesn't he? She'll try to tear him away from them, create a rift between them to strengthen her hold... and she'll strip him of all his assets, as she did to her previous husbands."

"Mark would never let her do this, I'm sure. I don't know him much more than you do, but he doesn't seem the type to fall for a woman like her!"

"Well, well, well..." Sarah said, her gaze focused beyond Olivia's left shoulder. "Speak of the devil..."

Olivia turned and saw Mark at the park's entrance, walking toward them.

"Morning, ladies," he said when he came closer.

"Did I miss a discussion of an important topic?" His half-smile tentative. "Or—by your guilty looks—was I the topic?"

"I must be off." Sarah said quickly and, turning to Olivia, said, "Bring Pinky when you're done here."

Olivia nodded, smiling gratefully.

"Wow! Was I the reason she left so swiftly?" Mark asked, smiling speculatively.

"No!" Olivia was quick to defend her friend. "Well... partly..."

They both laughed.

"According to Sarah, most of our neighbors are a bit apprehensive when it comes to you. Even in awe of you, mostly because you're too much."

"Too much?" Mark repeated, his tone questioning.

"I guess..." she said. "Too handsome, too famous, too highly esteemed, too..."

"I get it, I get it." Mark laughed, embarrassed. "Is this what you think, too?" he asked, turning serious.

"I don't respect people automatically, or stand in awe of them because they are rich or famous. Not until they prove they are worthy of respect," Olivia said. "I value integrity, honesty, good-heartedness, and kindness... things like that."

Olivia thought she sounded naïve. And patronizing. Not sure how the two could go together.

"I'm not saying you are not these things, too. I don't know if you..."

68

She stammered and blushed. "I... I evaluate people according to their traits, not according to their obtained possessions, so I need to know them a little better before deciding whether they have my esteem or not."

There was a different look in Mark's eyes when he gazed at her. Had his respect for her increased? He seemed surprised by her frank sincerity, as if he expected a light banter, not an insightful conversation.

"Is this what you were discussing with Sarah before I came?" he asked, his tone wistful.

"Not at all," Olivia replied, shrugging in embarrassment. "We were talking about your love life." She lowered her head so he wouldn't see her deep blush.

"The straightforward approach again..." Mark said, a slow, languid smile reaching his eyes. "And what were you saying about my love life?"

"Oh, Sarah told me about your dating Cynthia Morgan," Olivia said, uncomfortable at being caught gossiping.

She saw that his expression clouded. "Is it not true? You seem displeased."

"We're not dating!" Mark protested. "I've met her a few times. We've gone to the movies, and a mutual friend organized a party in Sacramento and asked me to bring her with me because she hates driving out of town! Nothing more."

"Well, that's enough to be considered 'dating' by most people, not that it is any of their business," Olivia said. She found herself amused by his discomfort and decided to probe it. "You're uncomfortable," she asserted. "Why?"

No beating around the bush. Always direct, candid communication. This embarrassed him even more. He could not evade her searching, open gaze.

"Because it's not 'dating' per se," he said. "Yes, I've taken Cynthia out several times, but I'm not emotionally involved." He seemed to be reflecting on what he said.

He feels a need to justify himself, Olivia thought. *Strange... why would he?*

"You don't need to justify yourself; you have every right to date whoever you choose. You're both free, mature individuals."

"I'm not justifying myself!" Mark responded vehemently, sounding annoyed. And he turned away, calling Tish, ready to leave.

Olivia was surprised, his outburst unexpected. "Mark, I'm sorry, I meant no offense. You're angry, though I don't really know why."

"You're intelligent enough. Figure it out!" he said curtly, and left.

Surprised, Olivia walked toward the exit, deep in thought, aware she must have hit a raw nerve.

12

Olivia's cellphone rang when she was on her way to the hospital.

Adam.

"Hi, son," she said.

"Are you on your way to the hospital, Mom? I think Dad's not breathing right!"

"I'll be there in a few minutes! Call the nurse!"

"I did, Mom. They are not responding; I went out to look for a nurse, and she said she'd be here in a few minutes, but that was five minutes ago!"

"OK. Call her again! I'll phone Orlansky. She's on my speed dial…"

Olivia parked illegally and rushed in. Pulling her cellphone from her handbag, she called Orlansky, reaching her voice mail. "Hi, Doctor, It's Olivia Anderson. Elliot has difficulty breathing, and we need your help at the hospital. Can you come right away? Thank you!"

She pressed the button repeatedly, wishing the elevator could fly down.

When the doors opened on the fifth floor, she ran as quickly as she could, not answering the nurse's call to slow down.

She entered the room, breathless. Adam was seated next to Elliot, holding his unresponsive hand, talking to him quietly. Elliot seemed agitated, his body jerking restlessly. His eyes were closed, an oxygen mask covering his face. He was breathing.

Adam looked up; his eyes were red-rimmed. "I was so scared," he said. "I came in, and he was thrashing around, his eyes closed. The mask was off. He probably pushed it away."

Olivia and Adam hugged tightly.

"He doesn't look too good…" Olivia said.

"No, he doesn't," Adam seemed distressed, "It's not similar to the other falls he had, is it?" He swallowed hard, the words sticking in his throat. "Are we losing him?"

She nodded and tried to calm the erratic movements by stroking Elliot's arm on the blanket. No response.

"I think we need to call Tom, tell him to come and say goodbye," she said, swallowing hard.

The nurse entered a few minutes later, glancing at Olivia and Adam sitting next to Elliot's bed, talking in hushed tones. Was it pity in her eyes? Sorrow, definitely… She took Elliot's blood pressure, checked his fever, ensured the oxygen mask was appropriately placed, and straightened the pillows.

"Can you give him something to calm him down? He's fidgety and seems so uncomfortable," Olivia asked.

"Sorry." the nurse said. "We can only give him the medication the doctor subscribed. But I can call Doctor Orlansky and ask her what she thinks."

Olivia nodded.

She looked at her restless husband, his legs moving, as if he dreamt he was walking. His eyes were half-closed, unseeing, and he was mumbling.

She couldn't take the sight. The proud man, her often silent, taciturn husband of many years, who already lost control over the flow of his life, was now losing the last vestiges of his dignity. Olivia wanted to scream her outrage at the unfairness of it all.

The nurse came back thirty minutes later with an injection in her hand.

"Doc said it was all right to give him a little something to relieve his tension," she said cheerily.

"What are you giving him?" Olivia asked.

"Just a minimal dose of benzodiazepine; it will help relax him in a few minutes."

Adam looked at his father, worry written all over his face.

"Tom said he'll try to find a flight this afternoon. He'll let me know as soon as he's booked a flight. I'll drive to the airport to pick him up."

"You probably need to go to work." Olivia looked at her son, feeling his pain. "Go. It will do you good. Nothing we can do here, really. It's out of our hands. All we can do right now is try and make him as comfortable as possible. I'll call you if there's any change. And when you hear from your brother—let me know his schedule."

"Work can wait… and how about you? Can your department wait?"

Your department… Yes, she was intensely involved in her work. Both her sons knew that. They paid the price of her career when they were younger because she was not always available to them… She wondered if they resented it. And her.

"The graduate program will wait. I put Andrew Kent in charge for now. You remember him, don't you? The friendly professor, you used to call him."

Adam smiled, nodding.

"I'd rather sit here with you. And Dad. In case there's a change. Maybe he'll wake up... even for a little while. I don't want to miss this if it happens..." He fell silent.

"You love him very much, don't you?" Olivia asked, more a statement than a question.

Adam shrugged. "We had a sort of unspoken understanding. Something profound that neither you nor Tom had. We're very much alike in many ways... Tom is more like you—easy-going, open, and sociable. He never knew what to make of Dad's silences. Never figured the nuances. I think you didn't either, Mom."

Adam looked at his hands, avoiding her eyes. "I think there was a lot he wanted to say but couldn't find the accurate words for his thoughts and feelings, so he kept silent. But I could see his feelings in his eyes. Sometimes, I felt he truly wanted to talk, express what he felt... then he would just make a gesture, which—for him—said it all. But you never seemed to perceive the meaning, see the love hidden there, so wanting to be exposed, and failing so miserably."

He fell quiet, gathering his thoughts.

Olivia sat motionless, shaken by her son's penetrating insights. Her silent son, the one who was so like his father, suddenly found the pungent words to describe his father's world. And probably his, too.

"He never said it, but he loves the three of us very much. We are his entire social world. There was nobody else for him. But we all had other people in our lives," he continued.

So true, Olivia thought. Elliot often said he didn't trust people; there was no such thing as "true friendship" according to him. Only needs and selfish considerations. He believed people formed relationships when their interests corresponded.

A sad way of looking at life, she told him once. He just shrugged.

After a while, Adam raised his lowered head and gazed at his mother.

"I often caught him looking at *you*... even when you just passed from the kitchen to your study, a cup of coffee in your hand. You were engrossed in whatever you were working on and didn't notice. There was so much love in his gaze… Forlorn love… As if he knew he couldn't reach you… and you hadn't even noticed… You never saw it."

There was no blame in his tone—only immense sadness.

It was true.

She liked Elliot. He was a good, decent man. But her love for him had died out a long time ago. Gradually, and unnoticed, it just faded…

The gap between them grew slowly. Olivia assumed that they both felt the same way, but apparently, what Adam saw indicated Olivia drifted away. It was not because she wanted to end the relationship or look for a change in her life. She had no romances and was not looking for one. She was immersed in her children and work; Elliot's role in her life had diminished.

"I wouldn't have left him. Ever!" she blurted.

"I know." Adam said. "Out of responsibility and obligation. Whereas for him, there was never a consideration of whether to leave or not. He stayed for love."

She looked at her son's vibrant, honest eyes, amazed at the depth of his understanding. So young—only twenty-seven—yet so mature and insightful.

"You are so much your father's son," she said pensively. "But a much-improved version. You have the dimension he lacked—you are so attuned to your feelings and the feelings of others. You don't do it frequently, but you talk openly and directly about how you see things… when you choose to. Your dad never could. Believe me, often enough, I tried to extract what *he* feels, what *he* thinks, what *he* wants—but he always found ways to sidetrack the conversation."

"I used to be like Dad, didn't I? It was easier to shut everything inside and hide my sensitive side, not to seem vulnerable. I have Ann to thank for the change in me. I'm still a project "in-process," but she helps a lot. With her understanding and patience, I feel I've come a long way already."

"And maybe this is why you could see him the way no one else could. And be aware of so much…" Olivia said, her eyes overflowing. "There's so much I failed to notice."

Adam put his arm around her shoulder; the gesture was both supportive and reassuring. They sat huddled, each gazing into a private distance, thinking of the strong bond between them, contemplating the complex meanings and undertones in the candid conversation they just had.

Adam's cellphone chimed.

Looking at the screen, he said Tom texted that he was just then boarding his flight. In about three hours, she'd see him again. After nine months…

Tom lived at home as a student because it was convenient, and he was in no rush to leave. They used to meet every Saturday morning in the corner coffee shop near their house; Tom would arrive from the gym, and she'd join him for the short walk to the coffee shop. They chatted about his week and hers, sharing insights about their lives. Sometimes they discussed social or political issues that interested them. It was a time capsule away from the flow of their existence, a time they both used to reflect on their choices, reconsider their actions. They hadn't missed a week since they started these meetings several years ago, and they only stopped when Tom got a lucrative job in Redmond. She still missed them.

Olivia and Adam sat, watching Elliot.

"He's much more relaxed." Adam said.

"Yes," agreed Olivia, "But his breath is very shallow. And slow."

"He's slipping away. I think he's decided to give up the fight. Like he's had enough."

"Yes." Olivia agreed again.

"Should we call a doctor? A nurse?"

"Why?" Olivia asked. "To revive him? Is this what you think he would want? And then what will happen? What quality of life will he have?"

Adam shook his head.

"Let him go, son… Let him go peacefully. And with dignity. It's time… No doctor can help him now… it's time for farewell, hard as it may be."

"Dad, hang on for just a little while longer! Tom is coming… He wants to see you! He needs to be able to say goodbye, too… stay with us… please, Dad!" Adam pleaded, not knowing whether his father heard or not.

The shallow breathing continued. Elliot looked relaxed and composed. At peace, finally.

Adam left a couple of hours later, promising to be as quick as possible, and return right back with his brother.

"Don't rush!" Olivia pleaded. "Drive carefully!"

***

The room seemed deathly quiet. The machines beeped and blipped, the flow of oxygen a soft hiss in the background. Muffled voices from the nurses' station could be heard from time to time. The solitude was complete.

Olivia moved closer to Elliot. Her hand stroking his face, her head on the pillow next to his.

"I'm sorry, hon. So sorry… for not being home with you most of the time. For not giving you my full attention. For wanting to live my life… I'm sorry for not trying to understand. Not that you made it easy, but still— I should have tried harder. Did I let you down in the end? Years ago, you told me you'd choose your life again, just as it has been, if you had to make the choice again. It meant you were happy with the way things turned out, right? Despite the big and small hitches along the way? And the boys turned out OK, too, right? You're very proud of them and the way they built their lives, you told me so, many times. What a pity you won't be there when they have children of their own… You would have been a fantastic grandfather, I'm certain… Will you watch us from wherever you'll end up? Watch over us?"

The pillow was wet, she realized. She wasn't aware that her tears were flowing freely.

"I wish I said all this, and so much more, before now," she continued the monologue, speaking softly, her lips close to his ear. "You deserve my gratitude for all your ungrudging support throughout the years, for always doing the right thing for the family, even when it was not the best thing for yourself."

Olivia straightened. There was a change. She couldn't figure out what it was, but she felt… something.

Looking hard at Elliot, she realized he wasn't breathing any more. Quietly and peacefully, unnoticed, he just let go and slipped away.

She'd never know if he heard her.

Olivia sat alone, crying miserably. No one came. No one noticed. *Maybe it's the way he wanted to depart,* the thought crossed her mind.

The instruments around her kept their mechanical sounds, the useless flow of oxygen—an undertone of futility. Her solitude was complete. She laid her head next to his again and waited.

Adam and Tom came hurrying into the room, and she raised her head slowly, wearily from the pillow. In a glance, the two young men—so alike and yet so different—grasped that their father was gone.

"No!" Anguished. In unison. They were too late.

Olivia got up and walked to the foot of the bed, where both her sons looked devastated, lost. She opened her arms and hugged the two tightly, letting her tears run again, mingled with theirs. The three of them were letting out the pent-up sorrow, profoundly feeling their loss, sharing the misery.

She kept them close for some time and then said quietly, "It's how *he* chose to depart. Maybe he didn't want you to see him take his last breath… he knew you loved him, and you cared, and you wanted to be here with him, but he needed his privacy to leave us… I was in the room with him, but he chose a time when I wasn't looking to slip away."

She didn't know whether what she said was right, but Olivia thought it might give them some solace to think so.

13

Two days later, on a cold, steely afternoon, they buried Elliot. Elliot had no family that Olivia and her sons knew about. Years ago, Elliot said something about having distant cousins, but he never got in touch with them. Old grievances, he said, but he was not willing to discuss the issue. Her divorced brother and his son were somewhere in Europe and could not arrive in time.

Her old parents were there, brokenhearted, unable to believe Elliot died before them, worried about their daughter and her sons. Adam and Ann escorted Olivia's eighty-five-year-old father, holding his arms; Tom and Emily did the same for her seventy-six-year-old mother.

The funeral was relatively small. Several of her colleagues were there, Olivia noticed, some neighbors, and a few of the boys' friends.

We hardly have any friends left, she thought. He'd pushed everyone away when he discovered he had cancer, not wanting compassion from anyone, shunning looks of pity.

They did not belong to any church, leading religion-free lives, and there were no prayers of any kind by the grave. The ceremony included the boys' eulogies, a few funny anecdotes of years ago, told by one of Elliot's oldest—and few—friends; a small number of poems that Elliot liked were read. Olivia said the final farewell. In a shaking voice, she talked about his loving nature and placing his family needs before his own, his uncomplaining acceptance of whatever life brought on, including the cancer. Tears were running down her cheeks when she ended quietly, "Rest in peace, honey, now that your suffering is over; we'll all miss you." Many eyes around her clouded, too, but she didn't notice.

The grave was filled up and covered with flowers.

After the brief ceremony, Olivia invited all present to come over to their house for some drinks, if they had time.

She drove home with Tom and Emily in her car; Adam and Ann followed, taking her parents. The house seemed gloomy, and she hurried to open the curtains and turn all the lights on.

Soon, the house was filled with voices, young and old. They were celebrating life, even in the aftermath of death. Gradually, the melancholy dissipated. People remembered stories related to a more youthful, healthier Elliot, sharing them with others. Olivia noticed how interested her sons were, as if they were collecting these anecdotes, adding them to their patchy memories of their father.

Olivia was in a haze, unfocused, her mind wandering. So many emotions fought for dominance in her soul—sadness and guilt, relief and worry, sorrow and loss. Despite the gloom and depression that were ever-present in the last years, she would miss him, she acknowledged. The memories of years past were sunnier and would flood her when she least expected them, but it was often the case with bereavement, she knew.

Moreover, there were so many issues she'd have to deal with, things she'd have to learn to do. After more than thirty years together, there were domains she knew very little about, she admitted to herself. She'd have to talk to the insurance company from now on, check their savings account, drive to the garage to service her car—all the things she hated to do, and Elliot relieved her from bothering with. There were probably many other functions she'd discover he took care of.

People talked to her, and she answered, but later she had no recollection of who said what or how she responded. She noticed both Adam and Tom watching her from a distance. They seemed worried.

I need to let them know I'm OK, not breaking up, she chided herself. *If they think I'm about to disintegrate, they won't be able to get back to their own lives.*

Straightening her back, pinning a smile to her lips, she pushed all irrelevant thoughts and feelings out of the way, turning her focus from her internal examination to her external surroundings.

She walked among her guests, moving around the big living room, talking to people, doing her best to put them at ease, showing everyone that she was managing.

It was a long time until the last guest left. Only the close family remained.

An hour later, the door opened again, and Sarah was there, bringing Pinky home. The little dog ran from one family member to another, barking ecstatically and springing from place to place. They started laughing when they watched her enthusiasm and antics.

Olivia sat down on the sofa, drained. The welcoming face she put on for everyone was wiped clean, the smile unpinned. Adam and Tom came to sit with her, letting her know she was not alone. Ann and Emily were clearing dishes and cups, loading the dishwasher, filling garbage bags, chatting softly. Olivia was happy to see that the two young women had become friends. It was a good sign of the future relationship between her sons, too.

Her mother, Rebecca, came to sit with Olivia and the boys, taking the adjacent armchair.

"I can't believe he's gone, and we're still here. That's not the right order of things," she said with a sigh. She looked at Arthur, Olivia's father, who was asleep in the farther corner of the sofa. "We loved him very much," she added.

"We know, Grandma." Tom said.

"We'll all miss him." Adam looked around, as if trying to memorize his house the way it was when his father was alive; his mother would change things now. It was only a matter of time.

Around ten p.m., the house was clean and perfectly ordered; the two girls came to join them.

Olivia's mother took that as a sign. She got up to wake her husband and leave. Olivia escorted her parents to the door. Her old father seemed exhausted. He was used to going to bed early; her mother was more the night bird.

Olivia was pleased to know they were happy to go home. They seemed to love their new apartment at the fancy Carlisle, the senior living community on Post Street, and adjusted well to the change from their big house to the beautiful, compact two-bedroom apartment. They made new friends in less than a year, her mother had new bridge partners, and her father enjoyed the gym and the swimming pool. It was reassuring to know that, in all respects, they were adequately taken care of.

Olivia returned to the living room. The four young people sat together, talking in a small, tight group. She joined them, though she was exhausted.

"When are you going back home?" Adam asked his brother.

"In a couple of days, if it's OK with you, Mom." Tom answered, looking at her. "That will give me a chance to spend some time with you, with Adam, and see some friends. Emily will have a chance to visit her folks, too."

Olivia nodded her assent.

"Shall we go to our coffee shop for breakfast tomorrow, like we used to? Adam, can you join us?" Tom asked.

Adam nodded, pleased.

"Sure, Tommy," she said. "I'm delighted you came home, and I'm grateful, and it will be great to go for breakfast." She smiled, her heart expanding a little, realizing how constricted it had felt in the last days... and, in fact, during the dreadful five-year period.

She added, her tone lighter, "You and Emily are welcome to use your old room, of course."

"Of course." He smiled.

When Adam and Ann left, Tom and Emily said goodnight and went to Tom's room. Olivia turned off the lights in the living room and went to her bedroom. She looked at Elliot's side of the bed. He would never occupy it again. She'd never again go to bed and find him there, lying on his side, his back to her.

I'm a widow, Olivia mused, trying to get used to her new status. *From now on, I'm on my own.*

She entered the bathroom to brush her teeth and saw his razor and toothbrush next to hers. She tossed both into the bin, removed his towels, and threw them in the hamper. She picked up his shaving cream and aftershave, ready to dump them, too, and then thought maybe Adam or Tom would want them.

No, she decided. It would be too weird if one of them smelled like their dead father.

The bathroom looked different without the visible signs of his occupancy. The single, lonely toothbrush reflected the loneliness that Olivia felt.

She was glad Tom and Emily were staying with her. The house would be less lonely.

Olivia turned the light off and returned to her bedroom. Only the small nightlight above her side of the bed was still on; the rest of the room was gloomy and dark. The silence inhabited the shadowed emptiness. She undressed slowly, knowing that sleep would evade her.

The thoughts and feelings she suppressed throughout the day now flooded Olivia. She allowed the emotional storm to wash over her, letting the tears she held back, flow freely. The strongest emotion, she realized, was vexation over her botched relationship with Elliot in recent years.

She blamed herself for all the missed opportunities, what could have been and would never be... so many things could have been done differently... It was not all her fault, Olivia conceded. Still, for years, she was the more resilient partner, so it was in her hands to alter what should have been changed in their relationship. But she didn't care enough, she admitted, and so she allowed the distance between them to grow continuously.

In the past, he helped a lot. Coming home early to be with the kids when they were young, cooking for them, helping with their homework. When they grew up, things changed. In recent years, he was not part of her academic life and showed no interest in it. At times, Olivia even thought that her advancement threatened him. He didn't try to stop or hinder her progress, but he seemed to resent her deep involvement in academic life.

If she had a chance to go back and make different choices, would she choose differently? Olivia wondered. No, she wouldn't, she admitted honestly.

So why did she feel so guilty about choosing the path of self-fulfillment? She was still pondering the question when she fell asleep.

14

Olivia slept late. Her sleep was troubled, and she was still tired when she woke up. Getting out of bed, Olivia padded to the bathroom. She took a quick shower, brushed her teeth, and put on a T-shirt and her old comfortable jeans.

The door to Tom's room stood ajar, no sounds from inside. They must have left early, Olivia surmised. She looked at her watch and saw the time was already nine forty-five a.m. They didn't leave early; she woke up late… and they must have taken Pinky out already. The little dog was in her basket, sleepily looking at Olivia, lazily wagging her tail.

She walked to the kitchen and turned on the coffee machine. Standing by the window, looking outside, she saw there was a lot of work to be done in her small garden. Though it was still winter, she wanted to get a few more seasonal flowers, add some color to the dreary place. She loved pottering in the garden but had no time for it in recent months.

Coffee in hand, Olivia went to Elliot's study. She had to go over all the documents he accumulated throughout the years. She was never interested in his business—the small company that manufactured medical equipment, mainly for the Bay area. He decided to sell the company with all its contracts and connections when he got ill. His pretext was age, saying he was too old to maintain the business, and as neither Adam nor Tom showed any interest in going into it, he'd rather sell it. Olivia suspected he wanted to control the sale's timing, not be forced to do it when it was less convenient or when potential buyers knew how sick he was.

Opening a few of the many files on the shelves by his desk, Olivia noticed how meticulously Elliot kept every contract, transaction, and receipt. Going over the papers, she realized he left her and the children much better off than she thought.

She also found the old letters she sent him over thirty years ago in his files. They were dating at the time but agreed to separate. She traveled east for her Ph.D. and had not decided whether she'd be back or not. They corresponded throughout that time. Olivia didn't know he kept her letters all those years. He always said he couldn't believe his good luck when she accepted the offered position at the University of San Francisco and returned.

Opening one of the letters, she read her doubts, her indecision... and her love. Yes, she did love him then. But she also figured there was already a gap between them, and it was bound to grow... It wasn't only the educational gap—he majored in economics, obtaining a bachelor's degree, which was enough for him—but a difference in attitudes. Her being more liberal, and Elliot a conservative, she was driven by an unwavering sense of social justice, and he was more practical and realistic. She wondered—even then—whether these differences would impact their relationship.

Her phone vibrated. Tom sent a message saying he'd arrive in a few minutes, asking if she was ready.

Of course, she texted back, *Meet you outside.*

***

They walked the familiar route to the corner coffee shop. "Is Adam not coming?" she asked, disappointed.

"He called earlier to say he'd be a bit late but will join us there." Tom smiled. "Don't worry. I'm positive he won't miss our meeting!" There was a glint in his eyes as if he knew something that she didn't.

They sat at their preferred corner, in the same positions they used in the past. Olivia decided to try and investigate, to find out what was going on.

"Are you and Emily getting married?" She asked half-jokingly. They were young—not even twenty-five, but she knew the relationship was serious and guessed they would formalize it sometime.

"Mom, are you probing or fishing?" Tom laughed. It was their usual code when either one was enquiring too deeply into areas where such an inquiry was too early or too private.

Olivia shrugged, embarrassed. Her flippant tone attempted to cover the seriousness of her question. She was worried they were too young to make such a decision.

"Don't worry, Mom. That's not the issue here. It won't happen yet. Em wants to finish her studies first, and we're in no hurry."

The menus were placed on their table, and Tom picked one up

immediately. "I'm starving!" he declared.

"Shouldn't we wait for Adam?"

"He wasn't certain when exactly he'll be able to join us, so I suggest we order, and eat slowly."

They ordered a full breakfast and talked about Tom's Ph.D. dissertation. He sounded enthusiastic, trying to explain the complex issues of the cybersecurity model he was developing, and she was happy to see his animated face.

Adam joined them before their food arrived. "Traffic was hell!" he declared. "But I'm glad you haven't started yet!"

Briefly looking at the menu, he signaled the waitress and said, "I'll have what they are having."

"Sure," she said, "Coffee for you, too?"

"Double espresso, please." Adam replied. "Thank you."

Olivia knew by the looks between the brothers that something was afoot, and she was anxious to find out what they were not revealing. "OK! What?" Olivia asked, her tone exasperated.

Adam looked into her eyes, and his face turned pensive, tender.

"You're going to be a grandmother in about seven months, Mom. This is the big news I wanted to share with you. Ann and I wanted to wait for twelve weeks, to be sure, before we said anything, but we changed our minds under the circumstances. I told Dad before I left for the airport to pick Tom up; I whispered the news in his ear. I don't know if he heard… or understood… I was so sorry I didn't tell him when we found out… before his deterioration! I wish I had… but we were told anything could happen in the first trimester… especially if it's the first pregnancy… and somehow, it did not feel like the right time to say anything when he was in such a bad condition. I told Tom yesterday, after the funeral, but there were so many people around you, I couldn't tell you."

Olivia was crying. Tears of happiness this time. She knew Ann was trying to get pregnant for some time and was overwhelmed by the joy she heard in Adam's voice.

"Congratulations! I'm so happy for you! And how does Ann feel?" Olivia managed.

"We're fine… she's fine… she's delighted. And relieved… The doctor confirmed that so far, everything looks OK. There will be lots of tests and examinations in the coming months. We'll update you, of course."

At that moment, three mimosa cocktails arrived at their table. Adam had called the coffee shop from the car when he was on his way, and asked them to bring it to the table when he signaled the waitress. Their breakfast followed the drinks, with the coffee shop staff smiling at them and sharing their celebration.

They raised their glasses, and Olivia relished the depth of the bond among them. Their small family was a tight-knit unit. A sense of harmonious calm engulfed her. She watched her sons conversing, animated. Not listening to what they said, she watched the interaction between them. Understanding and affection were noticeable.

We did good, Elliot, she thought, hoping somewhere, somehow, Elliot heard her.

15

Olivia took a few days off work. She needed time to grieve, adjust to the new situation, and create a schedule that did not include a need to rush home after a day's work.

Her days were slow, languorous, but not empty. She woke up late, went for long walks with Pinky when it was not raining, and dealt with Elliot's things. She prepared huge bags of his clothes and shoes for donation. She went through his desk drawers, pausing to remember the history of the items within—the collection of his old cellphones, the fountain pens he liked so much. In another drawer, she found his watches. The boys may want them, something personal of his. She'd ask them.

She sat on the carpet and polished them till they shone, remembering where each watch and pen came from, where and why they were bought: Birthdays, trips abroad.

The doorbell chimed, and Olivia got up slowly. She was not expecting anyone. Pinky was barking, but it sounded like a happy bark, a bark of recognition.

Sara, with Rex on a leash, was looking at her. "Come on." Sarah said. "You've been barricaded inside long enough! Were you brooding all day?"

"What time is it?" Olivia asked, surprised.

"After four p.m.!" Sarah said.

"Pinky didn't signal she wanted to go out, and I was clearing Elliot's study…"

"Let's go for a walk, for coffee, something!"

"Come in… Give me a minute."

"I'll wait here with the dogs. Hurry up!"

Olivia brushed her hair, put on a fresh T-shirt and came out of her bedroom.

"You *could* put some makeup on." Sarah said.

"Why?" Olivia asked, a wry smile on her lips. "Are we going on a date?"

"Well, you never know who you may meet!"

"Honestly, Sarah, I don't care who we meet. This is me, on a few days off, getting used to life on my own."

She *really* didn't care, she realized. And not because it was too soon. She didn't want anyone in her life right now. She had no idea how long she wanted this solitude to continue, but right now—it's what she needed most. Her home's peace and privacy formed a new order in her life, one in which she didn't have to rush home or hospitals.

Out of habit, they walked to the park. They chose a shaded bench, away from the kids enjoying the swings and the slides, squealing joyfully, distancing themselves from the indulgent mothers, who did not even try to keep some order in the mayhem they created.

"My daughter is just the same." Sarah sighed. "I'm not talking about strict control, but my grandkids have not learned the meaning of boundaries. They have no respect for other people's privacy and no consideration of their needs. It seems to me my daughter works just to get out of the house!"

Linda and Connor, Sarah's children, were a few years older than her sons. Her daughter married young and was a mother already, so Sarah already knew about "grandmother-ing". Olivia learned what to expect from her friend, especially what *not* to do.

Sarah always returned home angry and frustrated, telling Olivia about arguments and harsh words between her and her daughter. She couldn't help herself, Sarah said. Seeing how incompetent Linda was in dealing with bad manners, impertinence, fights over bedtime…

Linda, Sarah's daughter, had an autistic four-year-old son. He was diagnosed as a high-function autist, but with aggressive tendencies and frequent destructive outbursts. Sarah was frustrated by Linda's way of dealing with him.

Their minds seemed to have followed similar tracks, and, as if in response to an unasked question, Sarah said, "Linda is totally helpless when it comes to Ryan. She cuddles and spoils him as if she is trying to shield him from the harsh reality. Or to soften the frustrations created by the difficulties he encounters."

Olivia nodded to indicate she was attentive but said nothing. She understood Sarah's concerns for her daughter and grandson, and how helpless she felt. And her pain.

"There's nothing you can do about it, Sarah," Olivia said empathically, patting her friend's hand fisted in frustration. "At least you convinced her to get better professional help. The psychiatrist she's taking Ryan to is considered one of the best."

"The problem is not which psychiatrist he's seeing... I believe Linda herself is the problem. She is babying him! Neglecting the rest of her family."

"She may well be part of the problem which inhibits Ryan's development," Olivia concurred. "Linda has an older daughter, too, right? How is she taking it?"

"Zoe was really considerate, at first, when Ryan was first diagnosed. Protective... Supportive... Now? She's spiteful, self-destructive."

"Yeah, it often happens. I think that maybe Zoe is acting out, copying Ryan's behavior because she sees that it works for him," Olivia said. She waited for Sarah's reaction, for confirmation that it was OK to continue.

Sarah nodded.

"I believe that Zoe feels her brother receives much more love and attention than she does... and she's angry. She doesn't know how to explain what she feels, so she shows them."

Again, Sarah nodded. "I believe that is exactly what Zoe is signaling. She wants her mother's love and attention, too... but Linda is either at work or dealing with Ryan and hardly ever finds time to do things with Zoe."

They were silent for a while, thinking.

Another thought popped into her mind, and debating how to present it to Sarah, Olivia asked quietly, "Do you think Linda is using Ryan as a shield she can hide behind? Sort of a justification for all her inadequacies?"

Sarah seemed surprised, and Olivia was afraid she phrased her question too harshly.

After a reflective break, Sarah turned to Olivia and said, "Maybe. I'll have to think about it some more. Maybe this is why she won't relinquish control, won't allow anyone to limit her dominance. Ryan is completely dependent on her, and even when he's in kindergarten with other kids like him, he suffers when Linda departs. Somehow, he realizes she needs her work for her sanity, but other than her work—he behaves as if she is only his. He won't let her spend time with anyone, unless he is included and dominating her attention."

They sat, silent for a while, contemplating their talk, and then Sarah shook her head.

"How did we come to talk about me and my problems?" she said. "Tell me how you're holding up."

"I'm OK. Really. Getting used to having free time and no stress, with no domestic obligations."

Soft sunset colors permeated the park. Olivia noticed most mothers and kids were gone, and the birds, getting ready for nightfall, were heard clearly. The air became cold when the weak winter sun hid behind the low clouds. She loved it when it was so crisp, and the smells of trees and shrubbery infused the surroundings. Peace descended on the park. Olivia was reluctant to leave, but it was time to go.

She had a lot of work still ahead—she needed to finish sorting Elliot's office. Tomorrow morning, she'd donate most of his personal effects and get Ruby to clean the room properly. Top to bottom. She decided to turn it into a nursery so that when she became a grandmother, she'd be able to host Adam's baby, and any future kids he or Tom may have. Maybe the future grandchildren will want to stay for a sleepover.

You're fantasizing, old girl She chided herself. But it was so lovely to turn her thoughts to such a pleasant topic.

16

Olivia went back to work sooner than she intended. She wasn't cut out for idleness, and missed the action in the department, the interaction with colleagues and students, the intellectual challenges, and the ordered daily routines the intensive academic life necessitates.

Her days started early. Up by six thirty a.m., out for a short walk with Pinky. That hadn't changed. It was a time she spent thinking about the day ahead, planning her actions. Then, the gym—the treadmill first to warm up, the stepper next, maybe some rowing too, if she had time. She missed it so much and for so long! Now it was possible to work out properly. She took a shower and changed, and drove straight to work.

Her work schedule was loaded to fill her days, but also because there was so much to do. The new graduate specialization programs she planned were almost ready to be presented to the university's authorities. She dreamed of enhancing the graduate program's global impact in the diverse arms of the UN and NATO. They needed to recruit specialists in those organizations to act as mentors and reliable, well-known researchers. She had already met some high-ranking specialists and senior professors and interested them in the new initiatives. When—if—they'd join, the whole faculty would benefit, she knew.

We also need to review all the academic staff's advancement, see who needs further encouragement, who didn't take his or her share of mentoring, committees, etc., she thought.

The new routine she tailored for herself included time for socializing. She realized that the move to San Francisco and her demanding job, together with Elliot's frequent travels, had left her with hardly any friends. She wanted to create a new social sphere, go to concerts, movies, exhibitions.

She called the San Francisco Symphony and renewed her double subscription for the rest of the season. They couldn't give her the wonderful seats she had in the past, but maybe next season. Adam loved it, too, and went with her when Elliot didn't want to go. She was sure he'd be happy to join her again. Then, Olivia called the San Francisco Chamber Orchestra and reserved a single subscription. *I'll also renew my Opera subscription,* she decided. *I've missed it all so much…* It was like an immense void she had to fill, and fast.

Strange, I didn't allow myself to dwell on how much I missed this until it became possible to have it back in my life.

It was not entirely true, she knew. She *was* aware of how much she missed the concerts. She gave it up so as not to leave Elliot alone in the evenings as well as during the day… It was something she did willingly… couldn't act differently.

I *guess I was not* that *selfish, after all,* she thought.

Olivia was immersed in the report she had to submit to the university president, conveying the developments the academic council proposed for the graduate program. Sophie's phone rang frequently, but she didn't pass any phone calls to Olivia. She was very good at deciding the importance and urgency of calls. Therefore, Olivia agreed immediately when Sophie asked, "Can you take a call?"

There was something in Sophie's tone. Olivia had no time to figure out what it was when the caller was on.

"Professor Anderson?" A shy, young voice.

"Yes, who… Ruth—is that you?"

"Yes, Prof, it's me… I just wanted to tell you I'm fine… Aunt Judith said you'd want to know…and I wanted to say I was terribly sorry to hear about your husband."

"Thanks, Ruth. And your aunt was right—I'm delighted to hear from you! How are you, girl? Is everything OK?"

"I'm fine." Ruth said. "The pregnancy is going well, and the doctor said it's a girl!"

"Are you happy? Have you decided what you want to do?"

"I'm going to keep it. And raise my daughter by myself. Aunt Judith says she'll be happy if I stay with them even after my baby is born, and she'll help me. I love it here in the Valley; I love the vineyard, I love working with my uncle, taking care of the cultivation and harvesting, choosing the right varieties, using a refractometer to measure sugar levels."

"Hold it, girl, that's a whole lecture on wine-growing! You sound ecstatic, and it's wonderful! But what about your studies?"

"I found what I want! I'm going to be a viticulturist! I've been to university studying subjects I wasn't *really* interested in. I thought going to university was what everyone expected of me, but not something *I* wanted. I found out who I wanted to be and how I wanted to live, and it's right here. Napa Valley College has a program I can attend without leaving my new home. And finally, I'm sure my choice is utterly correct for me."

Olivia was pensive, absorbing the new twist. Ruth sounded so different… mature, and confident.

"Ruth… did you tell your parents?"

"Yes, I did. My father couldn't care less. He said, 'Do what you like.' Mom was more of a problem at first. But, luckily, she's busy with her new family and, if truth be told, she doesn't have time for me… I think what she hates most is the idea of me finding a home with her sister… It doesn't matter any more. It hurt at first… I'm going to have a baby, and she won't be there for me… but Aunt Judith will, so I'll be fine. And so will my baby!"

"Are you still in touch with your friends here? They were so concerned."

"Yes! They even came to visit me here! And they loved it, too! Aunt Judith said they could come to work with us in the summer and stay with us. That will be fun! They also loved the friends I made in Napa."

"And Rolf? Does he know where you are? And what about John?"

Ruth was silent. Olivia waited…

"Rolf doesn't know where I am. He asked Mason and Natalie, but they didn't tell him. They said he was furious when he found out I came by when he wasn't home and took all my belongings and vanished. I'm not ready to talk to him yet… And John. There is nothing I want to say to him after he dumped me as he did. I know it's *his* baby, but I am not interested in proving it."

"Sounds good to me, Ruth. I believe you found the right place for you. It sounds to me that Napa was the right decision."

"Yes, it *was* the right decision. And I'll always be grateful to you for helping me reach it. Thank you!"

Olivia smiled. "Keep me posted, OK? Take care!"

***

"Sophie, can you get John Kendrick for me? I tried getting hold of him several times! I want to see him in my office ASAP!"

"Right!" Sophie called. And then she mumbled quietly, "About time, too."

John was not in his office. Sophie left him a message to call her back. She entered Olivia's office and asked, "What are you going to do?"

"I don't think I have a choice," Olivia said. "I'll have to ask the university legal advisors what to do. John will have to resign at the end of the semester, of course. Otherwise—I'm afraid they'll fire him. The question is whether they will insist on pressing charges."

"He took advantage of the kid!" Sophie said vehemently.

"She's no kid. And she knew what she was getting into. So, it's two consenting adults. However, he *was* her teacher… I'd rather let the lawyers deal with this."

And the sooner he's out of here, the better, she thought. She was quite sure it wasn't a pattern, and he's learned his lesson, but still… he had a young family to support. She didn't want to deal with these concerns now.

When she later checked her daily appointments, Olivia found that Sophie scheduled a meeting with John Kendrick a few days later. According to Sophie, he called and asked for a meeting with her before she got hold of him. She wondered what he'd have to say about the whole affair with Ruth. What can a married professor say to explain such severe misconduct? How would he justify the breach of trust?

She invited Andrew Kent to join them—he was the dean of students, after all, and she filled him on the matter after Ruth gave her permission.

Olivia went to get a cup of coffee and met Andrew near her office on her way back.

"You look ready for a very unpleasant encounter," he said.

"Can't be avoided," Olivia replied and brushed her words away with a dismissive hand.

"And here he comes." Andrew said.

Olivia and Andrew entered her office, and John joined them a few seconds later. He looked haggard, stressed.

"Hello, John. You know Professor Kent, don't you?"

John nodded. "Hi," he said.

"Hi, John." Kent's voice was grave. "You know why we are all here. We would like to hear what you have to say."

"You wanted a chance to talk. We're listening," Olivia said, polite but distant.

"I did. Yes... I know my dismissal is inevitable. Although what I did was consensual, you know. Ruth wanted me as much as I wanted her. But, I know, it's still wrong."

Olivia only nodded and remained silent. At least he didn't deny the facts.

"You may not be aware yet, but the ripples reach much further than the affair. The gossip about it had spread, and one of my wife's friends told her about Ruth; I don't know how that woman found out. My wife is now suing for divorce. And I'm devastated. I begged her to reconsider, that it's not necessary—I've learned my lesson—but she's unwilling to listen. Mainly because Ruth is pregnant... I tried telling her I'm not sure I'm the father, but she doesn't care. Maybe, if I can prove to her it's not my baby, my wife will relent, I don't know, but there is a chance..."

John inhaled deeply, and his tone turned anguished. "I tried contacting Ruth, but she won't take my calls. I wanted to beg her to do paternity tests, that's all!"

He raised his gaze to meet Olivia's. "Please, can *you* talk to her? She would listen to you, I'm certain. At least we'll know undeniably if..."

"I won't try to influence her decision, and I can't convince her to talk to you, John. Nor do I wish to," Olivia said. "She's an adult and makes her own decisions. No one has the right to tell her what to do or what's appropriate. She makes her own choices. If she wants to share them with you—she will. As far as I know, she *did* try to talk to you, and *you* were the one who brushed her off."

"It was the shock of it!" John said, sounding anguished. "I didn't think she'd spring something like this on me! And you must agree it could very well be her boyfriend's baby."

"Spring it on you?" Olivia's temper flared. "Like you had no part in what happened between you?"

She saw his crestfallen face and relented. "I don't know why she refuses," Olivia said, looking at the distraught man. "I asked her before she left why she's so sure it's yours and why she does not want to ascertain paternity. She just shrugged."

"It's not only my wife..." John changed tack, sounding more insistent. "I need to ensure there will be no demands for child support. Especially now that I'll have to find another job, God knows where. Because you let everyone know about this mess."

"That's a baseless accusation, and you very well know it. I don't know how the rumors spread, but they did. Blaming Professor Anderson or myself would lead nowhere!" Andrew retorted angrily.

"John! What are you saying?" Olivia was furious, realizing John was trying to shift the blame to her shoulders. "I never told anyone," she continued coldly. "Except Andrew, of course. And he needed to know because of his role in the department. No one else heard anything from me. Of course, some students know, and I have no idea what they said or to whom. Don't try to find a scapegoat. Own up! And ask your wife who *she* told. She has no reason to keep your dirty little secret." Olivia turned acerbic and got hold of herself before she went too far.

John was taken aback. He didn't expect Olivia's harsh response.

Suddenly, before John could respond, Andrew, who was an avid reader of body language, noticed how John shifted his cellphone on Olivia's desk and asked him if he was using his phone to record their conversation.

Shocked, Olivia looked at Andrew, a question mark in her eyes. What made Andrew ask such a thing?

John blushed deep red, and this was answer enough. Andrew and Olivia exchanged a brief look, and Andrew said that the meeting was over as far as he was concerned.

Olivia crossed her hands in front of her.

"Yes, I agree," Olivia said. "Goodbye, John."

John sat frozen, desperate, at a loss. "My lawyer… he suggested it," he started saying and stopped. Then looked straight into Olivia's eyes.

"Olivia, please, help me. I know what I did was terribly wrong, and I'm so very sorry. I was petrified… And the way I responded when Ruth came to me was stupid and immature, but I need your help! Please—make her talk to me!"

"Is this why you're recording this conversation? As an indication of your trustworthiness?" Olivia asked angrily. She paused as she saw the desperation on his face. "I'll tell her of our conversation," she said in a softer tone. "If she chooses to, she'll contact you."

17

Almost six months after Elliot died, Olivia had a well-established, comfortable new routine. She liked her peaceful life. Her work was as demanding as ever, but all was going well—no dramas, no conflicts… She met friends, went to concerts, and visited her sons. She was content. Even the weather improved considerably and was much warmer.

I've learned to enjoy life again, she thought. *I gained the freedom to come and go as I see fit, without having to consider anyone else's needs. For the first time in so many years*—my *needs and wants came first.*

Liberty felt great, but it was also lonely at times.

She was thinking about the coming summer. The academic year has almost ended, and her administrative workload lessened. Soon, she'd have more time to write, travel, attend conferences—she longed for the stimulating options she missed in the last years and would now be able to enjoy. Maybe she'd fly to Italy to meet her brother? He was working there, and it'd been ages since she saw him. There was so much she wanted to do!

That evening, her phone rang. Her mother. Olivia forgot to call her as she did almost every afternoon.

She answered the call. "Hi, Mom." She sounded tired, even to herself.

Rebecca was oblivious to her daughter's tone and blurted excitedly, "Olivia—I want to suggest something! I'm going to take you on a cruise to Alaska! You know I—"

"Mom, hold it a second! Where did this come from? And why now?" Olivia was taken by surprise.

"You know I've been dreaming of going there and never had the chance. Now your father says he's too old and doesn't want to travel so far, and he hates ships! Now he'll be well taken care of here. So, please come with me! You deserve a vacation, some time for yourself, after all the hardship you dealt with in the last years! And you're too lonely with the kids away. Also—it would be a belated present for *my* birthday! I'll arrange everything! Can you take a week off?"

Her enthusiasm grew as she spoke. Olivia tried to slow her down, to say that it was not really a suitable time, but Rebecca wasn't listening. When she attempted to say she couldn't go, her mother—now sensitive to every nuance in Olivia's voice—asked what Olivia was concealing from her.

She's worried, surmised Olivia, probably assuming some health problems. Olivia was thinking fast. She didn't want to say how nervous she was about surviving an intensive week with her mother, but she had to respond somehow.

"Let me think about it, Mom, OK? I'd love to see Alaska, you know that. And the idea is so generous, but I need to make sure I can leave," she said. "I missed a lot of workdays in the last few months, before Elliot passed away, so I must check the possibilities."

Rebecca was too taken with her idea and the prospect of fulfilling her dream, she wouldn't consider failure. "Please, make it happen, darling! I'm not growing any younger, and who knows if I'll enjoy it so much next year. Or *when* an opportunity opens up in the future! I'll check availabilities!"

"We'll see, Mom. I'll come over soon, and we'll talk about it some more."

She had so many plans! And she wanted to be able to enjoy being on her own! But how could she disappoint her mother so? She knew her father was not in good shape, and also that he hated cruises. So, he wouldn't go… Maybe she should suggest that her mother take one of her friends instead? No… she knew that her mother would refuse…

***

A few days later, she was having coffee in Sarah's kitchen—a new habit they had on most Wednesdays when Olivia got home earlier—when all of a sudden, Sarah turned to Olivia.

"I think you are getting too comfortable." Sarah blurted.

"Ha?" Olivia was surprised. "What do you mean?"

"Just what I said—you're too comfortable with your solitary state. You're lonely, and you don't even realize it!"

"No, I'm not." Olivia tried, but Sarah cut her off with a stare.

"Yes, you are! You're getting used to being alone, doing everything by yourself, planning and organizing everything just for yourself. All too soon, you'll become a loner, like me!"

Olivia was stunned.

'Where does this come from? What makes you say that? *You*? Of all people? I thought you *liked* being alone!"

"Well, I do! It's right for *me*, but it isn't right for *you*. You're a people person, you know what I mean? You need people in your life. Not just at work."

"Yes, I do need people. And I *do* have people in my life. I have the kids and you, and I'm reconnecting with friends from the past... wait... that's not what you mean. Is it? You mean I don't have *a man* in my life, don't you?" Olivia finished, incredulous.

"Well... yes. But you need to go out with people in general. If you don't go out to places where you can meet men, you won't find one! The one who'll wake up your heart again."

Olivia shook her head. "I'm not sure I'm ready to form a new relationship..."

"You're too young to be a widow!"

"Sarah! You were widowed when you were younger than me! And you never thought of getting remarried or even finding a mate! I enjoy my independence, as you well know... Why push me?"

Sarah got up and walked to the window. She looked outside at the peaceful, drowsy garden, but the look on her face did not mirror the serenity she saw outside.

"It's different for me..." she said slowly, her voice sounding pained, hoarse suddenly. "My husband... I was glad when he died... relieved... I... I... for years... he was..."

She fell silent and shrugged.

"He was abusive?" Olivia finished for her.

Sarah nodded silently, a deep sigh escaping her lips.

"You never told me... but there were some small hints... and the way you avoided talking about these things..." Olivia said gently.

"What could I say?" Sarah shrugged again. "It ended before you came to live in the area..." She turned back to look at Olivia.

"There's another reason I never told you... whenever we hear about abused women, you seem so assertive when you say, 'She should have left him a long time ago.' Besides—it always seemed to me you had a perfect marriage, with a loving, considerate husband, so I didn't think you'd understand what it was like."

Shocked, Olivia considered her friend's words. "I'm so sorry, Sarah, truly... I strongly believe that no woman should stay in an abusive relationship, and tend to say this... without considering whether the abused woman can actually leave... And that's sort of insensitive of me."

She hugged Sarah tightly, and they stood together for a long time.

"Anyway," Sarah tried to switch topics, "We were talking about you, not me!"

Olivia refused to drop the issue.

"Most men are *not* abusive! The fact you were married to one doesn't mean you won't be able to form a very different relationship with someone else! And as for me—I don't know yet what type of person I want to find, so how can I search, or know where to search?"

After a reflective pause, Olivia added, "I don't know how long it will take, but I do need this timeout for myself. To decide what kind of men I want in my life. But you know something? You're right—I *will* want someone to share my life... someday... just not yet."

Sarah was still deep in thought when Olivia got to her feet and stretched.

"What time is it?" she asked.

"Late," Olivia answered and turned to leave.

***

Sleep eluded her. Olivia lay awake, thinking about her conversation with Sarah. Was she really turning into a hermit? No, she thought. She wasn't. But she did enjoy her solitude. Coming home after a hectic day at work, she needed time to unwind. And the house, which was so infused with sickness and depression in the past, was now a refuge, her safe haven.

But I'll want to change the house to suit me better.

When they moved in, five years ago, she made a lot of concessions. She knew Elliot's life would be more demanding because he'd have to travel back and forth between San Francisco and Sacramento, and that he was doing it for her. He never talked about sacrifices or tried to make her feel guilty, and she was grateful. So, when he wanted the dark, heavy furniture for the living room, and the dusky indigo velvet drapes, she hated it but conceded. She detested the beige and brown colors he wanted for the bathrooms but didn't fight it.

It will be airy and light colors from now on, she decided. *Oak*, she thought. *Lots of oak. And warm-colored cushions and rugs. This time, I want it to be entirely how I like it.*

Any man who'll be my partner in the future —if ever I find the energy to look for one—will have to like my home…

I don't know anything about finding a mate, she thought. She'd been with Elliot for almost thirty years. She didn't remember how to date. What do people do today? Where do they meet? How do they form relationships? How can one be sure he or she found the right person?

The main question was *what* to look for. Before the *where* to look, or *when* or *how*. She didn't know where to start.

Of course, like most women, I want "Prince Charming". The problem is, I'm no princess myself… so why would a "perfect specimen" want a less-than-perfect partner?

But then—nobody is perfect, right?

She'd need to find a partner whose imperfections are immaterial as far as she was concerned, and her own shortcomings—would not trouble him.

Olivia remembered telling Adam that people are never perfect. He was five years old at the time, and she got angry with him for fighting at school, then discovered he wasn't at fault. She apologized and tried to explain the fallibility of humans. She told him only angels were perfect and never made mistakes. Lucky for him, his mother was only human. If she were an angel, she'd be perfect. And living with an angel, when you are just a human being and, therefore, imperfect—would be very frustrating. She was not sure whether he grasped the complex concept.

She thought she should adopt her own ideas. *You're not perfect, so you don't want to find "Mr Perfect", because living with him would be just like living with an angel…*

She wasn't sure how to go on from there but finally drifted into sleep.

***

A couple of weeks later, her phone rang just as she arrived home.

"Hi, Mom," she said, attempting to sound cheerful.

"Livy!" Only her family members called her Livy. Rebecca sounded excited.

"Mom, what's up? Is everything OK?" Olivia was instantly worried by her mother's tone.

"Everything is great! Absolutely perfect! We're going! I've arranged everything! Well, my friend Barbara arranged it for us. Anyway, we have the flights, the cruise—everything!!!"

"Hold it, Mom! What are you talking about? Who's going? Going to where? When?" Olivia tried to slow her mother's enthusiastic outburst.

"You and me, of course! To Alaska! I told you I wanted to arrange it! You deserve a change of scene after all you've been through and all your hard work. And I deserve a break from your father... And now that we moved to the Carlisle senior community—I know he'll be absolutely fine... You know it was my dream! I wanted to do it last year as a present for myself, on my seventy-fifth birthday, but Elliot was so sick, I couldn't ask you to go with me... And I don't want to go alone. Not sure I can manage on my own."

"Mom, I told you I needed to think about this. It *really* is bad timing for me..."

"Livy, honey, it's *always* the wrong time for you! You're *always* busy. You haven't been away from home or your work in year. When was the last time you took a vacation?"

It was true. Olivia hadn't taken a vacation in years. But is this the vacation she wished for herself, after all this time? Would she manage, cooped up with her mother for days? Olivia's thoughts reeled.

"When, Mom, when is this going to happen?" Olivia asked.

"First weekend in September! I was lucky to find a cabin—someone canceled." Rebecca replied enthusiastically. "For a week! I told your boys about my plan, and they made a list of all the things we absolutely must see! So please, Livy, don't disappoint me! Make my dream come true! It's the last cruise of the season, and who knows what will happen in a year!"

Her sons collaborated with her mother to create the surprise she intended. The boys must have told Rebecca that, currently, there was nothing urgent in Olivia's life.

She didn't see a way out.

18

The park was tranquil when she arrived in the morning. The grass was still dewy, and the shadows hugged the trees. April blooms decorated the paths; their vibrant colors filled her with light-heartedness.

Pinky sprang forward. Olivia looked up and saw she was running to meet Tish. Mark raised his hand in greeting, walking toward her.

"Morning!" he said. "I haven't seen you for a long time! How are you? Keeping busy?"

"Very busy. Overworked…" Olivia smiled. "And you?"

"I'm fine…" Mark said.

For some reason, Olivia thought he wasn't. She wanted to ask him what was wrong but felt she had no right to invade his privacy.

Maybe he'll say something if he chooses to… when it's the proper timing for him. But something was wrong. She was sure of that.

"How are the renovations going?" Olivia asked, thinking that may be the problem. He told her some months ago that he and Helen bought a beautiful house in Seacliff, perched on a cliff overlooking the Golden Gate. He loved the peaceful vista, he said, the salty smell, and the sounds of nature.

"Great!" Mark's mood cleared. "The internal construction is almost finished; the bathrooms are all fixed, and so is the parquet. I chose oak, like you suggested, the light, blond kind. It's beautiful! When all the renovations are finished, I'll invite you to come over and see for yourself."

"You sound happy with the progress and the way the house is taking shape." This issue was not what bothered him, she realized.

"I am. It will be what *I* want. Uncluttered. No crazy decorating ideas. A house to live in and enjoy."

"Sounds good to me!" Olivia responded to his uplifted mood. "With cream-colored walls and some splashes of color in cushions and carpets— you'll have *my* dream of home…" She grasped what she said the moment the words left her mouth, and her face reddened. She averted her face, hoping Mark hadn't noticed and would not attach improper connotations to her words.

"And how is Cynthia? Does she approve of the choices you make?" Olivia changed the subject hurriedly.

A look of annoyance crossed Mark's face and was soon gone. "She hasn't seen it yet. And I do not involve her. I told you—this relationship is more for convenience, to go out, see movies. Anyway, I'll probably end it soon. I don't see her much, anyway."

No, Cynthia's not what he needs, Olivia thought. *If half of the gossip about her is right—she's definitely not…*

"I thought, at first, that the gossip was exaggerated, but I'm not sure any more…" He seemed hesitant. "Cynthia's beautiful, but it's not important… I'm bored most of the time."

"She's *stunning* and sexy," Olivia said, "And very *very* well to do. And well-connected, too—quite the high-society type, as far as I know. So, she has many advantages."

"Well, I don't think looks matter that much when you're older. I care more about a person being esthetic, not necessarily beautiful. I think that a woman who is intelligent, interesting to talk to, is much more fascinating."

What a revelation! Olivia thought. Both Helen and Cynthia represent the beautiful, elegant, bon vivants, but not the intellectual types.

"You seem surprised," Mark said. "Why?"

"Well…" Olivia stammered. "I am… I thought…" *What do I say now?* she thought, frantic. She took a deep breath.

"Well, truthfully?" she said and looked at him.

Mark nodded, so she continued.

"I thought Cynthia was *exactly* your type. She's much like Helen used to be, before she started drinking so heavily."

It was Mark's turn to look incredulous.

"I guess your friends thought so, too, or they would not have tried to couple the two of you." Olivia finished lamely.

"You don't think very highly of me, do you, Olivia?" Mark asked, pretending to mock her, but the tone of his voice sounded pained.

"No! No! Yes… I do… I mean, I *do* think highly of you. I mean…" Olivia raised her hands, pleading, searching for the right words.

"I do think highly of you. Honestly." She started again. "You're well-known as a brilliant doctor, a highly respected researcher, your appearances on TV command the respect of everyone. I'm always proud to say I'm your neighbor, and… It's just that I thought your taste in women was…" Olivia wanted to disappear, just melt away.

"Superficial? Shallow? Juvenile? Senseless?" Mark supplied the adjectives she couldn't voice.

Olivia shrugged, embarrassed.

"Well, well…" Mark said. "I guess appearances *are* deceiving, as they say, and what you saw justified your evaluation."

The perturbed look was back. Something was wrong. Olivia tended to trust her perceptions. People tend to call such discernments "intuition", but she always thought that intuition does not exist. That, consciously or unconsciously, humans notice subtle and often masked signals, that people can't hide even if they wanted to. It wasn't obvious what exactly were the cues she detected, but she was sure that her conclusion was correct—something was wrong.

But did Mark want to talk about it? She wouldn't know the answer unless she asked a direct question. Given their conversation so far, he was willing to open up and talk candidly.

"Mark, I sense something's wrong. Care to tell me what? You don't have to, of course, but…"

"Yes," he said, "I don't know what you perceived. But there's something very wrong."

He sighed heavily, and his shoulders dropped.

"I haven't told anyone yet. Not even my daughters. I went in for some tests, a regular checkup… and there were two round nodules on the chest X-ray. You know what that means?"

Olivia nodded, stunned. It meant he had some kind of lung cancer. Years ago, her father had it, and after they removed half of his left lung, he recovered. Fully. They caught it in time.

"The problem is, I had kidney cancer fifteen years ago and had half of my left kidney removed. The tumors in the lung look like metastases, which means that some cells managed to escape and lie hidden all those years… And now they have started growing. The expert I went to wants to do a PET-CT to determine if there are any other lesions." He stopped and looked to gauge her reaction.

She felt sadness, pain, and compassion mixed together. But she was not afraid or repulsed. And she didn't withdraw…

"Anyway, after all these years—this is bad news," he said.

"True, but maybe it's treatable, right? With radiation, or chemo, or an operation to remove the metastases?"

"It depends on where they are located. I'll know more in a few days."

"Why didn't you tell your daughters?" Olivia blurted, remembering he mentioned earlier that he didn't.

"Because they have their own lives to live, and enough problems without me adding my own. No need to worry them."

My sons would kill me if I didn't tell them something was so utterly wrong with me! Olivia thought.

"How old are your daughters?" She asked.

"Emma is forty; Clair is thirty-eight."

Olivia looked at him, surprised. "You don't think they'd *want* to know?"

A strange look crossed his face.

"You don't understand," Mark said, hastening to defend his daughters. "Their mother died when they were very young. Emma was fifteen, and Clair only thirteen, and they were traumatized. Victoria—that was her name—fought ovarian cancer for a year and a half, and it was terrible for all of us, especially the girls. And when I was diagnosed with cancer eight years after their mother died, it was too much... and they seemed fragile."

"They are adults *now*, Mark, not little girls... but I don't know them. Maybe you're right."

Mark shook his head. "When I know if there's treatment and what the prognosis is, I'll tell them. Not now."

They stood silently, companionably staring ahead, lost in thought. After a while, they simultaneously looked at their watches, noticed how late it was, and realized they needed to leave.

"I'm glad I told you," Mark said to Olivia, "It's difficult to let an almost stranger know your cancer has returned, but it felt good to share. You reacted sensibly but compassionately... You weren't intimidated or apprehensive."

"You seem relieved by my reaction. What did you expect?" Olivia asked.

"I don't know... but I like your levelheaded approach very much. And, as usual, our talks compel me to rethink issues I thought I already resolved," Mark replied, his eyes intently on hers.

I bet my comment about his daughters made him ponder how he was dealing with them, she surmised, but never considered asking in order to verify it was accurate.

Smiling at each other, they walked together out of the park.

19

"Sarah, hi!" Olivia sounded winded on the phone. "Can I bring Pinky over? I've got to rush to the hospital! Adam just called to tell me Ann's water broke, and he's taking her to the hospital… I want to be there with them."

"Of course!" came the immediate reply.

Olivia was sure that Sarah would help. It was past midnight, and she was glad Sarah was still up. Probably binging again… she loved those silly TV series…

In ten minutes, she was on Sarah's doorstep, with Pinky's bowl, bed, leash, and the spare keys. "I forgot to leave a note for Ruby," she said.

"Don't worry," Sarah was all smiles, "Go to your kids! I'll take care of the fort for you!"

Olivia started to speak, but Sarah cut her off, laughing. "Just go, and don't worry. You deserve some good news and some happiness. I hope all goes well, and I'll pray for you guys!"

Olivia clasped her friend tightly, knelt to hug the little dog, and rushed away.

***

Olivia arrived, breathless, and saw Adam and Ann before they saw her. They were sitting on the bed in the hospital room they were given. Their heads were leaning together. Her heart swelled, and she was reluctant to break the intimate tableau. A spasm crossed Ann's face, and she moved her body, searching for a more comfortable position. The contraction didn't last long, and was not very intense, judging by Ann's reaction.

Olivia knocked and entered.

They seemed happy to see her, and she was glad she came.

"How do you feel?" she asked Ann. "How close are the contractions?"

"I'm OK. It's not too bad… yet… so, I'm fine for now. There's still a lot of time."

"You're going to be parents very soon and make a granny out of me!"

she said cheerily. "Are you ready for the most important role in your lives?"

"I'm scared enough! Please don't amplify the situation!" Ann said, and Olivia knew she was only half-joking.

"You'll be fantastic parents. I've no doubts. You're both so sensitive and caring, I'm sure your baby will be just fine and have a bright future," Olivia said. "Are you going to tell me the name?"

"Only when the whole process is over, Mom, you know that!" Adam said impatiently.

Don't nag, Olivia reprimanded herself. *Let them decide when and where* She knew she tended to be a little bossy at times, and they would always reject her efforts. *I only want to help, even if they don't want my help.* She justified herself, but knew it was futile…

"I'm going to get some coffee. Can I get anything for you guys?" Olivia asked.

Both shook their heads.

Olivia went to look for the coffee shop. Passing close to the maternity ward entrance, she heard Margaret, Ann's mother, ask for directions. She wanted to be a part of the whole process, of course, and managed to arrive on time. Olivia went over to the entrance, and the two mothers hugged.

"Now Ann's joy will be complete!" Olivia said.

Margaret smiled; she was tense. "Where are they, do you know? Have you seen them yet?"

"Yes, I did. They are fine. The contractions are still far apart… So, I went for coffee. Do you want some?"

"I'd like to see them first." Margaret said.

"Of course," Olivia said, "It's this corridor, third door on your left."

Margaret hesitated for a second, then turned to Olivia. "Aren't you coming?" she asked.

"I'll just get some coffee and join you there," she said.

Margaret turned to look down the corridor, then nodded and walked away.

Once the birth process started, Olivia and Margaret went to the waiting room, where they sat for hours, expecting news.

***

Olivia fell in love with her granddaughter the moment she saw her. Leah

109

was lovely. She was a big, robust baby, with a mop of blond hair, and Olivia could hold her and talk or sing to her for hours. Ann took extended maternity leave, but Olivia was sure she'd want to go back to the law firm she worked for as soon as she could.

A new routine was established, and for three months, Olivia came every Tuesday afternoon to be with Leah. Even though it was meant to be free time for her to go out with friends or run errands, sometimes Ann stayed home on Tuesday afternoons, and the three of them went out for walks, to restaurants, or one of the parks. Adam took Thursdays off and came home early whenever he could.

It was a bright, sunny Tuesday in July. Olivia arrived to take Leah to the botanical garden. Ann decided to join them and arranged the big, heavy bag they'd need. Loading the car and strapping Leah in, they set out for a relaxed day of togetherness.

Leah gurgled happily in her pram, and they strolled leisurely. Ann said she was ready to go back to work and had found a young woman with excellent references to look after Leah every day until two p.m. Ann would be home with her and Leah for a week or two, to see how the nanny managed. She admitted she was worried it was too soon to leave Leah at only three months old, and Olivia had the feeling she was gauging her reaction.

"There is no 'right time' or 'wrong time' to go back to work," she said carefully. "The question is—do you *want* to go back to work, or would you prefer to stay home a bit longer? Don't think about what people might say. Think about what's right for you. And that's what you should do."

Ann nodded. "That's what Adam said, too."

Of course, he would say that. Olivia smiled in her heart. *He heard me speak on equality, women's rights, often enough... from the day he was born...*

"Do you intend to work full time, or return to a part-time job at first?" Olivia asked.

"McAllister, my boss at the law firm, said I could work part-time at the beginning, until two p.m., and when Leah is a little older, I can work longer hours. That sounds like a good arrangement to me... I really want to get back to work. Mothering is great, and I love being with Leah, but I need more... I think *you* understand me."

"I do," Olivia said. "I do. I did the same... after three months. And never regretted it. Of course, you'll miss a lot in your kid's life, but you'll gain a lot, too."

"Adam said you'd support me on this... My mom is not so sure... And most of my friends say I'm crazy."

"Look, Ann," Olivia stopped walking and turned to her daughter-in-law, "It should be entirely *your* decision. And there is a simple solution: I guess Adam will still be able to come home early on Thursdays, and, if you like, I can continue to come once a week to relieve the nanny at two. This arrangement would cover two days on which you can work late. Can your mother also come one day a week and give you an extra day? Then you'll have three full days."

Ann seemed flustered. Her body tensed, and she shook her head.

"I can't ask my mother," she said curtly. "She's not been well lately."

"I'm sorry, I didn't know," Olivia said, treading cautiously. "Complicated?"

Ann pointed to the bench they were approaching and sat down. Olivia sat next to her, worried, sensing Ann was distressed.

"Somewhat," she replied, not looking at Olivia. "I don't know yet." She bit her lower lip. "I'm worried... We'll see."

She hugged Ann, and they sat holding each other for a while.

"I'll tell you what," Olivia looked thoughtful, "We could try a somewhat different equation: If Adam arrived home early twice a week, and you come home early twice a week, and I come to relieve the nanny once a week, you'll both be able to advance your careers. This way, Leah will have a family member with her half days, all week, and both you and Adam on the weekends. And if there is a crisis along the way—we'll think of a solution, and one of us will be there! How does that sound?"

"It sounds like a plan." Ann said, and her brow cleared. "You are fully committed to the gender equality issue, aren't you?"

"Yes, I believe in equality. Not only for women. I think all individuals deserve a chance. Men too! They aren't equal when it comes to enjoying deep bonds with their kids—it's easier for women. Even considered 'natural.' Social norms discourage—even prevent—most men from preferring to stay home and be a full-time parent, for example. Society still looks funnily at men who choose that."

They looked at each other and smiled, sharing a feeling of deep understanding. Olivia thought that Ann felt relieved to find support.

***

That evening, Adam called her and added Tom to their WhatsApp video conversation. They often did a three-way call, so this was not unusual. However, after making sure that everyone was well and relatively happy, a surprise awaited Olivia when, after a pause, Adam said:

"Mom, Tom and I discussed it last night, and we want you to know that if—when—you decide to form a new relationship, we'll be OK with it. We wanted to tell you together. We know you were wonderful with dad. Always considerate and optimistic, simply *there* for him. But he's gone, it's almost a year since he died, and we had a long time to prepare for his death, and so did you. So, even if you consider it too soon, we thought you should hear this from us. It's not that you need our permission, but…"

Shocked, Olivia looked at her sons; both were nodding at her. *They can't be serious.*

"I… I…" Olivia stammered. She wasn't expecting this.

They both smiled. "You should see your face, Mom!" Tom said.

"We really mean what we say—if you ever want it, we'll be supportive. Not that you need our approval, but we thought you needed to hear this from us" Adam recapped the issue.

"Thank you, boys, I will take it under advisement, not that I'm quite ready yet."

20

The day was brisk for July, with high, scudding white clouds and a refreshing wind. Olivia set out with Pinky to the park to meet Sarah and Max.

Sarah was not there yet; Olivia started to walk, the invigorating fresh air making her skin tingle. The flowering shrubs created a riot of colors and smells and contrasted with the grass's cheerful, vivid green.

"Morning!" one of the neighbors she often met at the park said to her when he saw her on the path. "How've you been? I heard congratulations are in order! You have a granddaughter?"

"Thank you, yes, I do," Olivia responded. She couldn't remember his name, but she remembered Sarah told her he held a prominent executive position at one of San Francisco's banks. He was divorced and moved to their neighborhood a few months ago.

His beautiful golden retriever and Pinky were running in circles around them.

"And you? How do you like the neighborhood? Settled in? I think someone told me you came here from Davis? It must have been quite a change."

"I wanted a change. I needed one. After the divorce," he said. "It was complicated, like most divorces are, and I wanted a new start. I love it here. I love the people, the atmosphere, the culture... have you lived here long?"

"More than ten years," she replied, "And it is all that you say it is."

"Someone told me, your husband died a few months ago. Is it very tough for you? How do you manage?"

"I'm fine. Had a long time to get used to the idea of losing him, and life goes on... you know how it is." Then, sensing that he was too interested, she changed the subject and asked: "Do you have kids?"

"Three. Two of them left home, my youngest is still at home, but will leave soon."

He was interrupted in the middle of his sentence.

"Hi there." the low-timbered, cultured voice said on her right. "Haven't seen you in a while."

She stopped—Mark, as cool and collected as ever.

"Hey," she replied, "How are you?"

"Better now…" Mark said.

The man, whose name she couldn't remember, stopped walking when she did, and Olivia felt he was expecting her to cut short her conversation with Mark.

Olivia and Mark stood quietly for a moment, looking at each other.

"Better how?" Olivia asked after a while.

The man by her side seemed annoyed, mumbled something, and walked on, leaving Olivia and Mark in the middle of the trail.

"Well, the radiation sessions are over. I feel fine, the CT shows the tumors are considerably smaller, which is excellent news. It means they managed to destroy most of the malignant cells. It's a rare occurrence— renal cancer returning after so many years—and sending metastases to the lungs… And the best news is, it seems to be a slow-growing one."

"That is, indeed, good news," Olivia said. "Did Cynthia accompany you to the radiation treatments? Or your daughters?"

A strange look crossed his face, and Olivia paused.

"You didn't go alone, did you?"

Mark shrugged. "There was no need for anyone to come with me. I came in, I went out, drove to work…"

Olivia looked into his eyes, skeptical. She was about to say what was on her mind when she saw the loneliness and pain lurking behind the elegant façade and the enormous effort it took to cover them up.

"Oh, Mark…" She said, her eyes moistening.

"Well, I'm used to doing everything alone," Mark said slowly. "Even when I was first diagnosed with cancer, and Helen was well, she never came with me… she hated hospitals."

"Yet she chose to live with a doctor!" Olivia sounded indignant, even to herself.

Mark smiled. The embarrassed, self-conscious smile she remembered. The smile that evoked in her an urge to protect the little boy she saw behind the self-possessed, composed mask.

"And Cynthia? What's her excuse?" she asked.

Mark shrugged again. "It's over, well, almost… I'm phasing it out… Trying to do it as gently as I can. I want to end the relationship, despite her

114

attempts to maintain it. There's no real bond between us. There never was, and I guess there never will be."

"Oh." Olivia was surprised. They were seen all over the city, in all the prestigious occasions—gala concerts, exhibition openings—that's what the gossipers said.

"I know what people say, but believe me—it's not what it seems," Mark said, as if reading her mind. "We were seen together because she begged to attend these fancy occasions, and it was easier to give in than to fight... She pleaded with me to reconsider; said she'd do whatever I want, be what I want her to be... But I just want to leave, to end it."

"So why didn't you? End it, I mean," Olivia asked. She was still skeptical.

"Because I hate hurting people. And I'd rather go slowly."

Sarah entered the park, and Olivia waved, calling her over.

"Hi, how are you? How's Leah? I can't stay... must rush." Sarah said breathlessly, still at a distance. "I'm late... an appointment... I'm sorry." She apologized to Olivia and Mark. "We'll talk later?" this was directed at Olivia.

"Sure," Olivia replied, smiling at her flustered friend.

In seconds, Sarah veered onto a different path, which would lead her out of the park in a roundabout route.

"What was this all about?" Mark asked, his eyes laughing.

"I have no idea," said Olivia, bewildered. *That was so out of character,* she thought. *What got into her?*

"Leah is your granddaughter, right?"

"Yes." Olivia's face brightened as she thought of her bundle of sunshine. In a moment, she told him all about the baby's antics, how brilliant she believed her to be, and how proud she was of her son and daughter-in-law for the way they shared the task of raising her.

Mark looked at her, amazed. The transformation from a career woman, achievement-oriented, successful scholar, to a warm, nurturing, funny grandmother was complete.

She understood his surprise.

"What?" Olivia asked him, laughingly mocking him, pretending indignance, "You thought I was just an intellectual, researcher, academic director of a prestigious graduate program?"

She threw her chin forward, feigning haughtiness. "I can be Grandma, too, I'll have you know!" she said.

They both laughed.

"I believe you," Mark said. Was it astonishment in his look?

Olivia decided to inquire. "How about you? You're a grandfather too, aren't you? What kind of grandfather are you?"

Mark's face grew solemn.

"I'm more of a utilitarian grandfather." He saw that Olivia was expecting a further explanation. "I'm less involved in their daily lives; I get involved if I'm asked, mostly on technical issues. I help mostly by paying for things."

"Is it your choice?"

"To a certain degree, it is my choice. But not entirely."

He paused, as if considering how much to reveal.

"My daughters were grown up when Helen entered my life. I remained single for many years after their mother died and was not involved in a serious relationship until they went to university. I guess they got used to having me all to themselves. Suddenly, a beautiful young woman had a claim on my time and my loyalties. They were trying to fight my decision to live with Helen. So, when Helen and I bought the house and moved in together, a distance developed."

"You didn't have any significant relationships before Helen?"

According to the stories she heard about Mark, he was quite the 'ladies' man', a social butterfly, and, in the past, often appeared in gossip columns of various tabloids with different—always rich, beautiful, and elegant—partners.

"I did, of course, I did." He looked at Olivia. His faint smile did not reach his eyes; a silent plea for understanding lurked behind the self-mocking smile. "I'm sure you heard of my prowess, but trust me—the stories are vastly exaggerated."

A tabloid labeled him "one of the most sought-after, eligible men", she remembered. So, probably, anytime he went out with anyone, a romance was assumed.

"Olivia, please believe me… I admit, I was not a recluse after Victoria died. I was about forty at the time! But most of the stories are false."

He genuinely wanted her to believe him, she realized. And she was sure he was telling the truth. But, then, another consideration interrupted her thought process.

"Mark—how old were your daughters when you started seeing Helen?"

He thought for a second and said, "Emma was twenty-two or twenty-three, Clair two years younger. Why?"

"They had their own independent lives? Why should it matter to them who you went out with?" Olivia tried to understand.

"Yes, well…" Mark said, and she could see he was nonplussed.

She looked at him, waiting for him to continue and explain.

"As I said, they resented Helen's bossiness, and my daughters stopped coming. She was very different, not what they were used to. She was the total opposite of their mother… and they thought she was entirely unsuitable. Moreover, when they gathered that the relationship was more serious than those I had before, they felt threatened."

Olivia kept silent. Why would they hinder his attempt to rebuild his life? He was a well-to-do, fifty-year-old man, with a well-established career. Of course, he'd want to find a mate.

The silence between them deepened, each lost in his or her thoughts. Then, with a sigh, Mark said, "I waited until they grew up before I allowed any relationship to become meaningful… perhaps I waited too long."

Perhaps, Olivia thought. *Or maybe—you raised them in such a way that led them to believe they are the center of your universe, and they weren't willing to relinquish the position to anyone. Or maybe they saw something in Helen which you didn't—she* did *end up drinking and smoking so heavily. There could be other explanations, too… And perhaps I'm too judgmental.* He had to act as both father and mother after Victoria died, so maybe he needed to make allowances that other parents do not.

Olivia remembered that his daughters were married and had kids of their own. One of them was a well-known architect, the other a successful corporate executive. They must have grown out of the dependence Mark described earlier.

"Have your ties with them strengthened, now that Helen is no longer in your life?" Olivia queried.

"Somewhat, maybe," Mark shook his head pensively. "It was always a strong relationship, even when Helen was alive and well and antagonistic. They *are* my daughters, and nothing will change that. And if they need me—I'll always be there for them."

He paused for a second, staring into the distance. "They have their own lives, with kids of their own, and successful careers. I see them and their children once a week, on Saturday afternoons, for a couple of hours. Sometimes one of the kids is busy with friends, but I see them almost every week. And, of course, we talk on the phone if they need me."

"And are they involved in your life as much as you are in theirs?" Olivia inquired.

"Not really," Mark sounded gloomy. "Usually, they don't know about my needs, my desires, my concerns, if it is not related to them. But I never asked them for anything, never demanded their care or attention, so they never thought they needed to reciprocate. I thought they had enough to deal with after their mother died."

Olivia looked at Mark and decided to say nothing. She realized it was not a pleasant acknowledgment to make.

"There's another issue…" Mark continued after a while.

"What issue? Other than what?" Olivia couldn't follow his train of thought.

"Why I'm needed in their lives, but cannot burden them with my problems," Mark said. "Clair, my younger daughter, has a son—Jeffrey—who is problematic. And she often needs support, or financial help. Years ago, we found out his development is somewhat slow for his age, and he has severe learning disabilities. He is verbal, but even though he is fourteen, he reads like a third-grader… and he has no understanding of arithmetic whatsoever. Two years ago, he was diagnosed with a borderline personality disorder, with severe behavior problems both at home and school. You know what that means."

"What kind of behavior problems?"

Mark shrugged, dejected. "He's often aggressive, impulsive. He can't handle anything that remotely seems like rejection… it leads to dramatic outbursts, throwing things, hurting people. He even tried to choke his teacher once."

Olivia's mind went through the list of possible manifestations of the disorder, thinking how deeply the whole family would be affected by such a predicament.

"I'm sorry, Mark… I didn't know."

"He has terrible aggressive episodes, he loses control, and he's now five-foot-seven, weighing about a hundred seventy-five pounds, so you can imagine how difficult it is to cope with him. Since he's grown so big, even

Clair is afraid of him when he's in a tantrum. And Adel, her nine-year-old daughter, is terrified of him. Clair never leaves her alone with Jeff."

"Wow." Olivia couldn't find the words to express the depth of her sympathy.

She knew how profoundly the relationships among all family members could be affected by the challenging teenager... No wonder Mark was so concerned.

"Does he go to school? Special-needs classes?" she asked.

Mark nodded. "But he's problematic there, too, and Clair is often called to take him home when he's frustrated and aggressive. It's very tough for her."

"Does he receive medication to reduce his aggression?"

"Sure," Mark said and grimaced, "Doesn't help much."

"Maybe a higher dosage?" Olivia asked, though she thought it ridiculous to ask Mark—the expert—such a question.

She saw Mark's reaction and understood she hit a raw nerve. "Clair doesn't want to increase the dosage so as not to turn him into a zombie... when it comes to managing his medication, his day-to-day treatment—she listens to no one," he said.

"And you do not agree with her on that," she surmised.

"Clair doesn't want my advice... she decides... and I don't push. It's *her* son." His frustration was apparent. "But when there's some acute drama, she calls me and wants me to use my status and connections to help... Usually—to smooth things over and get Jeff off the hook. For example, he was violent at school last week and tried to choke his teacher... The school called Clair, but they also got the police involved... Clair called me for help. I left the hospital and rushed over."

Mark smiled sadly and shrugged. "I guess when the police officers saw me—many of them recognize me from all my TV appearances—they were more polite, more willing to be lenient, more considerate of Jeffrey's disability. So, whenever she needs help—Clair calls me or Emma, her older sister. Then Emma notifies me, and I try my best to deal with the crisis and its consequences."

He paused for a while and seemed far away. "It doesn't happen often," he said. "Usually, Clair manages just fine. She's brilliant and very competent. Very successful at her work and holds a senior position. She does wonders for the firm."

He seemed to be trying to improve her image of Clair, Olivia realized, to present her as an independent, capable woman. Raising a problematic child was a heavy load, a constant anguish one had to live with, never able to put the burden down and relax.

It's clear she needs her work, needs a life outside the home, needs the place where she is esteemed, achieving, successful, or she'll drown. I wonder how I would have dealt with a situation like hers. Could I manage a full-time, high-power career and raise a child like Jeffrey, who required constant monitoring?

Olivia was listening intently, considering the complexity of the dynamics in his family, feeling his pain. She said nothing. Instead, she looked at him, her empathy unmistakable. After a while, she said, "I'm so sorry for you, for them."

They were silent, deep in thought, each staring, unseeing, into a diffuse individual space.

After a lengthy period of unexpressed thoughts, Olivia asked, "And her husband, what's his role in all this? Doesn't he have a say? How does he relate to Jeffrey? He must have an opinion on what's happening?"

"Clair won't let anyone decide when it comes to Jeffrey. She makes all the decisions… Spencer, her husband, won't stand up to her when it's related to Jeffrey or Adel. He's also very busy with his software startup and travels a lot anyway, so he's often absent."

I wonder how Helen responded to all this? Olivia pondered. *Once the problems with Jeffrey became more severe, Mark probably became more involved in his daughter's life than he was before, and that must have infuriated Helen, pushing her to drink and smoke even more…*

"I can't believe I told you all this," Mark said. "These are not topics I talk about. How did we get to talk about these issues?"

He wasn't angry. Astonished, maybe.

"Sometimes, it's easier to talk with strangers than with close friends or family," Olivia said.

"You're no stranger," Mark responded, with a small, wry smile that reached his eyes.

"Relatively speaking," Olivia replied feebly.

He trusts me… and he acts as if he wants my company. Ignoring the immense differences between our social spheres. Well, maybe he's used to having female "buddies"? Sounds strange to me, but then, what else could this be?

21

The long and exhausting day was over, and Olivia was headed home. Though it was August, and the academic year had ended, her schedule was busy. She was still thinking about the paper she was working on. *It will be a significant breakthrough,* she thought. Several researchers were collaborating with her on the topic, and it seemed they'd have a substantial contribution to understanding people's willingness to invest in global ventures.

She was surprised to realize she had almost reached her street. Was there no traffic today? She looked at the car clock and understood that her mind was distracted again, and she drove without awareness of the road… *Bad habit,* she remonstrated herself, *very bad…*

She reached her house and got out of the car, her bag in one hand, the phone in the other. She tried to find the right key to open the front door when her phone rang. Juggling not to drop anything, she opened the door and hurried in. The phone stopped ringing. Frustrated, she looked at the screen and froze. The display showed the caller was Prof. Mark Wallace. She was trying to figure out what it meant, and why he was calling her, when the phone rang again.

"Hi," Mark said, "It's Mark."

"Yes, I know. I have your number from way back when you helped my father. How are you?"

"Fine. Great. All the renovations are finished, and the last of the workers left the house today, and finally, I moved in! I promised to call and invite you to come and see the house when it's all done. Can you come?"

"What?" Olivia was bemused. "Now?"

"Yes, why not? Are you busy?" Mark asked.

"I just got in after a grueling day, and—"

"You haven't eaten yet, have you? So, come, I don't cook, but I'll fix us a little something, with a glass of Chablis on the terrace… Please, come."

She was tired and wanted a shower, but she *did* need to eat something, and she *was* curious to see the house she heard so much about and observe the result of their discussions of color schemes, wood textures… still, she hesitated.

"OK, we'll make it a short visit—tomorrow I have to be at work early… but I *do* want to see it!"

"Great! See you soon!" Mark gave her the address and hung up.

It was already eight p.m. Olivia knew tomorrow she'd regret her hasty decision, when the lack of sleep would hit her hard.

Olivia changed her clothes and put on a comfortable ensemble of jeans and a top. She was back in her car in ten minutes. The streets were clear, evening rush hour long over, and the traffic was lighter as she reached Geary Boulevard heading west. She drove slowly, enjoying the serene beauty of the area. It was one of the less touristic neighborhoods, with no "attractions" such as famous locations or restaurants. It was not as posh as Pacific Heights, but the spacious houses afforded the best vistas of the ocean and Golden Gate Bridge, away from the city's bustle, which was why Mark preferred it.

He was out on the porch with Tish when she parked, a welcoming smile on his face and a tall, cool-looking glass of the promised Chablis in his hand. The sound of the ocean waves breaking on the shore below engulfed her, steady and deep, like a heartbeat. She crossed the beautiful front yard. Though she couldn't see much in the dark, the fragrances that reached her nose told her there were lots of flowers and shrubs around her, adding a subtle layer to the salty sea smell.

"Wow," she said when she reached Mark, taking the proffered chilled wine glass from his hand.

"Wait till you see the rest of it." Mark laughed softly.

They walked inside slowly, taking their time. Her limpid eyes were swallowing the view in front of her, his eyes absorbing her reactions. It was beautiful, indeed. More than beautiful. It was magnificent. Everywhere she looked, every detail was in understated but refined taste. The colors light and airy— cream-colored sofas, with a few coral pink and teal cushions, and marvelous Persian carpets.

"Amazing," she whispered. "Exquisite."

She wandered slowly through the house, sipping her wine, the oak floor drawing her in, inviting her to investigate further. She reached the kitchen and realized it was so neat that it bothered her.

Somehow, Mark understood. He was seeing his home through her eyes and reckoned why she stopped. "It seems too perfect, too orderly, right? Unlived in…"

"All it needs is time," Olivia said. "And somebody who'll break the perfection to make it seem alive. I'm sure you'll manage it in no time!"

She walked to the enormous, sliding-glass doors and gazed at the breathtaking vista of the Pacific and the lighted up Golden Gate Bridge in the distance, the view uninterrupted by other houses. A full moon was hanging low, casting a silver strip on the water.

"Dreamscape," Olivia murmured.

She felt Mark's hand laid gently on her shoulder, leading her onto the terrace.

"Come, sit down," he said softly. "I'll refresh your wine."

He was back a few minutes later with a tray full of cheeses, olives, cherry tomatoes, a basket filled with bread rolls and crackers, and assorted fruits, which he placed on the table. The wine bottle was in a bucket filled with ice by his chair.

They sat side by side, gazing at the open vista, immersed in private thoughts. Olivia was enthralled by the peaceful scene. Mark bent forward to take a slice of pear. His leg brushed against hers. She hadn't noticed at first; she was focused on the flickering lights upon the water. When he straightened and offered her half of the slice, without moving his leg away, she thought it might be intentional but wasn't sure. It felt too teenagerly and insecure, completely the opposite of the savvy image she had of him.

She concluded that he was probably not aware of it, or that it was just her imagination. *Or wishful thinking?* She chided herself.

They talked of his work and hers, about Elliot and Helen, about her sons and his daughters. The conversation flowed smoothly, without awkward silences, the long familiarity enabling her to relax.

He filled her glass again, and she saw the time on his watch.

"Mark, it's past midnight! I forgot myself… I have early meetings tomorrow! And you? How early do you have to be at work?"

"I play tennis tomorrow at six thirty," he said and smiled. "So what? I enjoyed the evening."

"Yes, so did I, but I'll leave you and your wonderful dream house to get some rest." She got up and stretched. "I'm delighted for you—it's a beautiful house, tastefully done, and in an exceptional location. Excellent choice, though we'll miss you in the old neighborhood."

"You can always come and visit!" Mark said, his eyes smiling sincerely.

"And you can bring Tish and come to visit us, too!" She smiled back.

***

Olivia was confused. She went over the evening, step by step, analyzing her perceptions and feelings, but no matter how she tried to interpret the events, she remained bewildered. Was this just a pleasant evening spent with a friend? Or was Mark trying to lead them somewhere else, deeper than friendly acquaintances?

Come on, be sensible, don't kid yourself, she scolded herself. *You know you're not his type. This was not a dinner date! No dinner at all, come to think of it...* But the little nuances she perceived indicated otherwise. She usually trusted her instincts, but she doubted them this time. The conclusion they led to was so improbable. Was Mark attracted to her?

Olivia didn't think so. She didn't see herself as "attractive". Certainly not the Olivia that Mark saw in the mornings in the park—with the old jeans and faded T-shirt, no makeup, and bleary-eyed. Not what she would have considered his "usual type".

She knew that he found her interesting, and he liked to listen to her opinions, the way she analyzed situations. She was an intellectual who read a lot, and they loved the same classical music. So, maybe, he was just bored and needed some refreshing conversation, which, according to Mark, Cynthia could not provide.

That's probably it, Olivia decided. *He had a free evening and wanted stimulating companionship.*

And what about me? Am I interested? I never considered him a potential partner. She wondered why not. He was good-looking—for a sixty-five-year-old man—intelligent, successful. Yet, she never thought of the possibility of taking their acquaintance further. What was the barrier? Olivia figured it could not be his personality traits, because she didn't know him well enough to know them. She knew he was open-minded, respected by his colleagues, but didn't know whether he was generous or warmhearted, for example.

Then she understood. The block was not Mark himself; it was his social world, which was so far from hers. According to rumors, there was something flashy, "show-offy," in the society he was associated with.

Do I want to belong to his social world? Olivia realized she did not. She was not interested in the lifestyle Mark seemed to lead, a life that included fancy designer clothes, grand openings, being seen in the right places, flashy cars. Being with Mark meant becoming part of his social life, and she wasn't sure she wanted to.

She liked Mark himself, as a person, as a friend, she decided. There was—potentially—much more depth of personality and intellect to Mark Wallace than she gave him credit for. So—her rational, analytical mind concluded: The evening together was an unexpected, enjoyable, and pleasant experience. It was nothing else.

That night, she dreamed of Mark, and in her dream, he was much more than just a friend.

She woke up in the morning, remembering the dream. Was her subconscious trying to tell her something that her conscious mind refused to grasp?

There was already a text message on her smartphone screen when she woke up.

"Last night was wonderful. Greatly enjoyed it. Thank you!"

It was sent at five thirty a.m. Mark wasn't kidding… his day *did* start very early.

"Enjoyed it too! Loved your house! And the view." She wrote back and added a smiley with hearts for eyes.

His immediate reply was a series of flowers, and a happy smiley, followed by a thumbs-up.

What a lovely way to start your day, she thought, smiling languidly.

***

A few hours later, Mark phoned.

"Can you talk?" he asked, knowing she was at work.

"Yes. How are you? How was the tennis?"

"I lost. No concentration. My mind drifted. And you—slept well?"

"Yes, indeed, though I had some strange dreams, which I remembered when I woke up… unusual for me," Olivia said, amusement in her voice.

"Shall we meet tonight so you can tell me all about them?" Mark asked.

Oh... What a surprise! Olivia thought, *and he sounded so eager, hopeful*! She planned to work tonight. There was so much she had to finish!

"Well…" Olivia began reluctantly.

"Don't hesitate!" Mark cut her off. "Please say yes!"

That eagerness again. He sounded like a happy sixteen-year-old.

"I really must…" Olivia tried, and again Mark interrupted before she could refuse.

"It's Friday, so you'll have the entire weekend if you need to do some work."

She faltered briefly. Then, surprising herself, she said, "OK. OK, eight p.m.?"

"Great!" Mark sounded enthusiastic. "I'll bring us a good bottle of wine! Do you prefer red or white?"

"The Chablis last night was wonderful," Olivia said, a smile in her voice.

"A chilled Chablis it is, then," Mark said. "See you at eight!"

Her mind was in a whirl, her heart beating madly. *What did I just do?* She was overwhelmed. *I'm never impulsive! What got into me? What was I thinking?*

Honestly? —she admitted to herself—*You're in the seventh heaven, as the cliché goes. And there's your solution to yesterday's dilemma of "was it just a pleasant evening or a beginning of something more?"*

Now she'd have to decide whether she wanted the "something more".

22

He was punctual. Olivia opened the door to find him there with a broad smile, red roses in one hand and a chilled bottle of Chablis in the other. A clear statement of "I came courting…"

"Hi," he said. Simple. Just that. And then he bent to kiss her cheek lightly.

Her heartbeat went crazy; she felt tense, flustered. Mark walked in and turned confidently to the kitchen, looking for a flower container. She handed him a crystal vase, and while he filled it with water, she unwrapped the flowers.

Saying nothing, he found the wine glasses and the corkscrew. He poured the wine and handed her one of the glasses. Leaning on the counter, he looked straight into her eyes and said, "To us!"

"To us." She whispered back, extending her hand to clink glasses.

They both took a sip, and he removed the glass from her hand, placed it on the counter next to his, and took her in his arms.

His strong arms wrapped around her tightly, holding her close. "I wanted to do this all day. You were constantly on my mind," he said softly in her ear.

She was trembling and thrilled. The long, lean body felt like a perfect fit. She barely reached his chin, and her head rested on his shoulder comfortably, as if it had always belonged there. "I thought of you too. A lot. Couldn't focus on work."

He turned her face to him and kissed her softly. "Is this OK with you?" he asked, but did not wait for a response and deepened his kiss.

Olivia felt she was melting, her knees unable to hold her body upright.

He let go, picked up the wine bottle, handed her the wine glass, and picked up his own, indicating the living room. "Shall we?" he asked, but again—did not wait for her response.

"So, how was your day?" he asked, his eyes warm, not leaving her face.

"It was fine until you called," she said, chuckling and embarrassed.

"Then I'm glad I didn't call you earlier. I wanted to, but held back, until

I couldn't any more. My day was ruined, too… Even my tennis!"

He took her hand, caressing it slowly. His hand was dry and warm, the touch feather-light.

"Did I really ruin your tennis?" she asked.

He nodded, "Unbelievable, but true."

He turned to her, and she knew he was going to kiss her again.

"Mark, this is so sudden. So unexpected… Surreal, even. I'm not sure…" She didn't know what she was unsure of, how to explain what she was feeling.

"I know," he said. "It's a total surprise for me, too. After you left, I realized this is absolutely, precisely, completely what I want."

"How can you be so sure?" Olivia couldn't believe he had such confidence after a single evening, pleasant as it was.

"I'm completely sure," Mark said, continuing to stroke her hand, his eyes conveying his confidence. "And it's not just after yesterday," he added as if he read her mind.

"I didn't even think of finding a partner yet…" Olivia tried to explain. "And it's more than thirty years since I dated. I'm so embarrassed. I don't know how to go about it."

Mark hugged her tightly. "I have enough experience for the both of us," he whispered in her ear. "Just flow with me, let yourself drift."

He kissed her ear, his breath warm on her cheek.

"Trust your instincts," he murmured, soothing her.

She was still tense, unable to relax into the pleasure his touch was providing.

"I'm trying to relax, but I'm so used to being in control, I'm unable to let go…" Olivia's stress was increasing. She was torn—her mind was dictating one thing, while her heart and body wanted something else.

Mark partially released her. His left arm was still around her, his right one caressing her face, throat, and shoulders. His lips moved softly on her hair, her brow, her eyes.

"Don't worry," Mark whispered softly. "I love your strength and independence and your spirit. I'll never try to break them. It's part of what attracts me to you, don't be anxious… Just let yourself feel."

He disengaged and bent forward to pour more wine into their glasses. Olivia missed his warmth immediately and wanted to snuggle in his arms again, but she held back.

"Mark…" Olivia wanted to explain her hesitation, her bewilderment. She didn't know where to begin. Mark turned to her as his hand crept to her thigh, his eyes holding hers.

"Go on," he said softly.

She shook her head slowly. "I don't understand… I've never seen you as a potential partner. I always saw you as part of a very different social circle, with very different values and preferences than mine. When I tried to imagine a future partner, you were never even considered. I never assumed there could be a real connection between us. It never occurred to me there's potential for you fitting in my world, or me fitting in yours… I'm not your style."

Mark was silent, thinking, choosing his response. His hand was still caressing her thigh, and she felt on fire, her insides melting. Olivia didn't move, praying he wouldn't stop, afraid of what would happen if he continued. She wasn't sure she was coherent.

"Do I make sense? Do you understand? Can you explain why you thought there could be anything meaningful between us?" Olivia looked at him, imploring.

Mark arranged his thoughts, and after a long pause, he said, "We talked often enough, and it was always a pleasure. Stimulating, intelligent, exciting, you made me think. I love your intellect and the way your rational mind analyzes situations. For me, that is a great source of attraction. When you talk, you are animated, your bright eyes so expressive… and I think I told you once that physical beauty doesn't mean that much to me… your kind of beauty, which derives from your brilliance, appeals to me much more than the skin-deep kind."

He was quiet, but Olivia could sense he was not done and waited for him to continue.

"You know, I think you completely misjudge me. You evaluate me according to the gossip you heard and the external, face-value factors or cues you perceive. It's not who I am. Not *all* that I am, certainly."

"Perhaps I did misjudge you," Olivia admitted softly, "Though I believe I'm pretty good at gauging people. It's hard to accept I made such a huge mistake," she said.

Yet, Olivia thought, *he seems so sincere and so vulnerable… Did I get the wrong impression of him? Have I taken him at face value? If so—what led me astray?*

"I hope you enjoy talking to me as much as I enjoy our conversations!" Mark's tone reproached her. "And I hope you'll give me a chance to prove to you that what you see is not the whole of me... Give *us* a chance."

"Well, I admit that you *are* much more experienced in such matters." unable to look at him directly, Olivia lowered her gaze. "I have no idea what to do, how to date, how to continue."

"So—let me steer for a while, because I know where I want to lead us. We'll take it slowly. You determine the pace, and we'll see where it takes us. Is that agreeable? Can you do this?"

Olivia nodded, still hesitant but willing to take a chance and examine the options.

"Yes, agreed." She gave him a tentative smile.

"Good!" Mark declared, looking pleased with himself. "I can now tell you the truth—I've *never* ever tried to start a relationship. I was always the one being approached... I wasn't sure what to say to convince you to trust me... and I'm very, very glad you said yes. And I think we'll call it a night. I won't push my luck, and it is a busy workday tomorrow."

Mark got up and pulled Olivia with him. He enveloped her in his arms and hugged her tightly, kissing the top of her head.

They walked to the door, their arms around each other. He turned to kiss her once more before he opened the door, his kiss deep and long. Her heart was pounding again, and the liquid feeling in her gut returned. She only had to say, "Stay." and he would, she knew. But she didn't, though she wanted it badly. *Slowly,* she told herself, *slowly!*

He kissed her again and murmured: "Until tomorrow. Good night, my love." and he was gone.

***

Sleep eluded her. She was too euphoric to relax into it, her exhilaration mixed with trepidation, physical arousal, and fear of waking up from a too-fantastic dream. Mark woke in her a fire she thought she lost a long time ago, believing it was extinguished forever.

She still had difficulty accepting the emotions he expressed, the desire she saw in his face. She was nothing like Helen or Cynthia. So how could she fit in where they did? She's the square peg in a round hole, as the cliché goes. His social circle would probably not be to her taste, if what she thought she knew about his elitist set was even slightly accurate.

However, if she was so wrong about him, maybe she was mistaken about his friends, too. Olivia would have to give them a chance as well... *But first—let's see whether I was so mistaken about Mark himself, as he wants me to believe...*

Finally, sleep conquered her exhausted mind and body. Olivia didn't see the clock, but the lightning darkness indicated that sunrise was near, and she wouldn't get much sleep.

***

The next morning, tired but elated, Olivia got ready to take Pinky to the park for her morning walk. Mark would not be there, of course. He'd be using the Seacliff parks. But that didn't matter—she would see him this evening. Light-footed, she crossed the sleepy street and entered the park. She was floating, looking ahead without focus, her mind on last night's events.

"Hi, there, Olivia! Are you sleep-walking?" She heard a call on her right. Sarah stood by the tall sycamore tree that shaded the pedestrian trail with two other women. Olivia thought she recognized them from the neighborhood.

"Good morning!" she called back cheerily and walked toward them. The heady summer smells of the flowering shrubs, and the myriad of colors lured her deep into the shady park.

Sarah eyed her suspiciously.

"What happened?" she asked, her eyes narrowed.

"What could have happened?" Olivia answered evasively, shrugging in mock nonchalance.

"I know you too well..." Sarah said. "If I didn't know better, I'd say you're in love."

Olivia smiled broadly, then turned to the other two women, saying, "Lovely to see the park so alive, so colorful, isn't it?"

"Olivia!" Sarah's voice was plaintive, questioning. She was sure something had changed for her best friend, something she was not part of, didn't even know about, and she was frustrated.

"All is well, Sarah, all is fine," Olivia said, trying to placate her friend without explaining. The three women were looking at her as if expecting further elaboration.

She would tell Sarah. Of course, she would. But not when there were strangers around. She knew that Sarah wouldn't betray her trust. Yet, she may feel this was too good a story and let it slip. Olivia didn't think she was ready for that. She needed more time to absorb the change in her life—if, indeed—there was a real and significant change. And she wasn't sure yet.

To change the subject and lead the others to focus on something other than herself, Olivia asked, "Did you watch the news last night? Our politicians are acting as if they are in the middle of an election campaign!" The three women lost interest in her immediately, which was precisely what Olivia wanted, and she was satisfied that she managed to find a polite way to move out of their focused attention. They returned to the discussion of traveling abroad and the most exciting places they visited, which they'd begun before she arrived. The shift allowed Olivia to return to her thoughts and reflections over last night's events.

It was real. Mark wanted her; confident they were a perfect fit. She was aware that this could only be right if she were very wrong. Did she get a false impression of him, while he had the correct one? Only if his outward persona was unlike his internal personality, and therefore misleading, she decided. She didn't think he *meant* to mislead her. The façade the world was familiar with could be his way of protecting a vulnerable inner self. Olivia believed that she was open and a "what-you-see-is-what-you-get" type of person, so if he evaluated her based on the little information he had, there was nothing to mislead *his* assessment. *Mark knows what he desires in a partner and who he really is, and therefore, he concluded that I fit the requirements.*

She didn't like the conclusion this train of thought was leading to, because then she'd have to admit her judgment was wrong. But if she *was* wrong, the reality may open up a possibility of something marvelous.

"Olivia, what's wrong with you today?" Sarah asked, exasperated. "You didn't hear a word we said, did you? Where were you?"

"I'm sorry, Sarah," Olivia said. "I *am* distracted. We'll talk later, OK?"

Olivia turned to leave, calling to Pinky.

"Olivia, wait!" Sarah called and hurried to join her, leaving her friends behind. "Tell me! You met someone, right? Do I know him? Someone at work? A colleague?"

"Sarah, I'm not sure what happened last night, so I don't want to talk about it yet. It needs further processing."

"It needs further processing..." repeated Sarah, her tone disbelieving, and she seemed irritated. "What needs further processing? Do you always have to analyze life till there's nothing left? Why can't you tell me?" Creating new combinations of metaphors was something Sarah was undeniably good at. Usually, it made Olivia laugh. Not today...

"Because I'm still trying to get a grip on what I feel and think, to figure things out." Now it was Olivia's turn to sound exasperated.

"Wow..." Sarah breathed. "You're in love! Can't be anything else! What—it happened overnight? You just met a guy and lost your head *and* heart? That's not the cool and rational Olivia I'm familiar with!" She sounded vexed.

Suddenly, Olivia figured out Sarah's reaction: *She's afraid of losing our friendship. If I fall in love and have someone new in my life—I'll have less time for her.* Olivia's irritation vanished; she turned and hugged her friend.

"Yes, it's a man, but I honestly don't know what it is yet, I had butterflies in my stomach, and my knees melted yesterday, but it is so farfetched—I'm not sure it's real and, therefore, can't discuss it yet. I promise I'll tell you when I *do* know!"

Round and wide open, Sarah's eyes gazed at Olivia in amazement. "A real Prince Charming, ha? Just tell me one thing, do I know him?"

Olivia smiled, neither confirming nor denying.

"So, I *do* know him!" Sarah concluded. And Olivia thought that her friend knew her too well...

The air between them cleared, and their parting was as warm as usual.

***

Olivia hurried home. After a quick shower, she dressed without paying much attention to the ensemble she prepared yesterday night and put on light makeup. She ran to the kitchen, left a note for Ruby about the shopping she needed, checked Pinky's water bowl, and was out of the house in twenty minutes. She'd be on time.

You're never late to a meeting with the dean, she warned herself. *Never!* She didn't know why he summoned her, but she'd find out soon enough... *Please, God, make the traffic bearable today...* she prayed.

23

Walking energetically, as was her custom, she still managed to stop for a brief moment to say a personal, "Good morning." to students and faculty members she met on her way to the office.

Sophie was at her desk, checking the mail, as Olivia entered.

"Good morning!" Olivia said cheerily.

"What?" Sophie said, a surprised look on her face. "You look different. What?"

Another one who can read me with ease, Olivia thought, *or is the change in me so noticeable?*

"All is well!" Olivia said, smiling. "I need to leave now if I want to be on time."

"And leave me hanging like this?" Sophie moaned.

Olivia entered her office, left her bag on her chair, and returned to Sophie's office. "If anyone calls—I'll be back in half an hour."

The dean's office was five minutes away. Knowing Olivia well, the dean's secretary smiled and said, "Good morning! You look... changed!"

Olivia was astounded. What did people see? She didn't think she looked any different when she got dressed this morning. There must be something, though.

"Right on time, as usual. Go right in."

"Please, come in," said Professor Williams, the faculty's dean. "I'm glad you could make it today, despite the short notice."

Olivia entered the beautifully furnished corner office, with its dark wood paneling, nodded, saying nothing, and sat in the comfortable armchair he indicated.

"I wished to tell you in person before rumors spread—did you know the student union conducted a popularity vote throughout the campus? They ranked all their teachers and professors, and I must admit I was surprised at how seriously they took it. They had to justify each choice to make the process transparent, and the final decision is obvious and clear."

He looked at her, making sure she was listening. Olivia nodded, saying nothing. She knew of the survey but hadn't paid much attention to the process.

"Two professors were ranked in the first place with the same number of votes." The dean continued, "The students came to see me, asking for advice and engaged me in the process. Together, we chose you because the arguments for your election were stronger. They were delighted with the final choice, and so were I and the president. We see in you the best we have to offer. Congratulations!"

Olivia was overwhelmed. There were so many excellent professors! It was humbling to know students were so aware of how much she cared about them and wanted to reciprocate and show her she meant that much to them. Still, the thought she was ranked so high was stupefying.

"May I ask what was the deciding factor?" she asked, humbled. She knew it was not only the quality of her teaching and the popularity of her courses that determined their choice, or her fairness or approachability. Many professors were at least as good as she was.

"You'll get a formal letter, of course, but I can tell you that the way you handled the situation with your pregnant student, and how you dealt with the offending professor, tipped the scales. You managed to deal with the issue fairly and humanely for both sides and maintained the dignity of all concerned, the university included."

"I don't know what to say." Olivia was at a loss for words. She was genuinely flustered. "I didn't know what to expect when I got the call saying you wanted to see me. I certainly did not imagine something like this… Thank you! I'm truly astounded."

"We are delighted we offered you the position and that you accepted it. The recommendations we received for you proved more than accurate. Congratulations again. And as the saying goes—keep up the good work!"

"Thanks again," Olivia said and got to her feet. "And to end our meeting with another cliché—you made my day!"

Olivia left the spacious office, walking on air. She felt she was floating. The last few days were so surreal! First, Mark; now, this. Had her life finally taken a turn, and new horizons were opening up for her? She thought back, remembering the problematic past years, and her eyes filled with tears. For the first time since Elliot died, she allowed herself to believe that maybe, just maybe, things will become brighter from now on.

Amazing herself, Olivia found herself thinking of Mark, wanting to share her award with him. He was probably swamped—she didn't know his schedule—so she'd wait till evening.

The people who'd be most pleased to know, were her mom and her boys, who paid a heavy price for her limitless investment in her work throughout the years. Telling them would be sharing the happiness and pride she felt, not boasting.

Olivia left the building and sat on a bench outside to avoid being overheard.

"Morning, Mom, how are you? How's Dad?" Olivia said when Rebecca answered the phone.

"We're fine; I just got back from breakfast with a friend. You never call me in the middle of the morning, is everything OK?" Her mother was immediately worried.

"Everything is great, Mom. I called to share something with you…" She joyfully repeated her conversation with the dean, her mother often interrupting with questions, happy exclamations, and asides to Arthur, Olivia's father, who wanted to be included. His health had deteriorated in the past year, and his failing hearing was a terrible hindrance, limiting his social contacts. It was sad to see the changes. He mellowed and became a pleasant and sociable man when he grew older. Now, as his health worsened, he was becoming taciturn and uncommunicative. His egotism and his self-centeredness reasserted themselves.

"I'm so happy for you, darling." her mom said, "I know your life was not easy for so many years. The kids' achievements were a source of joy, and your work, too. But the rest—was not fun at all. Such an acknowledgment of your investment is fantastic, isn't it?"

Rebecca was sensitive enough not to show all she perceived, but she was painfully aware of how forlorn Olivia was in recent years. She knew that Olivia tried to spare her the worst stages in Elliot's deterioration, or the difficulties she encountered while taking care of him because Rebecca was not strong enough to help.

Olivia was pleased to hear how delighted her mother was. Their relationship was not always smooth. Olivia's assertive, independent, sometimes impatient behavior and Rebecca's tendency to interfere in her daughter's life and her past grievances often led to conflicts between them. Their road to a better understanding was smoothed by their mellowing with age and the problematic health issues they both had to deal with—Olivia with Elliot's illness, Rebecca with her own, and Arthur's decline. It was Olivia who invited her mother to have coffee with her one day and changed the relationship's dynamics. Rebecca did not understand what caused the change, but welcomed the shift and adjusted her part in the complex dialog.

Her phone vibrated. Another caller. She looked at the screen—it was Mark.

"Listen, I've got a call waiting. I'll talk to you soon." Olivia ended the call.

A few seconds later, Mark called again. "I tried calling you; the line was busy. Long talk?"

No "hello", no "how are you?"

"Hello, Mark, how are you? I'm fine too, thank you," she replied, a smile in her voice.

"Yes, of course. I'm sorry. Just had to know all is well with you… are you OK?"

"Of course, I am. Why were you worried?" Olivia was surprised.

"I don't know. Just had the feeling something was up, and I wanted to hear your voice." He sounded relieved. "So—are you busy?"

"I am, rather… But I *really* want to talk… are you free this evening?"

"Sure. Will you come over? Let's say around eight p.m.?" He understood pressures at work.

"Great," she responded, and Mark hung up with a brief, "Bye."

Now I really must rush back, she thought. *I said I'd only be gone for half an hour…*

She entered her office, and seconds later, Sophie was in her doorway, a cup of coffee in her hand. "For you," she said, looking at Olivia, curiosity written all over her face, "So you'll be able to tell me what's happening right away!"

Olivia laughed. "Good strategy!" she said. And she told her secretary of the meeting with Dean Williams.

Sophie was impressed and delighted. Olivia realized that Sophie's joy was based on loyalty and tinged with pride in her contribution.

"I'm so impressed, Prof." Sophie said. "We must celebrate!"

"No, Sophie, absolutely not!" Olivia was quick to respond. "We'll do no such thing! There are probably many who are frustrated right now… and it's too boastful… besides, I think the president's office will issue a notice."

"Will you at least allow me to send an email to *our* faculty?" Sophie was not willing to give up so easily.

"Let's wait a little, OK?" Olivia hoped her tone conveyed the finality of her decision.

Sophie nodded, but it was clear she was disappointed. Then, she changed tack.

"And what about this morning? You came in looking so pleased with yourself! Haven't seen much light in your eyes in many months!"

"You don't miss much, do you?" Olivia chuckled, self-conscious.

"That's why I'm such a great secretary." came Sophie's immediate response.

Olivia smiled.

"I'll let you know when there's something to tell, OK?" Olivia felt ridiculous, embarrassed. Her tone changed, resuming her authoritative nuances.

"Sure, boss." Sophie got up; she was hurt.

"I'm sorry, Sophie, I didn't mean to sound so sharp... I was just uncomfortable."

Somewhat appeased, Sophie departed.

24

Olivia couldn't wait for the evening to come. Yet, she was shaking inside, afraid of the depth of her feelings, afraid to let herself go and allow herself to believe the relationship was possible and as real as it seemed to be. *Had anyone asked me, even a week ago, I would have said there's no way anything could exist between us. This turn of events is not only a change of perspective; it's a life-changing transformation! And it scares me... I'm so afraid of losing control...*

She took Pinky with her. Pinky liked Tish, and she was sure they'd get along fine. It would also serve as a distraction, should she need one...

She tried listening to the radio in her car, the dial, as usual, tuned to KDFC. She was unable to relax enough to enjoy the music, though it was one of her favorites—Schumann's piano concerto—and she was almost sure Martha Argerich was playing.

She wondered if she should remind Mark of their encounter years ago. She was so embarrassed at the time... He made her feel so young and foolish... and he didn't seem to remember any of it... *No,* she decided. *Not yet. We'll see where all this is leading...*

She parked in his driveway, behind his gleaming, sporty Audi, and opened the door. Pinky jumped out; she ran to relieve herself and leave her mark by the fence. They could hear Tish's excited barking inside, and a few seconds later, the front door opened, and an eager Tish came bounding out. Mark remained on the porch. he small, agile, tan mixed-breed Pinscher-type dog, and the big, clumsy blond Labrador were running circles around each other playfully, making their owners laugh.

Olivia strolled, crossing the gravel hesitantly. Mark came toward her and engulfed her in a warm embrace.

"Welcome, my love," he said softly in her ear. "I couldn't stop thinking of you all day."

"I thought about you, too," she admitted. "I couldn't avoid it even if I wanted to—people kept asking me what happened to me!"

"Really?" Mark seemed delighted with the idea. "And did you *want* to avoid thinking of me?" He asked, only half-joking.

Olivia looked into his eyes and whispered, "No, I liked having you within my mind all day."

Mark hugged her tightly. "I love your phrasing, and that image. Let's go in, it's a bit chilly, and I bought us some dinner; it was delivered a few minutes ago."

His arm still around her shoulders, they called the dogs in, and when he shut the door—he leaned down to kiss her. His lips were soft against hers at first but turned more demanding as the kiss deepened. She was aroused and breathless, wanting more, wanting the pleasure his touch provided, and the feeling of profound contentment he created in her, to continue.

He slowed the pace, and then released her, chuckling. "Let's eat first. And I want to hear what people had to say about how you looked, and why."

The table was beautifully set on the terrace overlooking the bay. Long, lavender-smelling candles were lit between the two exquisite filigree placemats, their light refracted in the tall, crystal wine glasses, the napkins neatly folded on the left-hand side of each set of plates.

"How lovely! I'm duly impressed!" Olivia's smile conveyed genuine pleasure.

"Good! I worked hard to create the perfect effect and the right atmosphere!" Mark replied, his smile matching hers. "I hope you like seafood."

"Mmm… the best cuisine for me!"

"Please, Madam, take a seat." Mark was mock-seriously standing behind the chair he drew out. "I didn't know what you prefer, so I ordered diverse dishes so you won't end up hungry."

He disappeared in the direction of the kitchen and returned with a huge tray loaded with small dishes, which he placed on the table between them.

Olivia giggled.

"What's so funny?" Mark asked. He seemed peeved, and Olivia hastened to reassure him.

"It's the quantities that made me laugh! It may all be delicious, but we'll never be able to finish it!"

"Well, we don't have to finish anything!" He was still standing by his chair; Olivia got up and went over to him.

"Thank you for doing all this for me. I do appreciate the effort. It's wonderful," Olivia said, and she gently laid her hand on his cheek.

"But," Olivia continued, "I must admit, you created a big problem for me—now I'll have to choose among all these wonderful dishes, and it's so difficult! It's like bringing kids to a candy store, telling them to choose whatever they wanted!"

Still standing by his seat, Mark looked hesitant, wondering how to interpret her comment until he saw the glint in her eyes. "You're pulling my leg again."

The sophisticated, famous doctor sounds like a little boy, at times, Olivia thought. She assumed that he trusted her enough to allow her to glimpse this kid, the most vulnerable, the most authentic part of him. She took his face in both her hands, stood on her tiptoes to reach his lips, and kissed him softly.

"Let's eat; I'm starving!" she declared as she returned to her seat.

And it was quite a dilemma. The feast laid in front of her was astounding: Grilled octopus, pan-fried scallops, fresh oysters, prawns in white wine sauce, crab cakes, steamed mussels, white fish ceviche—she didn't know where to start! It was all arranged beautifully, tempting her eyes, enticing her nose, and tantalizing her palate.

"Can we share all of them so that I can take a little bit of each dish? Would you mind?" She asked hesitantly. It was not proper etiquette, of course, but the temptation was too much.

"Great idea, and exactly what I hoped we could do." Mark seemed pleased with her enthusiasm and lack of pretense.

The food was, indeed, excellent. She enjoyed every bite and every dish. Now it was her turn to reveal the little girl within her, and she was not ashamed to do so.

After a while, Mark said, "What was it you wanted to tell me this morning? You promised to tell me when we met."

Olivia took another sip of her Chablis.

"I don't know how or why, but people saw me today and asked what happened to me. Sarah figured out I met someone and wanted to know who; my secretary told me I was glowing. It's as if my skin turned transparent today... I woke up happy, and people saw right into my heart." Olivia felt the blood rise to her face.

"Did it bother you that your emotions were so clear to others?" Mark asked, extending his hand across the table to take hers.

"No," Olivia said, "Not at all. The problem was they all wanted to know who was making me so happy, and I didn't know what to do or what to say."

"Why not tell them the truth?" Mark asked.

"Because I'm not sure what the truth *is*… yet," Olivia replied. "I want all this to be real, but I keep thinking I'll wake up and find that I made it all up. I honestly want to believe you when you say you know better than me who you *truly* are, and that I misjudged you. And this—" Olivia's hands indicated the table, the house, and Mark, "is not a fantasy. Not something that will vanish tomorrow. But I'm afraid *you'll* wake up and think you made a mistake, so I'm afraid to put my whole heart on the line here. I'm afraid I'm falling in love with you. And I'm petrified of getting hurt."

Mark listened attentively, and when she finished, he grinned broadly. He lifted her hand and kissed it.

"You can't begin to imagine how happy you just made me. Look, I know it is strange. A connection such as this is not something that happens to people our age. If you're lucky, it may happen to you when you're sixteen. Not when you're over fifty—certainly not when you're sixty-five, like me. Maybe in cheap, old-style, naïve novels, not in real life. But it *did* happen to us in real life. I feel it, too."

"You mean that the inadvertent encounters that brought us together— being neighbors, dog-owners, using the same park, at the same hours… maybe they were not just chance, or luck, or Karma…?" she asked, her eyes glowing.

He kissed the inside of her palm again, softly, stroking her long, narrow fingers.

"You know when I first thought we had a chance together?" He looked at her tenderly.

Olivia shook her head.

"Remember that day, at the park, when I said I was OK, and you asked me what was wrong, as if you saw right through my pretense?"

Olivia nodded, still silent. Then she said, "You told me about your cancer."

"Yes," Mark said. "And you didn't flinch. Or turn away from me, or reject me, or refuse to see *me*. My cancer didn't scare you away." Mark stopped, his gaze never leaving her face. "When you look at me, I can tell you don't see the sickness; you see *me*. Don't you understand? *This* is the real fantasy here —I'm much older than you, thirteen years is a big gap—

and I'm not healthy, yet you gave me a chance that you'll love me! Do you understand what that means to me?"

He stopped and inhaled deeply, his eyes never leaving hers, then he said, "You couldn't know this, but what I thought of myself is 'damaged goods.' Until you came into my life… But I'm not damaged when I see myself through your eyes. Will you give us a chance to be happy together? Put your reservations aside?"

Her eyes clouded, and she choked. She wanted to affirm it, but all she could manage was another nod.

Mark stood up and pulled her close to him, kissing her teary eyes, her face, her lips. Her hands rose to hug his neck, and she let her body melt into his. Sometime later, they moved to the bedroom—she couldn't remember how that happened—and he laid her on the bed. Opening the buttons of her shirt, he slowly stroked her breasts and lowered his soft lips to them. Her clothes vanished; she was not aware how or when; she was entirely focused on the sensations his lips and his tongue evoked. Olivia's body was on fire. Feelings she had long forgotten now flooded back and aroused every cell in her body. Every time she thought she'd explode, he slowed his caresses, prolonging the sweet agony. *He's an expert and knows all the right buttons to push*, she realized. And she let go…

***

She must have fallen asleep, naked, in his arms. Mark moved a little, trying to relieve his probably numb shoulder, and she woke up. His eyes were on her face, warm and tender. "Hello, there," he said quietly and kissed her again. Softly, undemanding. She wanted to stay there forever, curled in his embrace, but knew she had to get up and go home. She had to go to work tomorrow, and so did he.

"I need to go home," she said.

"I know. I wish you didn't. That you'd stay all night…"

"One day… maybe," she said, now fully awake.

She got up to gather her clothes and get dressed, and saw the dogs.

"Mark, look at them," she said quietly, nodding her head toward Tish's cushioned bed at the corner of the bedroom. Tiny Pinky had the bed, and Tish was lying on the carpet next to her. "The gallant host," Olivia said, "Like his owner."

***

Olivia woke up in her own bed; her heart was still in bed with him, at Seacliff. The whole scene still seemed surreal: The sumptuous, candlelit dinner, the physical ecstasy. It was all a too-good-to-be-true flight of the imagination. For a levelheaded woman like her, Olivia thought, the fantastic illusion he swept her into was too big of a contrast to her current life. She wasn't sure she'd manage to bridge the gap between the achievement-oriented, independent woman and the infatuated person she was yesterday.

She reminded herself that Mark was unequivocally sure that her perception of him was wrong. Based on mistaken assumptions. He kept emphasizing that he enjoys the comforts of life his hard-earned money could buy, but he's not a "jet-set", pleasure-seeking creature.

Olivia didn't know yet how to bring the two parallel life courses that she and Mark led close enough so they could span the void she sensed between them or whether she would ever be able to find a way to.

Based on last night, Olivia concluded, it was certainly worth a try…

25

I need to talk to someone… she thought when she returned home that evening.

She called Sarah.

"Well, well, well, look who's here! My old neglectful friend! I haven't heard from you in a while! And you don't return my calls!" Sarah answered her phone with a reprimand.

Olivia knew she deserved the explosion.

"Sarah, I need your help," Olivia said when Sarah stopped to breathe. "Will you forgive me so we can talk?"

"I'll be at your place in five minutes." Sarah said, as Olivia knew she would.

Olivia made fresh coffee and arranged her thoughts.

She let Sarah in, and they sat in their regular seats in the kitchen.

"Do tell," she said, looking expectantly at Olivia. Olivia started by telling her of the surprise trip her mother had planned.

Sarah was enthusiastic. "Fantastic!" she said. "I wish my mother had offered to take me! But she never did! What a sweet deal!"

She saw that Olivia was not as pleased with the planned cruise as she was.

"You're not entirely happy with the notion, are you? Why? It's a great opportunity! Is it because of Mr Wonderful? Will you tell me already?"

"Partially. You *do* know me," Olivia began. "And you suspected correctly—you do know him… It's Mark Wallace."

Stunned silence. And then Sarah erupted with, *"Who?"* she couldn't believe she heard correctly. Questions of where, when, why, how, and what followed soon after.

"All those talks in the park! They weren't so innocent, huh? You planned it all, right under our noses, and we never suspected!" Sarah was grinning gleefully.

"No, Sarah, believe me, I didn't plan anything. I wasn't aware of anything developing between us. For me—those were just chance encounters. Like any unplanned meetings with other neighbors!"

"I know!" Sarah chuckled. "I know you didn't! You were so blasé! I remember I told you one day to dress up so we could go to the park, and you asked, 'Why bother, we'll only meet neighbors!' How naïve! I'm sure he *did* plan it. He's calculating."

She saw Olivia's troubled face and hastened to clarify: "Not 'calculating' in a wicked way. I didn't mean he tried to lure you or seduce you. But he was gauging your reactions to his advances. You saw nothing? You? Of all people? Sensitive as you are?"

"I never thought I was his type or him, mine. So I misinterpreted the cues I detected. I thought he's arrogant... interesting, brilliant, but full of himself. And I was sure he was only interested in women like Helen or Cynthia, both of whom are so different from me. It never occurred to me there was anything in those talks but a few minutes' conversations, early in the morning, in the neighborhood park! I never thought it *could* lead to anything!"

"So—what happened? What changed all that?" Sarah asked.

"Mark bought a house in Seacliff and called me one evening to say that the renovations he had done were finished and all the new furniture was in place... and he invited me to see it. I was curious, and I went. And we talked and talked, and he was so different than the person I expected to see! He's totally *unlike* his persona, his public image. What I met was a considerate, sensitive, intelligent Mark Wallace. A real *nice* person." She finished lamely.

"Wow!" Sarah said. "Who would have thought! But the truth is, several people commented about your 'park conversations' and perceived that something was going on. Especially that banker, Teddy, who moved in from Davis? He was so frustrated; I think he wanted to hit on you himself. Anyway, the way you were standing together, Mark created 'closure,' excluding everyone but you. Didn't you realize he was always facing the entrance and had you standing with your back to the trails?"

Olivia shook her head.

"Well, several times, I, too, had the feeling you were in private conversations, and none of the other neighbors were welcome to join the discussion. Remember when I came over and then said I had a meeting and left right away? I sort of saw on his face that I wasn't welcome." Sarah continued. "But even I never suspected it could be this!"

146

They were quiet for a while, sipping their coffees.

"That's not *all* I wanted to talk to you about." Olivia smiled nervously.

"There's more?" Sarah groaned, but she was smiling.

Olivia nodded her head and said: "The timing of the trip to Alaska couldn't be worse, as you can understand, and on top of that—an intensive week with my mother scares me."

"Did you tell Mark?" Sarah asked, no longer joking.

Olivia shook her head.

"What do you think that he will say?" Sarah prodded.

"That I should do it, and fulfill her dream, and enjoy it as much as I can," Olivia said.

"He'll be right, you know." Sarah nodded her head vigorously. "I think so, too!"

***

Her phone rang early the following day.

"Morning!" Mark's voice sounded bright and full of life. "How are you? Sleep well?"

"Hi there," Olivia responded. "I'm fine, and you? Didn't sleep much, but I'm OK."

"Miss me already?" Mark asked, and she was sure he was smiling.

Olivia looked at her watch; it was seven a.m., the day had hardly begun...

"Not yet, but I'm sure I will in a little while," Olivia said, her tone playful.

"I'm wholly devastated! Shattered! I love my work, but these days, all I want is to go home and see you!"

His honesty and openness amazed her. No hesitation, no reservations, no games. She remembered that sayings like "don't wear your heart on your sleeve" were prevalent in her youth. She believed it, then, and was cautious... So—what changed? Was it Mark who was so different? The times? Or the fact they were older, more mature? Well, she'd respond with sincerity, too.

"The truth is—I do miss you, just too ashamed to admit it... I'm fifty-two, not sixteen. It's ridiculous."

"I know! And I'm sixty-five, so don't talk to me about being ridiculous.

147

It feels so good, though… I feel so alive!"

"Mark, I don't understand the switch from brief neighborly talks in the park to such a deep involvement, and so quickly. It's impossible, and I don't recognize myself!"

"Well, flow with the stream of emotions! I don't know how it all turned so fast, but it did. I know what I feel, and I know it's real. With no doubts or holding back. I can only hope it's the same for you."

It was, she realized, despite her fears. Textbook, classic, banal as it may sound, she was falling in love, she admitted it to herself.

"I have to learn to let go enough to drift with 'the flow,' as you call it. At least now I know that I want to!" Olivia said.

"That's a good start! We'll manage it together! Listen, I have to go. I'll see you tonight, and we'll discuss it."

A statement, not a question. He was sure she'd agree.

When they ended the call, Olivia remembered she'd said nothing about the trip to Alaska.

***

"Hello, Love, I'm in my car, headed home!" Mark said when he called in the afternoon.

"Early for you, isn't it?" Olivia said, amused.

"All your fault!" Mark sounded pleased with himself. "At long last, I'm alone and can speak freely. I wanted to hear your voice all day!"

Olivia laughed. "OK, drive carefully, and I'll see you soon!"

"What—you don't want to talk to me? You're brushing me off?" Mark pretended offense.

"No, silly, I want you to concentrate on the road! With your fast car, I want your attention undistracted!"

"I'll let you get ready and will be at your place around seven p.m." Mark laughed, and after a moment, he added, "If that's OK with you."

He said it as a matter of politeness, no question there.

She had a lot to tell him. It occurred to Olivia that they spoke only of the developing relationship last night, not about the day's events. And then they made love. She didn't even tell him about the award she received. And she was still debating how to reveal her mother's surprise.

Olivia took a shower and put on a new dress. She knew the lightweight, cornflower blue dress was the exact shade of her eyes. She was not beautiful, she knew, but she had big, beautiful blue eyes with long lashes. Her best asset. Together with her high forehead and fair complexion, they offset her slightly long nose and thin lips. She was slim and petite, with small breasts and straight legs. Luckily, it seemed to be enough for him.

By then, the pasta was ready, and her wonderful Bolognese sauce was simmering. She seasoned the salad and set the table. Not as fancy as last night, she thought, but it was homey. The smells will probably compensate for the lack of glitz... At least she hoped it would.

Pinky's excitement told her Mark was there, and she opened the door before he reached it. Tish ran in ahead of him, and, together with Pinky, went exploring around the house. Mark drew her close and kissed her deeply, hugging her tightly. After a minute, she broke the embrace and said warmly, "We're putting on a show for our neighbors; come on in!"

Mark entered and smelled the air. "You cooked? It smells wonderful!"

He made his way to the kitchen and opened the saucepan. He dipped the spoon she was using to stir the Bolognese and brought it to his mouth.

"Mmmm... divine!" A broad smile spread on his face.

"Hungry?" Olivia smiled.

"Yes!" he said. "I'm never hungry until I smell or see good food... An old habit."

"That's a surprise," Olivia said. "I thought Helen was a great cook."

"Helen was indeed an excellent cook, but she only cooked when we had guests. And she cooked very fancy, spicy food, which I hate. I like simple, fresh tastes. If you use fine, fresh ingredients, you don't need all the complicated spices and herbs, which were invented only to cover up the smell of rotten food."

Mark saw her bemused face and said, "It's true! The reason our forefathers used herbs and seasoning is to mask the odor of spoiled food!"

"Maybe that's how it started," Olivia retorted, "I don't think it's why we use them today—we use spices and sauces because our palates are used to more complex tastes. You may not like *some* of the herbs Helen used, but surely some may appeal to you! We'll need to find which are acceptable and which are intolerable to you!"

He came close, stroking her face, and leaned for a long and leisurely kiss. She smelled his excellent aftershave, and her "Mmm..." was appreciative.

"You like my Clive Christian?" he asked.

"I like it a lot, though I didn't know it was Clive Christian. I don't even know who Clive Christian is. From your response, I gather it's a well-known name, and I'm guessing it's expensive."

"Very…" Came the smug response.

"Let's see how you like my pasta," Olivia said and indicated the table. "Shall we?"

She was watching to see Mark's first reaction.

He beamed at her, and she let out the breath she wasn't aware she was holding.

"Excellent!" he said. "And you didn't put pepper in it! I hate pepper in my food."

Mark told her about the hospital and some of the dramas he encountered, recounting meetings with the department heads, administrators, donors, and lawyers.

"Sounds complicated, with so many conflicting interests! From what you just told me, it seems that you are a wizard at finding compromises that most people can live with, without offending anyone."

"Not always," Mark said but seemed to be pleased with her assessment.

Then, he added, as an afterthought, "I told my daughters about us today."

Olivia was surprised. It was somewhat soon, she thought, and she remembered their antagonism toward Helen.

"What did you tell them?" she asked.

"I said I think I found the right partner for me, and I hoped it would last forever. And I told them where we met, and how well I knew you before we started seeing each other. I also described you and told them what a wonderful person I think you are," Mark sounded very pleased with himself.

"What did they say? How did they react?" She wanted to know.

"With total lack of interest," he said. "It's so new, they probably thought it need not concern them; it was no threat to them. An affair that may not last. Maybe they think you're another Cynthia. Or—perhaps they remember that I changed many partners after their mother died, before Helen, and they assume that I'm going through a similar phase."

Maybe they know him better than I do? Olivia thought. Or, perhaps, like most people, they fail to see the real Mark Wallace? Not likely, they should know better, but then…

"Tell me about *your* day," he asked.

"Nothing as dramatic as your 'life and death' issues, but I had a pleasant surprise yesterday," Olivia said. She told Mark of her meeting with Dean Williams and the award she received. Though she tried to tone down the achievement and minimize its importance, she could see Mark's pride and sincere pleasure.

"Don't sound so modest!" he said. "This may have a significant impact on your career, on future advancements. Such accomplishments are highly valued by your colleagues, and other universities if you ever consider moving elsewhere. Besides, I know Frank Williams very well. He'll go crazy when he finds out about us… Which reminds me—I want to invite a few friends, some of my best friends, to introduce you and let them get to know you, sometime next week, if that's OK with you."

"Sure, it has to happen sometime… let's keep it to a few at a time, so I can really get to know them. But wait a minute—we can't do it next week; there's a problem."

Olivia fell silent. Mark was looking at her, puzzled, waiting for her to continue. She took a deep breath and said, "I'll be traveling with my mom to Alaska this weekend for a week. I had no chance to tell you yet, and I didn't tell her about us because it's so new… I'm so sorry, Mark, I said yes a few months ago before there was anything… and now I can't refuse to go—she arranged the flights, the cruise—everything."

"You're going away for a whole week?" Mark sounded upset.

"Mom wanted to do it last year, when she turned seventy-five, as a present for herself, but she can't travel on her own, and my dad doesn't want to go. And she couldn't ask me last year when Elliot was so sick… Mom thinks I need a vacation after all I've been through in the last few years, so she decided to surprise me and arranged everything…" Olivia finished feebly. She couldn't tell him she was worried about being cooped up with her mother for a whole week, in a small cabin.

"Yes. Well. OK… I understand," Mark said, and Olivia could see the forlorn little boy within him feeling rejected and left behind, hurt, and helpless.

Her heart went out to him. She got up and went to hug his head. She stroked the thick white hair, bent down, and murmured, "It's only a week, and I'll be back to love you forever."

Mark got up and took her face between his large, long-fingered palms, a soft smile in his eyes. "Did you mean what you just said?"

"Yes, I did. I didn't mean to say it… I hope I didn't scare you off just now. I can't believe it myself, but I know it's true. I love you. Completely and wholeheartedly."

He kissed her eyes softly and continued to tenderly kiss her forehead, her nose, and lips. "You made me so happy right now. I love you, too. I was afraid to say it aloud because I wasn't sure you were ready… Remember, I told you what we have is real. This is so right, so fitting!"

After a while, Mark said, his voice low and hoarse, "You must go with her. Who knows when you'll have another chance? She's quite strong, for her age—but who knows for how long… you can never tell. So, yes, go! I'll survive the week, and we'll meet my friends when you get back."

"And you better tell your mother about me," Mark looked at her, his face glowing, "Because I'll drive the two of you to the airport and come to get you upon your return."

She was going to say it wasn't necessary, they'd take a taxi, but Mark raised his hand, signaling he'd not argue the matter.

26

Olivia decided to leave her office earlier than usual and asked Sophie to come into her office. Time to arrange all the details before she left for Alaska, she knew. Sophie entered, notebook in hand, expecting instructions.

"Please sit," Olivia said, smiling.

Sophie seemed to relax; no drama was expected.

"You remember I told you that my mother wanted me to join her on a cruise to Alaska," she began.

Sophie nodded.

"Well, I meant to remind you a few days ago, but so many things are happening, I didn't find the time. So—beginning this weekend, I'll be away for a week. The academic year has ended, and there's nothing urgent right now, and I hope nothing dramatic will happen while I'm away."

"You deserve a vacation!" Sophie was enthusiastic.

"Yes, well…" Olivia's face showed her ambivalence. "I need to talk with Andrew Kent, so he'll cover for me. I'm sure he'll have no problem with that until I get back. Can you get him for me?"

"What's troubling you? Something seems to bother you, I can tell!" Sophie seemed worried.

"The timing. It's not really a good time…"

Then she told Sophie of the change in her life and asked her to keep the information for herself, at least for now.

Sophie nodded vigorously. She was ecstatic—her boss was dating a celebrity from TV… Olivia hoped she could trust her to keep the information to herself. She was also sure that Sophie would check the internet for more information about Mark.

She had to see her mother before Friday. Olivia couldn't shock her with such a revelation as Mark Wallace in her life just before the flight. Some preparation was necessary. She hadn't decided yet what to say or how to bring it up.

Her mother called her on Wednesday, wanting Olivia's advice on the clothes she should pack. Olivia promised to come by after work to help her decide and resolved to tell her about Mark when they met.

Olivia arrived at four thirty p.m. to allow her mother her afternoon nap. Her mother opened the door, smiling from ear to ear. The two-bedroom apartment, small but beautiful, tastefully furnished in ample shades of blue, had a serene atmosphere.

"Dad's not here?" Olivia asked, relieved. His failing hearing meant you had to raise your voice, and what she wanted to say was not something she wanted to shout out.

Her mother shook her head. She, too, needed some respite…

She knew her father was not happy they were going without him, but her mother insisted such a trip would be too much for him—the long flights, the sea voyage, the walks. Besides—he hated cruises. She was right, of course, and he had to accept it, willing or not.

Rebecca was ecstatic, excited, and nervous. "Oh, Olivia, I'm so glad you came! I took out all my winter clothes and couldn't decide what to take! It's so long since I traveled anywhere!"

"Easy, Mom, take it easy! Just remember—we're only going for a week. However, Alaska in early September is a bit cool. It's not ideal timing; it will be around forty-two degrees Fahrenheit during the day and twenty-eight degrees at night. I know you don't want to wait another year, but—"

Rebecca waved her misgivings away.

"The ship will be nice and warm, I'm sure," Olivia said. "Let's just hope it won't be too cold or too rainy, or too windy when we tour around."

Her mother seemed ready to explode at the thought of the experience. She kept saying, "It's a dream come true… my dream came true…" Olivia had not seen her so excited in a very long time and was glad she agreed to go.

After choosing a few outfits, Olivia asked, "Can we have some coffee now? Before Dad comes back from the gym, so we can talk."

Her mother loved those private conversations, loved being made a party to secrets Arthur didn't know and hurried to the tiny kitchenette to put the kettle on.

She then turned to Olivia, looking hard at her daughter, noticing the change in her. "Livy?" she asked. "Did you change your makeup? Your hair? Is this a new shirt?"

Olivia shook her head and could feel the blood rush to her face.

"Livy?" she asked again, baffled.

"Mom, I need to tell you something," Olivia began. "Something wonderful happened to me," she hurried to say when a worried look crossed her mother's face.

Rebecca nodded, allowing her daughter to continue.

"I met someone…" She began and was rewarded with a broad, joyful smile. "Well, he's not someone new. I've known him a long time. I never thought we'd be…" Olivia wasn't sure how to continue. Her mother put her hand on Olivia's arm, encouraging.

"Go on," she said tenderly.

"Do you remember Professor Mark Wallace, my neighbor? I took you and Dad to see him when you thought Dad was overmedicated?"

"Of course, I do." Rebecca said. "He saved him! Your dad was like a zombie, and when Dr Wallace reduced the number of pills he was taking, your dad became himself again! Well, what about the doctor?"

Olivia looked at her mother, saying nothing, her face radiant.

The understanding of what Olivia was hinting hit her suddenly. "I don't believe it!" Rebecca exclaimed. "It can't be! You said he's not your type when I told you to get your hooks into him."

"Unbelievable, right? But it happened." Olivia beamed. "We met many times in the park, walking the dogs, and we talked. I never thought it was anything more than neighborly conversations. He told me about the house he bought in Seacliff and its renovations, and a few weeks ago, he called me and suggested I come to see the completed house. And I did. And what I thought could never happen between us—just did."

"I knew he would be right for you!" Rebecca enthused. "I hate to say I told you so, but I just have to! It's wonderful! I'm so happy he had more sense than you!"

Olivia burst out laughing at her mother's elation.

"Have you told your boys yet?" Rebecca asked. "They'll be happy for you!"

Olivia shook her head. "It's all so new—haven't had time. I must admit I wasn't sure it was real… I don't know how I misjudged him so fully. I'm telling you now only because we're going to Alaska, and he'll take us to the airport for the flight to Vancouver."

They heard her father at the door. Olivia signaled, "Don't say a word," to her mother, who nodded her understanding.

A few minutes later, Olivia took her leave, knowing she'd see them again in a couple of days.

Olivia was driving home and knew she had to call her boys. There was so much she had to tell them. She decided to wait until she got home and talk to them together. *God bless whoever invented the group WhatsApp calls!* She thought.

***

She prepared a cup of coffee before she called them and sat at her kitchen table, gazing out, unseeing. What was she going to tell them? Olivia couldn't tell them she was in love… How to tell them how deeply she felt for Mark? She didn't want to sound as if she'd entirely moved on; it wouldn't be true… and Elliot was their father, after all.

She wrote a text message: *Can you talk? Need to speak with you guys.* Her finger hovered over the 'send' button. 'Need' sounding too strong. *I might scare them… they'll think something was wrong.*

Deleting 'need', she wrote, 'would love'. 'Would love to speak with you' sounded good. Nothing urgent. She was sure that knowing her, they'd understand that something was going on, and she *needed* to talk with them.

Sure enough, five minutes later, her cellphone vibrated. Adam had Tom on the line as well.

"Hi, Mom. How are you? What's up?" Adam began.

"All is well! Great, even," she responded with a smile. "I'm going on that cruise to Alaska at the end of the week with Grandma! It's the last cruise of the season, and she hated to postpone it for another year, just in case… you know, she's not getting any younger."

They were both delighted. They knew Rebecca planned it and were happy she convinced their mother.

"Mom, what a treat!" said Adam.

"Phenomenal!" from Tom.

"We leave on Friday, for a week," Olivia said. Both her sons realized at once that she was not as ecstatic as expected.

"Is there a problem, Mom? Are you worried the two of you won't get along? Is it a small, cramped cabin?" Tom asked.

"Well, yes… I'm worried about being cooped up with my mom twenty-four-seven, but it's a large suite, so maybe it won't be too bad. Let's just hope she won't ask too many snooping, interfering questions about my life and yours."

"Is there something else that bothers you, Mom?" Adam asked. They knew her too well, could read her so easily.

Olivia hesitated, searching for the right words.

"You met someone, didn't you?" Tom guessed first the reason for her hesitation.

Her face on their phone screens told them he hit the mark.

They started talking together, happy for her, congratulating. Then Adam asked, "Who is he? Do we know him?"

And Tom added before she could answer, "Where did the two of you meet?"

She was delighted to hear their genuine joy. "Do you remember my neighbor, who took care of Granddad's medication a few years ago? The one who recommended Doctor Orlansky when your dad was diagnosed with cancer?"

"*Him*?" They both cried together. And then they were speaking together.

"WOW, Mom!"

"He's handsome!"

"And famous…"

"How long has it been going on?"

"You've known him forever; why now?"

"Good catch, Mom!"

"Hold it, guys! Take it easy! I didn't catch him; he caught me! I didn't even see it coming… and yes—the fact I knew him made it easier. It's rather new, and so far, it's wonderful. Sometimes I feel like a character in a kitschy romantic novel. I'm not sure yet how it will develop, but for now—it's great. And I thought you guys should know."

"Aside from being handsome and famous—is he a nice person? I thought you considered him a sort of a high-society type."

Trust Adam not to forget anything… she thought.

"Yes, he's nice. Real nice," Olivia said. "Not at all what I thought. I don't know how I could have made such a massive mistake… luckily, he ignored my misguided convictions."

"Well, I hope it will last! You sound fantastic, Mom. Haven't heard you so happy for a very long time," Tom said.

"I agree. Completely." Adam said. "Keep us posted on how things develop. And we'd love to meet him!"

27

The rest of the week flew quickly. Olivia and Mark met every evening as if they wouldn't miss any opportunity to be together. He suggested dinner at the restaurant she liked for their last night before the cruise.

They were having desserts when Mark said, "You seem apprehensive. Expecting difficulties?"

Olivia looked at him and nodded.

"Difficulties with your mom? Are you worried it would be too difficult for her?"

Olivia shook her head. "No. I'm worried about us being stuck together. The most challenging part for me will be sharing a suite with my mother. I'm afraid we might clash and get into conflicts. Our relationship was not always stress-free. Growing up, I felt she didn't understand me, was constantly criticizing me. Never satisfied, no matter how talented I was academically. She wanted me to be more like her, I guess, and I was different. *Wanted* to be different. I was the brainy type even as a young girl. But my mom is a gregarious type and kept pushing me into social activities, like Girl Scouts, which I hated. All I wanted was to be left alone to read books, write. I wrote a lot. Short stories, dramatic plays…

"I was angry with her for years because her choices—when I was growing up—always favored my father and brother. When I was fourteen, my father worked in a corporation with branches in Africa. They wanted him to open a branch in Zambia, where there was no suitable high school for me. It was an excellent opportunity for him, with a significant pay increase, and he pressured my mom to support his decision to accept the job, though it meant kicking me out of the nest. She didn't stand up to him… she consented. So they tore the family apart. My father left and took my brother, Ben, with him—he was ten years old and intensely attached to me. I was the person he'd turn to if he were in trouble. My mother stayed behind to rent out our house, sell the cars… and put me in boarding school."

Olivia paused. Her eyes reflected the depth of her pain, her gaze fixed at a distant nothing. Mark realized she was remembering a traumatic event.

He held her small hand, his fingers caressing hers, as he waited for her to find the strength to continue.

"I was sent to boarding school..." she said after swallowing several times. "They allowed me to choose—a school here in Northern California, or England, or in South Africa, so I'd be closer to them. I chose to stay here, thinking that the few family members we had here—aunts and uncles and cousins—would be better than no one at all. As I found out, they were close physically, but did not always bother to include me in their families' lives. It turned out to be the loneliest time in my life."

With a deep sigh, Olivia continued, "It was the day-to-day life at the boarding school that was a total disaster for me. Young teenagers can be very cruel toward their peers, especially if their classmates don't fit the 'acceptable' mold. And I never learned how to fit a mold. Any mold. I was always a person who shaped her own patterns; a flexible mold that would allow me to change, not force me to be a certain way.

"So, throughout my time there, I felt like an outsider. Don't get me wrong—I learned to survive. Efficiently. It was clear that becoming 'officially' active would improve things for me, so I edited the boarding school's weekly, volunteered for several student bodies, and built a substantial status for myself.

"As it turned out, I was respected for my academic achievements, abilities, and contributions, but I remained an outsider because I refused to become *entirely* part of the group."

Olivia paused again and sighed deeply. Trying to lighten the mood, her tone self-mocking, she said, "Why am I telling you this sad story?"

"Because it's part of you. Part of what made you who you are," Mark replied, gazing into her eyes, his love for her apparent. "And because I want to know *you*. All of you. The better, happier portions and the sadder ones. Tell me more."

"The holidays were such miserable times." Taking a deep breath, Olivia continued. "I spent most of them alone when everyone left the boarding school to go home or to friends. I didn't want to go to friends' homes so as not to feel 'a charity case', and also because I could never return the favor."

She stopped again and shook her head. Her eyes were moist, and Mark could see how hard it was for her. Sharing the hardships and frustrations of this part of her life was something Olivia rarely did. A period she hated to recall, let alone speak of. He said nothing, but his eyes never left her face, encouraging her to speak.

"I remember one Thanksgiving…" her voice trembled. "It was cold and rainy, and everyone had left. I was all alone. I don't know how it happened, but none of the coaches or teachers invited me to have Thanksgiving dinner with them. I walked alone in the wet dark. The walkways were muddy and slippery. No one was out except me… The staffs' houses were all lit up, and I could hear sounds of laughter… and the smells of roast turkey and-" Olivia choked, took a sip of water, then, forcing herself to regain control, she said, "And there I was. Outside in the cold. Wet like an abandoned, miserable stray dog. Feeling lonely and unwanted… Excuse me." She got up and went to the restrooms.

When she got back, Olivia was composed again. Mark got up and hugged her, enveloping her in a warm embrace. "All right now?" he asked.

"Please, forgive me. I don't usually talk about that time, and it is—evidently—still an open wound even after all these years."

"Nothing to forgive," Mark said. "And I'm glad you told me. It explains why you were worried there would be clashes. Even if you resolved the issues with your mother, the scars are still there. And I can deeply relate to your story. I had similar experiences growing up— though not as harsh as yours. My parents' English wasn't perfect, and they had a terrible accent. That's how I spoke when I entered first grade… I was also small and skinny and weak, sickly. Kids harassed me, some were even physically abusive. I vowed then that I'd do whatever I could to develop abilities everyone will value and respect. And physical competence. Luckily, two years later, we moved to a different neighborhood, and I transferred to another school. And I grew taller and trained hard, so my status increased… But the trauma and the humiliation remained."

They were silent for a while, deep in thought. Then Mark said, "Why did you forgive her and not your dad?"

"I understood her motives, the reasons for her actions. I realized how weak she is, and was then. She would not have managed on her own and knew that if she decided to stay here, she'd pay heavily, whatever my father chose to do: If he elected to go alone, she'd be lost and have great difficulties providing for her kids. And if he decided to stay and give up the opportunity, he'd forever blame her for holding him back. Or even divorce her. You see, she's not an academic and would not have been able to find a high-paying job.

"As for my dad—I always knew he was a selfish, domineering egomaniac. It was always what *he* wanted, what *he* needed. Everyone else was secondary. So, I was abandoned when they left, and then—when the time came—they sent Ben away to boarding school, and broke his spirit completely. No fancy summer school in Montana, Switzerland, could compensate for the yearlong damage, at least he learned to ride horses there."

Olivia stopped, hearing the bitterness in her voice. She shrugged and continued.

"For many years, I was angry with him, resenting his callous abandonment, when I was a helpless adolescent. When I became a mother, and even more when I became a professor, my anger and resentment evaporated. Nothing filled the space that the anger once occupied in my heart—no love, not even compassion. There was only uninterested, dispassionate nothing. I wasn't even sad to realize the truth when I first noticed that the anger was gone, and nothing replaced it.

She stopped for a second and looked at Mark to gauge his reaction to what she said. It was not something she had told anyone outside the family.

"I'm not angry with him any more, but I don't like him, as a person," she continued when she saw he was listening intently, nonjudgmental. "I didn't forgive him, and I didn't forget what he's done to our family, but after all these years, it doesn't mean much. I'm polite, but that's as far as I go. He asked me once if I'll ever be able to move on and forgive him. I told him I have moved on, but there is no mending the damage he caused."

"Not a happy story," Mark said, looking into her eyes. "But you moved on. And it's part of what made you the person you are. At least you found a way to forgive your mother."

Olivia nodded. "Still, it's not always easy for me. She doesn't criticize me much nowadays—not with all my achievements, and I don't care even if she does. And maybe she accepted that I'm not like her, but I've turned out OK. Anyway, we're going, and we'll try to enjoy it as much as possible."

***

They came back to his house after dinner to pick up her car.

"Why don't you stay the night?" Mark asked.

"I'm OK now," Olivia said, a warm smile lighting her eyes. "We both need to be up early tomorrow, and I have to check the house, see what I need to buy."

Mark nodded, not pressing her.

28

Friday arrived, and Olivia was ready to leave, but her heart was heavy. Her flight was scheduled to depart at noon, and they needed to pick Rebecca up on the way. Mark showed up right on time.

"The first vacation I take in years, and I hate to go." Olivia was trying not to cry, her frustration visible.

"Only a week," Mark said, but she could see he was sad, too. She hugged him tightly, her hand on the nape of his neck.

"I miss you already, and we haven't even parted yet!" her voice broke.

"You'll have a wonderful time, you'll see. Alaska is amazing, and you'll love it." He was trying to cheer her up. "Come on, brighten up! You can't let your mother see you're so reluctant to go! She needs this vacation, and it's her dream, remember?"

Olivia nodded. She'd put on a happy face for her mother…

"Come on, Pinky, let's go!" Mark called, and the little dog came running, happy at the extra outing. Mark would take her home with him for the week. He picked up her handbag and suitcase and moved to the front door. Olivia dragged herself slowly behind him. He opened the door for her and took the keys from her hand to lock it. He stowed the luggage in the trunk of his car and came to open the car door for her.

"Don't worry, Livy, it'll be fine, you'll see."

Olivia nodded again, unable to speak.

They drove away, silent.

Mark was trying to lighten the atmosphere: "Come on, cheer up! You'll have fun there, discovering new places, and I'll be here, suffering and devastated without you." He looked at her and winked, and got a genuine smile for his efforts. She appreciated the truth in his words and straightened in her seat.

Her mother was waiting in the lobby when they arrived.

Olivia went to hug her, and Mark, by her side, said, "Hello, Rebecca."

"Hello…"

She didn't know what to call him, and as if reading her mind, he said,

"Mark, just Mark."

"Hello, Mark." Rebecca said with a bright smile. "So happy to see you!"

He smiled back. "Shall we go?"

He took her trolly and walked to the door when he saw Arthur, Olivia's father, seated further away.

Olivia saw the surprise on her father's face. She didn't expect to see Arthur there, and her father clearly didn't know how they were getting to the airport. *He probably expected a taxi driver,* Olivia thought. *Never mind, Mom will explain everything when she gets back…*

"Hi, Dad," Olivia said, hoping she sounded cheerful.

"Arthur," Mark said and went over to shake his hand, "How are you?"

"Hi, I'm OK." Arthur answered Mark, dejectedly.

"I hope you have a nice time in Alaska," he said in Rebecca's direction and turned to go.

Rebecca went to him. "Please, Art, let me leave with a smile to have some fun. You never wanted to do this with me. Now I have a chance to enjoy my dream-come-true. And it's only a week!"

Arthur nodded. "Eight days," he said quietly, seeming much older than his eighty-five years.

***

Mark took their luggage out of the trunk and placed it on the airport trolly for them. He straightened and said, a forced smile stitched to his lips, "All set? Papers ready? You have everything?"

Olivia could see his sadness underneath the attempted cheerfulness. He was hesitant, she saw, and realized he wasn't sure whether to kiss her in front of her mother or not. She stood on tiptoes to look him in the eyes, kissed him tenderly, and said, "I'll miss you terribly."

"So will I," Mark replied. "Have fun, darling, and come back soon."

Her mother pretended to look elsewhere, allowing them the brief moment of private parting, Olivia noticed.

"OK, all set, let's go," Olivia said, pushing the trolly forward.

"Bye, Mark! Thanks for the lift! I promise to take good care of Livy and bring her back in one peace!"

Olivia turned back to look at Mark again. She blew him a kiss and entered the terminal. Inside the building, she turned again to look out of the sliding doors. Mark was still standing there. Rebecca watched her daughter.

"Do you want us to cancel the trip?" she asked quietly.

Olivia looked at her, appreciating the gesture, shook her head, and walked resolutely to the United check-in area.

They boarded on schedule and found their seats. Olivia stowed their bags in the overhead bin and sat by her mother, who chose the window seat.

"He's just wonderful." Rebecca announced the moment Olivia sat down. "Absolutely wonderful. And a perfect match for you!" She didn't add "I told you so" this time, but Olivia could hear it in her voice.

"When had it all started?" Rebecca asked.

"Two weeks ago," Olivia said.

Only two weeks? Olivia couldn't believe it was only a few weeks since Mark called her and invited her to see his house. Surely, the intensity of their feelings needed longer to develop? Their relationship flared as if their souls recognized each other immediately and knew it was right, requiring no adjustment time.

Rebecca wanted details. Where they met, how often, what Mark was like… Olivia knew her mother admired the tall, handsome, distinguished professor and was delighted that her daughter was no longer alone. Rebecca and Arthur liked Elliot very much but knew how hard the final years had been.

***

Her mother arranged a mini-suite for them on one of the higher decks to ensure they had enough space on board, on the long cruising spans. They unpacked and decided to go and familiarize themselves with the ship's facilities.

When they reached the top deck, with its comfortable bar overlooking the ship's bow, Rebecca decided she had enough and suggested a cup of coffee.

"Perfect," said Olivia, "Exactly what I need."

They chose two armchairs facing the harbor and sat down. Rebecca was looking at her daughter, typing quickly on her smartphone. "Busy, busy, busy…" she said, trying to divert Olivia's attention.

"No, not busy. Just telling Mark we arrived safely," Olivia said.

They sat in the bar, talking about Rebecca and Arthur's new friends at the Carlisle and how pleased they were with the atmosphere and the staff. Rebecca didn't want to leave their lovely, roomy apartment in Pacific Heights, but Arthur wanted the gym a lift-ride away and the swimming pool for residents only. And Rebecca agreed, reluctantly. Now it sounded as if she, too, was happy with the move.

Soon, the ship lifted anchor, and they were on their way.

Rebecca turned to Olivia and said, "I want to thank you so much for doing this for me. It means a lot to me. I know it's not easy for you." Her voice shook with emotion.

"I'm glad you booked it!" Olivia said, a soft smile lighting her eyes. "I didn't get you much of a birthday present last year, nor on this years' birthday, come to think of it."

They looked at each other, the sorrows of last year fresh in their minds.

"It's fine, Livy; this more than evens the balance." Rebecca said, smiling at her daughter.

Olivia's phone chimed, indicating a message had arrived. She looked at the screen and smiled, and turned the screen so that her mother could read, too: "I miss you already!" it said, decorated with heart and flower emojis.

"You're lucky!" Rebecca said.

They laughed, and Rebecca said: "Let's go down and get ready for dinner!"

Dinner was fabulous—elegant and lavish; their table companions were a lovely couple from Chicago. They were discussing tomorrow's itinerary with Rebecca and left Olivia to her thoughts.

She contemplated the last weeks. She never expected such intense feelings. Meeting someone one day, a partner to go to concerts or movies with —that's what she anticipated. She never imagined anything more than that. Certainly not a relationship that would upset her well-organized life… *There's no telling where this relationship is going. Still, it will probably require significant changes. Am I willing to make such changes?*

"Olivia!" her mother looked at her. "You were a million miles away. You haven't heard me call you."

Dinner was over. Rebecca found out that the Chicago couple were bridge players, and they met another couple on board earlier, and one of them also played. They weren't sure how good he was but were willing to try playing with him. Would Olivia mind if Rebecca played with them? She loved bridge and was a good player, Olivia knew.

"Of course, Mom! Have fun! Don't stay up too late! She admonished jokingly.

She returned to their suite and texted Mark: "I survived dinner… miss you!"

His response was immediate, and her phone rang.

"I wanted to call you but didn't know what I'd be interrupting," he said.

"I just got back from dinner," Olivia said. "And I wasn't listening to the people at our table. Mom was frustrated. Anyway, I left her with one of the couples, to play bridge. She loves it, and it would provide me with some time on my own to talk with you."

"I'm glad. Sounds like she's having fun, and that was the whole point of the cruise, right?"

"Yes, she's excited and happy. It's just the timing…"

"I know. But it couldn't be helped. All you can do is try to enjoy it as much as possible. You're on a luxury cruise to Alaska, so it's not so bad, is it? And remember—you're doing it for her." He was trying to cheer her up.

"I guess…" she responded, then asked, "How about you? Did you eat?"

"Just grabbed some fruit. No appetite," Mark replied.

"You'll be as thin as a reed by the time I get back!" she said, laughing. He was already so slim.

"I never eat much. And without company, I feel even less like eating," Mark answered.

"Are you going to visit your daughters tomorrow?" He saw them every Saturday afternoon, she knew. Never for dinner. Even though the two of them, and their families, had dinner together almost every Saturday evening. As strange as that may seem, he was never invited to join them.

"As usual," Mark said. "I'll let you know tomorrow how it went."

She knew he was often frustrated by those visits and hoped tomorrow would be a good one.

***

She was still reading her Kindle when her mother entered their suite. She looked pleased with herself.

"Good game, huh?" Olivia asked.

167

"Yes, indeed!" her mother responded. Her pride was evident. The other man, Miles, her partner, turned out to be an excellent player, and Rebecca was delighted. They won and intended to play again tomorrow evening. She went into a detailed description of the game, the moves she and her partner made, and the points. Olivia lost her at the very beginning, but Rebecca went joyfully on, oblivious.

"Mom, you do remember I don't follow any of it, right?" She was happy her mother was having so much fun.

"It's not too late to learn." Rebecca huffed.

"Tomorrow will be long and difficult. I suggest we go to bed. What do you say?" Olivia tried to mollify her mom.

"Yes, you're right. Juneau, here we come!" Rebecca's good spirits returned.

***

As planned, they arrived after lunch; Juneau spread before them as they approached, with Mount Juneau towering above it. They disembarked and walked to the buses that would take them to Mendenhall Glacier. Her mother chose tours for every one of the ports the ship entered, Olivia knew, and braced herself.

Only twelve miles out of Juneau, they arrived at a different world. The massive, awe-inspiring wall of ice in front of them stopped the touristic babble of voices as all eyes turned to its immense beauty, with uncountable shades of intertwined blues and whites. Even her mother was silent. The track leading to the viewing point was narrow and steep, slippery in some parts, a strenuous hike for her mother, but the older woman was not ready to quit.

"This is it…" she said softly. "This is my dream come true. For so many years, I wanted… The beauty of this place."

***

Life on the large ship fell into a pattern—breakfast, lunch, and dinner; bridge for her mother in the evening. Olivia preferred her books and long conversations with Mark and her sons. And she texted her friends and colleagues, making sure she sounded happy. She missed Leah very much, and no matter how many pictures Ann and Adam sent her—she always wanted more.

As usual, her mother played bridge with her new friends in the evening, and Olivia had the suite to herself. She called Mark when she got back to the suite after dinner, alone, and had some privacy.

He'd been to see his daughters yesterday, Olivia knew. She asked how the visit was, "How did it go? Did you enjoy yourself?"

"Oh, the usual," he said.

She heard a change in his tone and thought something was wrong; she tried to figure out what it was… Sadness? Frustration? Loneliness?

"You don't sound happy… is Jeffrey OK?"

"I called them before I left the house, and they said they went to the mall in the afternoon, so they asked me to come later than usual. When I came, they were already busy preparing dinner, coming and going, moving around. I come to see them for a couple of hours once a week, and they are not very interested in talking to me; that's how I felt."

"Well, at least you had dinner with them, so that must have been nice!" Olivia was happy for him, delighted that because of the late hour, he did not eat alone.

"They didn't invite me to dine with them. So, I went home when they were ready to eat."

Olivia was disconcerted. Feeling his pain and sorrow. And shame. that's what she heard in his voice earlier. *He is always ready to provide them with whatever they need, and they don't see his needs…*

Mark told Olivia that his daughters knew he was no longer seeing Cynthia, and they knew he was now involved with her. They didn't care about Cynthia, and they didn't care about her either. But he was by himself that night.

"Did you tell them I'm away and you're alone?" she asked quietly, her heart breaking.

"Yes, I told them you're in Alaska, with your mother," he said.

"But not that you're alone, not invited to friends'," Olivia continued for him.

"No."

Of course not. He wouldn't show need, never asks them for anything, Mark told her in one of their conversations. She thought that a one-sided relationship—when one side only gives, and the other party only takes—

was not a real relationship, but she didn't say it, to avoid hurting him more than he was hurting already.

Attempting to correct the impression that he assumed she received, he hastened to add, "I'm sure they just didn't make the connection. They probably assumed I'm busy."

She understood that when Helen was alive, and they didn't want to see her—they didn't invite him. But now? Why didn't they *ask*?

Then she remembered that he often called them "the girls" like they were still five years old… and maybe, with him, they acted like little girls that never grew up. That could explain the discrepancy between their competence at work and their less mature behavior toward their father. However, if this was the correct interpretation, Mark was responsible for the skewed relationship as much as his daughters.

"Maybe," Olivia said sorrowfully. "Well… It's not easy to change old habits."

"No, it isn't. I'm fine, don't worry. Have fun tomorrow," Mark said and hung up.

Next, she called Sarah.

"Hi there!" said the cheerful voice on the phone. "How's it going? How's your mom? Everything going OK?"

"All is fine. As luxurious as one could wish for. The scenery is amazing, the sea is a little rough, but we don't feel it that much, only the waves cradling us to sleep. The food is fantastic and tastefully served. You would have loved it!"

"But? I hear a but…" Sarah could always read her so well, even on the phone.

Olivia swallowed hard.

"I miss him," she finally said.

"Are you insane?" she heard Sarah yell. "You go on a first-class, luxury dream cruise, all paid for, and you miss him? If it's as real as you made it sound—this relationship may be for the rest of your life! So come on, girl, make the best of it!"

"Exactly what I needed to hear," Olivia said. "You always manage to cut to the chase and focus on the main issues. Thank you, my friend. Talk to you soon!"

***

Like all the other tourists around her, Olivia took pictures repeatedly; most of them showed her mother, her pleasure evident. She was animated, happy, looked younger, and lively. She knew the memories would nourish her mother for years to come. She decided to prepare a photo album for her mother when they got back. Something she could leaf through and relive the pleasure she experienced. And show her friends, of course. She shared some of the pictures with Mark, her sons, and Sarah. They seemed happy to be included.

The Glacier Bay Basin topped all of Rebecca's expectations. The majestic glaciers surrounding the ship were as magnificent as she had imagined them. Although the blues and whites of the ice and snow were interspersed with black rocks, indicating the melting process, the view was still breathtaking, the vast frozen walls towering silently, feet above the calm water as grand and imposing as she imagined them to be. *Nature, at its most impressive manifestation,* Olivia thought.

They were on deck, filling their eyes with the clean, beautiful scenery, when all of a sudden, a segment of the iceberg wall in front of them calved, the deep rumbling sound drawing all eyes to the impressive sight.

"Now my dream is wholly fulfilled." Rebecca said, her eyes filled with awe, gleaming with joy.

Maybe one day, I'll take such trips with Mark, she thought. *Maybe— Galapagos? New Zealand?* She knew most of Mark's friends traveled a lot, and so did he. It was part of their lifestyle. She'd still have to deal with his friends and their lifestyle when she got back, she knew. The thought stressed her, but she made up her mind: For now—her unexpected new feelings of love and rekindled desire should be enough to occupy her thoughts.

29

Olivia was jittery and anxious and couldn't fall asleep.

"We'll be in port when we wake up in the morning." her mother said when she came back from playing bridge that evening.

"Yes. And we have to get up early to be among the first people to disembark so that we won't be late for our flight," Olivia responded. "Did you say goodbye to your friends? You seem to have bonded rather nicely!"

"Indeed," Rebecca said, "And I'm sure we'll meet again! Their daughter lives in San Francisco, so they travel once or twice a year to visit her and their grandchildren. They said they are considering moving into a community like ours, and maybe they'll move out of Chicago—it's getting too cold for them… and being close to the family will be good. I promised to introduce them to all the nice people in the Carlisle, and ease their entry into our social circle, to help them settle down. Miles also said they might move to the Bay Area."

"So—what do you say—all in all, was it a good trip? What you wished for?" Olivia asked.

Her mother looked at her, then shook her head.

"It's much more than I wished for! The scenery, the luxury, the pleasantness of the cruise—are what I dreamed of. But having you with me to share it—made it much more enjoyable… I'll be forever grateful… it will be a trip I'll never forget! The best trip I've had!"

Olivia went over to her mother and hugged her tightly. "I'm so glad we did it."

"I know how difficult it was for you. To tear yourself away… the timing was terrible for you… I truly appreciate what you did for me… and hope I didn't ruin anything for you."

"It's fine, Mom. Don't worry," Olivia said and smiled warmly. "If a week away can ruin a relationship, it's not the 'real deal' anyway. And I believe it ruined nothing. Maybe the opposite."

Olivia was glad she agreed to the trip and grateful it was over. And more than anything, she was delighted the relationship with her mother—

not always so easy and free of conflicts—had strengthened, while her mother was still alive and well enough to enjoy the love.

The plane approached landing, and Olivia couldn't wait to disembark. They gathered their hand luggage and checked to ensure nothing was left behind.

It all felt "slow motion". Anxious to reach the exit, Olivia felt that people went too slowly. Finally, the sliding doors opened, and they were walking out to the reception area of the arrival hall. Her eyes roaming, searching for him, she caught sight of him—his tall, slim figure and full, white hair—easy to spot in the crowd. Her heart beating exuberantly, Olivia ran forward and nearly knocked both of them to the floor. They laughed, and he kissed her joyfully. People around them seemed to share their happiness, as if they were glad to be reminded that such scenes existed and were still possible. His eyes smiled into hers, and his hand caressed her hair.

Rebecca couldn't stop talking about the delightful trip, the beautiful scenery, and the lovely people she met. Mark was amused and looked at Olivia. "Now I know where you get your exuberance from," he said quietly, so only Olivia could hear.

The drive didn't take too long, and they reached the Carlisle to drop Rebecca at home. Olivia got out of the car to hug her mother; Rebecca whispered in her ear, "Hang on to your man. He's one of a kind!"

Back in the car, Mark leaned over to kiss her and said, "I missed you… glad you're back!"

"Me too…" Olivia murmured.

Mark took her hand and kissed its palm. "Let's go home," he said.

She wondered which home he meant. They had two separate homes…

It was early afternoon when they reached his house, talking about his work and its demands.

So, this is "home", Olivia thought. *It's too soon*, she couldn't think of anywhere but her house as "home".

Mark opened the trunk and took her suitcase and handbag into his house. The moment he opened the door, the two dogs rushed out.

Pinky jumped around her, barking her happiness at seeing Olivia. More sedately, Tish followed her to welcome Olivia. She kneeled to hug the two dogs, laughing as both tried to lick her face simultaneously.

She followed Mark and walked inside. "Hello, house!" she said, her eyes drawn to the magnificent view of the Pacific. "Do you ever tire of all this beauty?" she asked, smiling.

"I hope I never will." He gathered her into his arms and kissed her again, his embrace tight, reflecting his need to feel her close.

"Welcome home," he said softly and warmly.

"So good to be back!" she responded.

They walked to the terrace and sat together, looking at the choppy water and the scudding clouds. It was a bit chilly but huddled tightly, they were warm enough.

"The house feels different, now that you're here," Mark said, his arm around her shoulders, his hand stroking her arm. "I wasn't lonely because I knew I had you to look forward to."

She looked up at his face and saw the depth of his feelings written there. She realized that she was no longer afraid she'd wake up from a dream. It was real.

"Finding someone intelligent and interesting, a partner to go out with, to be comfortable with—that was as much as I hoped for," he added. "Loving that someone—is such an unexpected bonus!"

"For years, I was told never to show how much I cared about a guy, never to say, 'I love you'. To avoid being taken advantage of," Olivia said gravely. "I'm so glad we don't play such games with each other. It feels so good just to come out and simply say—I love you!"

***

Hours later, Olivia woke up. She was curled in his arms, her body soft and warm, sated. His masculine smell surrounded her. She opened her eyes and saw him looking at her, his heart in his eyes. "What time is it?" she asked drowsily.

"Almost seven p.m.," he responded, "You must be hungry; you didn't even have lunch."

"Mmm… yes, some food would be nice."

"Well then, go and take a quick shower, and I'll reserve a table for us somewhere close. Seafood again?"

"Lovely!" she said and got out of bed.

***

The restaurant was not crowded. Soft music played in the background, muffling all conversations to allow privacy. Mark wanted to know more details about the trips they took, their daily schedules, and the difficulties.

Throughout dinner, she shared anecdotes and events from the cruise and the trips. Alaska was one of her dreams, too, Olivia said, not only her mother's. She tried to convince Elliot to go there for years, but he was not interested.

"At first, he said it was far too difficult—he didn't want to drive in Alaska, he was afraid of getting stuck somewhere in the wilderness, things like that… then Elliot said there were other places he wanted to see more than Alaska. Like Cost Rica, the Bahamas. We never got to those places either because he got sick."

"Well, you know the saying—people make plans, but God has his own plans," Mark said, his eyes smiling.

He took her hand in his, caressing her palm. "You love traveling?"

"One of the things I love most," Olivia responded with a smile of her own. "If I had all the time in the world to do what I like—I'd travel all over the globe. And come back to see the family in between, then go away again!"

"Where would you go? What's on the top of your list?" Mark asked.

"Galapagos. Definitely Galapagos! To see all the unique species. And Machu Picchu in Peru, while I'm in that neck of the woods. Then Antarctica, that sounds like another incredible place I'd like to experience and know more about. But these are far-fetched daydreams. These trips are so expensive, they are nothing but fantasies." Olivia's eyes were vivid, a dreamy look on her face.

"Sometimes dreams do come true… sometimes they are realistic enough, and it's not even that hard to fulfill them," Mark responded quietly.

30

When she returned to her home, Olivia discovered that life on her street had changed. Some building construction was taking place a few houses down the road, the noise of tractors and bulldozers was tearing every eardrum in the area. But worse yet—after years of the residents' begging, the city council decided to fix the tarmac covering the streets surrounding their park. The dust, the smell of hot tar, and the ceaseless noises were very unpleasant. No matter how often the neighbors said to each other that it would soon be over, and the suffering was for a good cause, they were all tormented. Most of them worked during the days, which spared them a few hours of anguish, but the work started early every morning and was dreadfully bothersome. It was utterly insufferable for those who worked from home or were full-time parents. According to the constructor, it would take them a couple of months to finish the job. Probably more.

Without deciding on the matter, Olivia and Mark created a pattern; they spent one evening at her place and one evening at his, going back to their own homes to sleep. She preferred it that way. She wanted to enjoy the changes she created after Elliot died. She wanted to feel at home at *her* place.

Mark tried to convince her it would be more convenient to spend every evening at his place where everything was clean, the air was fresh and smelled of sea and flowers, with a lovely lawn for the dogs to run around. But the best argument was the one he *didn't* use: he was suffering terribly from the dusty, smelly mess around her house. Olivia was aware of it and decided her wants did not justify the problems they were creating.

After two weeks of misery for both of them, Olivia consented to Mark's continued requests and decided to move in with him until the construction works ended.

By Friday afternoon, she packed a few clothes, her laptop, toiletries, and makeup case, not forgetting Pinky's bed, toys, and bowls. Mark came over to help her carry everything, and they drove away.

Is this the beginning of a different stage in our relationship? She mused while following Mark's car with hers. She wasn't sure she was ready to take things further… it was such a short time since it all began… it was August when she came to see the finished renovations. Was it not premature to move in with him by the end of September? Well, it was only temporary, she reminded herself. *And you can withdraw whenever you see fit.*

He rearranged his clothes in the walk-in closet and created a lot of space for her so she'd be comfortable. She was touched. He thought of everything. He wanted her to be at ease and happy by his side. She had to admit—his house was much bigger than hers and more luxurious. Yet, it wasn't *her* home. *We'll see,* she thought. *I'll give us a fair chance, and then we'll see.*

She unpacked and stowed her suitcase and went back to the living room. Mark arranged coffee with several small, individual cakes on a tray. "I didn't know what you preferred, so I bought apple strudel, cheesecake, chocolate cupcakes, and granola cookies."

"Oh, Mark, I didn't expect such abundance!" she looked at him, grateful.

"I wanted you to feel welcome, to know how much I want you here with me." He smiled at her, that old shy smile she loved.

She went to him and brought his mouth down to hers. "Thank you," she whispered, deeply moved.

They sat in the living room, watching the windswept Pacific, holding hands, totally relaxed, enjoying the quiet music he chose for them. "Moonlight Sonata?" Olivia asked.

Mark nodded.

The fallen leaves danced crazily on the grassy lawn, their browns, reds, and rusty yellows swirling in the shifting wind. Pinky and Tish were trying to catch the flying leaves, barking happily. Mark and Olivia watched their playful jumps.

"Look how careful he is not to hurt her—he moves out of the way so as not to collide with her," Olivia said.

"That's what a gentleman *should* do," Mark said. "Gentle-dogs as well."

They both smiled.

"I want to check your freezer, see if there's anything I can cook for dinner," Olivia said and got up.

"You cook?" has asked, surprised.

"Of course, I cook, silly! And I can do a lot more than just pasta! I had two kids to raise, remember? I couldn't have them eating pizzas, pasta, and hamburgers every day! So yes—I learned to cook. Nothing fancy, but I do quite well with basic food, and I'm good at improvising."

"I can dash to the store if you need anything—no problem," Mark said.

She found potatoes, onions, and hot dogs. In the fridge's bottom drawer, she found some tomatoes and cucumbers and a slightly wilted lettuce.

"Good enough for today," she said. "Tomorrow we'll go shopping, and you'll tell me what you like and dislike."

"Can I help you cook?" Mark asked, and she saw he was eager to have a reason to stay in the kitchen with her.

"Sure, you can!" She passed him two onions. "Know how to peel them? Chop them small? And after that, do the same to the potatoes."

"Wait and see! Watch an expert at work!" he said, and they smiled warmly at each other.

Olivia cut the salad and looked for lemons, olive oil, but couldn't find any condiments.

Mark seemed to know what she was looking for and said, "Check over there." and indicated a small cupboard. He was right. It was a treasure trove.

She looked at him, smiling her appreciation. He just shrugged, looking helpless and lost.

"I remembered looking for the espresso cups, and I met all those colorful bottles I didn't know what to do with, so I just left them there… I had an expert doing the packing and unpacking for me. She packed everything. I paid her nicely and didn't bother with arranging dishes and pots and the like. I'm still not sure I know where everything is, but it was better than having to do it myself!"

Dinner was fried potatoes with onions and sliced hotdogs added in, and the salad on the side. Mark was delighted.

"This is my preferred type of dinner—simple, nourishing, balanced. The fancy stuff is good for restaurants, once in a while. This is home food!"

They cleared the table and loaded the dishwasher together. When they finished, Mark suggested, "Gin and tonic?"

"Great." Olivia nodded and went to their intimate corner in the big living room, facing the vast windows overlooking the ocean and the bridge that decorated it.

Mark brought their drinks and sat close to her, drawing her closer to him.

They watched the lighted Golden Gate Bridge in silence, the Third Brandenburg Concerto playing softly in the background. His hand was roaming up and down her arm, and he bent down to kiss her head.

"Mark, I need to come clean and tell you something," Olivia said after a while, unexpected and unrelated to anything that happened that evening.

Mark tensed by her side but did not pull away. "Is it something devastating?" he asked, and she heard his apprehension. Maybe he thought she was going to say she had second thoughts?

"Nothing of the sort," she hastened to say.

"OK," he said, and she felt his body unclench, relieved.

"I want to tell you the truth about where I know you from, which may explain at least some of my primary assumption that we're so incompatible," she paused, choosing her words.

"Go on," Mark said.

"We met for the first time exactly thirty years ago. Almost to the day... October 17, 1989. Remember that day?" She looked up to see his reaction.

"How could I forget?" Mark queried. "The big Loma Prieta earthquake... the collapse of the upper tier of the Nimitz Freeway onto the lower tier. Thousands were injured... our hospital was completely swamped."

Olivia nodded, silent, allowing him to recall the details.

"We met that day. I was twenty-two years old. A student on my way home from Berkeley. I was driving close to the bridge when it collapsed. I was wounded; my injuries were minor, but the ambulance brought me to your hospital anyway. I was treated swiftly, my head and arm were bandaged, and I was released. There was such mayhem, and I saw how hard the nurses and doctors were working. People were rushing from one injured person to another, unable to make a dent in the inflow.

"I was about to leave when you appeared in the ER. Tall, young-faced, but you were white-haired even then, in a white coat, exuding authority. I didn't know who you were, but I saw the transformation in the people working there. The reaction was unbelievable. It was their relief that I noticed—sort of a total, profound, collective transfer of responsibility. And you walked in as if you owned the place. Like a ripple, the silence spread throughout the ER. They were waiting for you to lead. The frantic, hectic atmosphere changed in seconds.

"You started moving among the people on the stretchers, on the beds, giving orders, dividing the work, creating teams, arranging priorities, and all of that—in a calm, restrained voice, transmitting quiet assurance. Your suggestions were accepted without arguments, your questions answered swiftly and efficiently, and suddenly, there was a pattern, a system, people worked efficiently, and things improved rapidly.

"I stayed there, in a corner, fascinated. I've never seen anything like that. Someone came up to you—a nurse or social worker—and said several volunteers were waiting to do whatever was necessary and asked what you wanted to do with them. You stopped walking among the beds and told her that, of course, you needed them. And you told her to place any volunteer willing to take care of those the medical teams have already checked and treated, to aid the nurses."

Mark nodded to show he was listening, remembering the scene.

"Then you saw me there, watching you from the corner. Irritation was written all over your face, your eyes penetrating. 'What are you doing here?' you barked at me. 'Are you done? I can see you were already taken care of!' I felt so little, insignificant. A nuisance. 'Go and volunteer! We need all the help we can get! You're not *that* badly injured, so go! Make yourself useful!' you ordered me as if you had a right to do so."

It was evident that Mark didn't remember the incident; Olivia saw his attempt to recall it on his face.

"I was overawed, intimidated, and just waited for you to move on, remove your focus from me so I could vanish. And went to volunteer, of course… for five days and nights. There was a kid there, Zack. About five years old. His mother died in their car on the bridge, and he was trapped inside. The paramedics rescued him. He was badly injured and traumatized. The doctors later decided they had to amputate his leg. He was so confused and miserable and in pain, and crying pitiably! The hospital didn't know who his family was or how to reach any of them—and he was too young and couldn't tell them. I didn't think he knew. I guess the nurses were grateful I was there because they had so much to do and couldn't sit with the little guy. I stayed with him constantly, day and night, taking care of him until his father managed to find him. He was hurt, too, but not too badly. He was in a different car and was taken to a different hospital."

Mark didn't say anything.

"For years, ever since I moved back to San Francisco and realized we were neighbors, I prayed you wouldn't remember the incident in the ER. It would have embarrassed me terribly. But I needed to tell you now. It felt dishonest not to."

A strange look crossed Mark's face. She thought something had occurred to him, but he wasn't ready to share it with her.

"I didn't remember *you*," Mark said. "But I *do* remember the story of a young woman volunteer and her amazing dedication to the little orphan. All the nurses were talking about that. About what it meant to the little boy and how grateful *they* were for the help." After a while, he added with a smile, "It means we've known each other for thirty years! No wonder we got so close so quickly."

He hugged her tightly and said, "I was under a lot of pressure after the earthquake. I couldn't show it, of course, certainly not in the ER. So, I may have been too harsh."

Olivia shrugged. "It doesn't matter now. It was so long ago... never thought I'd talk about it. Certainly not with you. But now that we're together, I just had to... I believe that the memory of your authority, the cold efficiency, the no-nonsense attitude, influenced my perception of you."

They were silent, absorbed in their memories.

"I kept in touch with the boy and his family for a long time, while he was in the hospital and then in rehabilitation," Olivia said after a while. "They were broken... adjusting to the prosthetic leg, the loss of the mother. The father, too, needed support and compassion. I tried to help them until I noticed that the father sort of expected me to take his dead wife's place. Zack was intensely attached to me by then, and the two of them began to rely on me too much. Their broader family, too, sent signals they would be delighted if I stayed. But I was too young for that, and it scared me. Breaking away was one of the most difficult things I ever had to do." Olivia sighed. "I still think of Zack from time to time, wondering what has become of him, what's he like... how he managed to overcome the disability. He'll be thirty-five now... probably married, with kids of his own."

"Are you sorry you didn't stay?" Mark asked.

"No. Not at all. It wasn't right. And I didn't want to be a substitute for a dead woman. Unequivocally not!" she said with certainty.

They sat close together, gazing at the luminous moonlight and its shimmering reflection on the water, the play of silver hues on the liquid black creating a fascinating, dreamlike seascape.

After a while, Mark said, "Remember I wanted to invite some of my friends over, to get to know you? How about Saturday or Sunday, afternoon or evening?" Mark said, after a while. "Let's say—next week? Just three couples, my closest friends from way back. I want you to know them and hope you like them. I'm sure they'll like you."

It was vital to him, she realized. *He wants me to like them, and them— to like me. It's a sort of a test, without meaning to be... but I'll have to jump into his social circle sooner or later, so why not try it with just a few close friends?*

"Sure," she said, "Why don't you call them and see when they are free?"

"When I tell them *why* I'm inviting them, they'll be free whenever it's convenient for us." He smiled. "They'll be utterly surprised and curious!"

"Why surprised?" Olivia asked. "They know you broke up with Cynthia Morgan, don't they?"

"Of course, they do! And most of them are thrilled it ended."

"They were probably expecting you to find someone else, you're not the type to be alone for long!" Olivia commented.

Mark shook his head, the shy smile in his eyes again. "You won't believe how many women in our society tried to grab Helen's place when she died. When they found out it was over with Cynthia, the merry chase began again. Some of my friends tried to introduce me to eligible beauties... it was crazy," he said, shaking his head.

Olivia laughed, and he joined her. "And then you go and choose for yourself, and not only that—you 'import' a stranger into your society."

"And a lovely, brilliant professor, at that!" He chuckled. "I can't wait to see the faces of the society ladies... Don't get me wrong—none of them is an empty-headed beauty, just there for decoration, but they'll be somewhat intimidated."

"How many friends *do* you have?" she asked, worried all of a sudden, thinking of the many new faces and names she'll have to deal with.

Mark shrugged. "A lot. Some close, others—not so close. Many are acquaintances that we'll see in the bigger social events. I guess it's not a single circle, more like a series of concentric circles, in different degrees of intimacy. Some people I see often and at many social functions; others are more like acquaintances that I see only in bigger events. Some people I don't particularly like, but they are friends of some of the others who belong to my circle. I guess the same goes for all of them, too."

The thought of so many new people in her life was precisely what she dreaded. *However,* she thought, *if he likes them, and I like him, it is to be expected that I'll like most of them, too.* Simple, rational deduction, the rule of balanced relationships. *No reason to panic now,* she tried to convince herself. *We'll wait and see.*

For now—she'd deal with the three couples he wanted her to meet first—time to put their relationship to the social test. One of many, she was sure, but it had to begin sometime.

31

She woke up late the next day and was in no hurry to get up. The memory of last night's pleasures flooded her mind, and she turned to curl in his arms. He was covered to his chin and felt warm. Still drowsy, he opened his arms to fold her to him. Safe. She felt safe. And loved… *Whatever we'll encounter—we'll overcome;* the thought came unbidden to her mind. And she was sure it reflected deep conviction.

They decided to take the dogs for a walk in Land's End Park. The weather was chilly and cloudy, the wind bracing, but no rain was forecasted. They were sure the park would not be overcrowded in such weather. That only happened in summer, when locals and tourists swarmed the trails and the exhibitions area. They walked briskly, holding hands. She felt like a teenager, but it was a pleasant change from being the responsible, sober adult she always was with Elliot.

She said it aloud, and Mark laughed, happy to know how she felt.

"You know…" he began and stopped. "I don't remember myself laughing so much… for years, I had no reason to laugh," he said.

Olivia nodded. She understood perfectly.

They were talking about his work and hers, and their schedules. He had a much more massive load than Olivia's because, in addition to his role as medical director, he was still an active faculty member, teaching and directing.

"Why do you work so hard?" she wanted to know.

"I'm used to it," he replied.

"Are you afraid you won't know what to do with yourself if you had free time?" she asked. "It can't be the money, I'm sure your job pays well enough, and you have saved enough, so you'll be fine even if you decide to retire tomorrow."

"No… it's not the money," came his drawn-out response, as if he thought what to say, how to explain it to her. "I worked for long hours all my life. I had scholarships, when I was a student, but I needed to support myself, so I worked. Then, I worked hard to establish myself as a physician and scholar, and then I became chairperson of the internal medicine department, and that required long hours and a lot of reading to update my knowledge constantly. And when I became medical director of the hospital—the load just grew heavier because I wanted to keep practicing medicine, not just do management."

"When will it be time to ease up? I don't mean time to retire completely; just reduce the load." She looked at him and smiled to indicate she was not critical.

"When I'm old, I guess." He smiled back. And then he turned serious. "And I *do* need the money," he said softly.

Her look was inquiring, not understanding.

"You know, I have Clair and Jeffrey to think of. His treatments cost a lot. And it's complicated for them, so I help whenever they need me to. Clair never asks, but I sense it when she's in need."

"I thought she had a fantastic job, and so does Spencer, her husband. They must earn a lot by themselves. Don't they?"

"They do, but somehow—it's not always enough. And if I can help— why not? That's how I see it," he replied.

Why not, indeed? She thought.

Another thought popped into her mind—he was working hard because he wanted to. To be relevant, to feel needed, to remain updated. Or—maybe he wanted the security he didn't enjoy when he was young. And he wanted to be able to leave a lot to his daughters, so they'd lack nothing when he isn't there to help them.

Mark loves what he does more than any of the alternatives he knows, she concluded. Not that he had a chance to examine many options—he never felt a need to do that.

"Are you going to see them this afternoon?" She remembered he said he went every Saturday.

"If it's OK with you. I won't go if you don't want to stay alone in the house," he said. "But that's the only time in the week I *can* see them."

"It's certainly fine," Olivia said. "I'll change my meetings with my parents to Saturday afternoons, instead of Fridays. I'm sure they won't mind. My mother will be happy whenever I come; my dad? He's got his 'parliament' of friends and goes every day at five p.m. to meet them, whether I'm there or not. He sits with us for about ten minutes, and then he leaves." She shrugged, indicating her indifference.

***

On her way back from visiting her parents, Olivia decided to stop over at the Italian restaurant she loved to buy a few dishes she thought he would like for their dinner. She came back to the house before him.

By the time she set the table, Mark had arrived.

She immediately saw that he was in a bad mood. He hugged her tightly, his head lowered, and inhaled deeply as if trying to fill his whole being with her smell. He hung on, close, and she could feel the tension coursing through his body.

"What's wrong, Mark?"

"I'll be OK," he said, sounding miserable.

"Come on," Olivia said and pulled him to their preferred corner. "Tell me," she said, her voice filled with empathy.

"I don't know what I was expecting…" he said, shaking his head. "I told my daughters about you when we started seeing each other, and today I told them how happy you make me, how strongly I feel about you, and how much I wanted them to meet you." He paused and sighed deeply. "They said that they do not wish to meet you. It was too soon for them. They're still 'post-traumatic,' they said, getting over the damage Helen wreaked upon us. And besides—maybe it won't last, so why bother?"

His hands were twitchy, agitated, she saw, reflecting his inner turmoil.

"What was even worse—Instead of happiness for me, I was bombarded with questions and critical comments." He paused again, turned his gaze outside. She saw he was uneasy.

"What did they want to know?" she asked softly, encouraging him to continue.

"It began with 'Who is she?' and 'Where did you meet her?' I told them about us being neighbors for years, talking in the park while walking the dogs, and about Elliot and his death. And how I always found you fascinating, our intellectual conversations, and our similar taste in art and music.

"Emma wanted to know if you were beautiful, and I said you looked lovely, with stunning, shining, intelligent eyes. I thought they'd be pleased I chose a partner for her brains, not only her beauty. You know, they thought I chose Helen only because of her looks. She was gorgeous, but she was also vibrant and full of life, which I felt that I needed at the time, after so many years without a constant partner. But they didn't seem pleased."

Another pause. A longer one. Mark turned to look at her; his eyes darkened.

"Emma asked me if I intended to live with you, and I said we're living together now, though it's still temporary, and you needed to see if it suits you. And they reacted like I was crazy, with questions such as 'What do you need this burden for?' or 'Do you *truly* know the person you intend to live with after such a short acquaintance?' They made me feel like an old fool, a lovesick, irrational, old fool. I said you're no burden to me—on the contrary, and that I feel I know you well, after all our conversations, all our meetings that were so honest and without pretense."

Olivia realized he was not through yet and was finding it difficult to continue. She took his hand in hers, stroking it slowly, and waited patiently.

After a while, he said, "Later, Emma asked me what you were after, what you wanted from me, and why you chose to be with me. And I was shocked. Am I not worthy? I asked her, and she said that as you're so much younger than I, and I have cancer, you must have ulterior motives. As if my money and status are all I have to offer. That hurt. A lot."

Mark shrugged wretchedly.

She moved closer and hugged his bent shoulders. "We both know that we're perfect for each other, with all our imperfections," she said, her voice a whisper. "Maybe we're perfect together because our imperfections match so well." Her attempt to lighten his mood failed miserably. She remained by his side, hugging him, supportive, unable to alleviate the pain he felt, feeling helpless.

Olivia realized the whole conversation made her furious. She was sure they were not aware of his loneliness. Or perhaps they never grasped that underneath the handsome façade of the successful physician, with extensive social circles, hid a man who needed intimacy?

She also understood that there was a big difference between Emma and Clair. Emma was two years older and more dominant in the relationship. Clair was the brighter sibling, with more significant achievements, despite the heavy burden of Jeffrey and his disabilities. The two of them lived in beautiful big houses, next to each other, that Mark bought for them shortly after they got married. He wanted them to remain close, physically and emotionally. And he succeeded—the two were best friends and the primary support for each other. Clair would always side with Emma, in any conflict, she figured, because she needed her support and aid in everyday life.

She wondered what their husbands were like and whether the two women had close friends they trusted.

"Were their husbands there, too?" she asked.

Mark nodded. But said nothing.

"Well—what did *they* have to say?" She sounded exasperated.

"They did not interfere. Philip, Emma's husband, he's a decent guy, smart, too. Still, he won't go against Emma in front of people, so he's never antagonistic, and never expresses an independent opinion regarding *her* family. He loves and adores her, but Emma is the one who defines the dynamics in their family."

"So, she's the dominant one in their family?" Olivia was curious.

"Not always," he replied, and Olivia saw he was considering the question. "She's dominant when it suits her. Or when he doesn't care enough. When it comes to matters that he *does* care about—he'll make a stand and won't budge. For example, they have dinner together with Clair and her family almost every Saturday night. When his father and his wife came to live in San Francisco, he insisted that they be included. And his sister and her family too, when they come to visit. Emma tried to argue at first but gave in."

Why is it they never invite you to join the family dinners? The thought kept nagging on her mind. *Do they expect you to* ask *for an invitation?* He joined them only for Thanksgiving and Christmas dinners. She believed the thought had crossed his mind, too, for he fell quiet. Olivia didn't investigate further.

After a while, he continued.

"As for Spencer, Clair's husband, I think I told you—he's busy with the software startup he and some friends have initiated. He's a nice man, smart and funny, an excellent software engineer, topnotch. But when it comes to family and children—he's rather lost. He'll let Clair do whatever she wants. The problem is, sometimes he reacts rather immaturely. Like—when he gets angry with Jeff, they get into fights. With Jeff! Luckily, this doesn't happen too often. He travels a lot, so he is away from home quite a lot, which suits all of them. But it means that Clair is often alone to deal with all the complexities of their daily lives. Spencer is hardly there when the school calls, and it's almost always Clair who'll drop everything and rush over to take Jeffrey home. That's another reason why she relies on Emma so much. She's her first line of defense, the go-to person when she needs help or support."

Mark's head hung low, and he rested it on his hands, his palms supporting his forehead, elbows on his knees, his shoulders bent.

Trying to visualize Mark's situation, she suddenly grasped the depth of unease and the humiliation he must have felt. "So, the interrogation you went through happened when the whole family was there?" Olivia asked, dismayed.

"Not all the time… the kids were bored and left at some point. Sometime later, Philip and Spencer decided what they would prepare for dinner and went to their kitchens. My daughters don't cook. Luckily, their husbands do." He tried to sound whimsical but failed. "At some point—it was only the three of us, and it was very unpleasant."

Olivia could not understand the source of the ambivalence in his daughters' feelings toward Mark. Maybe they still bore a grudge because he chose Helen? Did they see his decision to live with Helen as a betrayal of them or their dead mother? He did say they defined themselves as "post-traumatic" because of Helen.

Maybe one day, she would understand better. Perhaps one day she'll be able to talk with Emma and Clair about such things? Perhaps their rejection of Helen was because they scorned her extravagant flamboyance? Or maybe they objected to her attempts to change his priorities and place herself as more important than they were? Olivia was neither flamboyant nor bossy, so perhaps she wouldn't encounter such antagonism.

Maybe they'll be able to form a "normal" relationship? She hoped it would happen, for Mark's sake. It would make him happy.

But they didn't sound like her type of people.

32

"My closest friends will be happy to come next Sunday evening," Mark announced a few days later when they met at his house after work. Olivia was tired. It was a difficult period at the department, with promotion committees and interfaculty political conflicts, and the thought of the additional burden of hosting his friends didn't appeal to her.

Mark read her mind.

"We don't have to do much. We'll buy some good cheeses and sausages, grilled shrimps with fancy dips, cut some vegetables, with good wines, and a selection of petits fours with coffee later—that's all it takes," he said. "We're all busy people, so it's quite acceptable, and I'll help, of course."

"Sounds doable," she said, marginally relieved.

"Were you worried?" he asked.

"Somewhat," she said. "I didn't know what to expect, what your friends are used to, or the acceptable style of hosting. And it's a challenging time at work, so I don't have time to invest in preparations."

He looked at her, questioning.

"Usual conflicts and issues. One of my professors doesn't want to be part of a certain committee, and another was offended that she was not asked to participate in another committee. Yet another is frustrated because he teaches unpopular courses, so his ranking suffers. Also, we had to cut a few groups of a certain course, and two professors wanted to teach the remaining groups of that course, fighting to be the one chosen. And on top of all this, the research on strategies to open new global markets is not going well, my research assistant is pregnant and wants to leave—she entered the ninth month—and I haven't found a replacement for her yet."

"I'm sure you'll manage very well, despite all the hassle. As you said—it's the usual conflicts and issues, so you must be used to it by now," Mark said, his smile soft and encouraging, hugging her warmly.

"Yes. I am," Olivia replied but shook her head. "Still, it's a lot of hassle, as you so aptly put it."

The smile returned to her eyes, feeling less tired once things returned to their right proportions.

***

Sunday arrived, and Olivia was tense, apprehensive. Knowing she's on display, put to the test.

The doorbell rang.

"Hi, Grace, Michael, come in, come in!" she heard Mark.

She walked over, extended her hand. "Hi, I'm Olivia," she said.

"And these are Grace and Michael Weber," Marked said.

Olivia shook hands with Grace and extended her hand to Michael.

He took her hand and held it, a baffled look on his face. "Hey, wait a minute—I know you!" He said, his voice booming.

Olivia looked at the tall, big man with a massive, grey-haired head and thick white beard. Her eyes were questioning.

"Yes!" He bellowed. "You're the academic director who got the dean's award last month! I'm the Dean of Management at USF, and Frank Williams told us about you in the last monthly deans' meeting. I checked you out and saw your picture! He said the way you handled the problem with the pregnant student was exceptional."

"Thank you," Olivia mumbled and felt her face blush.

Mark was immediately by her side, his arm possessively on her shoulder, and she felt his pride.

"Quite an achievement," said Grace, barely reaching her husband's shoulder, her wintergreen dress enhancing the vibrant green of her eyes. "I heard there were many contenders for the students' votes!"

They walked in, and the vista in front of them drew their attention away from her.

"What a view!" Grace exclaimed. "We can see the bay from our apartment as well, and the city, too, but this is so special! You have no houses between you and the ocean!"

Then she turned around. "And the house! So tasteful! You've done a beautiful job!"

"Looks comfortable, too." Michael said. "As houses should be, not just for show."

Mark came back with white wine for Grace and Olivia, a whisky for

Michael and himself.

He barely handed them their drinks, and the doorbell rang again.

Mark walked to the door, the tray still in his hand.

"Are we the first to arrive?" Olivia heard a familiar voice from the foyer.

"No, the Webers beat you to it," Mark replied, his voice merry. "Do come in!"

Olivia walked to the foyer and said, "Hello, Doctor Orlansky!"

The newcomer stared at her and then snatched her into a rib-breaking embrace. "You! How come you didn't warn me, Mark, you devil! Olivia, it's so good to see you, and in such different circumstances! It took me a minute to figure out it's you—in such a different location and different role." Then, she realized what she said and looked contrite, but only for a second.

She walked over to Mark and squeezed him, too. "I forgive you!" she declared. "But only because you made such a brilliant choice! Congratulations, you two!" The tall woman, with the mane of dark curls, seemed genuinely happy. "This is my husband, Teddy," she said, "This is Elliot's wife... ah... widow," she corrected herself and continued, unabashed. "Remember I told you about them, of her devotion to her husband? He's the one who always found the energy to banter with me!" Turning around, she added, her voice booming, "This house is magnificent! I want a tour, please!"

"Yes, I remember." Teddy said to Olivia with a warm smile. "Lovely to meet you."

She liked the mild-mannered man instantly. "Glad to meet you, too. I never thought of Doctor Orlansky—"

"Julia! My name is Julia! Only to my patients am I Doctor Orlansky! Or I'll call you Professor Anderson! I never made the connection, when Mark called to say he wants us to come and meet Olivia, the love of his life, I didn't put together the Olivia I knew from the hospital, as Elliot's wife, with *his* Olivia. Come, sit here, and tell me how, where and when you two met! We can take the tour later!"

At that instant, the doorbell rang again. Mark was there to open the door, and the last couple walked in. A beautiful woman with white-blond hair like a halo around her head, thin as a reed, walked into the living room and stopped as if thunderstruck. Her hand flew to her mouth; her eyes opened wide in shock.

Mark was by her side instantly, her partner on the other side.

"Nora?" Mark asked, bewildered. "You OK?

She didn't respond, still staring at Olivia, her eyes clouded with tears. "I know you! It is you!" she cried out, her voice choking.

Olivia stared back, not knowing what to say. She didn't recognize the woman who so clearly recognized her.

"I'm sorry," she said, confused. "I don't know who you are."

"Better sit down, and I'll tell you!" She grabbed Olivia's hand and pulled her into the living room.

"Hi, good to see you!" She said, briefly, to the other guests. The other two couples were also staring; the room hushed, expecting to hear the story she was palpably eager to tell.

"You're Zack's Olivia, aren't you?!" She said, and without waiting for a response, she turned to Mark. "The earthquake! Thirty years ago! Do you remember? The young woman who took care of the little boy whose mother died when the bridge collapsed on the car she was driving, and he was caught inside? The paramedics rescued him and brought him to our hospital! He was in shock and immense pain, and there was this young woman who was also injured but not as severely, and we patched her up earlier. She volunteered to take care of him! We didn't know what to do with him. He was all alone and wouldn't stop crying until she was there and managed to calm him.

"His father was also injured, in another car, and was taken to a different hospital. It took about a week before he found his son and arrived at our hospital to be with him! He was so lost—the father, I mean. His wife died so suddenly and traumatically, and he became a single parent to a five-year-old boy. I remember the heroic fight to save Zack's leg, but they failed... they had to amputate his left leg below the knee."

She took a deep breath, controlling her emotions. "Olivia is that woman! We all admired her dedication. She wouldn't leave the little boy's side for a second, even though she was injured, too! She slept in a chair next to his bed every night." She turned to Olivia without a pause. "You stayed there with them, helping them to cope. You were so heroic!"

Olivia blushed a deep red.

Mark nodded. "I remember the little boy. I never knew who the young woman was, until she told me a few days ago... reminded me that I yelled at her for loitering in the ER after they finished treating her injuries."

"For years, I wondered what happened to the young woman. You were no more than a girl, then, weren't you?"

"Twenty-two," Olivia said.

"My age!" Nora continued, "As I said—you were on my mind, I never forgot you, but I didn't know where or how to find anything about you. I don't think I even knew your full name."

She paused again, took a deep breath, and it was clear that she hadn't finished. The others were all expecting her to continue.

"Anyway," she said, "Last year, Natalie, my daughter, wanted to go back to university, for her graduate studies, and found it difficult to choose a program. So, she searched the internet and reduced the options. Then, she called me over to look at her selections and help her make the right choice. We were going over the alternatives when all of a sudden, I saw *her*!" She turned and pointed at Olivia. "Her picture under the title of 'Academic Director, International Economics Graduate Program'! And I said to Natalie—this is *her*! The woman I told you about! Because years ago, I told Natalie about the mysterious, courageous young woman who appeared like an angel after the earthquake. And I was so happy! I was delighted to know that you did so well. There was something special in you even then."

Now it was Olivia's turn to stare. She looked at Nora and took her hand. "Did your daughter choose my department?"

Nora was nodding vigorously. "Yes, she did! And she's delighted with her choice!"

Then she looked at Olivia, understanding it was not an idle question.

"Why?" she asked, flustered.

"You have a brave daughter, Nora," Olivia said. "Very courageous, and an excellent friend. She probably saved her friend's life. She came to see me about a month ago and confided in me, she told me about a pregnant friend in an abusive relationship, and enabled me to act and help out."

The two women sat gazing at each other, amazed. Nora was the first to react.

"Natalie told me about that. And how grateful they all were for what you did for their friend. Ruth is doing very well! You know she gave birth a short while ago? She has a lovely daughter, and according to Natalie— she's very happy."

Olivia was dazed. Before this evening, she was apprehensive, not knowing what his closest friends would be like. And it seems she knew all of them, or they knew her somehow, from different aspects of her life, before she even met Mark!

"Wait a minute," she said, "How did you recognize me? After thirty years? I'm amazed you even remembered what I looked like; I must have changed a lot!"

"You're still the same person, and your eyes haven't changed. They were an amazing blue then, and they are now." Nora said. "Besides, I was very young, too. It was my first year as a registered nurse, and you made an immense impression on me. That's also when I got to know Mark. He was sort of a mentor, the one who saw potential in me and pushed me to continue my studies."

Olivia shook her head, unable to believe the way the coincidences piled up, one on top of the other.

"Do you know what happened to Zack and his father? I had to pull away… but I felt so guilty."

"They are fine! Zack's father remarried. He married one of the nurses in rehabilitation; she was wonderful to Zack. And they have two daughters. They live in Noe Valley, not far from us! I think Zack got married a few years ago, but I'm not sure."

"What a story!" Grace said, her eyes clouded. "Unbelievable! Your life collided with ours in so many ways! It's sort of funny—Michael came in and said, 'I know you,' Julia came in, and she knew you, and Nora, too! It's too much of a far-fetched fairytale… but as it has a happy ending—we're all here together—I'll buy the fairytale!"

"I'll drink to that—if I could!" Michael said, raising his empty glass. They all laughed.

"Right you are!" Mark said. "Let's refresh the drinks for everyone. I know I need another! Even I did not know the whole story, and I really can't believe it—only a few days ago, Olivia told me her side of the story, now I hear it again, from a different angle."

The tension she felt all afternoon evaporated. These were no strangers, and the test was over.

There was only one person she was not introduced to. In her eagerness to tell her story, Nora took center stage, and there was no time to present her partner. Olivia went over and extended her hand formally to the dark-haired, handsome man, saying in a playful tone, "Hi, I'm Olivia. And who are you?"

"I'm Kevin Cohen, Nora's partner for the past ten years, and it's very nice to meet you. I, too, have heard about the mysterious angel who appeared after the earthquake and vanished later…"

"No angel, believe me!" Olivia said, her eyes glinting.

She went to help Mark prepare the drinks and replenish the refreshments. The others talked among themselves, and she heard snatches of their conversations, all of them realizing they were more closely connected than they ever thought possible.

Mark looked at her and smiled. "Flying colors, I'd say!" he said, his voice low, but sounding joyful. He knew she was nervous and could see that she was considerably more relaxed now.

"I'm still overwhelmed by the many coincidences. How our lives are interconnected."

The conversation turned to her when Olivia returned from the kitchen. They all knew each other and were curious to learn more about her. They asked about Elliot, and her kids, when they moved to San Francisco, whether she liked it better than Sacramento, and if she made new friends after the move.

The successful meeting with his friends revealed an additional dimension of their relationship. One she didn't expect: She no longer had to downplay her accomplishments so as not to threaten her partner. Mark was not intimidated by her achievements. On the contrary—he was proud of her… and it felt terrific.

33

"Tom and Emily are coming from Seattle for a few days next weekend," Olivia said to Mark one evening when they met back home. "For her brother's birthday. They'll stay at my house, of course. But as the fridge in my house is empty, and I'm here now, would you mind if I invite them and my parents for dinner before they go back?"

"By all means! Why not invite Adam and Ann, too?" Mark seemed happy. It was one step further toward making his house her home, and he liked that. "We should do it for lunch on Sunday so that they can bring Leah, too."

Olivia was grateful. She was certain Mark would not object, but the way he said it—the generosity, the willingness to embrace her family—was not something she took for granted. She hoped that one day, she'd be able to reciprocate and host his family, too.

"Great idea. Thank you for making me feel so good about this," she said and kissed him warmly. "I'll call them and see if they are all free to come. I wish my brother and his son were in the area too, but they are in Italy. Ben works with an international agricultural startup with a branch there, developing some kind of biological pest control. That's all the family I have close by. My family is spread around the world."

"I have even less than you. Both my parents are gone, and so is my dad's brother. My mother was a single child. My father came here from Sweden with his parents and younger brother a few years after World War II. At first, they lived in Boston, Massachusetts. He met my mother at Boston University, as they both studied Engineering. She was also of Swedish descent. My father's parents had some distant relatives who came to the U.S. years before them; that's why they preferred Boston, I think. I still have some relations out there, but we're not in touch. So nowadays—it's just my daughters and me."

"What was your wife like?" Olivia asked. She almost said, 'your first wife' then remembered he wasn't married to Helen.

"Victoria? She was smart and beautiful. And funny. Blond, thin, relatively short, so she always wore high heels. She was a very creative, brilliant architect. Her main problem was that she was a perfectionist, and somewhat insecure. Always thinking her designs could be improved, believing there could be a few more renovations that would make the houses she designed more interesting. She agonized over every presentation she had to prepare; it took ages before she was ready to release it. Emma followed in her footsteps. and she's just like that, too. With a similar sense of humor...

"In many ways, you remind me of her. Your honesty and depth; your analytical mind. It's as if after many years, I can be myself again. Thanks to you, I am more like I used to be."

"I believe what you just said was meant to be a huge compliment," Olivia said. "I know you loved Victoria very much, and both you and your daughters revere her memory. So, on the one hand, I feel truly complimented. On the other hand—the comparison puts me in the impossible position of competing with a myth. It's not a fair game... one can never succeed against a myth, as there's no way I'll be able to overcome the impositions of reality. I'm a mere human, with all the shortcomings and limitations of humans, whereas she is—and will always be—on a pedestal, infallible in your mind."

Mark nodded his understanding. "I don't compare the two of you. It's just... your question evoked the memory," he said, his voice barely audible.

She knew the association—and the comparison—were there, deep in his mind. And that Victoria would always be there in his memory—her daughters a constant reminder. She only hoped that one day, maybe, the shared experiences they would accumulate in their life together would tip the scales in her favor.

***

Her family gladly came to the Sunday lunch Olivia organized. They looked forward to the family reunion, and they were all curious to see where she lived now. Adam and Ann came earlier, per Olivia's request. She missed Leah and never got enough of her. She took her out to the terrace and stood with Leah in her arms, looking at the water and the ships sailing it. The baby seemed fascinated by the immense, shimmering blue expanse and held tight. Ann came out to join them, her eyes widened, like Leah's, at the view.

It was too cool to remain outside, and they didn't stay long.

"Wow," she said. "I expected beautiful scenery but never imagined."

"It will be heaven for Leah here in the summer," Olivia said. "If I'm still here."

Ann looked at her pensively. "I think you will be," she said quietly and walked in.

Adam and Mark were talking in the living room. Olivia examined their body language and was delighted to find both relaxed and at ease with each other. She came closer to them, and Mark extended his arms to Leah. The infant launched herself in his direction, gurgling happily. Mark hugged her, sniffing her baby smell with delight.

"You're a feisty one, aren't you?!" he said to the light-haired, round-faced, sturdy baby. "Who does she take after?"

"Her grandmother!" Adam and Ann said together, and they all laughed.

Tom and Emily arrived with Rebecca and Arthur. The hugs and back-pats among the men and kisses among the women brought them all close together.

Rebecca looked around her with delight. "What a beautiful place! Such good taste! I love the colors you chose! And the parquets! Exquisite!"

"I have your daughter to thank for those. She suggested the blond oak and the cushions. She didn't know she'd have to live with them, but at least it's to her taste!"

"Can I see the rest of the house?" she asked.

"Certainly," Olivia responded and looked, questioning, at the others. Both young women nodded eagerly and joined them. Left behind, the men could hear their cries of admiration and pleasure as they toured the big house.

"Lovely!" said Ann when they returned.

"Absolutely!" Emily agreed.

Rebecca was silent, but the admiration was written all over her face.

She went over to Mark, wanting to take Leah. The baby turned her head away and hugged Mark's neck tighter. Rebecca was surprised and tried to take Leah despite her rejection, and the infant gave a shrill scream of objection.

"Let her get used to you first," he suggested calmly. "She'll be happy to go to you then."

"How come she was willing to go to you?" Rebecca asked, frustrated.

"All little girls love me," he said, smiling. "Right, little one?" he said to the baby, but his real intent was obvious.

The dogs were ecstatic, too. Pinky ran from one family member to another, barking happily, demanding attention. Tish was shy but followed Pinky from one to the other. Mark lowered himself to the carpet. And holding Leah close to his body, he called Tish over. The big Labrador came to him to sniff the human bundle in his arms; his big head extended cautiously. Leah sent her chubby hands to touch him, feeling the softness of the blond fur.

Mark was speaking quietly to the baby and the dog. His tone of voice was warm, relaxed, coaxing them to become friends. Tish licked Leah's hand, and her curiosity became an apprehensive alarm. Her face contorted as if ready to cry, but Mark's continued ease, and his relaxed tone of voice, turned the grimace to a bright smile. She extended her arm once more and held it under Tish's nose to lick her again, then squealed her delight. Then she grabbed his ear and pulled hard. All heads turned in their direction, panic on Ann's face. The big dog licked Leah's cheek, and she squealed joyfully.

"He'll never hurt her, no matter what she'll do, so don't worry," he said. Pinky came over to see what the source of the noise was. Her tail wagging energetically, she joined Mark and Tish, trying to sniff the little girl. Leah waved her hand, trying to touch the little dog, the joy on her face evident. Pinky licked her, and Leah voiced her delight; it sounded like the baby was trying to communicate with the dogs. She touched Pinky, then patted her clumsily, but not aggressively.

Olivia was delighted. *One less worry,* she thought, she'd be able to bring Leah over to play with the dogs if Adam and Ann agreed.

They moved to the table, leaving Leah in the bouncer Olivia bought for her and placed on the carpet. Lunch was diverse, with dishes she knew they loved. After a creamy mushroom soup, she put on the table boneless fillets of sea bass that Mark and her father liked (still, there were enough fillets for everyone), lasagna her boys loved, stir-fried chicken and vegetables with noodles, mashed potatoes, oven-baked broccoli, and a big salad.

Conversation flowed around her. She looked from one to the other and felt content. The smooth interaction, the care they took of each other, and their joy at being together survived the change she brought into their lives. Elliot was no longer at the head of the table. Mark was. But they had all accepted the transformation and were OK with it. Her sons missed their father, she knew, and Mark was not a substitute. But they embraced him nonetheless, for her sake. And because they liked him.

Mark got up to clear the table, and she sent him a grateful look. Adam and Tom got up quickly to lend a hand, as they did at home. Mark tried to make them sit down again and enjoy the company, but they refused. Together, the three men cleared everything and brought fruit and ice cream for dessert in no time. Olivia gave Leah an orange segment to suck on, and they all laughed when the sour-sweet juice hit her palate.

It was soon apparent that Leah and Arthur were tired and needed a nap, and they all left.

"Maybe one day your daughters will want to come too," Olivia said to Mark, hugging him tightly.

He nodded and sighed.

34

Olivia slept badly. A rare occurrence for her.

She was troubled, and after much tossing and turning, she managed to fall asleep, only to wake up again and again. She looked at her cellphone, recharging on her nightstand. Four a.m. Exhausted and exasperated, she got out of bed quietly, taking her duvet with her. She tiptoed to the living room.

She sat down and curled her legs in the armchair facing the ocean, tired and miserable.

I can't do this… I can't live with Mark… I can't afford this lifestyle.

Her family's visit a few days ago showed her clearly the gap between her and Mark's financial means. She was well-off but not 'rolling in it'. Mark, on the other hand, belonged to a different bracket. He was much more than well-off. She knew she couldn't afford to split the expenses with him, but she didn't want to live with him if she couldn't contribute to their life together. Olivia was too proud.

Her house was lovely but much smaller, less lavish, nothing as high-class as his, and she couldn't ask him to move in with her when he had such a luxurious house that he invested so much in.

What do I do? There's no way for me to feel comfortable in such a relationship. The tormenting thoughts kept tumbling in her mind.

Do I want to live with him, as he apparently wants me to? I do, and I don't.

Do I want to leave him? I don't, but I may have to…

The tears were streaming down her cheeks, and she brought out a box of tissues, placing it next to her. She was staring at the sky, changing color from deep blue-black to a slightly lighter blue where the ocean met the heavens. Her body immobile, her mind in turmoil, her heart was beating crazily.

I never thought I'd fall in love again, she moaned in acknowledgment. *At my age? It's absurd! Yet it happened… how can I give it up now? I'm living a dream!*

Yes, you are, the other half of her mind responded. *A dream you can't afford. Just hope that the construction on your street has ended—or at least the noisy part is done—then go back home. To* your *home. Modest, but* yours.

It tore her insides. She'd be miserable if she left, Olivia was sure of that, but she might become miserable if she stayed…

And she was back where she started.

***

"Livy—what are you doing here? What's wrong? What happened?" Mark was awake. His distress at finding her curled up and crying like that was mounting.

Olivia could not answer; she just shook her head.

"Come on, Livy, talk to me!" he implored, crouched by her side. "What happened? What bothers you?"

What could she say? Even if she could speak—what could she say?

"Take a deep breath…" he used his 'doctor's voice'.

She did.

"Another one!" he said tensely. "Come on, take another deep breath!"

She inhaled deeply; her heartbeat slowed. Her eyes still clouded, tears streaming, she sniffed again and again.

"Tell me!" he said, his voice urging her softly.

"I don't know what to do. I think… I'm afraid I'll have to leave you." Olivia fell silent.

"What?" Mark was stunned. "Why?"

"I can't, Mark, I love you, but I can't…" she murmured.

"Can't what? You don't make sense! Livy, what's wrong?" Agitated, Mark turned her face to look into her eyes. "Please, baby, I don't understand."

Olivia took a deep breath, exhaled it slowly, and turned her body to him, though she was still curled in the armchair.

"I don't know what to do," she began, then fell silent. Mark took her hand in his, encouraging her to continue.

"Your lifestyle is way beyond my means, and I can't share the costs with you. I can't live with you if I do not contribute to our life together… I do not want to feel like a kept woman. I won't be able to tolerate it. And if I don't share the burden, you'll grow to resent it. Not now, perhaps… but gradually, maybe, one day—you may become annoyed by it. And I won't be able to bear it!"

203

Mark's eyes were full of compassion. He was still silent, allowing her to gather her thoughts.

"I'm torn," she continued after a while. "I'm truly, honestly, completely in love with you, and I wish I could live with you forever and ever, just as we are. What we share is much more than I could have ever dreamed possible, but I'm also proud. Not vain, but I need to be able to respect myself, and I'm afraid I won't be able to do that if…"

Olivia started crying again. Silently. Her shoulders shook, and her hand trembled in his.

"That hurts, and I can't find a solution to the dilemma…"

She looked up, searching his face for understanding, reading the compassion in his eyes.

I must look terrible with my eyes red, nose runny, and hair messed up, the irrelevant thought crossed her mind. As if it mattered.

Mark's expression changed. A subtle change. But he seemed less tense; his stress diminished; his eyes were bright. His teeth were no longer clenched, and his creased forehead relaxed.

"Make room for me," he said.

A question in her eyes, she lowered her legs to the floor but didn't know what he meant.

Mark stood up, her hand still in his. He pulled her up, then sat in the armchair, in her place, pulling her onto his lap, enfolding her in his strong arms.

"You miss the whole point," he said.

"If you think so, you didn't understand what I said," she replied sadly.

"No, Livy. I listened to you carefully, with my heart as well as with my mind. Now, please, listen to me, too. I understand what you said, I promise you. But as I said—you miss the whole point." He looked deeply into her tear-stained face.

"What point?" she asked, her voice agonized.

"I love you. I feel I gained another lease on life. For years I wondered, what's the point in going on? I had my work, and it was a source of fulfillment and a sense of achievement, but I was miserable at home. It's not that I thought of ending my life, but I felt like, 'Why bother?'"

Olivia was shocked. She didn't realize… she knew that his life with Helen was difficult for many years, but she didn't grasp how miserable he was. In the past, he covered up his anguish so well. Mark saw her reaction and forged on, pressing home the point he was trying to make.

"Since you entered my life, my joy at being alive has returned," Mark continued. "You gave me a reason to *want* to live. That's something no money can buy! I have a home to come to. I have someone who cares about me, and I care about her. Someone I can love wholeheartedly, and who loves me, too. Do you understand how much that means to me? For me—this is invaluable. Priceless."

Olivia sat in his lap, her body still tense, her heart still heavy, but the misery she felt earlier was oozing away.

"It doesn't matter who pays for things, money is there to be spent and enjoyed! And I want to enjoy it with you! If you ask me to live with you in your old house, I will—I swear it. But why should we, if we can enjoy this more spacious, beautiful house with the magnificent view we both like so much? I will not enjoy it if you take your love away from me. I want to live the rest of my life with you. And I want you to want that, too. So, you need to understand that giving is not only monetary. What you give me is no less valuable! It is worth the world to me."

His eyes turned serious again. "I want you to promise me something," he said, his tone both beseeching and demanding.

She looked at him, questioning.

"Don't ever do this to me again. Don't ever threaten to leave me. Don't ever think of leaving me for something that may be solvable, even if you don't see a possible solution. Together—we'll find the right answers to whatever we encounter. Not if you still love me, that is. And I believe you do, as much as I love you."

She straightened and hugged his neck.

"I promise," she whispered and kissed him with all her heart.

After a while, when they released each other, he whispered back, "Just remember—if you love me, leaving is not an option!"

She nodded, her heart lighter, at peace. She was thinking about finding ways to make it work.

35

Their life together assumed normality: working out early in the morning—going to the gym for her and tennis for him, showers and going to work, meeting at home in the evenings. She'd meet her friends or her mother in the afternoons, after work. Sarah felt she saw her less than in the past, but accepted the change in Olivia's life.

She loved coming home in the evenings. She never tired of the view of the constantly shifting colors of the ocean, with the scudding clouds changing shapes and shades of gray, casting their shadows upon the water, adding more hues to the glinting blues and greens of the Pacific. When the wind was blowing, the white crests of the faraway waves lent their shifting and churning shapes to the scene.

***

The barking of the dogs told her Mark was home.

"Hello, Livy," he said when he entered and kissed her. "Something smells good!"

"You're late today. Everything OK?" She asked.

"Fine. All is good—just some complicated but interesting cases, and lots of phone calls. Which reminds me—I forgot to tell you—we have a trip this weekend with my 'easy-walkers' group. It's to Sonoma and the surrounding area on the first day. The next day, we'll continue to The Shasta Trinity National Forest and Shasta Lake. We have a guide who's an expert on the history of Sonoma. Another guide, an expert on the northern California forest's fauna and flora, will join us the next day. As there's a lot to see, we'll spend two days in the area, with an overnight in one of the hotels there, near Fort Ross, I think. Can you make it?"

"How many people will we be? Who are they—friends? Close friends?" Olivia asked, worried.

"There are about fifty people in the group. I'm not sure how many are coming on this particular trip. Some are closer friends than others. They are more or less around my age, and we've been traveling together for about ten years. Some have retired already; others are in diverse occupations. We have several university professors, a few bankers, lawyers, a few other medical doctors, some engineers, too. All are well-off, some I would say are truly rich, and most of them are nice, which is more important."

Meeting fifty new people at once... Olivia hoped it wouldn't be an unbearable ordeal.

***

They woke up at five a.m. to get ready and be at the meeting area for the six thirty pickup. The dog sitter Olivia sometimes used when Elliot was sick arrived on time to pick up the two dogs. Pinky seemed happy to see him again, which Olivia considered a good sign. Tish was more reserved but accepted the guy that Pinky seemed to like.

"You're a little tense, Livy. Don't be. I'm sure they'll love you! And they'll all be nice!" Mark tried to help her relax when they were on their way.

I hope he's right, Olivia thought. She knew this had to happen sooner or later.

There were already a few couples at the parking lot meeting place. They seemed cheerful, chatting noisily despite the early hour. As Mark was removing their bags from the car's trunk, she noticed that several people were coming toward them slowly, as if haphazardly.

"Hi, Mark," said one of the approaching women, as she rose to kiss his cheek. "Introduce me!"

It sounded like a command, not a request.

"Hi, Sheila. This is Olivia, my partner. Olivia, this is Sheila, one of my oldest and best friends in the group. She may seem overbearing, but I assure you—she's a real sweetheart. And that's her partner there, waving at us, next to his car."

Olivia extended her hand. "Hi," she said, smiling, "Glad to meet you. And thanks for the explanation, Mark; I may have run away otherwise."

"I wanted to be among the first to come and greet you, to let you know you're very welcome to our group. We all knew Mark was bringing his new partner today and were curious to meet you. In fact, having met you now— I'm sure we'll all be delighted to have you in our group. I can see already we'll like you much better than we did Cynthia the Bitch! Obviously, you're nothing like her!" She paused, inhaling deeply. "The rumor on the grapevine is that you're a professor of international economics, is that right?"

Olivia nodded. "You mean all of you know of me?" Olivia was shocked. "It's not a secret, but how did you find out?"

"No secrets in our small town!" she laughed. "Besides, we all love Mark and care about him, especially after Cynthia, and we were a little worried you might be either a dry stick or a stuck-up bitch, full of self-importance. I believe you're neither!"

A few other women were approaching them, their men in tow, and the introductions repeated themselves.

Mark and Olivia were at the center of attention. The others were all acquainted for many years, and none of them were 'new couples.' Moreover, the gossip value was too good to let slip!

By the time the bus was ready to leave, Olivia was introduced to all of them. She tried hard to go over the names in her head, but there were too many. She needed cues that would serve as reminders. They were sharing a seat on the bus, and Mark told her little stories about each group member to help her distinguish among them.

"I'm sure they are all worthy people." Olivia sighed. "Still, some seem nice, and others seem more reserved. But these are just first impressions; I'll give all of them a chance to prove their 'friendability'. There's no such term, is there? But I think it's a useful concept. I guess that in time—some will become closer friends, while others will remain mere acquaintances."

She looked at Mark, gauging his reaction. He nodded, saying nothing. She saw he was thinking about what she said.

"I assume some of them were part of Helen's close circle of friends, and therefore yours?" she continued.

Again, Mark nodded, saying nothing, waiting to see where this was leading.

"Would it bother you if my closest friends are different?" she continued. "Maybe some of the people who'll become my friends were also Helen's friends, but Helen and I—we're so different—maybe some of my choices will be people that Helen avoided. Would that be OK with you?"

"Of course," he responded. "I want you to be comfortable, and you can choose whoever you like to befriend. Some of them are more distant acquaintances because they didn't bond with Helen, especially not in her heavy drinking years, but are fine people... as you said—we'll give all of them a chance and see who interests you more than others. The others, or most of them, we'll meet in broader social occasions."

They reached Sonoma in no time. Leaving the bus, they walked to the busy and colorful historic Sonoma Plaza. The guide directed them to City Hall, in the middle of the square, to recount the city's past. He described the tribes who lived in the area before the Europeans arrived, their diverse languages and cultures, and rivalries.

Then he turned to the Mexican rule and the missions they built along the coast, indicating the Mission San Francisco Solano on one side of the square, and Salvador Vallejo's house, occupying another side. Olivia noticed he lost most group members' attention when he talked about the 1848 Treaty of Guadalupe Hidalgo. Some women were eager to check the diverse quaint shops and galleries around the square; the men, looking forward to a coffee break in one of the many restaurants and cafés.

Sheila signaled from afar to ask if she wanted to join her and some other women; Olivia indicated maybe later. She preferred to stay close to Mark.

The tour organizers soon called everyone to move to the restaurant they booked for lunch for the whole group.

The conversation at their table soon turned to the plans for the rest of the day. Right after lunch, they were to return to the bus for the drive north to Fort Ross Historical Park.

Sheila caught up with them as Mark and Olivia walked back to their bus.

"How do you like us so far?" she asked, smiling.

"Quite," said Olivia. "I may disagree with some of the more 'political' individuals in the group, they are too extreme for me, but that's OK. I like some people already! Like you, for example!"

Both women smiled at each other.

"Yes," Sheila said "I like you, too. We'll toast the new friendship tonight at the resort!"

Laughing, they mounted the bus together. Mark saw the exchange and was pleased.

"You'll be part of the group in no time, I've no doubt!" he declared.

The drive to Fort Ross Historic Park was as relaxed and as beautiful as expected. Cold, windy, and intense, the ocean steered them on their way north.

The guide told them some parts of the history of the place they were about to see, emphasizing the Russian-American Company's role in developing the area. He spoke about the changing hands that took care of the place—first the Russians, then Aleutian Alaskans, and Californians until it was declared a historical site in 1828. Most of the area was rebuilt, not the original structures, but it still represented the 200 years of its existence.

The almost-empty road meant they made it in good time. The group toured the compound and its lovely chapel, the museum, and of course, the Rotchev House, the only original structure remaining from the Russian period.

They were led to one of the smoother trails around the compound. The walk in the beautiful park led to the San Andreas Fault, and the still-noticeable signs of the powerful and destructive 1906 earthquake. They all remembered the one in 1989, and soon people were talking of their own experiences, where they were when the earthquake occurred, the trauma.

Standing next to Olivia, Sheila noticed Mark lay a protective hand on Olivia's shoulder.

Her warm eyes searched Olivia's face, and she asked, "Big trauma for you? You lost someone you loved to that quake?"

Olivia looked at her new friend and shrugged. "It's a long story."

"We have time… tell me!" Sheila said in her semi-commanding, semi-joking tone.

"Maybe in the evening, drink in hand, once we've settled at the resort, OK?"

"Sounds to me there's a story worth listening to, waiting to be told," said one of the other women, who stood close to Sheila.

Olivia shrugged again, saying nothing, leaning more closely into Mark's side.

***

The bus reached Timber Cove Resort late in the afternoon, the beautiful hotel spread before them, the sound of the ocean accompanying them into the reception area. Redwood paneling everywhere, the atmosphere was warm and welcoming.

Olivia entered their spacious room and sighed with pleasure at the sight of the cove below. Waves rushed in, their heads foaming, the water dark in the dwindling light. The room's warmth and its brightness were comforting after the long day. Mark came over to stand by Olivia, looking out at the natural beauty surrounding them. He placed his arm on her shoulder, drawing her close.

"Happy that we came?"

"Very," she said, "Even if just for this…" she extended her hands as if trying to embrace the cove. "This is undeniably lovely… and your friends are nice, too. They are not what I was afraid they'd be. Most of them seem nice."

"Give them time, and you'll see that most of them *are* nice. Some are more restrained, maybe, so you don't know them yet, but we have a whole day tomorrow, and you seem to be doing just fine!"

"I guess so. I need a shower!" Olivia's eyes smiled mischievously. "Care to join me?"

"Would love to," Mark murmured. His hands wrapped around her, holding her close and tight. "I've wanted to do this all day," He said, kissing her ear.

"Let's go and take a shower before it's too late, or we'll miss dinner!"

Dinner was sumptuous and delicious. The noise level of the dining room was high, but no one seemed to mind. The wine was continuously poured, and the atmosphere was joyous. After the desserts, some group members left, too tired to stay up and talk. With teas, coffees, brandies, and liquors, the noise subsided. They were recounting the day's main events, trying to gauge which was the most exciting site, and which was most moving.

"You seemed moved by the San Andreas Fault area, weren't you, Olivia?" Sheila asked, remembering Olivia's promise to tell the story of the other earthquake they all remembered.

"Yes, I was," Olivia said quietly, directing her response to Sheila alone.

"Do tell." Sheila said, her tone imploring.

Olivia began the story of how she was in her car on the way home from Berkeley when the upper tier of the Nimitz Freeway collapsed, and she was wounded as her car swerved, when the earthquake hit, and slammed into the rail. She was not gravely injured, still, she was brought to the hospital. Then she told Sheila how Mark barked at her, saying she had to make herself useful and volunteer.

"That's just half of the story!" Mark said. "The thing is—she did volunteer. Do you remember the story of the five-year-old boy whose mother died on the bridge and we couldn't find his father? And the papers told the story of a young woman who took care of him? That was Olivia! And that's how we *really* met thirty years ago!"

She noticed that all the other conversations around the table died out while she was telling Sheila the story, and the others were all listening, too.

When Mark finished the story, many had tears in their eyes.

"What a story!"

"Unbelievable!"

"Amazing!"

"I remember the story…"

The emotional reaction was intense.

"And you met after all these years! Must be fate!" Sheila said. "Did you remember him, Olivia?

"Of course, I did!" she replied, smiling. "When we lived on the same street—before Mark moved to Seacliff—I was always afraid he'd remember that he met me before, and where… he never did. Well, after thirty years… And to be honest, it was only a brief encounter. Traumatic for me, but in the middle of the mayhem, it was probably insignificant for him. I only told him the truth about where we first met after we started living together."

They parted a short time after that, to be able to wake up early the next morning and be on their way to Shasta Trinity National Forest and Shasta Lake at seven a.m., after breakfast.

Walking to their rooms, Sheila said to Olivia, "Thank you for telling me. Us. It's a wonderful story, and I'm sure a lot of people will feel closer to you for it."

They hugged warmly and parted for the night.

36

The trip was a success in all its aspects. The diversity of topics they were exposed to, the amount of knowledge they acquired, the beauty of the varied landscapes contributed to the contentment people expressed. But most of all, Olivia thought, they enjoyed the social interaction, the feeling of togetherness, and being part of the group.

She enjoyed it, too, she had to admit.

Most of the people in the group were not what she expected, Olivia realized. The stereotype of vain, snobbish people was only partially applicable, and it applied only to a few of them. Most of the individuals she had a chance to talk to and get to know a little better were nothing like the stereotype.

Strange, she thought. *I allowed the stereotype to cloud my evaluation of Mark. I saw him as part of that group and decided he was not for me. I don't usually judge people like that. Do I loathe what the stereotype says they represent that much? It must be,* she concluded.

I was so wrong about him; maybe I was wrong about them, too...

One thing became clear to Olivia after meeting them—generalizing is never accurate and often misleading. She taught the principle often enough and now saw it in real life. Moreover, when you're an outsider, you can't see the group's variability or notice differences among individuals.

***

The social invitations started pouring in. Dinners, lunches, birthday parties, social gatherings—Olivia would need a social calendar if she wanted to manage it without mishaps. And they also had their subscriptions to the San Francisco Symphony, the Opera, and San Francisco Chamber Orchestra... and there was the family, especially Leah, and her work, with all it demanded of her!

And, of course, they'd have to invite people, too *if you accept invitations, you have to reciprocate.*

You entered his world, well—welcome to it! It comes with a lot of obligations!

37

Olivia's cellphone shrilled, and she woke up, confused. A second later—she was worried. She looked at the clock by her bed. Three a.m.… any call at this time of night means trouble, especially on the weekend. Mark was fully awake in an instant. He was used to emergency calls at all hours…

She picked up her phone. Her brother! It must be around noon in Italy, she realized.

"Livy!" An anguished, strangled cry. "Livy!"

She heard heart-wrenching sobs on the phone.

"Ben?" she asked. She knew it was her brother, but it didn't sound like him. "Ben?" she asked again. She sat up.

"Livy!" It *was* him; she was sure now.

"Livy… Nick is dead! I can't bear it… Nick… my son… Livy, Nick is dead!"

Ben was crying so hard, she wasn't sure she heard right. *Nick is dead?*

Olivia's eyes filled with tears. She was crying for her brother, and for sweet, good-natured, twenty-year-old Nick. Full of life, a loveable youngster—how can he be dead?

"Nick? Dead? Ben, what happened? Where are you now?" She asked, her tone anguished.

"In Milano, my apartment…" came the heartbroken, hoarse sigh. "They don't know what happened. They asked me if he was using drugs, and I said no. At least—as far as I know—he wasn't using. They took a blood sample just to make sure. They want an autopsy… it will be a few days before we can bury him."

"Does Cecilia know?" She asked immediately. Olivia didn't like his cold, bossy, know-it-all ex-wife, but she was Nick's mother.

"Yes, I called her first. She's on her way over here."

Ben and Cecilia divorced six years ago when Ben decided to accept the relocation to Italy. Nick was fourteen at the time and thought it could be an adventure to go there with his dad when they were sure there was a suitable international school he could attend.

"Do you have anyone with you now? Is Karen still with you?"

Karen, his girlfriend, was much younger than Ben. She was an Italian beauty, dark-haired and olive-skinned.

"Yes." Ben said. "At least I have her. I don't know how I would have managed without her."

Karen was thirty-three; Olivia remembered her brother telling her. She wanted children, but Ben was not sure... He was forty-seven and thought that he was too old to start all over again with babies, nappies, sleepless nights. Olivia didn't even want to think of the alternative. She liked the brash, fun-loving, coltish Italian.

"Can you tell me what happened? Where it happened?" Olivia asked.

"I'm not sure yet. All I know is Nick went up north for the weekend to visit some friends in a small town by Lake Como. It's still rather warm here, so they all went for a swim, and were all acting crazy in the water—racing each other, playing rough, and all of a sudden, they noticed Nick, thrashing, deeper in the lake, and they understood he was in trouble. So, some of the guys swam over and found him choking, unable to breathe. They didn't know if he swallowed water because he was tired, or had a cramp, or whatever, but they swam to shore, dragging him with them. By the time they reached the shore and dragged him out, he passed out. Or he may have been dead already. I'll never know."

Olivia could hear Ben's wretched sobs from the other side of the world, and her heart broke.

"It sounds terrible, Ben," Olivia managed to say through her own tears. "I'm so sorry for you."

"I keep thinking of my beautiful boy, in panic... alone in the water... unable to call for help... his friends so close yet so far and unresponsive... maybe he called me in his mind, and I didn't hear? It's tearing me to pieces, Livy. The pain is killing me!"

"I know, Ben, I'm sure. It's the worst thing... you were such a good dad, so caring. You always tried to do what you thought was best for him."

"Not true!" Ben's anguished cry sounded angry. "I often insisted I knew better than he did what's good for him." His voice cracked. "I didn't listen enough, and was often too critical... of his actions, his grades, his friends... and I was often short-tempered with him... now I'm so sorry, and I can't even tell him that... I'll never be able to tell him that."

What could she say? What could anyone say in such a situation? At a

215

time like this?

"Listen, Ben, we all have faults, and we're all human, so we make mistakes. I know you feel you could do more, be a better parent; it is normal to feel this way. But think about it—you couldn't have prevented what happened. Do you think that if you kept him protected, at home, you would have been able to save him? You probably couldn't. And he would have resented you if you didn't let him go with his friends. You had to let him live his own life as an independent person, and you did it as a good parent does."

Olivia wasn't sure she managed to penetrate the fog of pain that surrounded her brother, but he seemed to be listening to her empathic voice. She tried to shift his mood from focusing on his inadequacies to thoughts of the unavoidable accident and its consequences.

It will be years before he'll recover, she realized. Can you recover from such a blow as the death of a child? You learn to live with the pain, but she couldn't tell him that. Not yet.

"I'll find the first flight to Italy and come to be with you," Olivia said. "We'll talk again when I know which flight."

"No, don't," Ben said. "It will take time to book a flight, and about twenty hours of flight, even if you find a good connecting flight, so it will be more than a day before you can get here, and by then—we may be ready to leave for the U.S. Cecilia wants to bury him in upstate New York, in Albany, where she grew up, close to her dad. He loved Nick very much. This way, Nick won't be alone. I decided not to argue. Will you come to New York?"

"Of course, I will," Olivia responded without hesitation. "Adam and Tom will surely want to come, too, and our parents. Did you tell Mom and Dad? They'll certainly want to come, too."

"I haven't called them yet. I couldn't face the hysterics. I'm sure Mom will take it badly. Will you do it for me?"

"Fine... sure... I'll call Mom. Call me when you know what's happening and when you book your flight."

"Thanks, sis, I'll call." and he hung up.

"Livy, I'm so sorry," Mark said. "What a tragedy! I heard the conversation. It's the worst thing for any parent."

Mark walked around the bed and came to sit by her side, hugging her.

"He sounded so desolate," Olivia said in a teary voice. "Utterly distraught. And I can't help him from such a distance."

They sat together, silent, Mark's arm around her.

"We were very close when we were growing up. I took the role of big sister very seriously," Olivia said. "Then, life drew us apart. First, to Zambia with our parents. Then he moved to New York, and I was busy with the kids, my career. Later, he moved to Italy, and Elliot got sick. But he's my only brother."

She needed to focus and think: Cecilia wanted to bury him in Albany Rural Cemetery. Ben said the place was like a vast, well-maintained park, with tall trees and ancient graves.

"I'll need to book four hotel rooms for my parents, the boys, and one for me."

"Us," Mark said, still cradling her in his arms. "For us. You don't think I'd let you go alone, do you?"

"I won't be alone. I'll have the family around me," she said softly.

"True. And your family will need someone to lean on, and you'll be the one they'll turn to. Who will you lean on?" he asked, his voice warm in her ears.

"If my sons are there—I'll be fine. You didn't know Nick and never met my brother."

"Even if I haven't met Ben yet, I feel I know him through your stories, and your parents may need more help than you all will be able to provide, especially your dad."

She knew he was right.

Olivia nodded her assent. She looked at the clock. It was almost five a.m. Mark saw the direction of her gaze.

"I'll make us some coffee," he said and stood up. "Come on, go wash up; you'll feel a little better—nothing you can do right now anyway." Mark's eyes were filled with compassion.

She nodded, got up, and trudged to the bathroom.

***

It was a difficult conversation with her sons. They were shocked, but as she expected, both decided to attend the funeral. The call to her parents was even more problematic. She tried to soften the blow, but her mother became hysterical. She tried to calm her but failed miserably, the barrage of questions drowning her.

Mark took the phone. "Rebecca, good morning," he said, his tone calm, authoritative. "Please listen, and don't make it so much harder. We don't know any details yet. Only that he died somewhere in Lake Como, and the burial will take place in Albany. We don't know when yet, but Livy will book flights and reserve hotel rooms for all of you. OK?"

"Yes, OK." Rebecca responded. "But—"

"No buts," Mark cut through her words. "When we know more—we'll notify you."

"Fine," Rebecca said, "Put Livy back on."

Olivia took the phone from him before he could argue.

"Mom, we have to help each other preserve our sanity. I'll call you again when I know something. And I'll try to come later today and see both of you."

She called Sophie to let her know and cancel her meetings. Then she called Andrew Kent, the dean of students, to ask him—once again—to cover for her.

Her brother called an hour later. His voice was ragged. No drugs were found in Nick's system. *That's some kind of solace,* Olivia thought.

"Now they suspect ruptured aortic aneurysm," he said. "Who could have foreseen such a thing in someone so young? It's rather rare, they told me."

"And how are you holding up?" Olivia asked, worried.

"What can I say, sis? My life is ruined. My son is dead. I can't believe I'm saying it… he's never coming back… his whole future to look forward to, and he won't be there."

Olivia checked available flights to Newark and found a United flight that would arrive slightly after Ben's flight. They'd sit with him and accompany him and Nick's coffin to Albany. She sent her brother a message to inform him.

***

They all looked tired when they arrived at the terminal and met Ben. But none of them seemed as disheveled and miserable as he did. The bright blue eyes, so similar to hers, were reddened and bleary, his cheeks sunken and unshaved, his clothes rumpled. He seemed like a lifeless puppet, she

218

thought, going through the motions of life without awareness.

***

The small, sad funeral took place the day after they had all arrived. Cecilia's mother arranged the minister, the ceremony, and the gravesite. Ben seemed in a haze; he didn't care about any of it. He just wanted to know that there was a beautiful shady place for his Nick. The small family huddled in two groups, on both sides of the grave—Cecilia's on one side, Ben's—on the other. Brief, cordial head nods, murmured condolences, and they parted.

***

"Will you come with us to San Francisco for a few days before you head back to Milano, spend some time with the family?" She asked Karen after the funeral, sure that her brother would not decide anything.

Karen nodded, grateful. "Ben thought of staying in New York, but it's not his home any more. He doesn't have an apartment there any more. I like the idea of being with your family right now, not alone with him in an alienated hotel room, in an indifferent city."

"Settled." Olivia smiled warmly, appreciating the young woman's clear-headed resilience.

38

San Francisco in November was cold and gloomy, as usual. When they arrived back, late that afternoon, they were all tired. Olivia invited the family to come home with them.

When they entered the house, Olivia saw that Karen was overwhelmed by the deep blue vista that opened behind the sliding glass back of the house.

"I like your man." Karen said with half a smile. "You found a wonderful one. A really *good* one. Kind-hearted, considerate... and he loves you madly."

Olivia nodded. "He is all that. You have a good one, too. And I think you're good for him too, so I'll do my best to help you keep him."

The two women hugged. Karen moved to the living room and sat Ben in the armchair facing the ocean, speaking to him softly, as one would talk to a child. She sat close to him, caressing his back. Olivia went to the kitchen and joined Mark, already making coffee for everyone.

"Thank you for doing this. Bringing all of my family here for a while was a brilliant idea, and I'm so grateful you suggested it! Ben's so lost."

Mark said nothing, his eyes softly smiling. He picked up the coffee tray and went to the living room.

Ben had Karen on one side and his mother on the other. He was still mostly unresponsive, saying nothing. Mark placed an aromatic espresso next to him, and Ben looked up, gratitude in his eyes. He drank it in two gulps and set down the empty cup gently. Mark placed a tumbler with a generous measure of whiskey and ice in Ben's hand. Unquestioning, he drank this, too.

Little by little, a halting conversation about Nick started. Olivia's sons reminisced about trips they took with their father, Ben, and Nick to Yosemite Park, Big Sur, and Lake Tahoe. They treated Nick like a little brother, and it was a "boys only" kind of fun. Ben's head rose a little.

"He loved those trips with you guys. He said it was great to have big brothers... always wanted to live in California to be close to you. But my job… the firm."

Olivia left them to reminisce and went to organize the guest room for Karen and Ben, Mark by her side. They heard her sons slowly drawing Ben out of the shell he'd withdrawn into. Karen helped with questions about their happy experiences.

Olivia exchanged a smile with Karen. "Your room is ready; feel free to take Ben and leave us whenever you like. You probably didn't sleep much yesterday and must be dead tired. We'll talk tomorrow and see what you need and what you want to do."

"Good idea. Thanks for everything, Olivia." Karen said before they retired. "You're very thoughtful. And so is your wonderful man. I thought he looked distant, even condescending, when I first saw him, but he's nothing like that. I genuinely like him."

"Me too." Ben surprised her. "I'm glad for you, Livy. He's a thoroughly nice guy."

"I like him, too," she said, smiling at them. "Have a good night. I left some towels on your bed. If you need more—you'll find them in your bathroom, on the shelves."

***

A week later, Olivia was still in bed, not yet ready to start the day, when she heard her cellphone ping again. Picking it up, she found that many more condolences messages had arrived. *I'll deal with all that later*, she thought and went to the kitchen to brew some coffee.

Then she noticed a recorded WhatsApp message, a surprising and heartwarming one, and she stopped to listen. Ruth. The relocation to her nurturing family in Napa Valley worked like magic. The broken, lost student became a confident young mother.

She listened to Ruth, saying she heard about the tragedy and wasn't sure it was acceptable to do so, but her aunt suggested Ruth invite Olivia's brother and his partner to stay with them for a few days. The weather was excellent, and the peaceful environment will be pleasant for them. She'd be happy to host them; she owed Olivia her happiness, she said.

"Wow." Karen said. She was up and entered the kitchen. "Who was that?"

"An ex-student of mine. I helped Ruth a few months ago, and she

221

moved to Napa Valley. Her family has a prosperous vineyard there, and she decided to study viticulture."

"What a coincidence…" Karen said, bewilderment in her voice. "Did you know that the corporation Ben is working for focuses on developing an ecological solution to the European grapevine moth? It has spread to many areas of the world and damages vineyards, Napa too. It may be a good idea to go there.

"OK, when do you want to go? Ruth will be delighted, I'm sure."

"I'll ask Ben." Karen said, her face clouded, thinking about a way to convince him to go.

"Ask me what?" Ben joined them in the kitchen.

"We received an invitation to stay for a few days with friends of Olivia in Napa Valley; they have a big vineyard and a huge house." Karen said, looking hopefully at Ben.

It could be precisely what he needs, Olivia thought. *His area of interest and expertise, without the pressure of work…*

Ben began to shake his head. Karen changed tack. "I think they have a serious problem with your moth in Napa, don't they?"

Ben looked at her, a light of understanding in his eyes.

"Why don't we try it out? See if you can help them? You said you're reaching the testing stage, maybe…" it was clear that Karen managed to penetrate the haze Ben was in.

"Yeah, maybe…" he paused.

"Tomorrow? Or the day after?" Karen asked.

"I'll let Ruth know," Olivia said.

Yes! Olivia thought. *Maybe this is the helping hand he most needed to get him out of the dark vacuum. Coincidence, again?* There have been too many coincidences in her life lately… the universe? God? Karma? Whichever force was involved, she was grateful.

They sat down with their coffees. No one felt like having breakfast, each absorbed in their thoughts.

Ben stirred. "I keep wondering if he suffered… if the pain was terrible… if he was afraid… what were his last thoughts?"

"Understandable. It's a normal reaction, Ben, but you can't allow such painful and destructive thoughts to fill your mind all the time," Olivia said.

"It's true, but difficult to prevent the flooding of such thoughts, maybe a distraction will help. Like Napa." Karen said protectively. "Let's go for a walk! Come on, Ben! Let's change and tour the park! Will you join us, Olivia?"

"Thanks, but I'd better get in touch with my office to see what's happening."

***

Two days later, Ben and Karen rented a car and drove north. Olivia received a phone call from Karen saying they arrived safely, and the place was indeed as huge and prosperous as they were told. Judith and Joe, Ruth's aunt and uncle, were delightful people, and very knowledgeable in the areas that interested Ben, Karen said. They planned to stay there a day or two longer.

Good, she thought. She had to get back to work.

And then he'll be going back to Italy, and I'll miss him terribly. Olivia's thoughts turned to Ben's future. *I hope he'll manage to find happiness sometime. Karen will try her best, but will that be enough?* She hoped so. Karen was young and full of life, so maybe.

39

The weather was still nippy, but the spring sun was shining for lengthier periods, and the rains were no longer so heavy. *Soon, the flowers will begin blooming again. And Leah will be one year old! How time flies.*

I'll offer to organize a family party for her! Olivia thought. With balloons and a birthday cake. She loved the baby with all her heart. There were rules and regulations imposed by Leah's parents, and Olivia tried to comply. No sweets, limit the number of fruits you give her, put her to sleep in the afternoon… there were so many rules! As if she never raised a child herself. *Maybe they think things have changed a lot.*

She called her son right away.

"Yes, of course, why not?" Adam said when she suggested the birthday party. "But we'll do it for our family only. Ann's mother also wants to host a party for Leah. So, she can do their side, and you'll do our side of the family, OK?

"Sure," Olivia said. "Is she well enough?"

"Ann wants to let her do it, so we shall." came his decisive reply.

"Fine," Olivia responded. "Whatever." She would have preferred the whole family to gather together but decided not to argue.

She called Tom to see if he and Emily could come too, but he sent a text message saying he'd call her back later. He was in a meeting and couldn't answer. She texted back, offering to host him and Emily if they could come for Leah's birthday. His answer came back immediately: "Great, Mom. Of course, we'll come. Talk to you soon."

So, it will not be a big event, but she'll have the close family reunited for a while.

***

Olivia decorated the house with colorful balloons, 'happy birthday' signs all over the living room, and small surprises for the baby to find.

When they all arrived, and the happy, lively faces were all around her,

Olivia relaxed. Not a big event, but an intimate, heartwarming one. Adam and Tom were delighted to see each other and forgot about everybody else, updating each other, talking quietly in the corner of the living room. Both Ann and Emily helped out, and Olivia was grateful. Leah was the center of attention but hung close to Olivia, demanding to be picked up again whenever Olivia was busy serving her guests, or moving around. So laughingly giving in, she picked the little girl up and carried her wherever she went. Luckily, Mark saw her trying to manage a tray in one hand and the baby in the other and moved in to help. He took Leah in his arms, called Pinky to him, and went out to the veranda. A huge smile spread on Leah's face, who was ready to cry when taken from Olivia, and they all laughed with her when they saw Pinky running circles around the baby while Leah was trying to catch her waving tail.

***

The only one who didn't smile was Arthur. Olivia saw that her father had aged noticeably when her parents came to Leah's party. She didn't know what was wrong with him, but something certainly was. Mark saw it, too, she noticed. The change was too dramatic to ignore.

"Mom, is anything wrong with Dad? He lost a lot of weight, and he seems sluggish and sallow," Olivia asked.

Rebecca shrugged. "I have no idea. He lost his appetite. And he wants to sleep all the time. I have a hard time every morning trying to get him out of bed. He doesn't even want to go to the gym any more."

Mark heard her. "Did the doctors at the Carlisle see him? Say anything? Did they send him for blood tests? When was the last time he had a general checkup?"

Rebecca nodded. "I took him to the clinic last week. They wanted to send him for tests, but he refused. He said it wasn't necessary."

Mark shook his head, exasperated, and went to talk to Olivia's father. Olivia and her mother followed him.

"Arthur! I haven't seen you in a while. You seem to have lost weight since we met. Aren't you eating well? I thought you liked the food at the Carlisle better than your wife's cooking!" Mark aimed at a light, half-joking tone, but Arthur just nodded listlessly.

"What's wrong, Arthur? What bothers you? Are you in pain?" Mark insisted.

"No pain… just some discomfort." Arthur said, flapping his hand as if dismissing a pestering fly.

"Will you come to see me next week, so we can examine you, just to make sure, rule out any serious problems?" Mark refused to be brushed off.

"Yeah, OK." Arthur assented unwillingly.

"Good, I'll set it up. Rebecca, is the day after tomorrow a good time for you?" Mark asked.

"Whenever you say," came her immediate reply. "Thank you so much!"

***

"Your father's ultrasound and blood tests were not so good, Livy. We need some more tests… but I'm worried," Mark said when he got home after her parents visited the hospital.

"I expected that," Olivia said. "His yellowish color means there's something wrong with his pancreas or his liver, right?"

"Yes, I suspect so." Mark nodded. "I think your father has pancreatic cancer. But we'll need a CT scan and perhaps a biopsy to ascertain that. I'm sorry."

"I'm more worried about my mother and what will happen to her if— or when—he goes… she'll take it badly."

"We're not there yet!" Mark said. "We're not even sure it's cancer. Let's wait and see. If it is cancer, we'll have time to prepare her."

***

The additional tests were done, and the answer was unequivocal. Metastatic pancreatic cancer. Inoperable.

As gently as it was broached, it was devastating for her mother. She broke down and couldn't stop crying. She kept stroking his arm, as they sat in Mark's office with the specialist he brought in. Her father took the information with a shrug, as if unsurprised and indifferent.

Olivia, who accompanied them to the oncologist with Mark, looked at her father, stunned by his calm response. At first, she thought his hearing aid didn't work, and he didn't hear them properly. Then, she felt he misunderstood the information they had just revealed.

"Dad, do you understand what they just said?" Olivia asked, surprised to realize she felt deep compassion.

Arthur heard the empathy in her voice and turned to her. "I do, Livy. It's going to kill me." He shook his head, disbelieving. "It's astounding. There were pains, coming and going, in the past months, but nothing too overwhelming. So I ignored them… or swallowed some ibuprofen. Me, who worked out all my life, fit as a fiddle, never sick with the flu or anything. And it's the second time my body betrays me. Almost twenty years ago, I had prostatic cancer, and now this. I beat the first one, but I don't think I have a chance against this one." He fell silent, thinking.

Then, with a small smile, he added, "But I intend to give it a hell of a fight!"

"That's the spirit," Mark said.

That was the longest speech Olivia had heard from him in a long while. She knew it was only a matter of time. There was nothing they could do but alleviate the pain that may increase as the cancer spreads.

"Everyone dies, right?" Arthur asked rhetorically. "At least I know what I'll die of."

He didn't ask the doctors how long he had, Olivia noticed.

As expected, Rebecca took the news badly, her eyes streaming throughout the conversation. "Can't you do anything?" she asked, desperate. "Are there biological treatments or chemotherapy? Can you operate? Surely there's something we can do to slow the advancement?"

The oncologist shook his head. "I'm sorry. It's too late for surgery—the cancer has spread to remote organs. We can try chemotherapy and hope he reacts well to it."

"No," Arthur said decisively, "I want neither." He was resolute. "There is no point."

"It could prolong your…" Rebecca tried but was cut off brusquely by Arthur's gesture.

"It could, but I'll have no quality of life, so what's the point?" he said. As always, arrogant and full of self-importance, he would not have anyone see him as weak or helpless.

Even if it costs him his life, he won't relinquish his pride, Olivia thought. That's how he lived his life, and that's his choice of how to end it. She looked at him with new compassion.

That was unexpected. On finding that her father was dying, Olivia discovered the indifference was replaced by compassion for him. He could not fight his nature then—when she was growing up—any more than he could now.

40

The weather was warming gradually. The balmy air, scented by the first spring flowers, was more than welcome.

The construction and road work next to her house were almost at an end. *Time to go back home,* she thought—*my home*. Seacliff has become 'home', too, in the past months, but it wasn't *her* home.

Still, the long talks in the evenings, cooking their dinners together, going to sleep cradled in his arms every night were all habits she loved. She needed to make up her mind. Mark seemed to take her moving in with him for granted. They never discussed it, but they should talk about the issue. Did she want to give up her home and its familiar comforts? She loved her place, but did she love it more than she loved the pleasure of sharing her life with Mark?

She thought she'd talk with Sarah about it. Her practical rationality may help solve some of the complex, intertwined issues. And she'd have to discuss it with Mark, clarify his desires, even though she believed she already knew what he'd say—he'd want her to stay.

***

She called Sarah from her office before she left to go home.

As always, Sarah was happy to hear from her and suggested that Olivia come over after work.

They sat with their coffee cups in Sarah's kitchen. Olivia explained her dilemma and ended by saying, "The point is—I don't know whether to go back home or stay there and make his house my home."

"You didn't speak to Mark about it yet, did you?" Sarah asked.

Olivia shook her head.

"Is it because you know his answer, or because you are afraid of the answer?"

"I think I know… he'd love me to stay… Mark has repeatedly said that thanks to me, he has a warm home to come to, a home he *didn't* have for many years."

"And it matters to you, that you can provide it for him?"

"Of course," Olivia said.

"I don't know what to say; it's a decision only you can make." Sarah shrugged her shoulders. "I know that most women will not agree to leave their homes. Not for anyone. It's the home your kids come to. It's the place where a woman would normally feel most secure. But his house is bigger, more luxurious."

"The only thing I know for sure is that if we live together, I want a cohabitation agreement, or financial agreement, or whatever it's called. To prevent conflicts, or demands, or misunderstandings in the future if anything happens to either of us," Olivia said.

"Is that in your best interests?" Sarah questioned. "He has more than you. Much more. So why raise the issue?"

"Because I don't want what's not mine!" Olivia answered.

"I would have kept quiet in your place." Sarah responded.

"I know you wouldn't," Olivia said, smiling.

***

Olivia drove home slowly. As usual, the traffic was congested, and she had time to think, though she realized her mind was not on the road. She hoped Mark would not be too late or too tired tonight when he arrived home.

But he was. Both late and tired.

Over dinner, he told her of his hectic day. He spoke of attempts to acquire expensive new equipment for the labs, and the shortage of nurses in the Bay area. He also mentioned the resignation of the head of pediatrics, who was moving to New York.

He saw her pensive face, not entirely focused on what he said, unlike her usual intense listening and interest.

"And how was your day?" he asked.

"Not as dramatic as yours, that's for sure. I didn't save any lives today." Olivia didn't sound like her usual self, and she saw he noticed immediately.

"So—what happened to cause such a long face?" Mark's tone was sharp.

She looked up, not liking the tone. If Mark was in such a mood, it was not the right time to broach the subject of her dilemma.

She got up and gathered the dishes to clear the table, saying nothing.

Mark got up, too, and seemed flustered.

"You hardly speak, and when you do—it's sarcastic, and you don't answer my questions. I had a challenging day, and I don't feel like opening a new front, going into battle when I'm home!" he said, his voice hard and cold.

Olivia was deeply hurt. He must have noticed that something was wrong, but instead of trying to find out what bothered her, he attacked.

She left the dining room, leaving the table still laden with the remains of their meal. Not saying a word, she went to get her car keys and her phone. She picked up her coat and was on her way to the door.

"Olivia, don't!" She heard Mark call but did not stop.

"Livy, please, you promised me! We agreed that leaving is not an option!" There was sadness in his tone now, as well as fatigue. "Please, talk to me!"

She slowed, undecided… she did promise, but—

"I don't think you are in a mood to talk… and I need to think about what just happened here," she said, her voice low and miserable.

He closed the distance between them. "I'm sorry, baby. It's just… it was such a frantic day. I'm sorry I snapped. It was uncalled for. Don't leave like that."

She hadn't made up her mind and hesitated.

"Please don't make me beg," Mark said.

She turned to him. Angry now. "You never beg. You don't know how to." Olivia was so frustrated she had tears in her eyes, which made her angrier.

"I said I was sorry. I took my frustrations out on you, and I think I reacted based on past experiences. Helen used to annoy me with sarcastic comments and with disregard of the heavy load I carry, and I know you're nothing like her, but for a second there, I lost it and reacted as if…"

He hugged her. She was stiff, unyielding at first, but he didn't let go. Her body responded to his touch even though she didn't want to.

"Talk to me," he said softly, steering her back to the living room. He sat her on the sofa and sat close by. "Tell me."

"It's bad timing," she said, lost.

"It's never a bad time to tell me what's bothering you," Mark said.

Olivia looked up at his face, seeing the concern and attention in his eyes.

She sighed heavily.

"I was thinking… I went to visit Sarah today. It took them about six months, but finally, construction and road maintenance are almost finished in our street, and now that it's not as noisy and smelly, maybe I should move back home."

His surprise was apparent. And his distress.

"Aren't you happy here?" he asked quietly.

"Of course, I am. It's beautiful and pleasant, and I have you here—or what's left of you at the end of the day," she said, her tone joking, and then she turned serious again. "But we never discussed this as a permanent arrangement. It was supposed to be temporary until the construction ended; I didn't know it would take six months… and I'm not sure."

"Isn't what I want obvious to you?" Mark asked, sounding amazed.

"I learned not to assume what may be a huge mistaken assumption, remember? I almost failed to give us a chance because I made assumptions. Incorrect ones!"

Mark was still tense, but less so.

"Well, it should be obvious and not an assumption. I said it often enough—I love you, and I love sharing my life with you. And I'm delighted to go to sleep hugging you and waking up seeing you so peaceful next to me. How could you doubt what I want? Let me tell you something—I wanted to suggest you take out of your house anything you want with you, and bring it over here, and rent your house once the construction ends! You can have an added income, instead of paying city tax and all the bills like electricity, gas, or whatever."

He looked at her intensely. She kept silent.

"Do you still want to keep it vacant? Why? Is that where you intended to go tonight when you took your keys?" Mark asked.

"I didn't know what to do, but you seemed like a different person, and I wanted to get away from you… not go into a confrontation."

"Running away is not an option! We stay, and we talk things out!" he said vehemently.

"I hate arguments!" Olivia said. "And you seemed like you were spoiling for a fight, and I'm not good at that! So, I decided to give us space to cool down, to avoid saying things we don't mean and hurt each other." Olivia's voice dissolved slowly.

"I hate fights, too. I have enough of those at work," Mark replied. "But if we disagree on anything, or we think the other is being unfair or inconsiderate—we should talk and deal with it, and hey—we just had our first argument! And we survived it!"

The decision was hers again, as she knew it was. Mark made it clear—he wanted them to live together. *If I agree to that—it will be in his house, not in mine.* There were, in fact, two decisions to make... her orderly, rational thinking kicked into action.

Do I want to live with him? She wondered why this was an issue at all. Living together, so far, had been fantastic. Loving each other, feeling the deep bond between them, having someone to share everything with—was incredible. But it came with a price. They took care of each other, but did she truly want that? Did she want—or need—to be taken care of? And take care of someone else? Moreover, living together meant losing her freedom. She would no longer be free to come and go as she pleased, free to make all decisions concerning her life.

Freedom or intimacy? That was the essential question. It was the question all couples had to answer when they decided to live together.

What was right for *her*?

After the last years with Elliot, where she had no intimacy and no freedom, she gained her independence back when he died.

Was her time alone and free better than her time with Mark and less freedom?

Defining the dilemma in this manner—the answer to her dilemma became clear: she's staying. And she'll rent out her house.

41

"Mark, do you want to try and invite your daughters and their families for dinner one weekend? Maybe enough time has passed, and they'll be willing to come to terms with your having a woman in your life?" Olivia asked him one evening after dinner.

Mark looked thoughtfully at her.

"Maybe," he said, sounding cautious and uncertain. "I'll ask them."

"Don't be upset if they do not wish to come. I won't mind. If your daughters don't want to acknowledge my existence in your life, that's OK, too. I only suggest it because I believe *you* want it."

Mark nodded. He understood.

***

They agreed to come. Olivia guessed they were curious to see who she was. *Sort of 'know thy enemy.'* The thought crossed her mind when he told her they were willing. As if they were doing him a favor.

She decided to do her best to make the meeting a success.

They arrived together. Emma and her husband, Philip, entered first. Their beautiful daughters, Andrea and Audrey, followed. Then Clair came in with her son Jeffrey, and Olivia could see a little girl waiting outside, hesitantly, looking at the driveway. A man joined her. They had to be Spencer, Clair's husband, and Adel, their daughter.

Mark made the introductions, and the atmosphere was lively but still somewhat tense. *It's to be expected,* Olivia thought. *In their minds, I'm still a threat to them...*

Olivia was busy arranging the salads for their main course and watched her guests' dynamics and body language from the kitchen. Emma and Clair talked, but Clair's eyes were continually roaming, checking what her kids were doing. Philip was busy with his cellphone, alone, and Spencer occupied Jeffrey and the girls. Mark was preparing drinks. None of them tried to engage him, talk to him.

"Shall we sit down?" she asked, her tone friendly, inviting. She hoped she sounded sincere.

They all came to the table, and Mark allocated seats, placing Jeffrey next to his mother. His father around the corner, on his other side. Adel, on the other side of her mother. The girl wanted to sit with her cousins, but a look from her mother silenced her. Emma and Clair, seated on opposite sides of the table, communicated throughout dinner.

The talk turned to local politics, social issues of the day, and their representation in the local TV news. They were all concerned with the difficulties that homelessness created in their city. Philip said that the city spent millions trying to alleviate the problem. Spencer thought it was not helping at all. Emma felt the growing numbers of mentally ill and the drug addicts were frightening tax-paying citizens. The kids were not included, nor did they show any interest in the discussion. Emma's daughters talked quietly with each other, Adel looking longingly at them from the other side of the table.

The conversation then turned to their mother. Though dead for so many years, she was very much a part of their family, was the message they relayed. Olivia missed the turn in the conversation and how they managed to bring it forth, but she remembered it was their way to get under Helen's skin. They seemed disappointed when she reacted with interest, wanting to know more about Victoria. She told them that Mark had shared some stories of their dead mother, and she was interested in hearing their memories of her.

"It's not that important." Emma said and changed the subject.

Jeffrey was moving disquietly in his chair. Recognizing the signals, Clair got up and started clearing the first course dishes. Olivia was dismayed—it was evident that not everyone was done, but Clair decided the dinner should move forward without asking for her hosts' consent. Olivia didn't understand why Clair thought she had a right to do what she did but chose to let things slide by her and not wreck the fragile atmosphere. It made her uncomfortable, but she'd talk to Mark about it later.

A short time later, Clair said they had to go, and they all left.

The dinner was not a total disaster, Olivia thought, *but it was not a great success either...* no bond was created, and she felt they were not interested in creating one. *Well,* she thought, *at least you tried. It was worth it, for Mark's sake.* But if Mark had any expectations, his daughters sent a clear signal they had no intention of including her in their family, just as they were unwilling to accept Helen.

The split will be maintained. They had their father for a couple of hours on Saturday afternoons and whenever they needed him. They didn't care much who was in his life the rest of the time. Olivia hoped he wouldn't be too disappointed. He knows them well enough, and indubitably, he could have anticipated their reaction. They were not open to accepting any woman in his life.

They *didn't choose me,* Olivia surmised; their father *did. His choice does not bind them. And it goes both ways: I chose their father, not them.*

42

The academic year was almost over, and organizing the department before the year ended was demanding. Plans for next year were in full swing, and recruiting for the new programs Olivia devised was time-consuming. She was delighted to see new markets opening for her graduate department, extending new options for students: The World Bank, several countries in Africa and Asia were eager to create ties with researchers in the department. They were also willing to receive their students for internships.

It was a good year, she thought, pleased. She managed a lot despite all the changes in her personal life. Next year would be the end of her term as the academic director of the graduate program. Did she want to extend it? She believed she would, if it was offered.

She was working on several studies, but—she had to admit—not very diligently. There were so many changes in her life, and so much had happened in the last two years! Elliot's prolonged illness, and his death a year and a half ago, were the principal change. This year—Mark was, by far, the most significant change. But also—Leah's birth, Nick's death, her father's illness. No wonder she had less time for research. She loved this aspect of her profession, but it was the one aspect that was important but not critical in the day-to-day sense. Teaching classes, counseling graduate students, and managing the department—had to be performed according to schedule. She'd be happy to have time to immerse herself in the data her research on global business strategies produced and write the papers she planned.

Maybe they'd also take some time off and go somewhere? She loved traveling and knew that Mark did too. She'd see if Mark can take a vacation, and for how long.

***

Mark arrived late. He called earlier to say he didn't know when he'd be home. There was some kind of crisis, which he'd tell her about when he got back, but he was needed at the hospital.

She was going over a research proposal submitted by one of her students when she heard the dogs bark happily, telling her he was home. Olivia left her study and went to the door to greet him. Mark looked haggard. His face was solemn and gray, his shoulders hunched. She took him in her arms, and he dropped his head to hers, inhaling deeply.

"What a day!" he said, almost whispering.

"What happened?" she asked, worried.

"A terrible accident, on the I-80. There were four or five cars involved and a school bus. Several died. Many of them were brought to our hospital, and it was just so dreadful and crazy. I'm used to seeing horrid damages to the human body. Still, even I was shaken by the extent of the injuries, the number of people, the trauma, especially to the kids. And then the parents flooded the ER, looking for their kids. All were hoping their child survived… it was mayhem!"

"What were you doing there? How could you help? Were there a lot of internal injuries?" Olivia asked.

"Of course, there were. Most were multi-trauma cases, and some were in shock. In disaster situations, there is a crucial role for a leader to set priorities, organize teamwork, have the patience and empathy to talk to devastated relatives, and calm the victims themselves. And also—to give a hand in the 'bloody business' itself, to help with patient care, arrest bleeding, fix IVs, help to intubate. When you have twenty patients, and each one is a high priority, you really sweat."

"You look wiped out," Olivia said, caressing his back. "Can I fix you a drink?"

"Yes, please! Make it a big one!" A smile at last. A small, weak one, but still a smile.

She came back with a whiskey tumbler for him, a gin and tonic for herself, and took it to their corner of the living room. Mark sat heavily next to her, taking his drink from her hand, and he took a gulp. His body relaxed gradually, and he extended his arm to engulf her.

"I kept thinking that soon I'll be able to go home, to you, and envisioned us sitting just like we are now… and I didn't even have to tell you, this is what I needed most!"

He kissed her forehead and took another sip. "You don't know how much it means to me—to know that I have you to come home to… how often I say to myself, 'I'll tell Olivia about it when I get home'… and it gives me the energy I need to go on."

Olivia nodded. "I do know," she said, her voice caressing him.

"I need a vacation. I need to go far away, somewhere I can't be reached. to just be with you away from the world," Mark sighed.

"Antarctica, maybe?" Olivia smiled at the joke they often shared when they talked about abandoning the world behind them.

Mark laughed. "Not the right time of year, or I would say YES! It's winter down there now. But how about the Galapagos? Sounds far enough?"

"Are you kidding me?" Olivia turned to him, her eyes shining. It was the place she fantasized about, and Mark knew it.

"No, not at all. And you know what—it will be the end of the semester soon, won't it? Can you take two weeks off, so we can tour Peru, maybe Ecuador, too?"

"You're serious, aren't you?" Olivia was astounded, looking at Mark, her eyes alight.

"Yes, totally serious." He nodded, his eyes as bright as hers. "We deserve some time for ourselves, don't we? And as you said—it seems a great place to visit. Interesting and different, unique."

"It will be a dream come true for me!" she whispered.

"Then I'll be your dream fulfiller." He smiled, and it was a genuine, broad smile this time. "Will you search for a ship and some tours for us?"

Olivia nodded vigorously, speechless.

"Do it soon; I'm not sure there will be available cabins on any of the ships this late; they were probably booked way in advance. And the summer is the dry season in Ecuador, I think, so it's the best time to visit. Make it a private trip. I hate group trips where they have thirty strangers on a bus."

"It will be appallingly expensive this way," Olivia said hesitantly, thinking of the enormous cost she'll need to share.

"So what?" Mark smiled. "My idea, my way, my treat!"

Olivia looked at him, her eyes penetrating his, trying to figure out if he really meant it, and if he was wholeheartedly sure about it. She found no misgivings in his eyes, only enthusiasm.

A huge smile spread on her face. The immense joy that infused her was infecting him, too.

He pulled her over and sat her in his lap, kissing her face. Finding her mouth, he took her breath away.

"Oh, Mark, it must be a dream... am I dreaming?" she murmured.

"I hope not! Otherwise, it would mean I'm dreaming, too, and I want it to be a reality. *Our* reality. Besides, it would be a perfect birthday present for you, don't you think? And an almost-anniversary since you came to see the house for the first time, and it all began for us."

She laid her head on his breast, listening to the firm and steady heartbeat. She was afraid to acknowledge how happy she was. She couldn't ask for more.

"Are you hungry? I'm sure you had no time to eat anything today!" she remembered after a while.

"Famished!" he said, pulled her to her feet, and got up.

***

Olivia went online the next evening when she came home, looking for private tours of Peru and Ecuador, which included a cruise to the Galapagos. She found out it would have to be for more than two weeks. If they wanted to see enough of both countries and the famous islands, they would need more time. At least four days more. She could do it, she had enough vacation time, and the timing was right for her to take it. But could Mark manage it? She'd have to ask him before she decided on a tour.

Mark said he'd manage the extra days, and she showed him the tour she wanted. He looked at her animated face and was aware of her joyful immersion in the plans and expectations. "Whatever you decide," he said. "Just be sure we book first-class hotels. I'm past the age of backpacking!"

She booked the tour. Two and a half weeks in a different world, one she longed to see! She'd have to notify Sophie, though there was nothing in July that couldn't wait for two or three weeks. And she'd have to tell Adam and Ann that she wouldn't be able to take Leah. *I'll miss the baby so much!*

"I'll have to call Sheila and let her know," Olivia said. "She suggested we travel in July or August to Aspen, Colorado, or Banff, Alberta. It's out of the question now!"

She called Sheila to say they couldn't join them.

"Why? What's wrong?" Sheila asked.

"Nothing's wrong. Only we'll be in South America—Peru and

240

Ecuador!" She informed her new friend. "My birthday gift!"

"Quite a gift!" Sheila sounded happy for her. "Some of our group did it two years ago, and we couldn't go at the time. I hope we'll be able to go one day! I'd love to climb to Machu Picchu!"

"Yes, me too!" Olivia responded. "But the major attraction for me is the Galapagos! That was my dream. I even chose biology as one of my major subjects in high school because I was interested in genetics, especially after reading Darwin's *Origin of the Species*."

"Sounds even better!" Sheila said. "When are you leaving?"

"The beginning of July! I was lucky to find a suite this late on one of the ships touring the Galapagos; the tour organizers said they had a cancelation the day before I called them. The ship leaves Guayaquil in the last week in July, so we'll tour Peru first, then fly to Ecuador and board the ship after a few days in the Amazon jungle."

"Sounds great!" Sheila said. "You'll enjoy it, I'm sure. And we'll do Aspen next year!"

43

Mark arrived home relatively early. They were going out again. Dinner invitations kept coming, and she got to know more of his friends. She liked many of them. Some were more than acquaintances for her, too; they even became friends, people she enjoyed meeting, inviting home. As Mark said, some were status seekers and show-offs, but most were friendly, stimulating, intelligent people.

Some of his friends chose to arrange large parties with thirty or even fifty people; others opted for dinners for eight to twelve people. The smaller the gathering, the more Olivia liked it. The conversation was more interesting, and she got to know people better. It was more for pleasure and less for extravagant showing off.

Mark was used to both and felt fine in either type of get-togethers, but when he realized her reluctance to attend the more ostentatious celebrations, they skipped a growing number of those.

They entertained, too, of course. At first, Mark suggested they hire a catering service.

"They'd come with all the ingredients," he said. "They'll prepare everything in our kitchen, bring a few waiters to serve the food and drinks, and clear everything when the event comes to an end."

She agreed, reluctantly, because they had to return so many invitations. But after employing them a few times, she decided to try a smaller gathering of closer friends and cook for them. The evening was an immense success, and she was pleased.

Mark was delighted, too. Culinary skill was not one of the virtues he thought he'd find when they began their relationship. But he loved her cooking—he loved the twists she always had for the dishes he was familiar with—Spareribs that were marinated for hours in her special sauce then baked for six hours and melted in his mouth, the grilled jumbo shrimps with artichokes, the varied and surprising salads. The dinner wasn't as extravagantly decorative as the caterers could provide, but it was tasty, aesthetically presented, and allowed for greater intimacy and more interesting conversations.

Soon, the word was out that Olivia's cooking was not as elaborate as Helen's used to be; still, when it came to tastefulness, indulgence, and stimulating conversations, Olivia's dinners were among the best.

All in all, Olivia had to acknowledge, she survived the transition into his world. More than merely survived it. According to Mark, she seemed fully integrated to most of their friends. As if she had always been by his side.

Looking back at the last year, she realized how much she had changed, influenced by all that had happened in her life. She was happy and felt loved, treasured even. And she was much more relaxed than in the past years. More tolerant and patient. That was Mark's influence; she had no doubt. It was his way of looking at life, and it affected her, too.

He changed, too. Olivia was surprised when she realized that the reticent, introverted, always considerate of others, but standoffish man— opened up. People always respected and trusted him, but now they genuinely loved him. He smiled more, was ready to reveal feelings. She thought that Mark often surprised himself, nowadays.

She liked the change and loved him even more for inducing it in her, and she loved his willingness to show his feelings and speak openly more easily.

44

The trip to South America was organized according to their specifications. Mark and Olivia studied the maps to choose what they simply *had* to see and what they'd have to give up, knowing full well they couldn't see everything within the limiting time frame. As they requested, it would be private tours, with English-speaking guides, in both Peru and Ecuador.

The flight took them high above the Peruvian Andes to Cusco, the city built in a valley in their midst. A guide waited for them in the tiny airport and drove them to their hotel. The town, which served as the capital of the Inca empire around the fifteenth century, had impressive archaeological remains and Incan stonework ruins, the guide told them on their way. They'd have time to see it before they left around noon the next day on their way to Machu Picchu.

The guide also made sure they took the tablets to combat altitude sickness before flying to Peru. Cusco is three thousand four hundred meters high, and people who were not used to it may suffer shortness of breath, headaches, and weakness. Olivia remembered she read somewhere that it was eleven thousand two hundred feet and hoped they'd manage. She smoked heavily when she was young and worried that it might affect her ability to walk in the 'thinner' air with less oxygen.

They loved the scenery and the different culture all around them, enjoyed the tour of the Sacred Valley of the Incas, all the way to Aguas Callientes, and most of all—Machu Picchu, which was a must. Walking among the ruins of the most familiar icon of Inca civilization, built in their unique style and method, was overwhelming, leaving the many tourists in the area unable to believe that so many hundreds of years ago, the Incas managed such magnificent construction projects.

The walk was challenging, as expected. The altitude affected Olivia, but she refused to give in. Mark, in much better shape, was unaffected but insisted on a slow pace, his eyes continually watching her—the moment she started to breathe heavily, they stopped and rested. "What's the hurry?" Mark said, and the small, stocky guide happily complied.

***

When they finally boarded the ship that would take them to the Galapagos Islands, Olivia was enthusiastic. She couldn't wait to reach the islands. According to the information she had, they were not topographically impressive. It was the life on them that fascinated her—the unique species, the variety. And the fact that it was as primal as it was when Darwin first saw it. Untainted by human turmoil, technology, or progress.

The islands were as captivating as she expected them to be. Each island contained its exclusive, endemic species, which were not found anywhere in the world, all walking or swimming or flying unafraid of humans. They were warned not to walk too close to the wildlife, not to scare them with raised voices—humans were the guests, not the proprietors. Olivia was delighted with the change in roles.

They went down to the Zodiac speedboats from the ship to each island and arrived in small groups, a crew member and a guide accompanying them. On one of the islands, the guide suddenly signaled to all of them to stop and keep quiet. A massive sea lion cow lay across their path, and the guide said she was just then giving birth and should not be disturbed. Most of the group wanted to stay and watch; others opted to choose another path and look for more animals. Mark and Olivia stayed, fascinated by the process. Every now and then, the cow raised her head to look at the group, as if seeking help, but they could not approach her. When the pup arrived, suddenly popping out, and his mother turned to smell him, some people clapped, only to be silenced by the guide. Others had tears in their eyes, Olivia among them. Mark took her hand, twined their fingers, and they followed the others to continue the tour of the island.

Sitting on their balcony that evening, as the ship was cruising from one island to another, Olivia realized that in addition to the dream fulfilled, what made her pleasure complete was how easily they meshed together, and how considerate of each other they were. They were delighted when they managed to please each other. Moreover, they complemented each other: he relished her enthusiasm and ability to enjoy discovering new worlds, and she treasured his profound perceptions and generous, uncritical spirit.

She recognized another change in her, one that surprised and pleased her. She grasped that she was a little apprehensive before they started the trip, worried that they'd get on each other's nerves.

Olivia tore her eyes from the island sliding by, to look at Mark.

"You know, I thought I was not very good at having people with me day in and day out, many days in a row," she said quietly. "With Elliot, even with my mother on the Alaska cruise—I needed to get away and be by myself. For a few hours, at least. If not—I'd turn tense, unpleasant, even bitchy. It is so strange—I don't feel this way when I'm with you… it's an immense change which I can't explain."

"Maybe because there is no pressure? No need to do or go or arrive or whatever. We just flow, not compelled into any outside goals," Mark said, smiling at her. "And we enjoy the moment, every moment. Like now—we just appreciate sitting here, on our balcony, watching the waves and the birds flying above, at ease with each other and ourselves."

"True," Olivia nodded, "There is no pressure when I'm with you. Only pleasure of togetherness. And ease of being."

Mark took her hand and kissed her fingers one by one. "I love being with you, and I love making you happy, and seeing how enthusiastic you get, and how eager you are to try new tastes, reach new heights, meet new challenges!"

"And I love the way you make me feel about myself, and now there is another thing I love you for—you make my dreams come true! This trip has turned into a journey of discovery, encountering a new world, while discovering ourselves and each other!" She moved to his lap for a long, passionate kiss.

45

"Livy, how's your day? Everything OK?" Mark asked.

Olivia tensed. Alert and concerned. Mark hardly called her in the middle of a day's work; he might send a text message reminding her of his love, but he seldom called.

"Hi Mark, what's wrong? What's happening?" She knew she sounded apprehensive but couldn't help it.

"Can you talk?" It seemed to her that he was attempting to sound nonchalant, to cover up anxiety.

"Yes, talk to me!" She had already left the new program's staff meeting, asking them to continue before she exited.

"I received the blood test results this morning."

Olivia knew he took the test the day before, as he did periodically, because of the biological agent he received to retard the cancer progress. "And?" Based on his tone of voice, Olivia suspected the news was bad.

"The markers have gone up… significantly. It means that one or more of the metastases are growing."

Her heart plummeted. She knew it could happen, as the cancer was there, in Mark's body.

"It's not a catastrophic increase, but it means we need to do something. I'll do a PET-CT scan, and we'll be able to compare the previous one and the current one to see where the growth is. Then we'll be able to decide what to do."

"OK," Olivia said, "If I understand correctly, there are things we *can* do to stop the growth? It's a matter of finding the best one, right?"

"Exactly," Mark responded immediately, "As I said, it's bad news, but not a catastrophe. There are several options. I'll check the online medical sites to see the newest treatments possible, but we'll decide after the PET-CT scan."

"What time will you be home today?" Olivia asked. She sometimes arrived later than Mark but knew he loved coming home and finding her there, to welcome him with a warm hug. Tonight, she wanted to be there before him.

"Not late, I want to check the websites," Mark responded.

"Fine, I'll see you later. I love you!" she said.

"I love you more!" he replied.

Olivia kept thinking about Mark. She was sure he was a lot more concerned than he let on. Not a trivial thing—to know you have a malignant tumor in your lungs. One that could grow and begin multiplying, spreading itself. The unknown scared her. Not knowing what to expect. Or what were the chances that they'd be able to block the growth.

She'd be with him every step of the way—that goes without saying—whatever he decided to do. Her life would have to be rearranged to ensure that. It was too soon to know what would be needed, but she'd be there with him, for him, whatever it takes. She knew how to do that. She changed her life when Elliot got sick, and she'd manage it again.

These thoughts and fears threw her back a few years. Elliot was scared at first. Knowing that he had cancer petrified him. But then a process of denial kicked in, and he convinced himself his cancer was manageable. At least, he tried to maintain some outward optimism. But, deep down, he was a pessimist, and, at some point, he shut everyone out. Not knowing how he felt, whether afraid or worried, was very difficult for both Olivia and their sons. Now she'd have to go through emotional upheavals again. Luckily, Mark was more open about his feelings, more willing to share them, so she stood a chance of understanding better.

***

Mark arrived early. Early for him meant before five p.m. The dogs barked when his car entered the yard, and she went to open the door. She saw the stress on his face before he saw her, and her warm smile diffused some of his tension. He hugged her tightly, lowering his head to her, inhaling her familiar smell. His body gradually relaxed in her arms.

"You can't begin to understand how much it means to me, to be able to come home and find peace, and support, and warmth," he said, "To know that I'll have someone with whom I can share whatever troubles me, and find an understanding mind and empathic soul to listen and respond."

She had their drinks ready when he arrived, waiting in their private corner, and she led him to it. They sat together. His arms tight around her shoulders, pulling her close.

Mark sighed.

She looked at the handsome face and felt her heart growing heavier. Worried for him, helpless.

He turned to gaze at her as if he could hear her thoughts. "We'll get over this. The situation is not *that* bad. We'll find a way to beat it, you'll see."

Olivia nodded, not saying a word so that he wouldn't hear her brokenhearted voice.

"Livy, having you in my life makes me want to fight for what we have and win. You give me strength. And the will to live."

Her eyes teared; her emotions flooded her.

They sat together, slowly sipping their drinks, watching the high, soft clouds rushing above them, and the bright blue-green ocean below. The sun rays danced upon the surface, stroking the small waves and the low-flying seagulls that skimmed them. They were never tired of the ever-changing beauty of the scenery in front of their yard. It was their best way to put things in the right perspective and proportions.

Olivia pressed his hand in both of her smaller ones. "We'll fight and win! No other option!" She said it for both of them, trying to encourage him. She sounded more optimistic than she felt at that moment, but it's what she wanted to believe.

"I'll go to my study and check some treatments I heard about a while ago. We'll eat later, OK?" He kissed her forehead and got up.

She overheard him on the phone a while later. It sounded "professional". She heard his cellphone ring half an hour later, and it seemed as if he was given the information he was expecting. She caught, "Ah, ha," again and again. Then, "Thank you, that was very helpful... yes, of course, I will. Bye."

It took a couple of hours before he came to find her.

"Julia Orlansky sends her love," he said. His body language told her he heard some news that cheered him up.

"What did she say?" Olivia asked expectantly.

"She called some friends of hers in New York, renal cancer experts." Mark looked thoughtful. "The hospital they work for has been trying a new technique that may be effective for someone in my condition. I'll have to check it out and read their research and findings more thoroughly."

Thinking further on the matter, he said, "It's a large hospital with well-advanced technologies."

"OK, so they will be among the best in the world?" She knew they must be, but wanted it said, as a reminder… Mark seemed to understand what she was doing.

"Let's eat!" He said, more cheerful than he was when he came home.

Dinner was all his preferred dishes. He loved the most uncomplicated food, with minimum spices, and she had everything ready in no time—schnitzels with mashed potatoes, peas with fried onions, and a huge green salad.

They discussed the options over dinner. Well—Mark talked, and she listened, asking questions when something was unclear or unfamiliar. She knew that describing the alternatives and analyzing their merits and hazards helped him organize the information in his mind. It soon became apparent he liked the innovative New York option better than all the other alternatives. It was riskier, perhaps, he said, but the prospects are higher, too.

"I'll call Brian Campbell, Orlansky's friend, tomorrow. He was in charge of the experiments with the new technology, and now—for applying it to patients. I know him from way back; we met at several conferences. I'm sure he'll remember me."

"Let me know as soon as you find out, OK?" she requested quietly.

"Who else am I going to tell?" he asked, teasing her.

Your daughters, she thought, but did not voice it.

***

He called her around noon the next day. "Hello, Livy," he said, and she knew that he was pleased with the answers he received.

"I'm so happy to hear from you! I waited impatiently, knowing that if you didn't call—you had nothing to report," she answered breathlessly. "Well?"

"Write in your diary—September 25—New York!"

"Brian Campbell said yes?"

"Indeed, he did," Mark replied. "I sent him all the information by email, and he examined everything. A few minutes ago, he called to say I'm a suitable candidate for the treatment. But their staff is limited, and there's a queue, so it will take a few days before he can manage to squeeze me in."

"Do you know how long we'll be away?" Olivia asked, already thinking of all the processes that would have to wait until she returned.

"Three or four days, if all goes well, maybe an extra day before they allow me to fly, just to make sure."

"Fine… no problem… we'll do it!" He didn't ask her if she was coming with him. It was clear that she would.

Again, she had to look for someone to take her place while she was away, and the natural replacement, Andrew Kent, agreed. She was grateful that the steady, capable, and pleasant Andrew was her friend. She did not provide her colleagues with many details but explained the existence of medical necessity.

Her family was worried. They knew Mark had cancer in the past but knew nothing of the metastases still in his body. Olivia thought that they had enough dealings with cancer in their life and didn't need to handle Mark's, too. She knew they liked him and would be concerned if they thought he was not well, but she had to tell them now. When Olivia called to say they were going to New York so that Mark could be treated by the highly advanced technology that the New York hospital was trying out, they were as concerned as she assumed they would be. They were empathic, wanting to know if they could help in any way. She said there was nothing anyone could do, that she hoped that all would go well, and they'd be back in a few days.

It also surprised her that her sons were anxious for her, too. She dealt with their father's cancer for so long, and must now deal with it again. They understood the heavy burden she carried then and were troubled she'd have to bear it once more.

"Are his daughters going with you?" Tom asked.

"No, there's no need. And they are both busy with their families and careers," she said.

"Well, so are you," Adam responded drily, "But you're going with him."

"True… it's different for me. I'm his partner. Maybe it's better that way," Olivia remarked. After a pause, she said, "I don't think Mark asked them to come."

They knew his daughters avoided her and were not interested in seeing her as part of their family.

"Are they staying here because they know you're going?" Tom asked. "I mean—is it to avoid you or because they aren't involved in his life?"

"I don't know, Tommy. Honestly, I don't. But does it matter? It's fine with me," Olivia answered. "I'm not interested in their motives or desires. I do what I feel is right."

"That is so *you*, Mom!" was her sons' reaction.

"Let's just hope the procedures will be successful, and we'll see you back here soon." Adam said before they parted.

"And don't forget to take care of yourself, too, while you're there!" Tom added, knowing that she tended to ignore her own needs in such situations.

"I'll keep you posted and let you know what's happening." With that, she ended the conversation.

46

It was time to leave. Olivia went over all the details in her mind. The dog sitter would come to pick up the dogs soon. She paid for five days but said she wasn't sure when they'd return—it may take a little longer. The young man said there was no problem. He had a roomy house with a big yard, and he wasn't taking care of many dogs right now.

All was arranged with the department. Olivia informed her dean and her staff that she was taking a few days off, and all seemed to understand.

Her mother was upset and worried and hoped all would go well. "Don't worry about us," she said. She actually meant, *don't worry about your father*. Arthur was deteriorating but still refused any treatment.

"Let me know if anything happens," Olivia asked, but she suspected her mother wouldn't tell her anything until they returned.

She called Sarah, too. Sarah knew about the reason for their travel to New York, and Olivia was sure that Sarah would help from afar, no matter what Olivia needed.

Olivia checked again to make sure Mark had all the necessary medical papers, and that all the rest —flight tickets, hotel reservations, the number for the limo from the airport—was in her handbag. She went over the house to ascertain that all the windows and doors were locked properly.

She heard the taxi in the driveway. Mark was there before her, handing their suitcase and trolly to the driver.

"Ready?" he asked.

Olivia nodded, her anxiety rising.

***

They reached the hotel late that afternoon.

The hotel she chose was close to the hospital. A walking distance, in case she needed to come and go and didn't want to wait for a taxi. She chose a suite to allow them space, in case Mark needed an extra day of recuperation after the procedure.

Mark saw her staring out the huge windows overlooking the Queensboro Bridge and came to stand close behind her. His arms folded around her, and he rested his chin lightly on the top of her head. They stood silently, gazing at the bridge and Roosevelt Island.

"We'll be fine, you'll see, it will all work out OK." He spoke softly in her ear.

Is he trying to encourage himself or me? Olivia thought but didn't voice. She turned in his arms and cupped his face in her hands.

"I know," she said in the same soft voice.

"Let's leave everything and go out and enjoy the city. We can unpack later," Mark suggested.

"Good idea. There's still daylight!"

They walked out of their suite and rode the elevator down to the lobby.

Exiting to the broad avenue, she remembered how much she loved the city. Her previous trips were to Bleeker Street, where she shared a flat with Marsha, a colleague from NYU, when she came to work with her on their joint research on women managers in global corporations. She stayed for a week, and they did a lot of work but had a lot of fun, too. Her other visit was to a conference at the Hilton Garden Inn on West 54th St. Memories of the museums in the area, and the fantastic restaurants flooded her mind. *A lifetime ago, and so much has changed.*

"I don't think I've ever been to this part of the city," Olivia said.

They walked in silence, each immersed in their thoughts, among the beautiful boutiques, the delis, the small bookshops. They both needed to stretch their legs.

"What would you like for dinner?" Mark asked.

"I don't care, really." Olivia shrugged. "So long as it's a cozy place."

"We can eat at the hotel. They have a famous restaurant. It should be good, and the view will be great," Mark said solicitously.

"Sure... yeah... fine," she said.

"Come on, Livy, don't be so miserable. They've done hundreds of procedures already, and their success rate is impressive!" Mark was trying to reassure her.

"I know," Olivia said, "But that's the trouble—it's the *rate* I'm afraid of. It's never one hundred percent. I know I'm being silly, but..."

"You have every right to be worried," Mark said, taking her hand before crossing the road in front of their hotel. "But I'm in good health, other than these accursed metastases, so I have an excellent chance of adding to their success rate!"

She smiled at him, meeting the optimism in his eyes, answering him with her own.

They entered the restaurant, still hand in hand, and were given a corner table overlooking the street. The pedestrian masses had almost vanished. Only a few people were still out there, walking fast, looking ahead but avoiding contact with others, as if they had somewhere to go, *probably hurrying home*, she thought.

Waiting for their after-dinner espressos, Mark said, "I wouldn't have considered such a treatment in the past; it's only because I have you in my life. After a very long time, years even, I want to live. You infuse me with strength. Nowadays, I enjoy life. It's not just getting up in the morning, trudging through my routine. Each day is a treasure. You gave me a new purpose, a new lease on life."

Olivia's eyes were moist.

"Well, as I said before—you gave Victoria about fifteen years of your life, and you gave Helen about fifteen years, so I want at least that—fifteen years. At least!" She smiled through her tears. "I won't have it any other way! Promise me!"

Mark smiled and nodded as if agreeing, but she had a feeling he doubted his ability to achieve that. And, she noticed, he didn't promise...

"You know," Olivia looked at him, her heart in her eyes, "I never searched for love after Elliot died. As I told you, I had a vague notion that I'd find a partner or a friend one day. I never thought I could find anything like this... this total commitment to another person... so I never searched for it... but now that I found it, I'm afraid of losing it!"

"You didn't find it," Mark said as his warm, shy smile returned to his eyes, "It has found you! I found you, and I won't let go."

They went to their suite, his arm tightly around her. She felt safe, protected, needed... but she couldn't eliminate the fear that was nibbling a small corner filled with "what if's." in her mind.

47

Olivia slept badly. She found it difficult to fall asleep, and after she managed it—she kept waking up. She lay curled in his arms, her head on his shoulder, listening to his deep, stable breath. The hours crawled forward, uncaring, ignoring her desire for morning to appear.

She tried to figure out why she was apprehensive. Was it the newness of the procedure? The fact that it was not more widespread and known? Not knowing the doctor who would administer it? The thoughts kept rolling in her mind, running in perpetual circles, unable to reach a coherent conclusion. She was unable to resolve the complexity of what she felt and thought, and as a result, failed to find some measure of peace. Troubled, she finally fell into an uneasy sleep.

When she woke next, the sky had changed color. The morning was approaching. Sometime during the night, he turned over, depriving her of his warm embrace. Olivia realized that the forlorn feeling was partly due to the lack of his body wrapped around her. Slowly and quietly, she got out of bed. She couldn't postpone her need to go to the bathroom any more.

When she returned, she saw his eyes were open, looking at her. "Good morning, love," he said tenderly, opening the duvet that covered him to invite her in.

She climbed in, clinging to his solid frame, feeling his arms close around her.

"Slept well?" she asked.

"Quite," came his sleepy response.

"Good," she said.

At least one of us, she thought. Then she realized it must be a very good sign. It means Mark was relaxed, confident that all would be well.

Mark was not supposed to eat or drink before the tests that preceded the procedure. So, Olivia decided on a cup of coffee in their suite rather than a full breakfast. Taking the small trolly they packed the day before, they went downstairs, searching for a taxi for the short ride to the hospital.

Admissions' reception was crowded. Mark called Brian Campbell's cellphone to let him know he had arrived and would be up as soon as he arranged all the paperwork.

"Fine," came the curt reply.

Olivia didn't like it but said nothing. Campbell should have smoothed the way for them, she thought.

The line moved quickly, and it was their turn next. Mark was provided with the necessary paperwork, and they were directed to Dr Campbell's office.

The meeting with the doctor was brief and businesslike. Campbell confirmed that all was clear, elaborating the explanation about the planned procedure and its risks. He mentioned various possible sources of infections. The term pneumothorax was repeated several times, so Olivia opened her smartphone under the table and checked it out. She spelled it wrong, but Google understood what she wanted and offered her the correct term. A collapsed lung. Her heart seemed to stop. It sounded like a grave risk to her.

She put on a brave face, so as not to show Mark how afraid she felt. She tried to listen to the doctor and the percentage of cases in which pneumothorax happened, but her mind blocked the information.

The discussion turned to the tests Campbell wanted to perform before the procedure. Mark tried to express his opinion. Olivia noticed that Campbell was annoyed, clearly seeing Mark's comments as meddling. It was awkward, and again, she felt stressed. Mark was not an expert in the specific procedure, but he *was* a highly experienced internist. Undoubtedly, his opinions mattered?

Alienation. That, precisely, was what Olivia felt. Total lack of sympathy or empathy. Or collegial esteem. It was a novel feeling, and she was sure Mark was stung by it. The well-known doctor of the West Coast, recognized by peers and laypeople alike, reached the East Coast and encountered a lack of familiarity or respect. It was all cold, cordial formality.

When the meeting was over, they were shown to the private room Mark was given. He'd be there for the day, the nurse said. Tomorrow they'd come to take him for the procedure, and by evening—if all goes well—he'll return to it. Olivia arranged his toiletries in the small but convenient bathroom. Her heart was heavy. She felt like a big rock settled over it, squeezing the air out of her lungs.

She wanted to pray but didn't know how or to whom. The feeling of total lack of control over what was happening was new to both of them, and she hoped with all her heart it would end soon, and they'd be able to return home; being far away from their family and friends made it all even worse. They were so alone.

An orderly came to take him for another CT scan, ECG, blood test... Olivia was told to stay in the room. She sat there alone, looking outside the large window at the life going on in the street below her, oblivious and uncaring. Rush-hour traffic sped by; pedestrians seemed to hurry to get their lunch or arrive at unknown destinations. *You run around, hastening everywhere, not stopping to think if it's worth it, until life slaps you in the face with a tragedy or severe illness, forcing you to stop in your tracks and reevaluate your life choices.* She was one of those who were forced to stop and take a good look at her options... She sighed and turned her Kindle on, and tried to continue reading the book she started the day before, on the flight. Having read the same paragraph over and over, she realized she couldn't concentrate. Her mind was wandering, looking for him in the long, impersonal corridors of the large hospital.

The orderly brought Mark back to the room a few hours later, and she saw he was tired and depressed. He had a branula attached to the vein in his arm.

"Did all go well?" she asked, apprehensive.

"Yeah," Mark said and hung a wan smile on his face. His attempt to reassure her failed miserably.

"What did they say?" She tried to encourage him to share his feelings as well as the information with her.

"Nothing much," he replied, "Like I was a regular patient, not a doctor myself." He shrugged as if he didn't care much.

She knew he did care. She understood the anguish. Was there anything she could do? She wondered if they knew who he was. Or cared.

She went down and bought them some salads, a sandwich, and coffee. They'd had nothing to eat since yesterday's dinner, and after all the tests were done, he was allowed to eat. They sat together, eating very little, discussing the impersonality of the people around them. They knew who he was, Mark said, and that he came all the way from California because of the unique treatment they had to offer, paying a lot of money for it. Yet, they acted as if he was of no consequence.

There was a commotion at the door, and when it opened, Olivia saw Emma and Philip. They entered boisterously, smiling from ear to ear.

"Hello, hello! Surprise!" Emma called.

"I specifically asked you, girls, *not* to come!" Mark said.

"Well, Clair thought that one of us should be here with you. You can't go through this alone! And as she couldn't come, because Jeffrey was acting out again, she convinced me to do it. And you know how I hate flying."

"There's no need, and I'm not alone," Mark responded, both frustrated and embarrassed by her callousness.

"You know what I mean, alone without your family." Emma continued lamely, oblivious to the damage she was causing.

"Anyway, we're here now! And we'll take care of all you need!"

"I have all I need," Mark mumbled.

Olivia kept quiet, ignored by his daughter. The massive rock on her heart pressed down more tightly. She saw the stress on Mark's face. He wasn't happy, but what could he do? It was a fait accompli.

Emma was talking incessantly, Chatting about her work, her children, the flight over. Mark responded in monosyllables. Olivia sat by the window, sending WhatsApp messages to her family and friends back home. She didn't try to cover up her sadness and received encouragement in response, urging her to ignore the "noise" and focus on what was important.

Easier said than done, Olivia thought.

One of the nurses came in to ask them to leave. Visiting hours were over. Emma and Philip stood up.

"We should leave. We don't want the staff angry and unfriendly." Emma said, her tone overbearing, looking at Olivia.

"I'm staying," Olivia said quietly. Her tone suggested finality.

Emma looked at her father but saw he wasn't about to object. She shrugged, indicating indifference, but it seemed more like a deep annoyance.

"Suit yourself," she said haughtily, and they left.

"She means well," Mark said.

"She certainly has a funny way of showing it," Olivia replied.

"She does mean well. You just don't know her." He tried to defend his daughter, though he must have noticed how she reacted to Olivia.

Maybe he *didn't* notice, Olivia thought. *With all the tension going on and tomorrow's expectations on his mind, perhaps he wasn't aware.*

"You should go to the hotel, get a good night's sleep," he said after a while.

Olivia shook her head. "I won't be able to sleep anyway. And they may not let me in, in the morning. I want to be here tomorrow, to kiss you and wish you good luck."

She smiled at him but knew she couldn't hide her worries and fear.

There was no extra bed in the room. Olivia organized the armchair close to Mark's bed, raising her legs to the visitors' chair. It would be good enough, she knew.

48

She woke up early when the nurses' shifts changed. She went quickly to wash her face and brush her teeth, changing her clothes before leaving the bathroom.

A new head nurse appeared with the day shift nurses, looking even more unfriendly than the one who received them yesterday.

She had a look of, 'What the hell are you doing here so early?' but said nothing.

"And how are we today?" she addressed Mark, her tone condescending.

"I don't know about you, but I'm OK. Ready for today," he said. His attempted humor fell on deaf ears.

"We'll come for you when we're ready." Brisk, businesslike, uncaring.

Mark nodded curtly.

The entire entourage left, and they could hear them discussing Mark's case in the same professional cold tones.

Mark went to the shower and got ready, but it took a few more hours before an orderly came for him with a wheelchair.

They hugged, and Olivia felt she didn't want to let him go. The orderly was getting impatient, clearing his throat, expecting to get on with his work.

Mark moved a step backward, looking into her eyes. "I'll be fine!" he said and sat in the wheelchair.

"Let's go," he said to the orderly. Olivia started walking with them, but the orderly stopped her. "There's no place for you to wait there. Better stay here until they bring him back."

So, she wouldn't even be able to see him in the post-op recovery room? She sighed heavily and returned to the armchair. She moved it back to the window and sat wearily. She didn't know how long it would take before he was brought back or when the regular visiting hours were and decided not to leave the hospital. She went down to the cafeteria for coffee and a sandwich and returned to the room to wait.

It took hours, and she got apprehensive. Why was it taking so long?

Nobody came into the room, and she didn't think any of the nurses would make the inquiries for her if she asked them to check, so she didn't try to ask them for help. She had no one to ask, no one to consult with. She stayed in the room. Waiting. Afraid. Alone and lonely.

Finally, there were voices in the hall; some sounded concerned. The door opened widely, and Mark was wheeled in. On an operating room gurney, oxygen mask on his nose, infusion drip connected to the branula in his arm, his chest covered with ECG stickers, their wires attached to the machine next to the stretcher, and a drain entering the side of his ribs, linked to a mechanical instrument attached to the bottom of the wheeled stretcher. He was pale, almost gray, and seemed drained.

She got up immediately to go to him.

"Hold it, lady, let us fix him first," said the nurse who accompanied the orderlies and stretcher. "Please wait outside until we finish." She sounded unequivocal, but not unfriendly.

"Is he OK? What happened? What took so long?" she asked the nurse.

"The doctor will come and talk to you later," was all she said, hardly looking at Olivia, oblivious to her distress. They transferred Mark to his bed, made him as comfortable as they could, and left.

Hurrying to his side, Olivia bent over the bed, stroking Mark's hair, his sunken cheeks. She was choking but fought the intense need to cry so as not to scare him. *He can't see himself and doesn't know he looks terrible, so I mustn't let him realize it,* she scolded herself.

"I'm so glad to see you back here, Mark," she murmured close to his ear. His eyes were closed, still recovering from the anesthetics, his breathing was shallow and rapid, and she realized he must be exhausted. She was dying to know what happened but didn't ask him. She didn't even ask the trivial, "How do you feel?" She knew the answer to that…

She pulled the chair close to the bed and sat next to him, stroking his arm that lay motionless on top of the blanket covering him. Her eyes were continually shifting from his face to the monitor that stood slightly behind the bed, beeping softly.

'Still life', if someone were to paint us now, that is what they'd call the picture, Olivia thought, as her mind soared above them, looking at the tableau below it. Her hand stroking him, and the monitors, were the only moving elements, the beeping of the machines—the only sound in the room.

About an hour later, Mark opened his eyes. He sighed, and

immediately, a grimace shrouded his face, and he moaned. His eyes focused on her. He attempted a small smile; it hovered for a second over his pale lips and died.

"Hi," he said, his voice hoarse.

"Welcome back," she whispered, her eyes moist, "What happened?"

"Pneumothorax," he said, his voice barely audible, the mask blearing the sound.

"The lung collapsed? While they were treating you?"

A brief nod was all he answered.

Though she was not religious, the quotation from the book of Job popped into her mind: "*For the thing which I fear cometh upon me, and that which I am afraid of cometh unto me.*"

***

Emma and Philip arrived in the early afternoon. They were shocked to see Mark in such a state and late to cover it up.

"What happened?" Emma wailed. "What did they do to you?"

Mark looked at her, saying nothing.

"And where is the doctor? Why isn't he here? Why is nobody doing anything?" She sounded hysterical.

"When they brought Mark in, the nurse said the doctor would be here later but didn't say when that will be."

"Well, go and ask her again!" she snapped, her voice raised.

"Excuse me?" Olivia was shocked. "If you think it's necessary, why don't you go and ask? I don't think it's wise—but if you want to—suit yourself."

"You're stupid! Do you want my father to die?" Emma screeched.

"What did you say?" Olivia was stunned. She couldn't believe she heard Emma correctly.

"I said you're stupid!" she repeated her words, her stance belligerent. "And you are! We must act to save him! You'd let him die if you do nothing *now*!" Her tone rose further, her hysteria out of control.

Still shaken, Olivia got up and went to the closet. She took out the trolly, then went to the bathroom, brought her things from there, and packed them.

"I'm sorry, Mark. I won't stay here for such abuse. Your beloved daughter can take care of you better than I can, apparently. So, I'll go back home and let her do it."

"Livy, don't go!" Mark was fighting for breath.

Olivia looked at him, tears streaming down her cheeks.

"If you leave, I'll die!" he said weakly but clearly.

She shook her head.

Then Mark turned to Emma.

"Apologize immediately!"

Olivia didn't know how he found the strength to command her so forcefully.

"Yes, Daddy, whatever you say," she replied, sounding like a scolded little girl, afraid of the adult she has just angered.

She turned to Olivia, and her stance changed to one of haughtiness, her face angry and hostile.

"He wants me to apologize, so, here, I apologize. And you accept it, right? So—all is well now, agreed? See, Dad? All is well!" She hurried to the chair that Olivia vacated and sat down close to her father, snatching his hand.

"I'm sorry," Olivia said. "That's not an apology. And no—I do not accept it."

"What? You—" Emma was stopped by her husband, who pulled her out of the chair.

"Enough!" he said gruffly. "Let's go. We'll take a walk to cool off. We'll be back later." The last sentence was said in Mark's direction.

They went outside.

Olivia went to the bathroom to wash her face and returned to his side to kiss him goodbye.

"Livy, please... I know for certain... If you leave, I'll die..." he repeated. His eyes were willing her to understand the seriousness of his words and to relent.

She hesitated, torn between the desire to flee and his expressed need. Then the internal battle was decided, and she nodded.

And she put the trolly away.

Olivia came back to sit by his bed. He raised his hand weakly to place it on her arm.

"I'm so sorry," he whispered. "I guess anxiety turned to hysteria... it's just too stressful for her... Emma didn't mean it."

He was trying to defend his 'little girl.'

"Yes, she meant. I have no doubt what she thinks of me now. Being hysterical reduced her inhibitions and revealed the hostility she tried to cover up to please you, but nothing justifies such uncouth behavior. Anyway, don't worry—I'll stay because *you* want me to."

"Please, don't get into a fight with her when they return. I don't have the strength to deal with such arguments right now."

"I'll do my best," Olivia said.

Mark nodded and closed his eyes. *The drama was too much for him,* she thought, and sat quietly, not moving, to let him sleep and begin to recuperate.

He dozed fitfully. Olivia kept vigil, making sure that he was breathing properly and that the saturation was not dropping.

The doctor came for a brief visit. He said there was quite a large pneumothorax, but he expected it to drain soon and heal, so they'd be able to leave. For now—the drain had to remain in place, so he wanted Mark to stay in the hospital.

"For how long?" Olivia asked.

The doctor shrugged. "I don't know yet, we'll see how he improves. He's not young, you know, a lot can happen."

He was stating the obvious.

Olivia hoped their stay would not be overextended. He'd recover much faster at home, by the ocean.

Emma and Philip returned in the evening for a short stay.

"How are you, guys? Was the doctor here for a visit? Any news?" Philip asked.

Mark opened his eyes briefly, then closed them again tiredly, half of his face covered by the plastic oxygen mask.

"A pneumothorax, quite a large one; the drain will not be removed until they see improvement," Olivia said quietly, her face reflecting the apprehension that filled her heart.

She got up, vacating the seat close to Mark's bed. "I'll use the interlude and go to the hotel, take a shower, and come right back," Olivia said to Mark quietly, and kissed his hot forehead. He nodded.

She uttered "Bye." and left, not waiting for a reply.

***

Olivia walked the few blocks to their hotel, oblivious to her surroundings, her mind still in the hospital. She hoped Mark would be all right and that Philip would do his best to keep his wife in check. She wasn't sure his best was enough, as the recent events proved.

What was the explosion really about? What made Emma so aggressive and unrestrained? Was it anxiety, as Mark had supposed? Or was it her anger that there was another woman that he cared about? Did that threaten her position? She was not going to fight for the right to take care of Mark. Not with his daughter. Mark understood her decision to avoid escalating the fight when she prepared to leave, and he made his choice clear and evident: He wanted her to stay by his side.

Olivia decided it didn't matter what Emma's reason was. Nothing justified what Emma said and the way she acted. Olivia might have forgiven Emma if a sincere apology was offered when she returned, with either a heartfelt acknowledgment of guilt or a genuine attempt to explain. Olivia would never forget and would forever distrust her, but some semblance of civility must be maintained. Olivia doubted she would receive an apology of any kind.

A different reflection penetrated her mind: *How will Emma explain what happened?* People tended to shift the blame to others rather than assume responsibility for blunders. Will Emma present what happened as Olivia's fault? She supposed Emma would. *Do I honestly care? Definitely not,* she concluded.

However, for Mark's sake, she'd be civil.

***

Olivia grabbed a sandwich at the deli, close to the hotel, and took the elevator to their room. The quick shower revived her. Feeling revitalized, she used the room's machine and made a cup of coffee. Taking her sandwich, she sat by the window. She ate slowly, not hungry but aware that some food in her stomach was necessary. She felt so desperate and lonely.

Stop it! She scolded herself. *What's all this self-pity? You're miserable? So what? Mark is in terrible shape, and you need to buckle up and do all you can to help him fight his way back to health! And you're the one he wants here!*

The pep talk helped. Olivia smiled at her reflection in the enormous window and finished the coffee. She looked at the pristine bed with longing, then turned her back on the temptation and walked to the door.

Half an hour later, she was at the hospital again.

***

Mark's face lit up when he saw her. *Did he think I wasn't coming back?* Olivia thought. *Maybe he believed I'd take the opportunity and walk away?* She came close to kiss him, but Emma was blocking her access. And she didn't move.

"Excuse me," Olivia said, coldly polite.

No reaction.

"Emma!" Philip barked, calling her to him.

She moved away unwillingly, avoiding looking at Olivia.

"You're back!" Mark said, relieved. "What took you so long?"

Olivia looked at her watch. "It was less than two hours, Mark, but I missed you, too!"

She smiled, and he made an effort to smile back, but a deep cough caught him, and she could see the immense pain it was causing him. He tried to raise himself to a sitting position, and she supported his back. Black phlegm appeared on his lips. She found a box of tissues on his nightstand and handed it to him. He coughed again, and the tissue turned black and moist. Groaning and breathless, he sank back to the pillow.

The phlegm didn't seem like just a matter of a pneumothorax. Olivia didn't know what the coughing indicated, but she didn't like it.

Some dinner was brought for Mark a little later. He didn't want any. Olivia managed to convince him to swallow a few teaspoons of yogurt, but he agreed to nothing else. He was weak and helpless. Maybe a good night's sleep would do him good. She hoped he would sleep well.

She dimmed the light in the room and went to brush her teeth.

"No, no, no," he said, breathing hard. "Go back to the hotel. Come back in the morning!"

Olivia shook her head.

"Please, Livy, you need your strength, too!" he whispered.

"Enough!" Olivia responded passionately. "Right now, it's your life versus my comfort. So, the equation is clear, and so is the answer."

Mark stopped arguing. Not because he agreed with her, but because he didn't have the strength to continue, Olivia surmised.

She took his hand in hers and softened her tone. "I'll be fine, Mark, don't worry about me. I'll sleep much better here, on the chair next to you than in the lovely bed in the fancy hotel. Believe me!"

Mark pressed her hand in reply.

Emma and Philip were still in the room, leaning on the cabinet in the corner, whispering to each other. Their tones changed gradually, and Olivia heard them argue. She looked at them. Philip moved away from the cabinet, extending his arm to his wife. She moved reluctantly toward her father's bed. Olivia moved to the window to allow her privacy. Emma leaned down, close to her father, and spoke to him in hushed tones. His eyes were closed. She patted his shoulder, but he did not respond. Emma shook him lightly; he opened his eyes, trying to focus on her face. Then he nodded weakly and closed his eyes again. She straightened, turned away, and walked to the door.

"Bye," she said reluctantly, inaudibly, her back to the room.

Philip turned and raised his hand in a weak wave.

"See you tomorrow," he said and followed his wife.

Olivia arranged the armchair closer to his bed again so that she'd be able to see him, and he could see her. She checked the monitor, the drip into his arm, listened to the sounds of the suction pump attached to the drain coming out of his lung, sucking cloudy yellowish fluids which dripped into a small plastic bag. All seemed to be working properly. She sat wearily, her phone in her hand, and closed her eyes with a sigh.

The night nurse came in to check Mark's temperature and replace the drip bag.

"He's still feverish," Olivia said, her tone accusatory as she looked at what the nurse scribbled in Mark's chart. It said 103°F… The nurse nodded, saying nothing.

He opened his eyes for a moment. He looked at Olivia as if he was making sure she was still there and closed them again tiredly.

The nurse turned the light off before she left the room, but enough light was coming through the glass wall between the room and the unit in which it was located and the open door.

"Good night, my love," Olivia said quietly. He moved his hand slightly, as if trying to wave at her. His eyes remained closed.

49

Olivia hardly slept. Hospital noises woke her up every time she drifted into a snooze. She managed to nap again when the noise subsided, only to be awakened again. Early in the morning, the light streaming through the huge window and the changing of the shifts taking place woke her, and she went to wash up.

Mark's eyes were open when she reentered the room.

"Got some sleep?" she asked tenderly.

Mark tried to smile under the oxygen mask still attached to his mouth and nose. It seemed more like a grimace than a smile. "On and off," he said, behind the mask.

"Let's hope there will be a significant change today, so we can abandon this place and go home." She tried to sound cheerful, but then she stroked his face and felt his fever burning.

"I'll be right back," she told him and left, looking for a nurse.

***

The nurses' station was empty. She turned, aiming to search for help. The door behind her opened, and a sharp voice asked her, "Can I help you?"

"I hope so!" Olivia said. "Good morning, I'm Professor Wallace's partner. I just checked, and I think his fever is very high. He seems lethargic, unresponsive." She sounded apprehensive, her eyes imploring.

"We'll be coming to check all patients' temperatures in a few minutes, before shift change. Go back, and we'll be with you shortly."

She returned to Mark's side, concerned.

"I think your fever is high," she said, touching his forehead again.

"I know it is," Mark responded weakly. "I can feel it."

"The nurses will be here soon, at least that's what the nurse I met told me," Olivia said, attempting to reassure him.

Mark nodded listlessly.

Time passed, and no one came. She was about to search for help again when she heard voices outside. Two young nurses entered. They went about their work, hardly looking at the patient. One of them checked his temperature but continued her conversation with her friend.

"How high is it?" Olivia asked pointedly.

"A hundred and three," the young nurse replied, indifferent.

Olivia's heart sank. *Does it mean an infection? Or was it related to the treatment he received?* She didn't know enough… the former, she guessed.

"When will the doctor be here?" she asked.

"In a couple of hours, probably," came the vague response.

***

Half an hour passed, and a group of nurses entered. Shift change, Olivia realized. The nurse in charge of the night shift spoke in an efficient, professional tone, exchanging information with her colleagues, not addressing the patient.

Olivia decided to interfere. "Excuse me," she said in the same quiet voice the nurses used. "He has a high fever, and he's very weak. Can you please tell me when the doctor will be here?"

They all looked at her coldly. Some of the younger ones, Olivia noticed, seemed shocked by her audacity. The nurse in charge looked at the chart, then turned to Olivia, her tone softer. "Soon. We'll be doing the rounds soon, and the doctors will check him."

"Thank you," Olivia mumbled haltingly, relieved to get some acknowledgment.

"But you can't stay here. You need to leave right away! Before the doctors arrive. You're not allowed to be here." One of the staff nurses said, her tone harsh and cold.

Olivia looked at her, searching for a shred of sympathy, finding none.

"You can return at eleven a.m," said one of the other nurses, a little compassion in her tone, realizing Olivia's distress.

They were still looking at her, expecting her to leave immediately. Olivia wanted to say she'd leave soon, but noticing the mounting antagonism, she nodded her head and went to Mark to tell him she had to leave and would return as quickly as she could.

She was desperate. What was going on? What kind of treatment was this? Didn't they care?

She left the hospital, her head bent low, her eyes streaming. She felt devastated, totally powerless. Knowing that she was entirely in their cold hands, she felt like screaming in anger. She entered the hotel, dejected, her shoulders bowed. She smelled coffee and turned automatically to the cafeteria. It seemed a good idea to have a cup before she went up to their suite.

Olivia chose a quiet corner and waited, her elbows on the table, her hands holding her face, her eyes unfocused, staring forward. A waitress approached her, ready to take her order, but seeing Olivia's doleful eyes— she asked, "Are you OK, ma'am? Do you need help?"

"Thanks," Olivia said, looking up at the kind face with warm eyes. "I just came back from a long night at the hospital, and I'm worried, that's all. I'll be fine. Can I have some coffee, please?"

"Sure, honey. How about some breakfast, too?"

Olivia shook her head. "No, thanks."

"A croissant, maybe? They're freshly baked!" She genuinely seemed to care.

Olivia was touched.

"OK. A croissant would be nice." She attempted to smile at the older woman.

The coffee and a fresh, warm croissant arrived quickly, with butter and strawberry jam. Olivia took a sip, and holding the hot cup in her hands, she gazed ahead, her mind reeling.

What can I do? The thought kept tumbling in her mind. She needed to do something. His reaction to the treatment was not what she expected. She didn't think it was the usual reaction. Something was wrong; she was sure. But there was no doctor to talk to; no information was provided. Can she demand to meet the doctor who treated him and ask for explanations? And when will they remove the drain? It was causing him so much pain and inconvenience! And what was that black phlegm she saw yesterday?

Well, she decided she would insist on getting some answers. And one thing was sure, Olivia decided: She would not be kicked out of there again!

She signed the bill and left a generous tip on the table. She left.

Back in their lonely, impersonal suite, she went to take a shower. Standing under the pounding stream, she felt her mind clear. Assertive-Olivia reappeared. It must have been the tiring, sleepless night and the emotionally distressing day that sapped her energies and left her devoid of resilience, she thought. *No more!* She decided. Dressing quickly, she put some makeup on. No reason to look neglected and bedraggled, she reprimanded herself.

Walking resolutely, she returned to the hospital before ten a.m. The automatic doors to the department were closed, and no one answered when she pressed the bell. She tried again, with the same result. The staff had magnetic cards they could open the doors with, and visiting hours began at eleven a.m., she remembered, so they were not answering. Luckily, an orderly with a keycard approached the door. She followed him in, and he did not rebuke her. She walked confidently to Mark's room. A nurse called to her. Olivia turned; her gaze was ice cold and arrogant.

"Yes?" she asked haughtily, her tone signaling, 'Don't mess with me.'

"Oh, it's you," the young nurse mumbled. Olivia nodded and walked on.

"Finally!" Mark greeted her. "I missed you!"

Was he breathing better? She noticed they removed the mask from his face, replacing it with a thin, flexible hose providing oxygen only to his nostrils. His voice was less raspy.

"I missed you, too, so I didn't wait till eleven and snuck in; the doors are locked, and they do not answer when you ring the bell. Luckily, someone with a magnetic badge entered, and I took my chance and followed. Were the doctors here?"

"Yes. The resident doctor told me that Campbell said that the treatment was successful, and they are sure they destroyed the tumor they aimed at. But the pneumothorax complicated everything, and they encountered a few more problems. Probably an infection, too. That's why my fever rose. They started antibiotics and gave me something to bring the fever down. They expect my situation to improve in a few days."

"All right, you're strong. So, it's just a slight delay. You'll beat it, I'm sure! When will they take the drain out?"

"A few more days." He tried to sit up straighter and grimaced in pain. Another coughing attack seized him. His thin frame shuddered intensely. Olivia was ready with the box of tissues and saw him wiping black phlegm again.

"Did you tell them about this?" she asked.

"No." He shook his head. "It's a reaction to the treatment."

They sat silently, holding hands. Mark needed his strength, and Olivia tried not to tire him. Mark dozed between coughing spells, and she used these pauses to keep in touch with family and friends back home. No conversations, only texted messages, so as not to disturb him. She needed the contact. Though only electronic, it provided her with an anchor. Something to keep her moored to reality. Any contact was priceless in the cold, uncaring situation she found herself in. And when her mother or her sons wrote back their encouragement, their messages warm and empathic, offering to help any way she wanted—she felt her constricted heart expand again. They conveyed complete confidence in her ability to deal with the situation, boosting her falling spirits. Sarah's messages were supportive and full of desire to help. She even offered to come to New York and be with her when she was not by Mark's side.

Emma and Philip arrived in the afternoon. They seemed well-rested and buoyant. Olivia moved aside to let Emma sit by her father and sat with Philip by the window.

"How is he?" Philip asked her quietly.

"Not great," Olivia replied. "He caught some infection here and has a fever and a terrible cough."

"Not good signs," he remarked, shaking his head.

"No. Not good signs," Olivia concurred.

"Were the doctors here? What did they say?"

"Campbell, the specialist who treated him, didn't show his face. The physicians in the department said it would take a few days, and his lungs will recover." Olivia's face betrayed her skepticism.

"Let's hope so." Philip sounded optimistic. "We do have to get back to SF in a few days."

"What did you do today?" Olivia asked, keeping the conversation light, her eyes on Mark, checking the signs.

"Did some shopping in the morning, walked around, visited the Frick Collection on our way to the hospital. Amazing! You should go and see it yourself! It's not far from here. In fact—why not do it *now*, when we are here and can look after Mark? Or go to the hotel, get some sleep. You need to conserve your strength, or you'll be of no use to him!" He looked at her, his face open and honest. He seriously meant it.

"I was at the hotel in the morning, but I'm too restless to sleep. And I'm certainly not up to going to a museum or a gallery right now," Olivia answered candidly.

They were silently watching the world outside, passing by their window, indifferent and uncaring. They heard Emma talk incessantly, Mark nodding from time to time or answering in monosyllables. His eyes were closing more and more often, Olivia saw. He was getting tired. But he didn't tell his daughter that.

"I'll go to the cafeteria for some coffee. Can I get anything for anyone?" Olivia asked, no longer able to sit and listen to the vacuous verbal stream.

Mark shook his head.

"No, thanks, we had a huge lunch." Philip said.

Emma didn't bother to answer and kept talking.

Olivia walked to the elevators, deep in thought. She wouldn't say anything about his need to rest; she made up her mind. His daughter should understand this by herself. And if not, it was up to her father to say something. If pleasing her—or avoiding hurting her—was more important to Mark than his own needs, there was nothing Olivia could do. Whatever she said, she knew, would be interpreted as offensive...

She bought coffee and a salad for herself and cold chocolate milk for Mark. Maybe he'd agree to sip a little. She returned to the department a few minutes later, carrying the food. She heard the terrible, deep, wet cough while still outside his room. Hurrying in, she noticed his hand signaling for a tissue. She placed the food on the small table and rushed forward. Supporting Mark's back, to help him sit up, she plucked a tissue from the box by the bed and handed it to him. After a while, the cough subsided, and Olivia helped him lie down again.

"Oh, that sounded terrible, Daddy," Emma said in her little girl's voice. Her face could not hide the disgust she felt.

They left when Mark's dinner was brought in, promising to return the next day. He did not touch the food.

50

No one tried to kick her out any more. In the mornings, when the shifts changed, she provided vital information to the nurses. When the doctors came on their rounds, she made herself scarce. When they entered the room next to Mark's, she left his room and found a place to sit, out of sight. She suspected they knew she was there but said nothing, to avoid conflict.

It took three more days for them to see that he was not improving. Quite the opposite… his cough worsened. He refused to take the ibuprofen that the doctors wanted him to swallow to reduce his fever; he wanted to know how high his temperature actually was. Or how strong the infection was… it still reached one hundred and two or three every day.

Olivia decided not to leave when the doctors came the next day. To ask questions. She wanted to know when they'd remove the drain and whether the pneumothorax vanished. But mostly, she wanted to know their prognosis.

No one asked her to leave when they arrived. And although they responded to her questions, they had no definite answers to any of them. Mark made an effort and tried to talk with them, suggest treatment.

"We use steroids in cases similar to mine," he said calmly. "And administer diuretics, like Furosemide, as treatment of edema, which I already have."

"Well, we don't do that… that's not in our protocol," one of the attending physicians replied. "Unless the edema is associated with congestive heart failure, and thank God, you don't have that."

"And there is no indication whatsoever for the administration of steroids," added another doctor, haughtily.

If they are so obtuse, I'm going to be rude, Olivia decided in her desperation. She trusted his immense knowledge and could see they were not listening. Do they have some other treatment to help him?

"So, what *do* you intend to do?" she asked, her tone assertive, almost aggressive.

"We're considering transferring him to ICU," said the distinguished, kind-faced, elderly physician she assumed was the most senior doctor among them.

"ICU?" Olivia repeated. "He needs intensive care? Why?"

"Well, he's not responding to the antibiotics as well as we expected, and the lung infection reduces the saturation of oxygen in his blood. We may have to intubate," he replied patiently, avoiding medical details. "Besides," he added with a small smile, "The doctors in ICU are much better suited to dealing with an acute situation such as his than we are, and he'll receive more attention, day and night."

Olivia nodded, not knowing for sure if that was a good or a bad thing. *But,* she thought, *maybe they'll be more willing to listen to Mark. After a week, maybe things will improve…*

She shared her thoughts with Mark when they left. He just nodded. Olivia assumed he was not very hopeful.

***

Three hours later, two orderlies walked in. "We'll take you to ICU now," one of them said. It took them some time to unhook him from the monitor, transfer the drip, drain, and pump, and hook Mark to a portable oxygen generator.

Olivia packed their trolly in advance and was ready to leave when they were.

***

The intensive care unit was quiet. A single nurse attended the department's nurses' station in; the patients' rooms spread like a fan around the hub. She stood up when the orderlies entered, steering Mark's bed.

The nurse glanced at the papers they handed her.

"Room seven," she said. Turning to Olivia, she told her assertively, "Please wait outside until we settle him."

Olivia went to one of the empty rooms and sat in a chair that the nurse could not see. When she heard the orderlies leave, she went to room seven. Mark seemed somewhat comfortable. *Well, as comfortable as one can get with so many tubes entering his body,* she contemplated.

She went to him, not saying a word. He opened his eyes when he heard her.

"I'm so sorry for causing you all this trouble." He sounded anguished.

"Are you kidding?" Olivia gazed at him, pain in her eyes for the shame she thought she detected in his voice. "Where else do you think I want to be right now?"

Then an understanding hit her: he was afraid she was not fully committed to their relationship. That after just a year together, she'd leave him rather than get stuck with a sick person once more. Especially after the ordeal she went through with Elliot. Mark would never express these fears, so as not to reveal weakness or need, but they were on his mind nonetheless.

A worn-out smile drifted for a second across his lips at her response.

"I must admit that seeing your eyes whenever I search for them, makes me want to fight on. I'm so tired… the cough is so painful; it's tearing my insides every time. But I want to live. I want to return to our life together… if not for you—I would have given up already." Another bout of coughing forced him to stop talking, and he was fighting for breath when it ended.

"Rest, Mark… rest. Catch your breath. I'll always be here. As long as you want me by your side, I'll be here!"

She kissed his forehead and realized it was hot and sweaty. His fever was still high.

Groaning, Mark lay back and closed his eyes, his hand still gripping hers. His breath eased a little, and his body relaxed. Olivia hoped he dozed. Slowly, she took her phone out and, one-handed, checked for messages. There were several. Adam was worried she wasn't taking good care of herself. Tom wanted to know if there was anything they needed. Her mother asked when they were coming back. Sarah offered again to come and be with her when she was free. Sheila wanted information. Sophie sent love and begged her to say what she could do to help.

She began to answer when Emma and Philip appeared at the door. Olivia tried to signal "keep quiet" with a finger against her lips, but she was too late.

"Why didn't you call to let us know they're transferring him? Why was the transfer necessary? Do they think his condition is deteriorating?" Emma entered, firing questions and accusations in a shrill voice. *No hello, good afternoon…*

Mark opened his eyes with a sigh.

Walking to his side, Emma kept talking. "How are you, Daddy? How do you feel? Are you still feverish? What are they giving you now—have they changed the medication they give you?"

Olivia moved away from the bed to the window and looked down at the busy avenue. They were now facing a different view. Life hurried by, unaware of the pain and suffering it passed. As if those inside the building were in a parallel universe.

"Hi, Olivia." Philip stood next to her.

She nodded without averting her eyes, saying nothing.

"Did you have a chance to speak with the doctors?" he asked mildly, following her gaze.

"Yes, and it was very frustrating. They don't know what to do, but they don't admit that. Mark tried to suggest a treatment, and they just ignored him; it's not in their protocol of treating patients in his condition, they said."

"What do you mean by 'they ignored him'?" Emma's raised voice sounded belligerent.

"Sh… sh… sh…" Mark tried to curb the storm he saw coming.

"What do you mean by 'they ignored him'?" Emma repeated her question aggressively.

"Lower your voice," Olivia said coldly. "It's just that. They ignored him. Mark seems to know what needs to be done. They do not. But still— they won't heed his advice. I don't know if it is because they never listen to patients, or because they are too arrogant, or they don't trust his knowledge."

"And you did *nothing*?" Emma's voice rose again, her disdain apparent.

Olivia looked at her, astounded by the rudeness.

"I'll go and deal with it." Emma said haughtily.

"Stay here!" Mark barked. "Don't exacerbate the situation. Maybe the doctors here, at the ICU, will be more willing to listen," he added in a milder tone.

She sat down again and started talking. Olivia tuned out. She thought she heard Emma say something about their visit to the Museum of Modern Art.

Mark was fighting to keep his eyes open. When it was too much for him, and he closed them, Emma called him, shaking his hand. Olivia couldn't stand it and wished Mark would say something, even though she knew he could not admonish his 'girls.' And, as usual with him, he didn't.

Not my place to interfere, she decided, though she was seething inside.

"I'll go down and get some coffee while you're here," she said to Philip. "Want anything?"

He shook his head and mumbled, "Thanks."

"I'll be back soon," she said to Mark and went out.

***

Olivia saw Emma and Philip in the hall, outside Mark's room. The senior physician arrived when she was getting the coffee, Philip said, and asked them to leave the room and wait outside.

A few minutes later, the doctor came out, his face grim.

"Are you his family?" he asked. "I need to talk to you."

"Livy!" Mark called her.

"I'll be with you in a minute," she said to the doctor and went to Mark.

"The physician just told me they might have to anesthetize and intubate me. I asked him to wait with it. I'm doing my best—coughing most of the mucus out. He asked who'll be in charge if they'll have to intubate despite my efforts, and something goes wrong. If they can't wake me later... he needed a name, someone who'd be my guardian or custodian when I can't make decisions for myself. I gave him your name. I want you to promise me you won't let them bring me back a cripple. You know I don't want to live dependent on others. So, promise me!" he grabbed her hand and held it tightly.

"Mark!" Olivia cried out, her heart bursting. "No... Mark!"

"Don't argue... just promise me!" She didn't know where he found the strength to say it so forcefully.

She nodded, unable to speak. Her throat hurt from the tears she was trying hard not to shed in front of him.

"Say it! Promise me!" He demanded desperately.

"I do... I promise," Olivia whispered brokenly, and Mark released her hand.

"I'll be right back," she managed to say as she left the room hurriedly, barely holding her tears back, looking for a place to cry.

"Can you join us, please?" The doctor sounded impatient. She forgot all about him...

She swallowed hard, her eyes brimming, and walked over to where he was standing with Emma and Philip.

"I started telling them and will reiterate for you. Your husband's lungs are not supplying enough oxygen. We may have to intubate, so we'll need to anesthetize him. There are always risks in such situations, and sometimes weaning intubated patients is problematic."

He looked from one to the other, ascertaining they followed what he said. Olivia bit her lower lip hard to hold in the gasps that threatened to escape.

"He asked me to postpone the procedure, and I agreed to wait a while. But I told him that if his condition deteriorates—and it can happen quickly and dramatically—I need the name of the person who'll make the decisions for him should he be unable to make them."

He turned to Olivia. "You are Professor Olivia Anderson, right? He named you as that person."

Olivia nodded, unable to speak.

"What? What did you say? It can't be! I'm his daughter!" Emma was screaming hysterically, waving her hands in the air.

The doctor raised his hand commandingly, shutting her up.

All sound died throughout the ICU. Only the beeping monitors continued unimpeded and uncaring. She saw the nurses and other personnel glued to the tableau they created, frozen—horror and shock on their faces.

"You should understand—it's not my decision to make. That's what Professor Wallace wants, and his decision is final, as far as the hospital is concerned. His signature verifies his will." The doctor looked at Emma, his disapproval apparent.

"She's not even his wife! She hardly knows him! He's my father!" She screeched, standing belligerently in front of the doctor.

Then she turned to Olivia, her face red and contorted. "*You? You* will decide *when* my father will die? *You* will decide *if* my father will live?" Arrogance, hysteria, and aggression were mixed up in her tone.

Olivia was overwhelmed. She had yet to deal with the agony of knowing there is a possibility that the man she loves so much may die, and now she had to deal with this cruel outburst in front of the whole staff.

Despite the anguish in her breaking heart, the tears choking her throat, and the shame she felt because of Emma's appalling display, she held her head high. She promised Mark she would not leave him. As long as he wanted her there, she would not desert him and would not be chased away by anyone. Not even his daughter.

Philip understood the devastation his wife created, and pulled her to the exit. She resisted at first, but he leaned closer to her and said something. The tone sounded sharp, and she walked out.

Olivia wanted to walk into one of the empty rooms and cry to let her torment flow out of her body, but she thought Mark heard the exchange and might be distressed. She needed to be there for him and returned to his side.

"I'm so sorry, Livy," Mark said weakly. "I'm so very sorry."

So, he heard the abysmal exchange.

"It's OK, don't worry," she replied through her anguish, her throat clenched, and her voice cracked. *He has enough to deal with!* The thought repeated itself in her mind.

"It was inexcusable, and wholly uncalled for; it was my decision. She shouldn't have taken her frustration on you, and should have respected my decision!"

Olivia nodded and tried to smile. It came out as a grimace more than a smile.

"She's just hysterical with worry." As ever, he tried to defend his daughter.

Olivia's temper flared. "Stop it, Mark! Nothing excuses such behaviors! *She's* worried? *Really*? What did she think *I* was feeling? What do *you* think I feel? And right after you dropped a bomb on me, telling me *you may die* from the intubation? Making me the one who'll decide whether you live or die?" She lost control, and her tears coursed down her face. She was fighting to regain command of her emotions, failing miserably.

"No, Livy, please, don't cry. You're tearing me to pieces, please, Livy." He was distraught.

"I'm sorry… I'm sorry. I lost control," Olivia mumbled and walked to the sink to wash her face. "I'm sorry."

"You're right, of course. Nothing excuses what Emma said. Or how she behaved. I can't believe she allowed herself to erupt and rave like this."

Olivia nodded, saying nothing.

She sipped her coffee, cold now and tasteless.

She looked up and made a face.

"That good, ha?" Mark smiled weakly.

"Try to rest," Olivia said. "Quite a tiring visit."

He closed his eyes. The remnants of the smile were still turning up the corners of his mouth.

***

Olivia was glad they did not return that evening. She didn't even go to the hotel, she realized. *In the morning, I'll go and take a shower and change my clothes,* Olivia thought. She ran out of clean underwear and needed to wash a few shirts too.

She arranged the armchair next to his bed after the nurses finished the evening procedures. His fever was still high, oxygen saturation low, his cough still terrible. But he was fighting to clear his lungs, not giving in. Not willing to provide the doctors with the justification to intubate him.

The pain of coughing with the drain stuck in his lung was excruciating, she knew. Yet, he sat up in bed to clear his lungs as much as he could. She was there to help him sit up and lie down again when the bouts were over.

She dimmed the light and sat down. "Good night, Mark," she whispered.

He smiled for a second and wiggled his fingers.

He woke up several times during the night. Whenever he did, he found her looking at him. Her eyes were open, encouraging, and loving.

She remembered that when Adam was born, she woke up the moment she sensed that he began to move in his cot, aware that he was about to wake up before he actually did. And she was ready to go to him the moment he needed her. She did the same now.

51

Olivia was apprehensive. Two more days passed, ten days since they arrived, and instead of improving, she thought Mark's condition continued to deteriorate. Slowly but continually, he grew weaker with each passing day. And he wasn't eating. She managed to convince him to swallow a few teaspoons of yogurt, but not much more. Not a proper diet for a grown man; and despite the lack of food, his body was puffed up. He was retaining fluids, the edema spreading.

Orderlies came three times a day with Mark's meals and must have seen the tray was untouched every time they came back to take the tray. They did nothing with the information. No nutritionist came to discuss diets with Mark.

The staff around them—doctors and nurses alike—seemed indifferent, not only the orderlies. Did they give up on him? She was not ready to accept that, but they were not fighting to improve the situation. They continued with the same treatment, hoping it would work eventually, though it seemed futile.

Mark looked worn out. How long would he manage to hang on? There was no change in sight, and the threat of intubation loomed menacingly in her mind.

The morning rounds began, and Mark sat up in bed. He wanted to talk about changing the protocol. He tried that before, but they were convinced their method would work, given time. Maybe now, after a few ineffective days, they would listen.

The physician in charge checked the charts.

"No change," Mark said.

The physician shrugged, her plain-featured face blank and indifferent. She looked at him for a second and was about to turn and leave when Mark asked her, "The antibiotics you're administering don't work, so—what do you intend to do?"

"I don't know," she said, shaking her head.

"You don't know? What treatment are you considering? What are the options you're thinking about?" Mark asked, his voice insistent. "It's obviously *not* an infection. It may be a form of acute lung reaction that would respond to steroids."

She shrugged again.

So, they are not going to change the ineffective procedures? Olivia was frustrated.

"Why not try Furosemide, then?" Mark asked her. "It can't do any harm in my condition, and as you can see, the edema is spreading. You know what it may lead to!"

"As I told you, we only administer diuretics to patients with congestive heart failure, and you don't have that," she said it patiently, as if speaking to an errant child.

"I know what you said. But the edema is growing. It indicates the loss of albumin and may lead to pressure sores. It may have already led to the formation of pleural effusion, which is why I find it so difficult to breathe! Don't you think it is an ominous sign, *especially* if there is no heart failure involved? It is the hallmark of catastrophic deterioration!"

"Maybe," she said, unconvinced. "There is no indication that Furosemide may help you."

"Well, we tried your way for several days now. We know it is *not* working. Maybe we should try *my* way for a few days and see if I improve?"

"OK, I'll give you a ten-milligram injection, just to prove you're wrong," she said, her tone indicating she was trying to get rid of a substantial inconvenience.

"Ten milligrams won't do it! Not for a man my size, and not in my condition!"

"That's as much as I can do." With that, she turned and left.

"Unbelievable," Mark muttered.

"Why won't they listen? They don't know what to do and how to treat you, so why won't they try it your way?" Olivia asked, agitated.

"I don't know," Mark sighed, shaking his head. "Maybe it's, 'Don't tell us what to do'? Or 'We know best'? Or some other type of ego trip? I simply don't know."

"When will they take the drain out? They haven't even set a time for that. Is this something else they don't know? I can see how much pain it causes you every time you cough, and it would be a sign of *something* getting better!" Olivia was beside herself.

"It's frustrating: things like that, behaviors such as these, would never happen in my hospital," Mark said glumly.

"I can't believe she acknowledged that their treatment protocol doesn't work and then said she doesn't know what to do!" Olivia answered, annoyed and frustrated.

***

It was eight p.m. already when Emma and Philip arrived. Olivia looked at her watch. *How long do they intend to stay?* She was so tired, and she was sure that Mark was, too.

"That's it! We've finished all our shopping and the museums we planned to see!" Philip said merrily. Olivia thought he meant to be funny or sarcastic, but it came out lame. Saying this in front of Mark a few days after being told he might not come out of the hospital alive was somewhat callous.

They were leaving early tomorrow morning so this evening would be their last visit. Emma and Philip spent their mornings walking the streets, visiting museums, going shopping, then they went to their hotel for a shower and some rest and came to see Mark.

They must have noticed the deterioration in his condition, but they didn't change their intentions and were going home as planned. Olivia couldn't understand the absurdity.

And Clair didn't come at all. Her sister must have told her their father was in a terrible state, still—she didn't arrive. Olivia couldn't understand that, either. They had to know he was in a life-threatening situation… Or perhaps they didn't? *Not possible,* she decided. *Emma heard the doctor… that's why she exploded.*

It's none of your business, she chastised herself.

Emma sat next to her father, chattering, her husband behind her. Olivia sat at the corner, going over emails and text messages. Tuning out the prattle, she waited for their departure.

It was torture. Mark tried to keep his eyes open, but his eyelids kept dropping. Then, he didn't even try. He lay exhausted, his eyes closed, his breathing shallow. Emma posed questions, expecting answers, not realizing how tired he was…

At nine fifteen, Olivia asked, tiredly, "I hope you won't mind if I dimmed the lights?"

"Not at all! It's time we left anyway." Philip said. Was it a tone of relief she heard in his voice? "We still need to pack everything," he added.

Emma disagreed. "We'll stay a while longer. Maybe Daddy will wake up again, and I'll be able to say goodbye properly." She sounded petulant.

They argued by the window. Olivia looked at Mark and hoped he was asleep. She closed her eyes, trying to doze, but the sounds of their argument intruded on her thoughts and bothered her. A few minutes later, Philip managed to convince Emma to leave. She returned to Mark's bed, intending to wake him up to say goodbye.

Philip grabbed Emma's hand and pulled her to the door. "Bye," he said quietly, and they walked out. Emma said nothing, and neither did Olivia.

Olivia sank deeper into the armchair, raising her feet to rest on the chair she placed in front of her. She realized she was relieved. Though she would have to leave Mark alone when she went to the hotel to take a shower, it was only for an hour or two. Now they'd focus only on the factors related to Mark's illness.

52

Twelve days… twelve days since they arrived, Olivia pondered. Six days in the Intensive Care Unit, without improvement. *No,* Olivia thought. *That's incorrect.* Not only was Mark *not* improving, but his condition was deteriorating. Still, the doctors maintained the same routine.

Each day, Olivia asked when the drain would be taken out. It was clear that Mark was tortured by it every time he coughed. No answers were available. She told the doctors that he hardly ate anything, but they did nothing with the information.

He was growing weaker. *I wish we were home… maybe in the hospital that he managed, they would listen to him?* She thought. However, with the drain still in his lung, she didn't know if traveling was possible.

Late that night, he woke up with a terrible bout of coughing. Groaning in pain, he lay back down—his suffering eyes on hers.

"Maybe we should fly home?" she asked quietly, in desperation.

His gaze crystallized, became more focused.

"Well…" he said, contemplating the idea. "Maybe we should."

"There are a lot of dangers we need to consider," Olivia said. "The main one being the drain in your lung. And they do not intend to take it out any time soon."

"No, the main problem is the flight home. Changes in air pressure may collapse the lung," Mark said.

"It was a crazy idea, huh? I knew it," she said, her voice hollow, devoid of hope.

"It wasn't… isn't," Mark said. "Not crazy at all… think about it: If we stay here, I'll surely die. If we leave, I have a chance."

"What are you saying? What do you mean by if you stay here, you'll die?"

"Livy, they are not doing anything to help me. I'm not improving—quite the opposite—if this trend continues, sooner or later, I won't have the strength to cough any more. So, they'll have to intubate, but that would be futile, because my lungs will fill up with the mucus I'm now fighting to rid them of. And I'll die. If we fly home—I have a chance. The trip *is* dangerous. But if we manage to get back to my hospital in San Francisco, and get people to listen to me, I have a chance."

She sat forward, her face distressed. "If I understand correctly, you are saying that if we stay here, you'll surely die?"

Mark gazed deeply into her eyes. "Don't you think it's obvious? I'm getting weaker… how long do you think I can still cough like this and hold off the intubation? I nearly gave up earlier."

He stopped for breath, and she looked at him, silent and tormented.

"The last bout of coughing almost made me decide to give in," he continued a moment later. "If not for your face in front of me—I would have given up… the pain is unrelenting. And excruciating."

She got closer to him. Taking his hand in hers, her eyes were misty. "I love you," she whispered, infusing him with the strength of her feelings.

"I mean it," he responded. "If not for you—I would have given up already."

They sat together, their eyes locked, ensuring each other of the deep commitment they shared. Mark raised her hand, still clasping his, to his lips and kissed it.

"Can you arrange it?" he asked.

"You're serious, aren't you?" she asked, probing his eyes for certainty.

"Absolutely." came his reply.

"Then I'll find a way to arrange it!" Olivia said. Her mind was already searching for contacts. Who can I call? Who'll be able to arrange it quickly? It can't be a regular flight anyway. They'll need an ambulance flight.

She looked at her watch and saw it was past midnight. She can't call anyone.

Mark was exhausted. He closed his eyes, still holding her hand.

She texted Sarah: *Do you know a travel agent who can arrange a private flight from New York To San Francisco?*

Air ambulance? came the immediate reply. Sarah was awake.

Olivia was surprised but then remembered the time difference between the two cities.

YES, she wrote quickly, *Or Medical evacuation… whatever it's called… Just so long as we can get the hell away from here. ASAP!* she added another message.

On it! Sarah wrote back.

Her phone pinged a few minutes later, indicating an incoming text message. She flipped the cover to see it.

All the agencies are closed, but I have a friend who has one of the biggest travel agencies, and he'll arrange it for you. It won't be cheap. He'll be in touch tomorrow morning with more info.

Do I know him? she wrote back.

Maybe, Sarah wrote, *Jack Lawler. Rings a bell?*

Not sure. Olivia responded.

He's fantastic. I wish he were single. A smiley with hearts for eyes, typical Sarah.

OK. I'll wait for Lawler's call, Olivia texted, *Thank you for saving me again!*

A line of winking smileys, tongues lolling, appeared on her screen in reply.

Freeing her hand gently from Mark's clasp, she went back to the armchair, moving slowly not to wake him up. He slept so lightly. Even her silent moves woke him up.

"Why aren't you asleep?" he asked.

"I just got us a ride home," she said, her voice muted, but with a smile.

"Really? So quick? How did you manage that?" Mark sounded encouraged, which filled her heart with joy.

"I texted Sarah… she knows Jack Lawler, who's the owner of one of the big travel agencies back home. She contacted him. And he'll call me tomorrow with details," she said, maintaining the hushed tones because of the hour.

"I know him,' Mark said. "He's very good at what he does."

Her phone pinged again—another WhatsApp message.

"It's from Jack Lawler," she said, surprised.

'Sarah gave me your number. I'll be in touch tomorrow morning to ascertain what you need exactly, and we'll arrange it for you. Don't worry. Good night. Jack Lawler.' she read the message to Mark.

"That's a nice thing to do!" she said, pleased.

"Yes, reassuring," Mark concurred.

"Well, he sure put my mind to rest," she said. Raising her eyes from the 'thank you,' she wrote back to Jack Lawler, she looked at Mark and asked: "So—we're going forward with this?"

"Yes, we are! Whatever it may cost. And it won't be cheap, but you don't put a price on life, right?" Mark smiled. The first smile in a very long time.

She felt like crying. Her heart was brimming with happiness for the hope they suddenly had, for the change in him, for defeating the desperation.

Choking, she only nodded.

"Now I'll be able to sleep," Mark said. "I don't know why I didn't think of this before now. It just shows you how scrambled my mind is, my brain doesn't function fully. You're amazing for suggesting this flight!"

He looked at her and smiled again. "Good night, love!"

"Good night," she whispered, astounded by the change in him. He seemed confident again, convinced that things would turn out well.

She rested her head against the armchair and closed her eyes. But she couldn't sleep. All the things that could go wrong flooded her mind. She couldn't stop her imagination from producing catastrophic scenarios.

Her tired mind shut down some time later, and she fell into a deep slumber.

Morning hospital noises woke her a few hours later. She opened her eyes, turning immediately to check Mark. His eyes were open, and he was watching her.

"Good morning, my Livy!" he said, sounding more cheerful than she had heard him in a long time.

"I slept too deeply! I didn't hear you wake up!" She was annoyed with herself.

"No, no, no! It's fine! I enjoyed watching you sleep so soundly!" he said. She noted a significant change in his attitude, and his eyes were shining as if he was infused with hope.

She went to the sink to brush her teeth and comb her hair.

His breakfast arrived soon after. "Will you make more of an effort today?" Olivia asked, her tone cheery.

He nodded. "I'll try!"

She placed the tray close to him, and he made a face. She looked at him sternly. "Eat!" she said.

"Yes, ma'am," he replied and tried the fried eggs.

***

The nurses didn't enter his room during shift change. They stood outside, speaking softly. What information were they exchanging? Olivia wondered. Nothing was different; nothing changed. Olivia went to them. They all turned to her when they saw her at the room's door.

"Good morning," she said politely. "Can you please let the attending physician know that we wish to speak with her when she arrives?"

"What about?" asked one of the older nurses; Olivia assumed she was the one accepting responsibility for the coming shift. Her tone was businesslike, devoid of interest in Olivia or the person she was with.

"Just let her know I asked to talk to her. Please," Olivia responded. The "please" was added as an afterthought. Still polite, but as cold and authoritative as the nurse sounded.

The nurses looked surprised. Olivia was no longer courteous and friendly, attempting to get similar behavior from them. She turned and walked back into the room.

***

A short time later, Olivia's phone chimed, a text message on her WhatsApp: "*Can we talk?*" The sender was Jack Lawler.

"Lawler is up early," she commented, smiling at Mark.

Instead of texting back, Olivia called him.

"Good morning," she said.

"To you, too," came his raspy-voiced reply, "I'm Jack. Sarah told me you need help to get Professor Wallace from New York to Frisco. Is that right?"

"Yes, it is. May I put you on speaker so that Professor Wallace can listen to our talk, add information if necessary?"

"Of course." came the immediate reply.

"Twelve days ago, Professor Wallace underwent a procedure here in New York. During the procedure, a pneumothorax was created, and his left lung collapsed. A drain was inserted. It is still in place. We are not pleased with the treatment he receives here, and wish to go back home to continue treatment in the hospital he manages."

Olivia stopped, looked at Mark to ensure the details she was providing were concise and accurate. He nodded.

"I see," Jack interrupted, "And if I understand correctly, you can't take him on a regular flight because of the differences in air pressure at high altitude?"

"Exactly," Olivia answered.

"And time is a critical factor here, I presume?" he asked.

"Of course," she replied. Mark nodded his assent.

"Then, train travel is out of the question. The travel duration is long, with stops and starts, shaking and swaying, while getting in and out of stations." His tone was efficient, and she liked it. She trusted him.

"I didn't even think about trains. I thought of an air medical service, or whatever it's called."

"Medevac," he replied. "Medevac by ambulance aircraft."

"Yes, that's it. I think a train will be too painful," Olivia said.

"A train will also take a few days. It's about eighty hours, with a transfer in Chicago. With a lot of yanking and flinging on the way. However, it is much cheaper than a flight. Even if we take into account the doctors that I'll fly out to you so they can accompany you on the way home."

"Money is not an issue here," Mark said forthrightly.

"Fine," said the voice on the phone. "Let me check out all the details, and I'll get back to you with the information ASAP. You'll need at least two doctors on board the flight—intensive care specialists. Do you want someone specific, or are you willing to trust my teams on that?"

"I don't want to waste time searching for available doctors," Mark said. Olivia knew he was incapable of the effort right now.

"Good. No problem. I'll be in touch soonest. Take care!" He hung up.

"He knows his business," Mark said, relaxing for the first time in days.

"Sounds like it." Olivia felt immense relief. At long last! Help was on its way. In a few minutes of conversation, she found an ally. "He sounds very competent, doesn't he?" She beamed at Mark. He looked relieved, too.

His smile was all the answer she needed. Mark closed his eyes, but she saw he was restful.

She texted Sarah: *Thank you!!! Talked with Jack. He's on it! Hope he calls back soon!* She added a big red heart.

I'll make sure he stays on it! She texted right back.

Olivia wrote: *We're coming home. Ambulance flight. Will let you know the exact time when I get the info. See you soon. Don't call, can't speak. Love you!* She sent it to her mother, then copied the text and sent it to her sons. She deleted the "Love you" and sent the message to Sophie at the department and Sheila, her new friend. Sheila would probably tell all their other friends too.

The answers came back soon, despite the early hour.

Finally! Sophie wrote. *We miss you! Be strong and see you soon! All is well this end.*

Good idea! Adam wrote. *Long time! Waiting to hear the details. Love you, Mom! Regards to Mark.*

At long last, from Tom. *Hope it means he's well enough to fly. Talk to you soon! Love you! Say hi to Mark.*

Her mother did not reply. *She's still asleep,* Olivia surmised. It was around seven a.m. on the West Coast…

***

The doctor arrived later than usual and entered Mark's room at around eleven a.m.

"You wanted to talk to me?" she asked in her usual impersonal way, and looked at her watch, to indicate she had no time to waste.

"Yes," Mark replied in the same tone. "I'll be leaving the hospital in a day or two. Please prepare my discharge papers. And I'll need all the information on disk to take home."

"What? You *can't* leave!" she said. Her surprise complete.

Finally, some emotion there! Olivia thought.

"What do you mean by you're leaving?" She looked at Mark suspiciously.

"I'm flying home and will continue treatment there," Mark gazed at her serenely.

"You can't fly in your condition! I won't allow it! You might die!" She seemed distressed.

"I'm not asking for your permission," Mark replied. "I'll get the treatment I don't seem to be able to receive here. You said you *don't know* what to do. You have rigid protocols. And *they don't work*! That's obvious by now. But you stick to them and won't think of alternatives!"

He was angry, Olivia could tell. A rare occurrence… The doctor's insolence must have gotten under his skin.

"I mean it—your lung may collapse in high altitude, and they won't be able to save you, not in the air, away from a proper hospital!" The doctor's eyes misted. Anger? Frustration? Affront? Maybe a combination of those, Olivia realized. She didn't feel sorry for the doctor who was so arrogant before. *Perhaps that will serve as a wake-up call for you,* she thought, *make you a better doctor—a more empathic one.*

"We can't remove the drain yet." The doctor tried another tack. Her tone changed. She was almost begging.

"I didn't ask you to. There will be doctors accompanying me on the flight; they will monitor my condition throughout the ambulance flight at a lower altitude," Mark said in a kinder tone, seeing her distress.

"Please, reconsider! The flight might kill you!" she tried again.

Mark gazed straight into her eyes. "If I stay here, I'll surely die. If I leave—I have a chance to live. So, yes, there is some risk in flying, but there is also a chance. I'd rather take a chance, despite the danger, than have no chance at all. Don't you agree?"

The doctor shook her head, saying nothing.

"Moreover, you can tell Doctor Brian Campbell I'm very disappointed. He didn't show his face here. Only once—right after he performed the botched procedure. No explanation, no show of caring, and I don't mean he should have apologized and assumed responsibility, even though I deserve that, too. I came here for *him*! And I'm a colleague! Not to mention, I paid a lot of money for his expertise. The least he could do was to come and see his patient!"

"It's not his department." the doctor mumbled, sounding pitiful.

"I know it isn't! But how about caring for your patient whose condition became complicated because of the treatment you administered? Or even common courtesy toward a colleague?" His tone was sharp, demanding.

She looked at him miserably, shrugging helplessly.

"Yeah, right... please have my papers ready, with the entire medical record. By tonight, if possible."

She hasn't moved.

Mark said sharply, "Thank you!"

Her head dropped, and she walked to the door. Stopping on the threshold, she looked back as if going to say something. Then, changing her mind, she left.

"I've never seen you so assertive... bossy," Olivia said, a small smile on her lips.

"That's because you haven't seen me when such behaviors are required."

"Is that how you act at work?" she asked, only half-joking.

"No! Of course not!" Mark responded, aghast. "I don't need to, in a rational organization like the one I work in, most problems are solved when people discuss the issues at hand and work out a solution together. Normally, there is no need to force people to do things they *should* be doing."

Olivia smiled and nodded, still bemused.

They performed all the tests needed to provide the most accurate, up-to-date information before releasing him. Was it to cover themselves against a possible lawsuit? She didn't care. She just wanted to bring him home, help him recover, and put the whole episode behind them. She just hoped that the procedure they performed successfully reduced the metastases in his lungs.

53

"Good afternoon, Professor Anderson," said the unfamiliar voice, the number on her phone's screen — unrecognized.

"Good afternoon," she replied.

Before she could ask who was calling, the caller said, "My name is Catherine. I work for Mr Lawler, and he gave me your number. I'll be your liaison with the company, the ambulance, the flight crew, and the doctors that will accompany you and your husband."

"Oh!" Olivia was surprised. "You mean you have everything ready? That was quick! I'm so glad!" She turned the speaker on to include Mark in the conversation, in case he had any questions.

"Well, I understood that time is of the essence here, so we all did our utmost to get you home as quickly and safely as possible. And here is how it will work: An ambulance will arrive at the hospital around eleven a.m. tomorrow, with the doctors and an orderly to take you to the aircraft. They'll come to your husband's room with a gurney. OK, so far?"

She was just making sure Olivia was listening and absorbing all the information.

"So far—it sounds simply great." Olivia's relief was immeasurable, her heart pumping wildly.

"You need to have all the paperwork, the release forms, etc., ready so you can leave quickly. You will be taken to an airfield. We'll take care of all the necessary arrangements. Just have some form of IDs ready. The flight home will be longer than the usual flights because you'll be flying low. An ambulance will wait for you in San Francisco airport and take you and your husband to the hospital, which I know he manages."

"Yes, OK, but…" Olivia was going to say Mark's not her husband; as if reading her mind, he stopped her, signaling "leave it" before she could continue.

"Yes?" Catherine asked.

"How long will it take? When will we arrive?" Olivia changed direction.

"Ah, that depends on how long it will take to get you to the aircraft, and you take off. The flight itself will take approximately eight hours. And you need to take into account the time difference between the two coasts."

"So, we'll be there late afternoon, right?"

"Let's hope so!" the efficient voice replied. "Do you have any other questions? You can always reach me on this number if you need anything or want to clarify any issue. I'll keep you informed every step of the way."

Olivia looked at Mark, searching his eyes to see if there was a question in them. He nodded, seemed happy with the arrangements.

"OK, fine… great… let me know when the team lands in New York, OK?" Olivia asked.

"Of course!" Catherine said. "Bye for now, and please keep my number, Professor Anderson."

"Olivia," she said.

"Great, thanks. Bye, Olivia. Call anytime if you need me."

Was there a smile in the unfamiliar voice? Olivia thought she heard one.

She was so happy! She got up and kissed Mark, noticing the new glint in his eyes. They were both relieved. One more night, and they'd be in familiar territory!

They talked about the risks again. Olivia wanted to make sure Mark didn't change his mind.

"I'm unequivocally, positively, one hundred percent sure we're doing the right thing. Livy, they gave up on me here. They don't know what to do, and they are incapable of thinking outside the box to find a new idea to improve my condition! And they won't deign to try the treatment I suggested. I don't know if it's arrogance or obtuseness, but if we stay here, the result will be the same—I'll die. If I survive the flight home—I have a decent chance to live."

"Then we'll take the chance…" she said quietly, the dread numbing her joy. *But there is hope,* she kept telling herself.

He ate a little of the soup they brought with his lunch and some of the dessert. Tired as if this was a considerable effort, he lay back down and closed his eyes.

Olivia removed the tray and leaned over him. "I'll pop over to the hotel and pack our things, settle our bill, and come back here with our suitcase, so we don't have to do it tomorrow. OK? I'll be as quick as I can, Mark."

He smiled at her and raised his hand to hug her. Olivia noticed how thick his arm looked. The edema was unquestionably spreading and growing. *He's gained at least fifteen pounds,* she thought, *all fluids*.

Her step was lighter, she noticed. Despite the fear of the dangerous flight, her hopes were high for the first time since the complication occurred.

Arriving at the hotel, she went to the front desk. The young woman at the reception desk looked up and smiled.

"Good afternoon, Professor Anderson! How are you today? How's your husband?" she asked.

Did all the staff know? Olivia wondered.

"We're not doing so well," she said haltingly. "So we'll be going home tomorrow to continue treatment there. I need to check out."

"Really?" She sounded genuinely surprised. "I thought New York hospitals were among the best in the world, if not *the* best!"

"Well, you know, sometimes… maybe at home…" Olivia stammered, unsure what to say.

"Yeah, sure, I understand," came the compassionate reply.

"I'll just go up and pack. And take a quick shower. Can you have my bill ready?"

"Sure thing," she said.

She was back down in about twenty minutes, her suitcase wheeled by her side. "Can you call a taxi for me, please?" she asked as she drew her credit card out.

"Right away," the young woman said.

By the time all was settled, the taxi had arrived. Olivia thanked the kind woman and left the hotel, not looking back. In less than ten minutes, she was at the hospital again. She rushed up but slowed down when she neared his room, afraid to wake him if he managed to fall asleep. And he did.

She tiptoed in and placed the suitcase by the window, next to the trolly they brought to the hospital on the first day.

Still standing by the window, Olivia sent messages to family and friends: *Leaving tomorrow. We'll arrive in SF early evening. An ambulance will take us to Mark's hospital. I'll update along the way.*

Be kind, she told herself, *send the message to his daughters, too.* She sent it to Clair, knowing she'd tell her sister also.

Her phone vibrated a moment later, and she was glad it was always in mute mode. Clair. She wrote: *Can't speak. Mark asleep. More info later, when I have it.* She knew Clair was shocked, not knowing of the change in their plans. But she'd have to wait. Olivia didn't want to leave the room in case Mark woke up and needed her. Also, she had no energy to spare. Elaborate explanations, questioning the decision, dealing with other people's fears—were too much for her now. Moreover, she wasn't sure what Emma told her sister when she returned from New York and had no wish to go into any arguments or discussions.

Text messages kept popping on the phone's screen.

Have a safe trip home! from Tom.

Very brave decision. Safe trip! Waiting to hear more, from Adam.

So scary! Love you. Take care of yourself, too. Her mother.

Sheila, Sarah, Sophie, Andrew Kent, Julia Orlansky, Grace, Nora—all sent similar messages of support and encouragement.

She sent another message to Sarah: *I owe you, big time! You're a lifesaver... in more ways than one.* She added a series of hearts and pressed the send button.

She looked outside and sighed. The city spread in front of her, full of life, energy, and action. Never resting, unrelenting. She used to love it but now felt like a stranger. Out of sync. Maybe, in the future, she'd enjoy the city of unlimited options again.

She turned around. Mark was awake, and he was watching her.

"Are you sorry we're leaving? You didn't have a chance to enjoy the city. We'll be back, I promise. If I recover—we'll come back and see all the shows we missed, all the exhibitions," he said.

"Don't, Mark, don't think for a second I'm sorry to leave, or feel that I missed much," she said and went to sit by his side. "I'm not sorry and not sad. In fact, I'm glad we decided to go back home. As you said—it improves your chances of getting better. For me—that's reason enough to leave. And the sooner, the better."

She bent to kiss his cheek.

"I must admit—the flight scares me. What if something happens during the flight? What if the change in air pressure collapses your lung? Or causes an embolism?" She looked into his eyes when she raised these issues to gauge his reactions.

"That's why we're taking a medical flight and not a regular one. It means we'll be flying low, to maintain minimal changes in air pressure. And we'll have two doctors on board. Our chances are good," he said and smiled at her. "I'll fight fiercely, and do whatever it takes to win the fight!"

Olivia smiled. "No way you stop fighting!"

"You can't begin to imagine how many times I considered it. In the last few nights, every time I woke up choking, needing to cough those deep and very painful coughs, I wanted to stop fighting… But then I saw your eyes on me, encouraging me, and I coughed as hard as I could to clear up my lungs."

He brought her hand to his lips and kissed her fingers. "With your suggestion of going home, you probably saved my life again. I was already so far gone, my mind so confused with pain and drugs, that I failed to come up with the idea myself. I could not think of any possibilities to help myself."

"You're a fighter! Besides, remember: I said that as you gave Victoria around fifteen years of your life, and you gave Helen about the same number, I want at least the same! *At least* that. I'll be greedy and admit I want even more, but I'll certainly not settle for less!"

He smiled, saying nothing.

"Well, promise me!" she demanded, her tone light but her face serious.

"I'll do my best." He evaded her request.

Her phone vibrated again. One of her colleagues; Olivia declined the call.

"What's going on?" Mark queried, amused. "Did you tell the whole world we're coming home?"

"No," she said, acting offended, but her tone was cheerful, "Only a small portion of it, and they are all happy we're coming back!"

He turned serious. "Please let my daughters know, too. I know you're angry, but as I can't do it now."

Olivia cut him off in midsentence. "Do you think I didn't? Do you honestly believe you need to ask me something like that? Clair knows. And I promised to provide more details when I have them."

"Thanks," he said and sent her a grateful, slightly apologetic look.

"What happened here is not Clair's fault. I know they are innately united in your mind, but even you make a clear distinction."

"Yes, I do," he acknowledged. "And after New York, even more so."

She was sure Mark would not say a word to his daughters about what happened in New York. He'd not confront them. It was not his way.

54

She woke up to the usual morning noises. Mark was awake, too, and she came to sit by his side. "Just a few more hours," she whispered to him. He nodded, looking more relaxed this morning.

"I feel hopeful for the first time in a very long time," he said quietly.

"Me too," she said.

***

The physician came in around ten a.m. Her stance was no longer arrogant. She looked at the info the nurses entered that morning and saw no improvement in his condition.

"Can I persuade you to change your mind?" she asked. "It's not too late."

"Why?" he replied with a question. "Have you finally decided to change treatment?"

She shook her head miserably and shrugged.

"So, you cannot change my mind," Mark responded, "Besides, the doctors who'll accompany me on the flight will be here in an hour or so. This means that, by now, they are close to landing in New York."

She nodded helplessly.

A few seconds elapsed, and she stood there as if undecided. Then she said, "Let me emphasize—this trip is against my better judgment. You'll have to sign the forms saying you were notified of the dangers and decided to assume responsibility for discharging yourself against our medical advice. I'll prepare your discharge papers."

"It's the first time since I came here that she appears to care. Really care," Mark said once she left.

"Do you wish to reconsider?" Olivia asked. "Maybe she's ready to listen now."

"No!" Mark answered immediately. "No way. I need some good doctors who'll listen to me and be open-minded and critical, and think about what I say, just in case. I'm in no condition to take full responsibility yet, and it's not my area of expertise."

Her phone chimed. Catherine. She read the incoming message aloud: *The plane has landed!*

She looked at Mark, anticipation mixed with apprehension in her eyes.

"Not long now…" he said. His eyes echoed Olivia's feelings.

She smiled tentatively.

"Don't worry. I think we're doing the right thing. We'll be OK."

We must be! she thought. *I cannot cope with the alternative… I will not!*

She forwarded Catherine's message to her sons, to Clair, and Sarah.

Sarah was the first to answer: *I know,* she wrote. *Jack keeps me informed. He's on it, every step of the way. You're in good hands.*

The others wished them bon voyage.

"The ambulance and crew are on their way to you." A new text message arrived from Catherine in San Francisco. *Reaches you in about 1.5 h.* Laconic, but enough to tell Mark and Olivia that their homeward journey has begun.

55

Olivia heard the commotion long before seeing the two doctors and the orderly pushing the stretcher into their room. She heard one of the doctors demanding to talk with the resident in charge.

"I'm taking charge of one of your patients, and I'd like to receive all the details pertaining to his case from a doctor, not a nurse. Or do you not extend common courtesy to doctors from other hospitals?" His voice boomed throughout the ICU.

Olivia didn't hear the nurse's answer, but the doctor's retort was unmistakable: "Then call her back here now! We have a plane to catch, and I know she was notified we'd be here this morning. What kind of unit do you run? Or should I call your superiors?"

Another mumbled reply, to which the doctor responded with a stilted, "Yes, do that!"

When he entered Mark's room, the small, heavyset doctor walked right to the bed. A big smile spread over his broad face. "Professor Wallace! Delighted to see you again, despite the circumstances! It's been a long time since I was your student, but I never forgot you. You taught us how to think and to ask questions. And not to be afraid to criticize or reason independently."

Then he turned to Olivia, offering his hand. "Hi, I'm Doctor Joshua Brendel, an intensive care specialist, and this is Doctor Caroline Kiel. And we'll take good care of your husband and you! Don't worry. We've worked as a team several times before, and we're good at what we do!" There was pride, and confidence, in the voice of the fast-talking, energetic doctor.

"Thanks, Doctor Brendel," Olivia said, relief in her eyes.

"Josh," the doctor said, the big smile returning to his face, "I'm always Josh to my friends!"

Olivia smiled in return, saying, "Thanks, Josh!"

The orderly—Larry—was working quietly and efficiently, releasing Mark from the machines he was hooked to, connecting him to the portable ones—heart monitor, IV drip, an oxygen tank.

"Do you have the release papers and the medical summary?" Josh asked.

"No," Olivia said. "Not yet. The resident said she would prepare it but didn't bring it yet."

"No kidding." Josh replied, turning his eyes up, exasperated, as if looking for help from above.

Then, looking at his partner, he said, "Can you check if she's here yet, Carol?"

The physician, the opposite of Josh in every way, turned to go to the nurses' station. The resident physician bumped into her as she reached the door.

"Ah, there you are." Josh said to her as if speaking to a wayward child. "I'm Doctor Brendel, from San Francisco. What's your name?"

"I'm Doctor Elizabeth Collins, and I'm in charge of the ICU in this hospital," she said, attempting to regain the authority which Brendel so expertly stripped of her.

"Nice to know," he said, his tone dripping acid. "Do you have all the paperwork ready for me to sign?"

"I need my patient to sign some of them, including his statement that he is leaving the hospital against our advice," she said, attempting to sound in control.

"Well, may I have the papers that he doesn't need to sign? And may I view the disks I expect you to provide for his continued treatment elsewhere?" He was giving her no chance to recover. The little man acted like a pitbull who wouldn't release his prey once he got his jaws into it.

Doctor Collins turned on her heels; her desire to flee was unmistakable. "Please follow the good Doctor Collins, Doctor Keil, and make sure we have everything we need." His tone turned sweet and polite, the sarcastic nuances intentionally noticeable.

"I hate these pretentious, stuck up, know-it-alls, who think they can condescend on us 'mere humans.' They bring out the worst of my temper. And Jack told me a little about the way they treated you here," he said to Mark and winked and, turning to Olivia, he added, "I'm an adorable guy in everyday life, believe me… better yet—ask my ex-wife!" He laughed merrily.

He checked Larry's work while he talked, ensuring all the connections were made safely and correctly. His expertise was evident. Olivia liked him.

And more importantly—she trusted him.

An excellent beginning, she thought. *We're in good hands.*

"I'm glad you chose intensive care, Josh," Mark said, smiling underneath the oxygen mask Larry attached to his nose and mouth.

"I didn't choose it; *you* chose it for me! You said it suited my temper and personality. And you know what—I never regretted it and never stopped blessing you for it. I don't travel much nowadays, but when Lawler called me to say he needs to bring *you* back home, I didn't think twice!" He checked Mark thoroughly, noting his vital signs, then straightened and gave him a thumbs-up.

They were all set to leave, but Doctor Keil had not returned yet.

"Now watch me in action and see the fireworks," he said and left the room.

"Doctor Collins!" Mark and Olivia heard him bellow, his voice ringing throughout the unit. A hush followed.

Another, much softer voice replied, "In here, Doctor Brendel." The silence returned to the department.

"He was always like this," Mark said, his eyes alight. "A volatile firecracker... charming when he wants to be, but if you cross him—he's unpredictable. But he's brilliant, so many hospitals wanted him, and he rose like a shooting star. I feel so much safer, knowing he'll accompany us!"

Several minutes later, Josh came back, brandishing the papers in one hand and the disk in the other, a beatific smile spread on his face. Caroline Keil followed, still shaking her head from side to side, attempting not to laugh.

"All set! Let's go! Do you wish to say goodbye to anyone?" Josh looked from Mark to Olivia, both of whom shook their heads. Olivia took hold of the trolly and suitcase, but Josh seized the more massive bag, saying gallantly, "Allow me, madam."

"If you intend to be formal, Josh, it's Professor Anderson," Mark said, his eyes merry.

Josh turned to look at her. Surprise and admiration on his face. Olivia shrugged, embarrassed. "One of us?" he asked.

"International economics! She's the head of the graduate program at USF," Mark said, pride in his voice.

"Wow." Brendel said, awe in his voice. "No kidding! Such a small woman in a tough men's world." Then he blushed. "I didn't mean to belittle you, but you are small… well, I mean your height… no offense. I'm also small, but I'm a barracuda. And you seem so nice!"

"It's OK, no offense taken," Olivia said, embarrassed by the compliment she knew he intended.

The ambulance sped toward Newark, New Jersey. Traffic was heavy but not congested. The ambulance driver was careful, avoided abrupt stops and sharp curves, and made good progress. Brendel and Keil discussed the details of the X-rays and ultrasounds the latter saw at the ICU, Brendel nodding and asking questions. He seemed satisfied with the information but not with Mark's treatment.

The ambulance plane was waiting on the tarmac, its doors open. The pilot came out to greet them, shaking hands with Olivia, patting Mark's shoulder. The flight attendant took the papers from Olivia and went to the offices to clear them for the flight. The stretcher was brought inside in no time and fastened to the aircraft's wall. Mark was tightly strapped in. Olivia boarded next, and Josh asked her to take a seat toward the back, leaving the places closer to Mark's head free for him and Kiel. In half an hour, they were ready to go.

Bon voyage! her phone indicated a new message from Catherine a few seconds later, another notification arrived, this time—from Sarah: *Lawler told me you're aboard the plane! Safe trip! Waiting to hug you!* A huge, pounding heart emoji followed.

Despite her confidence in the doctors and the reassurances that they'll be flying low with no significant changes in air pressure, Olivia was stressed. So many things could go wrong! She loved flying, but this time, her grip on the armrests tightened until her knuckles turned white during take-off. The small plane soared effortlessly and straightened at the designated level. Her eyes were glued to Mark, checking that his color still indicated he was all right. From time to time, her eyes darted to the doctors in front, checking that they were awake, with their eyes on the monitors, deriving from their expressions that the situation was unchanged. An hour into the flight, when things seemed settled and unchanging, she felt her body somewhat relax. She was not aware of how tightly she clenched her body until she allowed it to uncoil slightly.

Mark was trying to relax, too. With his eyes closed, he breathed slowly, trying to avoid the terrible fits of coughing. On occasion, he opened his eyes, searching for her gaze. She puckered her lips as if kissing him from afar, to send him a message from her heart—*I'm here, I'm watching over you and your doctors, I love you and won't let go.*

The doctors talked in low tones, their eyes on the monitors, and the tension in the aircraft diminished, the atmosphere stable. Brendel caught her looking at him and sent her a thumbs-up signal, then placed both palms against each other and placed them next to his cheek, lowering his head upon them as on a pillow, indicating Mark was asleep. She nodded back to show she understood; a flighty smile appeared and vanished on her lips.

She couldn't relax—not enough to read a book or to take a nap. She tried closing her eyes and meditating, listening to her breathing, trying to reduce her muscles' tension one at a time. Nothing worked. Her eyes flew open, and her body refused to unclench. She decided not to fight it and sat back in her chair, her eyes on her man, urging him—in her heart—to breathe, to fight on, not to give up.

A few hours into the flight, Brendel offered her a sandwich. Wordlessly, she waved her hand, rejecting the suggestion. He tried again, his expression one of insistence. She sent him a feeble smile but shook her head, still refusing. He pointed to a thermos in his hand and mouthed, "Coffee?" She nodded tiredly, and he poured the strong brew, its subtle aroma spreading throughout the plane.

Finally, exhausted by the prolonged lack of sleep and the tension, she succumbed and drifted asleep. Not a deep sleep, but she managed to neutralize her brain partially.

An air pocket woke her up, confused and in panic. Her eyes flew open, and, instinctively, she searched for Mark. He was also awake, his eyes met hers, and he signaled he was OK.

Olivia saw that he wasn't. Pale as a sheet, his face was scrunched tight. The sharp movement must have shifted the drain, causing immense pain. The doctors saw the signs on their monitors as well and jumped up. However, after the initial jolt, the level of the agony returned to the bearable one. They were not needed; no intervention was necessary, but Olivia saw they were on edge, and she was glad to see how ready they were.

Some conversation with the cockpit ensued, but she couldn't hear what they said—something about a route change to avoid more turbulence.

***

Time crawled. Other than the minor turbulence, the flight was uneventful. Mark was not suffering more than he agonized at the New York hospital, and that—for her—was a great reason to rejoice.

"How long?" Olivia asked the flight attendant, who was bored without work throughout the flight, playing with his cellphone.

"About an hour or so," he replied, offering a professional yet pleasant smile.

May the rest of the flight be monotonous, she wished in her mind, *especially the landing...*

"Time to strap yourselves; we're approaching the airport," the attendant told them.

Brendel rechecked Mark, ensuring all the equipment was secure and that the tubes going into him were securely fastened. Then he, too, sat down, buckling his belt.

Again, Olivia wished she knew how to pray...

The aircraft wobbled and swayed on its way down. Olivia's heart was beating fast, her eyes locked on Mark's face. His eyes were closed, and she thought he was preparing for another jolt. She could see the plane approaching rapidly to meet the runway, and she gripped the armrests with all her might. No bounce, bump, or jolt occurred. Just a smooth glide to greet the surface and a continued taxiing along the runway, smoothly and gradually slowing down.

56

They made it. They were safe. Relief flooded Olivia, and with it—all the tension she wasn't aware she was holding so tightly in check—poured out. Her teary gaze returned from the San Francisco airport to Mark's face. He was removing the oxygen mask from his face.

"Don't cry, Livy! We made it! From now on—things will improve, you'll see!" Mark said, his voice croaky but happy.

Only then did Olivia realize that tears were streaming down her face. In the seat in front of her, Caroline Keil handed her a pack of tissues and a smile. "All is well," she said. "He's fine, we made it, and all is well."

Olivia wanted the tears to stop and had to fight hard to achieve that.

"What happens now?" she asked.

"Now we take Professor Wallace to the ambulance that's already here and waiting, and I'll take both your papers and his, and clear all the formalities. That will take about half an hour, and then you can be on your way to the hospital." The flight attendant responded.

Olivia nodded. "That was a terrific landing," she said, still choked.

"I'll let the pilot know you enjoyed his skillful and gentle touch on the stick," he said and smiled.

They came to a complete stop in front of a small terminal building. As promised, the ambulance was waiting, its gurney out on the tarmac. The doors opened, and Olivia was asked to disembark to allow more room to maneuver the stretcher off the plane. She went down the few steps and onto solid ground, her legs trembling.

It was dusk, she noted. It took longer than the eight hours Olivia expected. So that's what the pilot asked Brendel—if it was OK to choose a longer route. But that didn't matter now—they were safe, on the ground, and soon would be whisked to the hospital.

"Olivia!" a familiar voice called, and a figure exited the small building on her left, hurrying in their direction.

"Sarah? How did you get here? You got permission to be out here?" Olivia asked as her friend gathered her into a bear hug.

"Jack managed it. I kept nagging, and he had no choice. All he wanted was to get rid of me, and all I wanted was to be here to hug you!"

Typical Sarah... but she was delighted to see her friend there.

"Come, hot coffee and some sandwiches are prepared for you inside the waiting hall. I'm sure you didn't eat anything during the flight."

"I can't leave, Sarah; we'll be moving shortly!" Olivia said, tense.

"It will take time until they unload Mark and arrange everything in the ambulance and all the paperwork. Rest for a while! You've still hours before you can relax!" Sarah insisted. "By the way—what about your luggage? Did you take it off the plane?"

Olivia shook her head. She completely forgot about their bags.

"Well, I'll take them home with me and bring them to you tomorrow. You don't want it with you in the hospital, do you?"

Mark waved at them from the gurney as they wheeled him to the waiting ambulance.

"Forget the coffee," Olivia said, "Though I could use one. I better join them now... we'll text later?" she hugged her friend tightly and turned to leave.

Sarah nodded and returned to the small private terminal. Seconds later, she was back, holding a steaming Styrofoam cup in her hand. She handed it to Olivia, who was already in the ambulance, sent her a kiss, and said, "Safe trip! See you soon. Be well, Mark!" and she walked to the plane to get their suitcases.

Evening traffic was dense. The ambulance sped whenever possible, his siren blaring.

***

Olivia didn't know what to expect once they reached the hospital, and she was tense. Her phone vibrated again. She looked at it and saw another message from Catherine: *Welcome home. Hospital waiting for you! All the best! Be well soon. Best wishes from Jack Lawler, too.* Olivia told Mark what the message said.

He removed the oxygen mask from his face and said, "Did you have any doubts?"

Olivia nodded. He smiled.

She sent a text message to Clair: *Landed in SF. On our way to the hospital.*

***

The ambulance reached the entrance to the ER. Many people were milling around, and Olivia wondered why the ER was so busy at this hour. When the ambulance stopped, and the doctors stepped down, everyone halted. Out of the window, Olivia saw that a hushed, subdued standstill fell on the place. The gurney was brought down, and she followed.

A doctor tore himself from the frozen crowd and approached hastily. "Professor Wallace! Good to have you back with us! As you can see— we've been expecting you." The freeze broke, and the crowd approached, offering welcoming smiles, cries of greeting.

The doctor said aloud, "Give the man some space!" and signaled two orderlies to bring the gurney into the ER.

"You must be his partner?" He looked at Olivia. She nodded, still overwhelmed by the reception they'd just received.

"We'll check you out first, take all the measures we need, and whisk you up," he said to Mark, radiating professional confidence and determination. "We have a room prepared for you in the Pulmonary Critical Care Unit."

"Livy, meet Professor Robert Conti. Bobby was my student years ago and advanced so nicely—he's now the head of the entire Pulmonary service," Mark said. Under the oxygen mask, relief was written plainly on his face, and her heart lifted. He was telling her he was in excellent hands.

The young professor smiled broadly and placed his hand on Mark's shoulder. "You taught me well!"

Mark was transferred to a hospital bed, and a nurse approached to draw some blood. She, too, was smiling broadly, welcoming Mark back home. Professor Conti moved aside to confer with the two doctors who accompanied them on the flight. Olivia saw him nodding as the two doctors provided information and handed him the disks and paperwork from New York. They shook hands, and all three approached the bed.

The two doctors said their goodbyes and departed; Brendel promised to be in touch before he left.

Many more people approached Mark's bed just to say hello and wish him well, or promise to come and talk to him later, imploring him to tell

311

them if he needed anything.

Mark's second in command came, too, and was the only one who dared to express what must have been on everyone's mind: "You look like you've returned from hell!"

"I did," Mark said. Then he introduced Olivia.

"From what I heard so far, you were the one who suggested the trip home? Brilliant! I talked to Brendel, he said you would have died there, if not for her."

Mark only nodded. He was exhausted.

"I'll come to see you tomorrow and consult with you about several urgent issues if you are up to it," he said as they were entering the elevator.

"Wait!" They heard the cry from the hall leading to the elevators.

Emma and Clair were rushing to enter the elevator with them. They were all over their father, asking questions about the trip, talking about how much they missed him. Mark smiled, happy to see them.

***

The Pulmonary Critical Care Unit was quiet. The lights were dimmed, the nurses speaking in hushed tones at their station, all the patients in their beds.

"Last room on your left," one of them said to the orderly when he wheeled the gurney in. "We'll be right there to help you settle him in." Two of them came to follow the gurney, and one of them turned to Olivia and Mark's daughters, saying, "Please wait outside until we finish."

They stood outside impatiently. Clair asked about the flight back home, and Olivia tried to describe the tremendous risk, his pain and discomfort, her fears. She thought that they had not realized how perilous Mark's condition was until now. Maybe now they'll have a better idea.

When the nurses exited Mark's room, the three of them walked in.

"Today, I'll be able to sleep in a bed next to you! Sleeping in an armchair, even in one you could slightly recline, produces a very light sleep."

She hoped she would be able to relax enough to sleep better, despite hospital noises and her need to hear Mark.

"No, Livy. Absolutely not, and please don't argue. Tonight, you sleep at home. In our bed. I'll be able to sleep much better, knowing that you're able to relax and sleep properly."

312

"Out of the question!" she argued. "You need someone to help you raise yourself when you cough!"

"Not where we are. I can promise you. I'll have the best possible care! And you need to get back to work. You've been away for so long, and they surely need you there. Come to see me when you finish work."

She decided not to argue, so he would not waste energy.

Olivia's nerves were on edge, unable to desert him. She came close to Mark's head and whispered her goodbye, promising to come back in the morning. "I hope you'll be able to get some sleep," she said aloud, hoping the other two women would understand, but had the feeling they ignored her words. *His problem*, she decided. *He needs to learn to express his needs.* And if they didn't see for themselves how desperately he needed rest, and he can't tell them—she's unable to help him.

Her watch showed it was eleven fifteen p.m. She took a taxi home and was on her phone, texting friends and family to let them know the news. She didn't call anyone; she had no desire to answer questions.

The city seemed almost deserted. The recent rain drove people indoors, and the dripping cars owned the streets. Trees swayed, their branches dribbling soundlessly on the already drenched sidewalks. The taxi tires were whooshing on the wet asphalt. Olivia's eyes ran dejectedly over the cityscape as the car sped on. So familiar, yet so inaccessibly alien right now. On her way to an empty, cold home. Without Mark. Lonely and worried, she remembered that even the dogs wouldn't be there.

"Thank you, good night," she said as she paid and got out of the car.

The driver turned his car around and vanished down the street, his blood-red taillights receding in the distance. She turned around and faced the dark, brooding house, and the feeling of alienation hit her even harder. Alone and miserable, she walked up the path, her steps slow and cumbersome, as if her legs refused to cooperate.

She turned the lights on and walked in, turning on more lights as she went. The house was spotless and flawlessly ordered. The maid did her job properly.

Olivia went to the spot where they always sat when they relaxed together, having a drink and talking. Standing by the glass wall, she looked at the rain-swept yard and the distant, familiar bridge, her loneliness increasing.

I need you here so badly, she thought. *You must be well soon and come back home to me!*

Weary to the point of ache, Olivia padded to the bathroom to take a shower.

She wondered if she'd be able to fall asleep, but the familiar bed hugged her, and after two weeks of sleeping intermittently, she dropped into a deep, dreamless sleep the moment her head touched the pillow.

57

Gray morning light woke her up. *People always say that things look better in daylight,* she thought, *and there's truth in that.* Despite the low-hanging gray October clouds and the seething ocean, both harassed by the raging winds, she felt better than she did the night before. Dressing quickly, she rushed out, hoping her car would start so that she could drive to the hospital.

Traffic was still tolerable at six a.m., and she made the way to the hospital in no time. Hoping that their schedule would be similar to the New York hospital, she believed he'd be awake. And he was. Washed and shaved, he lay relaxed, with a clear plastic tube under his nose instead of the mask. His eyes were brighter than she'd seen them in a very long time. Her heart lifted, and a bright smile spread on her face.

Mark smiled back. The transformation in him was overwhelming. Was it the familiarity? Feeling of security? Responsiveness of the staff? Whatever it was, the change was miraculous.

"Livy! You're back!" Mark's tone was upbeat. "Did you get home all right? Sleep well?"

Olivia nodded, speechless. She went over to hug him, noticing that the canula was still in his vein, and so was the drain. She kissed his forehead and realized his fever was down.

"If you had any doubts whether we did the right thing flying home—forget them! They gave me a massive dose of Furosemide last night, and it worked like magic! My body has been releasing fluids ever since, and I can feel the difference already! And a nutritionist came early this morning to discuss my diet—I need a lot of protein to rebuild the reservoir I lost. They'll do some more tests and X-rays today, and then we'll know when it will be possible to remove the drain."

She couldn't believe her eyes. Never one to believe in miracles, Olivia had to admit that what she was seeing was one, or as close to one as you can get. Mark was not yet out of danger, she understood, but unquestionably on his way.

"Seeing you now, no one would believe the condition you were in a few hours ago!" she said, with tears of happiness in her eyes. "The change in you is simply unbelievable!"

"It is believable," he said, pleased and proud. "Conti knew, *precisely*, what to do, and it was, exactly, what I told the New Yorkers that should be done! The doctors here acted immediately, and you can see that it worked like a charm!"

She was so happy! Relief and a sense of reprieve dislodged the massive rock that had suffocated her heart for so long.

"Let's hope you'll be able to go home soon! It's so lonely without you!" Olivia whispered to him, taking his hand in hers.

"We're not there yet," Mark replied, "But you have to promise me something. As you can see—I'm on the mend. So, I want you to go back to your life. You must go back to work, bring the dogs back home. Come and visit me, but you're not going to sit with me day in and day out! Believe me—I'm well taken care of here. I lack for nothing!"

She was about to argue, but he cut through her as-yet-unsaid objections. "Please, Livy, I'll feel much better if I knew you have your life back. You've been my guardian angel when I so needed one, and I'll be grateful forever for the way you cared for me. However, what you need now—and I do, too—is to restart your routines!"

Olivia nodded. She was elated. If he was so confident that he could manage independently, it was the best possible sign that he was getting better. Her heart expanded, and she knew she'd wait for him to come back, however long it takes.

***

A couple of hours later, she drove to her office. She called her mother while on the way to let her know all was fine, and promised to phone again later. Then, she called Sarah and vowed to stop by on her way back to the hospital, for a brief cup of coffee and to pick up her suitcases.

Sophie was delighted to see her and had tears in her eyes when she said, "What a hassle you've just been through! I can't imagine myself doing what you did! It's so good to have you back! We need you, too, you know."

"Of course, I know. And I need you, too—for my sanity more than anything!"

She entered her office and found a pile of mail waiting for her attention.

316

Arranging each one in order of priority, and separating letters into those she could let Sophie answer, and those she'd need to respond to herself, she decided the issues were not urgent enough. She turned her computer on.

Sophie came in a few moments later, her notebook in hand, ready for instructions. Olivia handed Sophie the pile she thought she could handle, with specific instructions on what to do with each letter. She also requested Sophie to get hold of Andrew Kent and Frank Williams, their faculty's dean, on the phone.

There were so many issues she had to deal with! She began with the most recent ones, working steadily.

Her phone rang. "Andrew Kent for you." Sophie said, and a second later, his rich baritone voice boomed, "Welcome back!"

"Thanks," Olivia responded. "It's good to be back!"

"I heard it was quite a traumatic trip," Andrew said. "Sophie didn't tell us much, but we know it was more than you bargained for."

"To put it mildly," Olivia said. "But tell me what has been going on while I was away. Any particular dilemmas I need to know about? Any conflicts or glitches?"

"No, none, nothing special... I think our colleagues were very considerate and accommodating while you were gone. And I believe you managed to solve most of the major problems before leaving. I'll come up later—I'm teaching in a few minutes—and fill you in regarding the minor details."

"Fine, thanks!" Olivia said and hung up.

The hours flew rapidly. Phone calls and emails, and many welcome visits from colleagues and staff members, all interested in what happened, wishing her the best and offering help should she need anything.

It was early afternoon. Olivia called the dog sitter to ask if she could come to pick the dogs up later. Come anytime, he said, and that was settled.

So—to Sarah's first, the dog sitter second, then home to drop the dogs and the luggage, and then—the hospital.

It was a good day, after so many miserable ones.

She reached Sarah's house a few minutes later and parked. The new, asphalted street looked pleasant and calm again. The construction down the road was yet in progress, though, and there must still be a lot of noise and dust during working hours.

Coffee was ready, and a steaming cup was handed to Olivia the moment she entered, right after the warm hug.

"Wow, I need this! Had no time to drink or eat today," she said.

"I was sure you wouldn't. Come—I have some pasta and meatballs ready for you!"

"Oh, Sarah, you're the best. I'm famished!" Olivia said, only now allowing herself to acknowledge her hunger.

They sat down at the kitchen table, and Olivia poured out her heart, telling Sarah about the fear and misery, Mark's suffering and the sleepless nights, the obtuse doctors, and the encounters with Emma.

Sarah responded with warm-hearted support, always taking Olivia's side.

Olivia then revealed to her friend how desperate she became that night when she requested her help getting back home. All alone, with Mark's condition deteriorating and no assistance in sight, she didn't know what to do.

"When I suggested we fly home, and he said yes—I wasn't sure how to arrange it and called you! Luckily—you knew who to turn to, and Jack Lawler worked out just great!"

"It worked out even better." Sarah said, with a glint in her eyes, her face turning red.

Olivia looked at her friend, failing to understand.

"Jack is in the middle of getting divorced. Well, it's almost a fait accompli." Sarah said, her eyes glowing. "He is miserable and lonely, and we got talking… he said he always thought very highly of me, and he loves my funky sense of humor." Taking a deep breath, she added, "There might be something brewing, I don't know yet."

"Oh, Sarah! I'm so happy!" Olivia erupted. "He sounded like such a nice guy! It's so wonderful!"

"Hold it! I'm not sure yet whether I want to get into any relationship. Moreover, with a guy after a messy divorce?" Sarah shook her head, her face clouded with doubt.

"Well, give it a try!" Olivia said enthusiastically. "Remember how you pushed me to think positively about the possibility of meeting someone? And it was less than a year after Elliot passed away! It's so many years since your husband died; time to move on and give yourself a chance!"

Sarah nodded, still doubtful and hesitant. "We'll see," she said.

At least it's not a total NO, Olivia thought, *and that's a significant change.*

***

Olivia entered the hospital that evening in a hurry, wondering how he managed without her all day. They texted each other several times, even talked twice, but that was not a good enough alternative to being there.

He was sitting up in bed, his glasses on, a newspaper in hand.

"Mark! What a change! I'm so happy to see you like this!" Olivia bent to kiss him, her delight apparent.

"I feel much better, too," he replied, a soft smile playing on his lips. "The Furosemide and the steroids worked like magic, just as I said they would."

His face darkened, and Olivia understood that something was troubling him. She waited patiently, knowing he'd share his doubts with her.

After a while, Mark gazed directly into her eyes and said, "We may have a problem, though. I may need to be continuously hooked to an oxygen generator. I tried removing the oxygen tube last night—I thought I could do without it—and woke up panting and breathless in the middle of the night. It was a scary feeling, and it showed me that my lungs couldn't supply enough oxygen. There are portable generators, and I'll need to get one before I can go home."

"So, we'll get one! That's not a big problem, is it? We'll adjust! It's no big deal," Olivia said, returning his gaze with conviction in her eyes and voice. She stroked his hand. "We'll manage the transition, you'll see! The main thing is—you'll be home again!"

"It will be noisy at night... and I won't be able to play tennis any more... many additional limitations," he said, despondent.

"None of that matters! You can still work, meet friends, and take walks with me and the dogs... we'll rearrange our lives around it... and establish new routines!" She sounded positive and confident.

Mark lowered his eyes, then raised them again and looked at her, amazement, happiness, and surprise mixed in his gaze.

"Are you aware of how unbelievable what you just said is?" he asked. "I wasn't expecting you to stay. I may be an invalid... a disabled old man... I didn't presume. I thought you'd leave rather than be encumbered by another sick man... you deserve so much better! And it's only about a year

319

since we connected."

"I have 'better'! I don't care about the oxygen you'll need. And that doesn't turn you into an invalid. A little limited in options, maybe, but nothing significant. I love *you*! Your mind, your soul, your heart; I'll take your meager lungs, too, so long as they are attached to you," she said, smiling, her eyes misted. "I mean it, Mark. I won't give you up as long as you want me by your side. And we'll make the best of what we have!"

He pressed her fingers and raised them to his lips—relief and happiness suffusing him, visible in his eyes and his relaxing features.

He never requested anything for himself. Perhaps he didn't know how to ask. The man who was so ready to help others never expected anyone to do anything for him, Olivia realized, and not for the first time.

And I meant every word, she grasped. She was sure that he'd be a fantastic partner, even with an oxygen generator.

They sat talking about people approaching him with problems, about her work, how happy the dogs were to come home and how well they looked, and about Sarah and her surprise. It was so pleasant to be able to relax together!

Emma and Clair arrived around eight p.m. *A little late to come for a visit!* She thought, but, as usual, she said nothing.

"Hi," they both said together, sounding jolly.

"You already look better, Daddy!" Emma said, hurrying to his side to kiss his brow.

Clair approached more slowly, smiling shyly.

Olivia got up to leave, and Mark grabbed her hand, his eyes begging her to stay. She looked at him, shaking her head imperceptibly, and he understood.

"Oh, you're leaving already?" Clair asked, sounding disappointed.

"You need time alone with him, too," Olivia said, "Besides, it's rather late." She hoped they'd draw the right conclusion but doubted it.

She kissed Mark goodnight and said, "I'll come to see you in the morning; I do hope you'll get some sleep tonight." then she left, thankful he was looking better, more reassured, and felt hopeful for tomorrow.

58

The drain was removed four days later, and the additional X-ray showed the pneumothorax had almost vanished. Astonishingly, he regained enough capacity to breathe independently during the day, needing oxygen aid only after exerting himself. He was growing stronger with each passing day, enjoying walks in the halls of the department.

It took another week before he was declared fit enough to be released. Olivia picked up fresh warm clothes for him and obtained the oxygen generator he needed, and she came to take him home. Mark insisted on leaving the hospital without an oxygen tube dangling under his nose. He entered her car, tall and proud, free of the pipes that had been hooked onto him for almost a month.

She drove slowly and carefully, avoiding sharp turns and sudden brakes. They could hear the enthusiastic barks of both dogs when they entered the front yard parking area. Opening the door, Mark extracted his legs but remained seated. "How I missed the smell of the ocean!" he said, his eyes closed with pleasure, listening to the waves crashing not far below them.

Olivia walked over and, smiling broadly, extended her hand and said, "Welcome home!"

He refused help and got to his feet. She knew he must still be frail but respected his need for independence.

They walked together toward the house, his hand on her shoulder, hugging her without leaning on her for support. "Our garden suffered while we were away," he said. "Some tender loving care will restore it in no time."

Entering the house after such a long absence, he looked around, loving the sight: The attractive colors, the peaceful atmosphere, the welcoming view of the terrace and the garden, the ocean close by.

"Home," he said.

Olivia looked at him, a tender smile on her lips, realizing he was happy.

"There were a few times in New York, when I doubted I'd ever be able to come back to it."

"I know," she said quietly.

He walked over to Olivia and hugged her tightly. No words were needed to explain how they felt.

"A drink in our corner?" she asked.

"That would be more than a great idea!" was his immediate reply.

It was a bit early for her, but she'd make an exception this time—they needed to celebrate.

They sat together, contemplating the clouds rushing by in the gray sky, kissing the surface of the ocean, and the seagulls that were skimming the waves.

"To new beginnings!" she said and raised her wineglass.

"And to the rest of our lives!" and raised his whiskey goblet to meet hers. "It is so good to be back. Now, all we can do is hope that the treatment *was* a success, as they said, and they managed to destroy the tumor they treated. I'll do a CT scan in three months, and we'll see whether the tumor is still there or not."

"If you had to decide now—would you have chosen to undergo the treatment, now that you know the dangers and pitfalls?" Olivia asked. Her voice had a tremor in it.

"Maybe," Mark said, contemplating. "It depends on the outcome. In three months, I'll be able to give a better answer. If the tumor was dramatically affected, then yes—maybe I would have chosen again to do it, despite what I went through. It's all theoretical, anyhow."

He turned to look at her, then added: "I want to live. It's something I haven't felt in a very long time, but I *really* want to live… to be with you… to enjoy our togetherness. I thought I lost it, but you brought the desire back."

"I'm glad!" Olivia responded, her eyes bright. "I was afraid I'd be blamed for this 'adventure' we went through, if—…"

"Why would it be your fault? Or guilt? I decided to do it, my choice, and nobody else's. And I did it even though I knew the risks."

She put her arm through his and moved closer, saying nothing.

After a while, he sighed deeply and said, "I need to check my emails. There'll probably be hundreds of them to deal with, after almost a month. I need to do this before I reach the office tomorrow."

She released his arm and turned to look at him, astonished. "Tomorrow? You intend to go to the office *tomorrow*?"

"I've been away too long. Besides, if I stay home, I'll just feel useless. And what good will it do? I'm not sick!" he responded.

"Let your body rest for a day or two!" Olivia was exasperated.

"What do you think I was doing these last few days?" he asked, smiling at her protective attitude. "I'll go for a few hours and come back home," he compromised.

Olivia understood his need to regain normalcy, and she nodded. "OK," then she added, "If you intend to go and check your emails, I should do the same and go and communicate with people," she said and got up.

She answered her many emails and turned to her WhatsApp, only to find many more messages requiring information, sending best wishes, offering any help they may need. She answered all those that a texted message would satisfy. Still, she realized, there's no avoiding it—she had to tell people they were home. She wanted to give him a few days to recuperate, but their close friends would want to see him, she was sure. *Maybe over the weekend, just for afternoon coffee or drinks, nothing lengthy that will require preparations.*

Soon after she sent the messages, the doorbell rang, and an enormous bouquet of chrysanthemums and baby's breath was delivered. She hadn't found a vase before the bell rang again. This time, it was a fabulous potted white orchid with huge flowers. Within two hours, their house was filled with abundant flowers of many colors and shades, big and small. The cards attached expressed good wishes and a desire to see them soon.

Deeply touched, Olivia surveyed the colorful exhibition of friendship all around her, and it warmed her heart. She started calling friends to thank them and invite those who were closer to come during the weekend. It would be great for both of them to return to their ordinary life!

59

"Clair called me today and suggested that we celebrate Thanksgiving together. I told her I'd have to ascertain your plans before I could accept. What do you think?" Mark asked her one day in early November when he returned from the hospital.

Was she suggesting that Olivia and Mark would host them or that Clair would prepare the Thanksgiving dinner?

"I'm sorry, but that won't be possible. Ann asked me last Tuesday—when I came to take Leah—if we'll celebrate together, and I said yes. Tom and Emily are also coming home, and while she'll probably celebrate with her family, Tom will want to celebrate with us. My parents, too. We didn't do anything last year because it was so close to Nick's death and the funeral in Albany."

The invitation took her by surprise. She wasn't invited last year—the relationship was too new to be taken seriously, she explained it to herself at the time. Why now? Was it his daughter's way of acknowledging her existence in his life? Or Emma's way of apologizing without actually doing it or ignoring the incident altogether? She didn't believe that Emma thought she had anything to apologize for.

Combining the two families was out of the question. Of that—she was sure. There would be too many unconnected people. Mark understood that also; she could see the recognition on his face. And that left him in a dilemma—who does he celebrate with?

"If they do not wish to be burdened with the preparations and want to celebrate with you here, that's fine! I can go home and prepare everything for my family there if you want to host them here," Olivia suggested.

"Go *home*? This is *home*!" He erupted passionately. "Do you still think of your house as an optional home?"

"No, Mark, that's not what I intended! I meant—we have options to celebrate with both our families. I know you're always celebrating Thanksgiving and Christmas Eve with them. You're more than welcome to celebrate with us, but I thought you'd prefer to be with your daughters and their family. Both my sons and my parents like you a lot, so it would be nice if we could be together, but I'll completely understand if you choose otherwise."

"If you prepare Thanksgiving dinner for your family, you do it here," Mark said.

He meant that his daughters would prepare their own dinner, in their own houses.

Olivia nodded her understanding. "The fact that we consider ourselves so compatible and we choose to be together doesn't mean our families would harmonize too, you know. We both know they won't."

Mark nodded dejectedly. "I wish we could be a united family."

"Listen, Mark," Olivia said, taking his hand in hers, "It's not because my sons accepted you willingly, while your daughters did not. From what I know—it is often the case with fathers and daughters. Daughters tend to reject their father's new partner. So, it's not just your daughters. I have no idea why that happens, but it does, it's not that you did something wrong, it's just the way of things."

Mark hugged her and murmured in her ear, "Did I tell you today how much I love you?"

"Yes," she said softly, "But you may say it as often as you like, and I'll always be happy to hear it."

***

Olivia called her mother the next day to tell her she'd be hosting Thanksgiving dinner at Seacliff with the boys and that she and Arthur were invited, too. Rebecca was overjoyed until she thought of her own son.

"I wish Ben were here, too. I hope he's not too lonely in Milano. Do you think they celebrate Thanksgiving over there?"

"No, Mom," Olivia said. "They have enough holidays of their own."

"You know your father is not well. Maybe he doesn't have another Thanksgiving left, so I wish we could enjoy it together, with Ben, too."

Olivia didn't know her father was doing so poorly.

"What happened, Mom, and why didn't you tell me?" Olivia asked, worried. "Did something happen in the last month when we were in New York? Did you hide a change in his condition because you knew we were fighting for Mark's life? You refrained from sharing so as not to add to my burden?"

"Nothing drastic." Rebecca said, dismissing Olivia's concern. "I can see the slow decline, but he still refuses treatment or too much attention. There was nothing you could do for him anyway, so why bother you when you're so far away and so stressed?"

"I appreciate the consideration, but we'll ask Mark to check Dad to see if his cancer had advanced," Olivia suggested.

"No rush. Your father is not going anywhere, and he won't die tomorrow."

"Oh, I understand…" Olivia sounded relieved.

"I forgot to tell you!" Rebecca continued, exuberant. "Remember the lovely couple who were our dinner partners on the Alaska cruise? Well, they came to visit us last week! They are considering moving to San Francisco and into a senior citizens' community! They came to say hi, and check the Carlisle! I believe they were highly impressed, and I took them to meet some friends, showed them around. I hope they'll join us here! And Myles and his wife are also considering it. Remember, Myles, my bridge partner? Well, I kept in touch with him, as well. And they are considering a move, too; only his wife prefers Florida."

"Mom, I've got to go!" Olivia said, knowing her mother could talk a mile a minute.

Her call to Ann was next. Olivia wanted to invite Margaret, but Ann said her mother refused to celebrate Thanksgiving this year, and she was not in the mood to be among many strangers.

"So, it will only be the three of you?" Olivia asked.

"Uh-huh." Ann replied sadly.

"We'll try to make it as happy an occasion as we can!" Olivia said.

Tom was his usual cheery self.

"Hi, Mom!"

Her heart lifted. She missed him so! She got a chance to see Adam every week, but Tom was often too busy to come home.

"Hi, son! I just called to make sure you *are* coming on Thanksgiving and ask if Emily decided to join us here or go to her family," she said.

"Sadly, it will be only me this time," he replied. "Maybe once we're married, we'll organize it differently."

"No problem, darling, don't worry! It will be just us and your grandparents."

"What—Mark won't be with us?" Direct as always.

"He'll join us later, but he'll be with his daughters and their families first. They invited me too, but I preferred to celebrate with my family."

"Nice of them to offer," he said drily. "Especially after New York. But I understand your reluctance. I'm sure Mark does too...' After a moment, he added in his usual positive tone: "Hey—we're going to have a proper traditional Thanksgiving dinner, right? With all the trimmings? Like we used to have?"

"Of course, Tommy! Of course!" she answered. "No fancy postmodern stuff, I promise!"

She called Sarah, too, inviting her to join them. No way she'd allow her to be alone on such a day. But Sarah was driving to her daughter and her family. She'd stay with Linda and her family for a few days and see Connor and his partner while she was there.

***

A few days later, unable to postpone it any longer, she made the most challenging call... to her brother. How do you wish someone happiness a year after such an inconceivable tragedy as his? But there was no avoiding it. She checked to make sure it wasn't the middle of the night in Italy.

"Hey, sis," he said when he answered the phone.

"Hi, brother," she said cautiously, trying to gauge his mood. "How are you doing over there, on the other side of the world? How's Karen?"

"We're both OK. Karen's terrific and very patient, work is going all right, and I miss you terribly! You are all the family I have now... you and Karen... There isn't a day going by when I do not think of Nick... but life moves on, and I drift forward. Luckily, Karen is forever the optimist, so she's my ray of sunshine."

He still sounded dejected, but not as lost and brokenhearted as he was in the past months.

"I wish you were here, with us," Olivia said. "But I understand the constraints and pressures of work. How is it going, by the way? Have you started experimenting yet?"

"Yes!" he said, sounding more upbeat. "For now, it's just small local testing of chemicals and procedures, but we'd be ready to broaden the scale of analyses shortly."

327

"Where will you do it?" Olivia asked, interested.

"You won't believe it—but we may choose Napa!" Ben said. "I've been in touch with them throughout the year after I visited the area."

"Will you be in charge of the experiments?" Olivia inquired, hope in her voice.

"Maybe..." he replied. "I may surprise you sooner than you think and appear for Thanksgiving!"

***

She knew what her family liked, precisely: A whole roasted turkey with her special recipe for the stuffing, candied yams and mashed potatoes, green bean casserole, and pumpkin pie. And she'd ask her mother to make the cranberry sauce... Olivia would make an extra effort to make this holiday a happy one. One to remember. The first one away from their home. In what had become *her* new home. She'd show them that nothing had changed for their family, except Mark was there instead of their father. But that couldn't be helped—their father was gone.

It would also be a first for Leah, and that meant a lot to Olivia. She was just a few months old last year and didn't miss the family get-together, but this year—maybe she'd remember. *And I'll make sure we have plenty of new toys for her to play with, to keep her busy and happy!*

***

Mark left early on Thanksgiving evening. She was sorry he wouldn't be there to greet their guests, but accepted his choice.

The house filled up slowly. They were all thrilled to see each other, with hugs and kisses all around. The delicious, homey smells delighted everyone, and the atmosphere was what she aimed for.

Her father was the only exception—he was excruciatingly thin and looked sallow and lethargic. They were all shocked by the transformation. Olivia looked at her mother and saw her absorbing the dramatic effect Arthur's appearance had on the family. He chose to sit in a corner, away from the noise and the action, saying little except to inquire where Mark was. When Olivia assured him, that Mark would join them soon, Arthur nodded, saying, "Good." And he rested his head against the back of the coach.

The three young people were seated on the floor, Leah in the middle of the circle they created, and the dogs running crazily among them. They were all laughing at their antics, Leah more than anyone. Rebecca was seated on a chair, looking at the happy bunch, trying to be a part of merry-making, contributing her share of playfulness to the reunion.

They were all hungry, Tom said. "Are we waiting for Mark?" he asked.

"No," Olivia responded, "He'll join us when he can."

She was going to say, "Let's eat!" when the doorbell rang. All heads were raised, looking at Olivia in surprise, searching for an explanation. They were not waiting for any other guests, and Mark wouldn't ring the bell, surely?

"I'd better get that," Olivia said, a small smile decorating her face. She left them there, looking at each other, baffled.

"Hello, hello," they heard her say, "So good to see you! Welcome!"

They were all standing, expectant.

Ben and Karen entered the living room, disheveled and tired, but smiling. Rebecca screamed, and Olivia was afraid her mother was having a heart attack when she flew past Olivia to hug her son tightly.

"Ben! Oh, Ben! You're here! Why didn't you tell us you're coming?" she cried.

Tom and Adam came forward, Leah in Adam's arms, and they hugged Ben and then Karen.

The welcomes and surprise exclamations continued, and many questions were asked about their arrival, how long they intended to stay, and the plans for the future. Ben answered patiently, explaining they were coming to Napa for his work.

After a while, Rebecca said quietly, "Come and say hi to your father!" She pulled Ben to the living room. Arthur was slowly getting up, obviously needing help, a broad smile on his face, his eyes bright with tears.

Father and son hugged for a long time. It seemed that Ben was holding his father up, the old, sick man leaning heavily on his son. They said nothing. Nothing needed to be said.

It was apparent to all those watching the tableau that such a meeting would not happen again, and Arthur was happy to see his son before it was too late.

***

It was late when they finally sat at the table, but no one cared. The Thanksgiving dinner was a success before they took their first bite. Mark arrived and sat at the table with them, but didn't eat much. Leah, as usual, was on his lap.

Leah was tired, and Ann took her to the crib Olivia bought for her and kept in the guest room. The others stayed late, talking effortlessly.

Olivia mostly listened, not saying much. Adam was telling Tom about the project he was working on, and Tom was sharing his advancement on his doctorate, both of them knowing they would each understand the complex issues the other dealt with.

Then her brother was included in the conversation, and they asked him about the research he was involved in. Ben told them about the ecological solution his biotech startup was developing to contend with the devastation that the European grapevine moth was causing to vineyards worldwide. The others were listening carefully, trying to understand the developments he seemed so excited about. He was more animated when he talked about his group's advancement in finding the solution than she saw him all evening.

And then Ben surprised all of them. "Thanks to my dear sister, I had a chance to visit Napa Valley last year, and I got to know some remarkable people there, and Karen and I will move to the area so the in-field experiments will commence there. We'll stay with Judith and Joe, Ruth's aunt and uncle, for a little while, until we find our own place. And we hope it won't take us too long. We'd want to move to our home in time, before…" he looked at Karen, who nodded at him and smiled, "before the baby arrives!"

The cries of happiness and congratulations reverberated around the table. Rebecca was elated, Olivia could tell. Her father had tears in his eyes, and he sat straighter in his chair. Would this provide him with an additional incentive to live? Olivia knew how hard he took Nick's death and how devastated he was to see his son so brokenhearted. He didn't talk about it, but her mother often caught him looking at pictures of Ben and Nick, pain and compassion evident in his eyes.

Her sons were happy, too, pleased to broaden the family again.

He'll be close to the family again! A family united. Olivia thought. "A Thanksgiving to remember," she said quietly. More to herself than to anyone.

60

"We did it! We did it! We did it!" Olivia flung herself into Mark's arms as she returned home that evening. She arrived late, but her radiant face and her exuberance indicated it was worth it.

"What did you do?" Mark asked, laughing.

"The new graduate programs! We finalized all the details! We'll have the specializations that I worked so hard to include in our curriculum!" She seemed ready to explode with exhilaration at the achievement.

"Slow down! Begin at the beginning! I know you planned new specializations, but there were so many issues to resolve, so what happened?" Mark asked, still smiling.

Olivia took a deep breath, trying to slow down.

"We had a visit today. We had a meeting with one of the senior members of the International Monetary Fund board of governors today! The dean and I. And they will take our graduate students as interns in their seventeen departments! Can you imagine the opportunities this opens for my students? I sent the IMF the details of the courses I planned for the new programs, and they had some comments, which I took into account and revised to suit them. So—we'll have specializations in Capacity Building and Development, Monetary Cooperation, Sustainable Economic Growth, and International Trade! All in accord with the IMF's charter! The dean told me after the meeting ended that the university expects substantial growth in the number of applicants to our faculty, and a considerable increase to its ranking!" Olivia stopped for breath, her face beaming.

"Wonderful!" Mark said. "What an achievement! I'm duly impressed!"

"My colleagues were simply incredible. They worked with me so hard to make this happen! Remember I told you of my efforts to induce collaboration and a feeling of shared goals? Well, it paid off! The department members are cooperating like never before, and the atmosphere is one of camaraderie and sharing, not only competition for advancement, though we have a lot of that, too."

"It sounds great. I know how much it means to you, and it's such a

331

pleasure to see you so happy. I'm intensely proud of you!" He hugged her again, his face as delighted as hers. "We should celebrate! I'll check which of the fanciest restaurants has a last-minute table available just for the two of us!"

It was almost eight p.m., and she doubted he'd find any availability, but it was worth trying. They could always drive to their favorite seafood restaurant close to home.

"Do you want to call some of our friends to see if they can join us this weekend and celebrate with us? We'll order some fancy cocktail catering, so you won't have to work too hard, and we'll invite as many as you like!"

Olivia was overwhelmed. She already knew he was proud of her abilities and achievements and was never stingy when it came to praising or showing his admiration, but it still surprised her when she encountered it. It's not what she was used to. And it was an incredible feeling, one she cherished and was immensely thankful for.

61

Mark's health improved gradually. No longer needing the oxygen generator, not even at night, he considered taking up tennis again. Olivia wasn't sure it was wise, but she would not argue. It was something he intensely desired and—for him—a clear indication of his full recovery. Mark looked much better, too. Only two months after he was released from the hospital, he seemed to be his old self again! An excellent sign for the beginning of the new year… though she knew there were still a few more small metastases in his lungs.

Her father, on the other hand, was doing worse. The deterioration was sudden and rapid. Arthur was moved to the hospital for some tests, but Mark asked Olivia and Rebecca not to get their hopes too high. In private, Mark told Olivia to look for an appropriate hospice.

There was no need for that, she told him. The Carlisle had a particular unit for those who needed assistance and would care for him until the end. It would make it easier for her mother and save her traveling back and forth to visit him.

After two days in the hospital, they brought him back to the seniors' community and into a private room at their assisted living department. Rebecca was devastated. Her eyes red from crying, Olivia took her to a coffee shop close to their residence after settling Arthur. She tried to comfort her, but Rebecca was inconsolable. After more than fifty years together, she didn't know how to live her life without him, as a single person.

It was raining again. This December was wetter than usual, she thought. Though it was early afternoon, the sky was already dark, as if it was much later. The wind picked up again, and the bare limbs of the trees along the street were bending and twisting crazily. The coffee shop was almost empty of people. Olivia was afraid it would be overflowing with the after-work hoards, but the cold, heavy rain and the blustery wind must have sent them home early. *Too bad,* Olivia thought. *A crowd would have inhibited Mother, stopped her crying.*

"Mom, you knew it was bound to happen, didn't you?" Olivia asked patiently.

"Yes, I did." her mother responded. "But knowing it is different from having to deal with it concretely."

"I know, Mom, but dad refused treatment—and maybe wisely so—and his suffering will end soon. You know he is suffering terribly, don't you? The pain must have been excruciating lately."

"Yes, I know. I saw it in Art's eyes, he said nothing and never complained, but I could see it every morning from the moment he got up, and all through the day," her mother said and sighed deeply. She swallowed her tears and looked at Olivia.

"Do you think it's time to call Ben to come home to part with his father?" Rebecca asked, melancholy, and it was apparent to Olivia that she knew the answer to her question.

"Yes, I think we must, though there is no telling how long it will be. Ben should know what is happening and decide for himself."

Rebecca nodded, saying nothing.

"Do you want me to do this, or will you call him?" Olivia asked, knowing how hard it would be for her mother.

It won't be easy for him, either, Olivia thought. Only a year after he lost his only son, he was going to lose his father, too. He hadn't healed yet and had a lot to deal with right now, Olivia knew, with Karen's pregnancy, the move back to the States, creating a new home... She was afraid to break the news to him, but maybe it would be better than her mother's tearful diatribe?

"I'll tell him." Rebecca said. Relief and worry warred in Olivia's mind. Glad she wouldn't be the bearer of bad news but concerned about the harm her brother may suffer.

"I'll let Adam and Tommy know," Olivia said. "They will want to be here too, I'm sure."

Again, Rebecca nodded, saying nothing, her gaze distant, her face gloomy.

They drank their coffees in companionable silence, after which Olivia escorted her mother back home, making sure the umbrella was covering her properly. She knew Rebecca would go to see Arthur before she went to the apartment, and that their home would seem empty and sad, but that could not be helped.

She went home and called her sons, choosing a group video WhatsApp call to see both of them as she told them the sad news. As she expected, Adam took it harder than Tom. Of course, they would both be there, they said.

"And how are you holding up, Mom?" Tom asked.

Olivia shrugged. "You know I wasn't very close to him, so I'm fine. More worried about your grandmother. And I don't know how Ben will be affected, so soon after Nick's death."

"It will be tough for him, I'm sure." Tom said.

"How old is grandad?" Adam interjected. "He's not that old!" There was immense pain in his voice.

"He's eighty-six years old," Olivia said. "And no—he's not that old. But pancreatic cancer doesn't care about age. And, as you know, we only discovered it when it already reached the stage where there were metastases in the liver, and your grandfather refused treatment. Any kind of treatment. So, his cancer just grew until…"

"Can I go and see him? You said they transferred him to the assisted living unit; do they have visiting hours or am I free to come whenever I can?" Adam asked.

"I'm almost certain you may come whenever you like," Olivia replied. "He'll be delighted to see you whenever you come."

"I'm sorry, Mom, but I can't come right away… unless it's entirely necessary." Tom said, meaning he'll come for the funeral, she assumed. "Let me know the arrangements, and I'll do my best to arrive before the end."

***

"Are you OK?" Mark asked her that evening.

"Yes. I am. It's sort of sad, but it won't break my heart. I was not close to my father, and we sort of avoided each other's company for years. It wasn't only me. I believe that his pride prevented him from reaching out, afraid I'd reject him, or something like that. Even after I let go of the anger I harbored against him for so long, and found some compassion toward him, I wasn't searching for his acceptance. Or his company."

She looked at Mark, seeing a distant, thoughtful look on his face, his eyes gazing at the ocean, unfocused.

"I'm glad you lost your anger, it will make the healing process easier," Mark said.

"There will not be a healing process," she said quietly, her tone assured. "There will not be pain or mourning. I let go of the anger and even managed to feel sympathy for him and his pain. But the void created by the antagonism of the past was never filled with anything. There's just that— an emptiness. I'll be sorry for my mother and my sons. Especially Adam, who was more firmly attached to his grandfather. He saw something beyond the selfishness and egotism and arrogance that neither Tommy nor I could see."

"It is rather sad," Mark said, "I understand what you're saying, but it makes me sad. And I wonder what my girls will say when I'm gone. They'll overcome the grief and, before long, go on with their lives."

"I think it's the natural way of things," Olivia said.

"Yeah, certainly," Mark responded.

She wondered what it was like for him when his father died. Having no siblings and his mother dying many years before his father, he only had his daughters. And now her. But no one who knew him throughout his life as a parent or a sibling, would. It would have been more difficult for him. Having to arrange everything alone. She didn't know if Mark's father belonged to any church or parish or community. She assumed that, like Mark, he was related to none. She didn't even know where he was buried.

Well, I still have a lot to learn about my man, she thought. A brief smile lighted on her lips and was gone in an instant.

***

Arthur died three days later, in the afternoon, surrounded by his family. The Carlisle helped with all the arrangements. Getting Rebecca's permission, they conferred with Olivia and her sons to find their preferences. Adam took charge. "I think he'd want to be buried close to our dad. They loved each other a lot."

Olivia didn't argue. Neither did Tom. They were sure Rebecca would concur. He'll be buried in two days, they said, and that would give them time to notify family and friends.

The social worker took Rebecca under her wing and took her home. She stayed with her until her best friends arrived to sit with her. Olivia and her sons departed, needing to make phone calls to contact Arthur's more distant relatives, his and Rebecca's old friends and neighbors. Her sons would decide which of their friends to call, too.

Olivia was considering whether to let any of her new friends know. Some were closer than others, but she wasn't sure how to go about it.

She needn't have worried. Mark was waiting for her at home when she arrived, and he had already notified some of their closest friends, knowing they'd tell the others. All she'd have to do was call her friends unrelated to Mark's social circles, and, of course, Sophie, who would notify the department.

***

The funeral took place in the afternoon. The weather was still freezing, but it didn't rain, and Olivia hoped it wouldn't be too muddy by the gravesite. Mark and Olivia drove to the Carlisle to pick up a tearful Rebecca. Tom and Emily were staying with Adam and Ann and came together. Ben and Karen arrived soon after.

Many people came to the ceremony, many more than Olivia expected. Distant cousins mingled with new friends, colleagues from her work, her parents' old neighbors, new friends from the senior community, and her sons' closest friends. And Mark's two daughters with their husbands. *An odd, diverse mixture of people. It's rather surprising—I believe he was very well-liked at the Carlisle, though.* She understood this from the comments she heard. People there found him entertaining, good company. They admired the fact that at his age, he still worked out at the gym every morning. Olivia thought that he might have mellowed with age. Or he became more adept at hiding his domineering, aggressive nature.

Olivia moved among the guests, talking to everyone, thanking them. She saw her mother seated with her close friends and went over to make sure she was holding up all right. Rebecca nodded. She was fine, she said, surrounded by love and attention.

They all went to the open grave, where Ben talked about his father. He described significant events in his life, military record, financial successes in Africa and America, and hinted at the substantial price the family paid for Arthur's ambition.

Adam got up next and spoke of the grandfather who took him to

337

museums, told him stories about Africa, and taught him tennis, expressing love and gratitude, leaving no eye dry in the crowd.

Tom surprised her by walking to the coffin, wanting to speak. He talked of pain and a feeling of missing out, knowing there was so much more to the man they were saying goodbye to, but that he never had a chance to enjoy the grandfather his brother knew in his younger years. The tears kept streaming.

Her mother was last. She chose to speak directly to Arthur, thanking him for so many years of togetherness, with no end to the ups and downs they encountered together, and how sad she was that the road they traveled together now came to an end. She admitted she didn't know how to continue walking on her own, but that, with the help of their friends and family— she'd manage. "Don't worry, Art, I'll tell you all about the things you miss until we meet, when we meet again," she said at the end.

"You aren't going to say anything?" Sarah whispered to Olivia.

Olivia shook her head. "I can't say what I feel or think, and I can't say anything positive, so I'd rather keep quiet," she whispered back.

They departed soon after. With many people coming with them to the Carlisle, where refreshments were organized, seats were arranged in various corners of the vast lobby for the diverse crowd attending. Olivia saw her mother surrounded by friends and knew she'd be all right.

62

Spring was back, and so were the longer, warmer days with more sunshine. Colors filled the gardens. The air was filled with the sweet fragrance of hyacinths and lilacs, and the beautiful elegance of daffodils and tulips, with lots of other flowers and bushes Olivia couldn't name.

What would she get for Leah's second birthday? Olivia wanted something unique. Maybe a bed? The kind of transition bed from cot to toddlers' beds? Or power wheels—the type of tricycles with a small motor? Or maybe the unpowered type? She'd have to ask Adam and Ann what they would prefer… and what about a celebration? Would they have a separate one for each side of the family this year, too?

She came on Tuesday, as was her habit, to take Leah and release the nanny. Olivia knew that soon it would be time to place Leah in a supervised nursery school with a small number of children her age. She hoped they would still allow her to come and pick up her granddaughter every Tuesday.

She decided to bring Leah home and take her and the dogs for a walk in the park. Leah loved it, and they often stopped along the way to rest and eat some fruit while watching the dogs playing, running freely. They always made Leah laugh. The little girl was shy with strangers but loved talking with her grandmother, who could understand her baby talk.

Adam was home too, and the nanny was gone. Olivia was worried. *Was something wrong?* She never saw him at home this early on her Tuesdays, only in the evenings, when she brought Leah back home. Every second Sunday, they came over to her house for lunch, playing in the backyard if the weather was nice, using the inflatable pool if it was warm enough. Otherwise—they communicated over the phone.

"Don't worry, Mom, all is well!" he said when he saw her troubled face. "I'm on leave, and using my vacation days."

"What do you mean by 'on leave'?" she asked, worried.

"I quit my job." Adam said. "Looking for something more challenging."

"You had a wonderful job!" he said. "Do you have another job to go to?"

"No," he said calmly. "I'll find one when I'm ready. No rush, I'm in no hurry."

"I'm sure that in your field, you'll not have a problem finding a good job, but still. You have a family to support."

"Don't worry, Mom! We're fine, and it's something I've been thinking about for quite a while. And it's the right thing to do."

Olivia said, her voice tense, "But why not line up a new job before you quit?"

"Because it doesn't seem right. To me, at least." Adam said, smiling. "Besides, I'm entitled to some vacation time, why not enjoy it?"

Olivia didn't know what to say.

"What were your plans for today, anyway?" he said, looking at Leah clinging to her grandmother, wanting to be picked up, and Olivia bending down to do so without thinking.

"I thought I'd take her to Seacliff and take her for a walk in the park with the dogs. She loves it there. Care to join us? It would be lovely to have you there!"

"Sure. Why not?" Adam said. "Let me just pack a bag for her, and we'll go."

Olivia didn't say she was used to preparing one and left him to it.

On their way, she asked Adam about a suitable birthday present, discussing her ideas with him.

"A transition bed—is what we thought we'd get for her. But the powered tricycle sounds fantastic. I'll ask Ann what she thinks, if that's OK with you. Before you buy one."

"Good idea," she said. "And how about a party? Have you decided if it's going to be a separate one this time, too?"

"We'll do it at our place this time." Adam replied. "For all the family together. I hope Tom and Emily will be able to join us, too!"

When Leah reached the point where they usually stopped for fruit and a break, she stopped, as always. And Adam stopped too, looking at the beautiful vista spread before them.

"Wow, what a spot for a picnic!" he said.

"Your daughter loves it, too; that's why she stopped here," Olivia said and spread the mat she brought, and they all shared the rug and the basket of fruit she brought along.

They had a wonderful time together.

"Don't forget to ask Ann about the present!" she reminded her son as he was leaving the car to take Leah home.

"Will you stop worrying?" he said, and she wasn't sure he was only pretending to be exasperated.

"And tell me as soon as you find a new job!" she couldn't help saying.

"Of course, Mom," he said, his back already turned.

***

Mark was helping her to prepare the birthday party for Leah. It was supposed to be for their family only, in addition to the party Adam and Ann arranged. It was always a pleasure to work in the kitchen together. He declared himself her sous chef and awaited directions. Olivia found various jobs to keep him busy and by her side. They were working silently, touching each other gently when their paths crossed, moving around the kitchen, commenting on their work from time to time.

While he was chopping onions and she was preparing the marinade for the shrimp she intended to grill, Mark said quietly, as a matter of fact, not raising his head from his task, "Would you like to get married? I think we should."

Olivia's mind was occupied, and she was sure she didn't hear properly. "Sorry—What did you say?" she asked.

"I asked if you'd like to get married," he said.

She looked at him, incredulous and speechless, trying to figure out what brought this on, and why.

As she didn't say anything, Mark added, "We don't have to, of course, it was just an idea. I'm fine with the way things are. I just thought that maybe—"

"You're serious, aren't you?" Olivia asked, still doubtful and hesitant. "Why? And why now? This proposal is so sudden and unexpected…"

What was his face conveying? Olivia tried to decipher his expression. Was he disappointed? Or feeling rejected because she didn't say "yes" immediately?

She hurried to explain, "It's not that I'm saying no, I just need some explanation. Would you mind if we took a break, had a drink, and talked about it?"

She went to the sink and washed her hands, removing her apron. Mark nodded and went to pour them some wine, then he followed her to their corner.

"OK, now, tell me. What brought this on? What has changed? Why do you want this? We never discussed it before. Marriage was never an issue. So—why now?"

"Well, we don't have to, I understand you're not interested. It's all right," Mark said.

"Mark—I didn't say no, I just need to understand!" Olivia was edgy. Did he think she'd change her mind and leave him at some point? "You know what—I don't mind. If you want us to get married—we will. But tell me why."

"No! Not 'I don't mind'! That's not a matter of 'I don't mind.' I asked if you *want* to get married!" He sounded agitated.

"Yes! Okay, if you want it, then yes, by all means," she responded, trying to reassure him of her sincerity.

"Not because *I* want it! Do *you* want it?" He demanded.

She'd never thought about it, and now had to give a clear, direct, unambiguous answer. Apparently—it mattered to Mark. She wasn't sure why. It never seemed an issue in the past. Something must have changed.

If it mattered enough for him to suggest it—without preparation or warning—she'd consent. She figured that he would wait for her answer before he'd explain.

"Yes," she said. "Yes, I'd marry you any day, anytime, in any circumstance," she said with a smile.

Mark nodded, satisfied.

"Now tell me—why?" she asked.

"After New York, it was on my mind, with all that happened there. I thought it would be a statement," he said, his response fragmented, as if he wasn't sure how to explain himself. "We don't have to tell anyone."

That was even more baffling. *Why do it at all, if it would be a secret?* And then she thought—

"Are you afraid of your daughters' reaction if they knew of your plans? Is that why you want it kept a secret?"

He shrugged. "Not afraid, but I'd rather not deal with the outburst."

For some reason, that fired her anger.

"Even if you don't tell them beforehand, you'll have to deal with it afterward anyway!" she stated. "Besides, I *have* to tell my sons and my mom. I won't do something as significant as this behind their backs! That's not in accord with the trust our relationship is based on."

He only nodded, silent.

"Mark! Your daughters need to know you have *a life of your own*, and you have *a right* to make *your own* decisions when it comes to *your* life!"

"They know it! But they don't always think I make the right decisions," he said, sounding despondent.

"Well, we can choose *not* to get married and continue as we are," Olivia said, allowing him to withdraw his proposal.

"No," he said forcefully. "No. I want to do it. It's something that has been on my mind ever since we came back. If I had any doubts about our relationship initially—because of our age difference and my medical problems—they evaporated. We deserve it!"

"So, we'll do it! It's more a public statement than something we need for ourselves, but sometimes such statements have great value!"

Mark pulled her onto his lap, hugged her tightly, and kissed her wholeheartedly. Then he said: "You're a very wise lady, you know?"

"And you are too, my love forever!" She cupped his face in her small hands. "Now, let's go finish preparing dinner! And we won't say anything tonight, not to mix the two celebrations. And—we won't make a big issue of the matter, with no huge announcements. We're too old for that," she said, smiling.

"Speak for yourself!" he said, returning her smile.

***

The birthday party was a great success, with high spirits, great food, and excellent wine.

A few days later, she called her sons to let them know that Mark proposed, and they were getting married.

"Really? Congratulations!" they said together.

"Why?" from Adam.

"At your age, it's quite redundant, don't you think?" from Tom.

Their tone was amused, not critical.

"I think maybe Mark suggested it as a statement of how deeply he feels," she said, slightly embarrassed by their reference to her age.

"Or he wants to make sure you'll always be there?" Tom, forever the pragmatist, remarked.

"After New York, I'm sure he knows that," she replied.

"Is that what you want, too?" Adam asked unexpectedly.

"Well… I was surprised when Mark popped the question, but I guess I do, it is a strong statement, especially after what happened in New York, and because he never agreed to marry Helen. So, in truth—yes, I do," she said.

"Well, in that case—you have my blessing! If you were looking for it." Adam said.

"Mine too!" Tom added his support. "If it'd make you happy—go for it!"

***

Her mother was overjoyed. Being more traditional, she had a sense of it being more "suitable," she said. Never bothering to ask why it was necessary, or why now, she was just happy. What bothered her was when it would take place and if she'd be invited.

"I don't know when, Mom," Olivia said, "but it will be a private occasion, at the registry office. It's not a celebration. Just something we're doing for the two of us."

Rebecca was disappointed, but she'd come to terms with it, Olivia knew.

She thought again of her conversation with her sons, especially about Adam's question. "Is that what you want, too?" he had asked. She stammered and hesitated when she responded, but the more she thought about it, the more certain she became of her willingness to do it. It was a profound, significant statement of their commitment, aimed at their entire social circle. She was doing what she felt was right. Right for her. And for Mark.

63

They chose a date for the wedding—July 7. Almost two years since the day Olivia came to see the Seacliff house. It seemed like a perfect date to her, especially as it happened on a Saturday. Triple seven.

Olivia wanted a small, private place, without long queues. City Hall in San Francisco would be crowded, she assumed.

"How about Sonoma?" he asked. "You liked the place, said it was "quaint", if I remember correctly."

"Lovely idea!" She loved the place. And it meant a lot—the first trip they took together, the first time she met his broader circle of friends. And she had delightful memories of that trip. "I'll find out who we have to arrange it with, and see if they can accommodate us on the date we chose—it seems appropriate, somehow."

***

"We'll need a marriage license," Olivia said a few days later. "Do you think we can obtain it right before the ceremony on Saturday at the County Clerk-Recorder Office? I wonder if it'd be open on a Saturday, or if we'll have to appear there during business hours another day."

"I'll inquire tomorrow," Mark replied. "And if he's still in office, the mayor of Sonoma is an old acquaintance of mine and owes me a favor, so maybe he'll be happy to perform the ceremony."

"That would be lovely!" Olivia was pleased. "Where do you know him from?"

"His daughter-in-law came to see me a few years ago, and I've been taking care of her ever since... I even had to hospitalize her a few times, and met the mayor several times when he visited her," Mark said, his small, shy smile lighting his eyes.

"One more thing,' Mark said, still smiling. "Shall we make it a weekend away from home? How about a night at the same hotel we were at—The Timber Cove Resort? Would that make you happy?"

"Yes, indeed!" Olivia whispered, emotional. He was so considerate… and he knew her so well.

***

They drove north early on Saturday morning, though the wedding was planned for eleven a.m. Taking the 101 North, the trip was supposed to take about one hour, but they took no chances with traffic, problems on the road. They'd have a coffee in the square if they arrived early.

Olivia bought cream-colored pants and a matching lightweight jacket and matching high-heeled pumps for the occasion. Mark had his beautiful dark gray Armani jacket on, and a very light blue-gray shirt. She had butterflies in her stomach, and her hands were trembling.

"Are we doing the right thing, Mark?" she asked, her voice hesitant.

"What—you have second thoughts? You don't want to marry me?" he looked amused.

"It's not that! Marriage is such a strong statement!"

"You're right. It *is* a strong statement. And that is why we're doing it. For our kids, for our friends. I love you and want you always by my side, and I don't need a wedding to make it happen. But it seemed the right thing to do. Besides—it's a little late for that, don't you think?" he said, smiling, and he took her hand, brought it to his lips, and kissed it.

"I love you, too, and sometimes I still can't believe that it is not a dream. I'm glad you were so confident that we're a good match!" The smile returned to her face, too. "There are so many inadvertent encounters in our lives, opening options we never dreamed of, closing others we were sure of. They make life more interesting. Sometimes—they bring out the best in us; sometimes—they pose challenges we have to face."